PENGUIN CLASSICS

SERIES ADVISOR: PAUL POPLAWSKI

THE WOMAN WHO RODE AWAY
ST. MAWR
THE PRINCESS

DAVID HERBERT LAWRENCE was born into a miner's family in Eastwood, Nottinghamshire, in 1885, the fourth of five children. His first novel, *The White Peacock*, was published in 1911. In 1912 Lawrence went to Germany and Italy with Frieda Weekley, the German wife of a professor at Nottingham University College, where Lawrence had studied; she divorced, and they were married on their return to England in 1914. Lawrence had published *Sons and Lovers* in 1913; but *The Rainbow*, completed in 1915, was suppressed, and for three years he could not find a publisher for *Women in Love*, which he first completed in 1917. After the First World War he travelled extensively in Europe, Australia, America and Mexico. He returned to Europe from America in 1925, and lived mainly in Italy and France. His last novel, *Lady Chatterley's Lover*, was published in 1928 but was banned in England and America. In 1930 he died in Vence, in the south of France, at the age of forty-four.

JAMES LASDUN was born in London and now lives in Woodstock, New York. He has published several books of poetry and fiction, including *The Horned Man*, a novel. His story 'The Siege' was adapted by Bernardo Bertolucci for his film *Besieged* and is included in a selection of his stories published by Vintage. With Michael Hofmann he co-edited the anthology *After Ovid: New Metamorphoses*. He is the recipient of a Guggenheim Fellowship in poetry, and currently teaches creative writing at Princeton and the New School.

PAUL POPLAWSKI is a Senior Lecturer at the University of Leicester. He is a member of the editorial board of the Cambridge Edition of Lawrence's Works and his recent publications include the revised third edition of *A Bibliography of D. H. Lawrence* (Cambridge, 2001), and *Encyclopedia of Literary Modernism* (Greenwood, 2003).

D. H. LAWRENCE

The Woman Who Rode Away
St. Mawr
The Princess

Edited by BRIAN FINNEY, CHRISTA JANSOHN *and* DIETER MEHL
With Explanatory Notes and additional editing by PAUL POPLAWSKI
With an Introduction by JAMES LASDUN

PENGUIN BOOKS

PENGUIN CLASSICS

Published by the Penguin Group
Penguin Books Ltd, 80 Strand, London WC2R ORL, England
Penguin Group (USA) Inc., 375 Hudson Street, New York, New York 10014, USA
Penguin Group (Canada), 90 Eglinton Avenue East, Suite 700, Toronto, Ontario, Canada M4P 2Y3
(a division of Pearson Penguin Canada Inc.)
Penguin Ireland, 25 St Stephen's Green, Dublin 2, Ireland (a division of Penguin Books Ltd)
Penguin Group (Australia), 250 Camberwell Road, Camberwell,
Victoria 3124, Australia (a division of Pearson Australia Group Pty Ltd)
Penguin Books India Pvt Ltd, 11 Community Centre,
Panchsheel Park, New Delhi – 110 017, India
Penguin Group (NZ), cnr Airborne and Rosedale Roads, Albany,
Auckland 1310, New Zealand (a division of Pearson New Zealand Ltd)
Penguin Books (South Africa) (Pty) Ltd, 24 Sturdee Avenue,
Rosebank, Johannesburg 2196, South Africa

Penguin Books Ltd, Registered Offices: 80 Strand, London WC2R ORL, England

www.penguin.com

St. Mawr Together with The Princess first published 1925
The Woman Who Rode Away first published 1928
Cambridge University Press edition of *St. Mawr and Other Stories* (including *The Princess*)
published 1983; Cambridge University Press edition of *The Woman Who Rode Away and
Other Stories* published 1995
Published with new editorial material in Penguin Books 1996, 1997
This edition published with new Chronology, Introduction, Further Reading, A Note on
the Texts and Explanatory Notes in Penguin Classics 2006

014

Copyright © the Estate of Frieda Lawrence, 1983, 1995
Introduction copyright © James Lasdun, 2006
Chronology, Further Reading, A Note on the Texts and Explanatory Notes
copyright © Paul Poplawski, 2006
All rights reserved

The moral right of the introducer and editor has been asserted

Printed in England by Clays Ltd, St Ives plc

ISBN-13: 978-0-141-44166-5

www.greenpenguin.co.uk

Contents

Chronology

1885 11 September: David Herbert Lawrence born in Eastwood, Nottinghamshire, third son of Arthur John (coalminer) and Lydia Lawrence.

1898–1901 Attends Nottingham High School.

1901 October–December: Clerk at Nottingham factory of J. C. Heywood; falls ill.

1902–5 Pupil-teacher in Eastwood and Ilkeston; meets Chambers family, including Jessie, in 1902.

1905–6 Uncertificated teacher in Eastwood; starts to write poetry, shows it to Jessie.

1906–8 Studies for teaching certificate at University College, Nottingham; begins first novel *The White Peacock* in 1906.

1907 Writes first short stories; first published story, 'A Prelude', appears in the *Nottinghamshire Guardian* (under Jessie's name).

1908–11 Elementary teacher at Davidson Road School, Croydon.

1909 Jessie sends selection of Lawrence's poems to the *English Review*; Ford Madox Hueffer (editor) accepts five and recommends *The White Peacock* to a publisher. Writes 'Odour of Chrysanthemums' (–1911) and first play, *A Collier's Friday Night*.

1910 Engaged to Louie Burrows; death of his mother. First drafts of *The Trespasser* and 'Paul Morel' (later *Sons and Lovers*).

1911 *The White Peacock* published. Second draft of 'Paul Morel'; writes and revises short stories. 'Odour of Chrysanthemums' published. Third draft of 'Paul Morel' (–1912). Falls seriously ill with pneumonia (November–December).

1912 Recuperates in Bournemouth; in February, breaks off engagement, returns to Eastwood and resigns teaching post. Meets Frieda Weekley (née von Richthofen), the wife of a professor at Nottingham University, and in May goes with her to Germany and then to Italy for the winter. *The Trespasser* published. Revises 'Paul Morel' into *Sons and Lovers*.

1913 Drafts Italian essays and starts to write 'The Sisters' (which will become *The Rainbow* and *Women in Love*). *Love Poems* published. April–June in Germany; writes 'The Prussian Officer' and other stories. *Sons and Lovers* published (May). Spends the summer in England with Frieda, then they return to Italy. Works on 'The Sisters'.

1914 *The Widowing of Mrs Holroyd* (play) published (USA). Finishes 'The Wedding Ring' (latest version of 'The Sisters') and returns to England with Frieda; her divorce finalized, they marry on 13 July. At the outbreak of war (August), Methuen & Co. withdraw from their agreement to publish 'The Wedding Ring'. War prevents return to Italy; lives in Buckinghamshire and Sussex. Rewrites 'The Wedding Ring' as *The Rainbow* (–1915).

1915 Writes 'England, My England'; works on essays for *Twilight in Italy*. Moves to London in August. *The Rainbow* is published in September but withdrawn in October, and prosecuted as obscene and banned a month later. Hopes to travel to USA with Frieda but at the end of December they settle in Cornwall (–October 1917).

1916 Rewrites the other half of 'The Sisters' material as *Women in Love*; it is finished by November but refused by several publishers (–1917). Reading American literature. *Twilight in Italy* and *Amores* (poems) published.

1917 Begins work on *Studies in Classic American Literature* (hereafter *Studies*). Revises *Women in Love*. Expelled from Cornwall with Frieda in October under Defence of the Realm Act; they return to London. Begins the novel *Aaron's Rod*. *Look! We Have Come Through!* (poems) published.

1918 Lives mostly in Berkshire and Derbyshire (–mid 1919). *New Poems* published; first versions of eight *Studies* essays published in periodical form (–1919). War ends (November). Writes *The Fox*.

1919 Revises *Studies* essays in intermediate versions. Revises *Women in Love* for Thomas Seltzer (USA). In November leaves for Italy.

1920 Moves to Sicily (February) and settles at Taormina. Publication of *Women in Love* in USA, *Touch and Go* (play), *Bay* (poems) and *The Lost Girl* in England.

1921 Visits Sardinia with Frieda and writes *Sea and Sardinia*. *Movements in European History* (textbook) and *Women in Love* published in England; *Psychoanalysis and the Unconscious* and *Sea and Sardinia* published in USA. Travels to Italy, Germany and Austria (April–September) and then returns to Taormina. Finishes *Aaron's Rod*, writes *The Captain's Doll* and *The Ladybird*, revises *The Fox*.

1922 February–September: Travels with Frieda to Ceylon, Australia and USA. *Aaron's Rod* published; writes *Kangaroo* in Australia.

Arrives in Taos, New Mexico in September; rewrites *Studies* (final version). *Fantasia of the Unconscious* and *England, My England and Other Stories* published. Moves to Del Monte Ranch, near Taos, in December.

1923 *The Ladybird* (with *The Fox* and *The Captain's Doll*) published. Travels to Mexico with Frieda. *Studies* published in August (USA). Writes 'Quetzalcoatl' (early version of *The Plumed Serpent*). *Kangaroo* and *Birds, Beasts and Flowers* (poems) published. Rewrites *The Boy in the Bush* from Mollie Skinner's manuscript. Frieda returns to England in August; Lawrence follows in December.

1924 In France and Germany, then to Kiowa Ranch, near Taos. *The Boy in the Bush* published; writes 'The Woman Who Rode Away', *St. Mawr* and 'The Princess'. Death of his father. Goes to Mexico with Frieda.

1925 Finishes *The Plumed Serpent* in Oaxaca; falls ill, nearly dies and is diagnosed with tuberculosis. Returns to Mexico City and then to Kiowa Ranch. *St. Mawr Together with The Princess* published. Travels via London to Italy. *Reflections on the Death of a Porcupine* (essays) published; writes *The Virgin and the Gipsy* (–January 1926).

1926 *The Plumed Serpent* and *David* (play) published. Visits England for the last time; returns to Italy and writes first version of *Lady Chatterley's Lover*, then second version (–1927).

1927 Tours Etruscan sites with Earl Brewster; writes *Sketches of Etruscan Places*; writes first part of *The Escaped Cock* (second part in 1928). Suffers series of bronchial haemorrhages. *Mornings in Mexico* (essays) published. Starts third version of *Lady Chatterley's Lover*.

1928 *The Woman Who Rode Away and Other Stories* published. Finishes, revises and privately publishes third version of *Lady Chatterley's Lover* in limited edition (late June); distributes it through network of friends but many copies confiscated by authorities in USA and England. Travels to Switzerland for health, and then to Bandol in the south of France. *The Collected Poems of D. H. Lawrence* published; writes many of the poems for *Pansies*.

1929 Organizes cheap Paris edition of *Lady Chatterley's Lover* to counter piracies. Typescript of *Pansies* seized by police in London. Travels to Spain, Italy and Germany; increasingly ill. Police raid exhibition of his paintings in London (July). Expurgated (July) and unexpurgated (August) editions of *Pansies* published; *The Escaped Cock* published. Returns to Bandol.

1930 2 March: Dies of tuberculosis at Vence, Alpes Maritimes,

France, and is buried there. *Nettles* (poems), *Assorted Articles, The Virgin and the Gipsy* and *Love Among the Haystacks & Other Pieces* published.

1932 *Sketches of Etruscan Places* published (as *Etruscan Places*). *Last Poems* published.

1933–4 Story collections *The Lovely Lady* (1933) and *A Modern Lover* (1934) published.

1935 Frieda has Lawrence exhumed and cremated, and his ashes taken to Kiowa Ranch.

1936 *Phoenix* (compilation) published.

1956 Death of Frieda.

1960 Penguin Books publish the first unexpurgated English edition of *Lady Chatterley's Lover*, following the famous obscenity trial.

Introduction

On the question of happiness, literature has always tended to play Virgil to the Dante of the reader's imagination: leading the way to the gates of paradise, but not often venturing past them, and usually falling flat when it does. Comedy ends in a wedding, but seldom concerns itself with the nature of the marriage that follows. The great tragic novels of the nineteenth century state their high ideals of fulfilment in terms of what their large-hearted heroines are ultimately denied, or punished by society for wanting. Happiness in these books exists largely in the negative space of what has been forbidden or lost, or what might have been.

Society no longer has that kind of power over us. Already with Chekhov a bad marriage is more a nuisance than a tragedy. The adulterous couple in 'The Lady with the Little Dog' (1899) may not have it easy, but they are more likely to succumb to boredom than throw themselves under a train. Every other conceivable taboo has been broken in the decades since, to the point where it requires special pleading for an author to present a character in any way constrained by the social order, except perhaps economically. What to do with this freedom, what to make of it, how to propagate it into a compelling narrative (a form that thrives on obstruction) is a question that has faced every serious novelist for some time now.

For D. H. Lawrence it was *the* question, and unlike some of his contemporaries or successors, he had no interest in evading it behind an attitude of irony or melancholy, much less a plot full of circumstantial misfortune. 'I hate [Arnold] Bennett's resignation,' he wrote; 'Tragedy ought really to be a great kick at misery. But *Anna of the Five Towns* [1902] seems like an acceptance – so does all the modern stuff since Flaubert. I hate it. I want to wash again quick, wash off England, the oldness and grubbiness and despair.'[1]

By 1924, the year in which all three of the stories in this volume were written, Lawrence's own life was an advanced study in the art of washing off 'oldness'. He had broken from England, eloped with a married mother of three, lived on five continents (in a number of variously configured *ménages*), become a fully self-supporting writer;

even, in a sustained miracle of defiance, warded off the constraining symptoms of his own ailing body. As in life, so in his fiction: a similarly unshackled independence characterizes the inhabitants of his stories in this period. Total freedom is no longer the wistfully imagined end of the struggle, but more or less the point of departure. The underlying impulse, as in a controlled experiment, seems to be to see what human beings can make of themselves under the best possible circumstances.

Typically the protagonists are women: well-off, 'liberated' in the old parlance, superficially content, but at a deeper level dissatisfied, and existing in a benumbed state of vagueness or detachment. The story of Sleeping Beauty is the not-very-hidden subtext of their lives, with the built-in expectation that a prince will come along and wake them with a kiss. Lawrence plays repeatedly with and against that expectation, using it to probe and expose the dead matter in various defunct notions of love, and then to feel his way toward the articulation of a more vital idea of fulfilment. 'Man must find a new expression, give a new value to life, or his women will reject him, and he must die,' he had declared,[2] with his usual apocalyptic vehemence, a decade earlier. Story after story attempts to substantiate that 'new value', sending its spellbound heroines out in search of it through a variety of landscapes, ranging from the Italian Riviera (*Sun*), to the English north country (*The Virgin and the Gipsy*), and, most vividly, the high desert and mountains of New Mexico, where the present stories are set and were largely composed.

Like the side panels of a triptych, 'The Woman Who Rode Away' and 'The Princess' (respectively the first and last to be completed) have obvious symmetries. In each the heroine is established in the characteristic state of deadlock or dreamy inertia. In each a half-conscious desire for salvation compels her to undertake a journey on horseback into the mountain wilderness. In each, through a series of precise, beautifully transfiguring descriptions, the landscape becomes the expression of successively deepening states of consciousness. In each the journey culminates in a momentous, shattering encounter. And in each it has to be said that, while the presentation of the heroine and the depiction of her journey are stunning examples of Lawrence's ability to accelerate a narrative from the mundane to the visionary in a few pages, the denouement seems to falter.

The main difference between them is in the terms in which the heroine's quest is conceived. For Dollie Urquhart in 'The Princess', glaciating in her virginal intactness, 'impervious as crystal' (182:2), the terms are sexual. The pretext for her journey is to see the 'wild animals' in the mountains, but it is clear that what she really wants, or at least what a part of her wants, is to broach a further level of intimacy with her Mexican guide, Romero, whose delicate instincts for her needs and desires – 'a subtle, insidious male *kindliness* she had never known before' (189:32–3) – mark him as the first man she has been able to contemplate as a mate. Unfortunately for her (and ultimately for the story itself), another part of her – the fey, 'changeling' side of her that shrinks from human contact – causes her to recoil from Romero at the moment of consummation, fatally humiliating him. This splitting of Dollie's nature into opposing drives, while psychologically fascinating, also creates two opposed lines of tension in the story, demanding contradictory resolutions. Lawrence tries to reconcile these in the person of Romero, turning him abruptly from tender lover to maniacal brute (a sort of mockery of Dollie's imagined 'wild animals'). This might have been manageable in a longer piece (and the elaborate, almost novelistic account of Dollie's complicated family circumstances at the beginning suggests that Lawrence was originally planning something more expansive). As it is, Romero's violent transformation seems forced, while the ending, with its gunshots and hysteria, feels truncated and a little melodramatic.

In 'The Woman Who Rode Away' the terms of the encounter are primarily religious rather than sexual: 'I want ... to know their Gods', the woman says very simply (34:1–2), as she goes off in search of a hidden tribe of Indians. And in its sardonic way, the story proceeds to oblige her.

The opening is a marvel of compressed social portraiture – the kind at which Lawrence excelled. Poet and seer that he was, he was also an acidly witty observer of the prosaic world. We may never learn the name of the heroine (and the interests of this proto-existentialist tale of a woman casually abandoning her husband and children without a backward glance are clearly served by presenting her as something of a blank slate), but how vividly the circumstances of her marriage are evoked in that opening sketch of her husband, the mine owner, with his forlornly self-sufficient childhood, 'thrown out on the world, a little bachelor, at the age of ten', and his pointless dynamism that manifests itself in a view from the house of 'the huge pink cone of the silver-mud refuse, and the machinery of the extracting plant, against heaven above. No more' (pp. 39–40). How perfectly his biography accounts for her psychology; his bleak, barren monumentality predicating both her 'stupor of subjected amazement' and the jolt of wonderment that stirs her at the mention of these Aztec descendants worshipping the old gods in a remote valley.

If it doesn't quite account for her blithe unconcern at their alleged practice of human sacrifice, that is perhaps because this whole aspect of the story – the playing out of a prophecy that a white woman will offer herself as a sacrificial victim so that the Indians can recover their connection to the sun and moon gods – suffers from a certain crudeness, even cheesiness, in its conception (Lawrence, rather surprisingly, was an avid reader of the pulp magazine *Adventure*). For all its insistently visualized detail, the long process of self-surrender beginning with the woman's arrival in the valley – the stripping, the imprisonment, the Huxleyesque drug-taking that enables her to 'hear' the flowers unfolding and the planets revolving – seems unconvinced of itself and finally preposterous. The phallic imagery that surfaces in the last scene, while clearly an attempt to incorporate the story's latent sexual energies into its religious climax, merely gives the action a lurid colouring.

Seized on by Kate Millett in her influential book *Sexual Politics* (1970), this scene was used to indict Lawrence of a pervasive misogyny, and helped lose him a generation of readers. A better way to look at it would be as a partial, provisional statement: one of a series of works in which Lawrence struggled to express an extraordinarily complex cluster of intuitions concerning the sources of vitality in both the human and the wider cosmic order – the 'circumambient universe' in his famous phrase.[3] It is no more the last word on its subject than *The Princess* is on *its*. The latter was reprised, with greater artistry, in *The Virgin and the Gipsy*, while the former laid the groundwork for many of the ideas that are brought to consummate expression in *St. Mawr*, the magnificent centrepiece of this trilogy.

The literary critic F. R. Leavis considered *St. Mawr* one of the great works of the modern period: a prophetic poem in prose to set beside T. S. Eliot's *The Waste Land* (1922); as potent in the affirming vision it wrenches out of near-despair – its 'great kick at misery' – as Eliot's is in its negations. The estimate seems indisputable, the only mystery being why this book, among the most concentratedly powerful as well as humane that Lawrence wrote (no act of edifying violation required for the heroine here), remains relatively unknown.

Perhaps its most immediately striking feature is the astounding amount of life – human and otherwise – contained in its 130-odd pages. As if the central nucleus of Lou Witt and her entourage –

mother, husband, the two grooms Lewis and Phoenix – each with their competing, richly individuated ways of looking at the world, were not already enough to occupy a story of this length, there is an irrepressible flow of minor characters through its pages: the Manby girls, Dean Vyner and his wife (figures who demonstrate Lawrence's casual mastery of English satirical comedy), and beyond them a host of incidental characters, all incandescently rendered in their brief moment: the servile postmaster, Mr Jones, delivering his message to Lou 'in the mayonnaise of his own unction' (52:26–7), a pair of bilberry pickers seen from afar 'pick—pick—picking with curious, rather disgusting assiduity' (90:18), the maids in Shropshire, the Havana tourists, numerous others, their presence giving this short novel a feeling of almost epic amplitude. Then there is its teeming underworld of animals and plants: the many horses (and in St. Mawr himself Lawrence creates one of the few great animal 'characters' in serious fiction, complete with his own tragic psychology); the flying fishes on the sea voyage, that 'came like drops of bright water, sailing out of the massive slippery waves', the wonderfully awful pack-rats at the ranch 'bouncing on her ceiling like hippopotami in the night'; the multitude of flowers and trees, most notably in the final bravura evocation of the seething 'living landscape' in which Lou and her mother make their last bid for a meaningful life (or in the mother's case, a meaningful death).

Almost as remarkable as the abundance itself is its dense coherence. Every creature exists luminously, not only in its own right, but also in a precisely modifying relation to the whole. The unctuous postmaster adds a comic flourish to a larger picture of an 'unworthy, ignoble' humanity, typified by the Manbys and the Vyners, whose little snobberies and vanities and cruelties coalesce in the ghoulish conspiracy to geld St. Mawr. The marvellously described pine tree up by the cabin – 'a bristling, almost demonish guardian' – is incorporated into the backdrop of radically alien modes of existence against which the human story unfolds: 'Its great pillar of pale, flakey-ribbed copper rose there in strange callous indifference ... A passionless, non-phallic column, rising in the shadows of the pre-sexual world' (164:22–6). Even the prohibition-defying Havana tourists, 'imbibing with a sort of fixed and deliberate will' (149:3–4), develop a line of thought concerning the mechanical pursuit of pleasure – 'lots of fun' (e.g. 83:25) – that drains the life out of everything and finally reduces the mystery of death itself to a larky line in a popular song: '*Oh Death where is thy sting-a-ling-a-ling?*' (112:24–5).

This coherence is partly a matter of the sure-footed rapidity of

Lawrence's late style, which had evolved by now into a kind of hiero-glyphic alphabet for transcribing the living world at high speed, every phrase and image condensing formidable accumulations of knowledge, observation and reflection. Descriptions, while beautifully perceptive as to the surface of things, are never static or merely pictorial. They analyse as they present, transform through metaphor as they analyse, impart very precise emotional tonalities to every image, crack startling little jokes, then ripple on seamlessly to the next subject. And although the prose in fact consists of numerous, highly accurate little jabs and thrusts, it gives the impression of being a current of pure verbal energy that seems simply to swirl on itself into the image of, say, a mariposa lily here, a lightning bolt there, a group of riders or little scene of haircutting elsewhere, all hard-edged and discrete (Lawrence is never 'impressionistic') and yet all unmistakably part of the same fluid, sinuous continuum.

Partly also the coherence is a result of the inspired use of St. Mawr himself as a unifying, interpetative counterpoint – part mirror, part refracting lens – to the rest of the novella. Everything finds its mean-ing in relation to him. Even before Lou's first, fateful encounter with him in the Westminster mews, the dissatisfactions of her life are expressed in terms that subtly prepare her (and us) for the impact this stallion will have on her imagination. The bloodlessness of fashionable society is staged, in a wittily pertinent paradox, on horseback: 'awfully well-groomed papas, and tight mamas who looked as if they were going to pour tea between the ears of their horses, and converse with banal skill, one eye on the teapot, one on the visitor with whom she was talking' (46:3–7). And the carefully repressed inner tensions of Lou's husband, Rico, are given in explicitly equine terms – 'He didn't want to erupt like some suddenly wicked horse' (47:11–12). (This heralds what becomes a sustained parallel study of the reciprocally out-of-kilter temperaments of master and horse, culminating in the scene where St. Mawr topples backward on Rico, crushing him).

In the mews, as St. Mawr swings his great head into Lou's con-sciousness for the first time, he is evoked in terms of purely animal sensitivity and vitality, beautifully registered in that instant when the stable owner touches him and Lou sees 'the brilliant skin of the horse crinkle a little in apprehensive anticipation, like the shadow of the descending hand on a bright red-gold liquid' (48:14–16). Thereafter he becomes the subject of a series of extraordinary, transfiguring portraits, each one reaching through some aspect of his appearance or behaviour, to new regions of metaphorical resonance. Already by the time Lou gets home, his presence in her mind has gone beyond the purely creaturely to the hieratic: 'The wild, brilliant head of St. Mawr seemed to look at her out of another world' (50:362–7). Elsewhere that head reappears in a passage of exquisite, almost amorous tenderness, where Lou escapes from the flirting and affectation of the Manby entourage, to look at St. Mawr. At first he seems 'a little bit extinguished':

> But when he lifted his lovely naked head, like a bunch of flames, to see who it was had entered, she saw he was still himself. Forever sensitive and alert, his head lifted like the summit of a fountain. And within him the clean bones striking to the earth, his hoofs intervening between him and the ground like lesser jewels. (84:6–10)

And meanwhile, beneath these lyrical notes an opposing suggestion, of something primitive and dimly saurian, has also been quietly orchestrated into the imagery. There is an early glimpse, again of St. Mawr's head, with its 'exquisite fine lines reaching a little snake-like forward'; an observation of horses' heads in general having 'something of a snake in their way of looking round' (4:37–8, 55:18–19). Later, in the scene where St. Mawr falls (or is pulled) backward on top of Rico, Lawrence abruptly brings this submerged primeval imagery to the surface, activating its latent charge of horror in the picture of St. Mawr giving 'a great curve like a fish . . . his face in panic, almost like some terrible lizard' (96:28, 31–2). This double aspect of St. Mawr – in Lou's eyes 'almost like a god'; but under Rico's weakly domineering hand 'Reversed, and purely evil' – is a crucial point of uncertainty in the complex argument Lou conducts with herself in her subsequent 'vision of evil' (98:39, 6); one that she resolves by taking the measure of her own civilization, attributing St. Mawr's behaviour to Rico's 'impotence as a master' (99:7) and concluding, with glorious misanthropy, that 'The horse is superannuated, for man. But alas, man is even more superannuated, for the horse' (104:7–8).

The expectation is that in some way Lou and St. Mawr will end up together in America. But instead, with perfectly judged nonchalance, the story leaves the horse in Texas, trotting off after a mare, while Lou continues her journey without him. By shrugging him off in this casual way, the book avoids the kind of over-insistent loading of significance (and plot-function) into its leading male character that mars the other two stories. Metaphorically, St. Mawr may be at different times snake, fish, lizard, god, 'bunch of flames', 'summit of a fountain', but literally he is also a flesh and blood stallion, and a measure of the book's confidence and genial spirit, is that it allows him his natural destiny in that capacity instead of forcing him to conclude his role as a symbol in some human equation.

But that isn't quite the end of it either. At one point Lou thinks of St. Mawr as being 'like some living background, into which she wanted to retreat' (61:23–4), and by an alchemy that only a novelist of genius could have contrived, everything he has come to mean for Lou – as animal, as window on to another world, as embodiment of an idea of divinity radically opposed to that of Dean Vyner and his like – turns out to be in some way extended or reiterated in the Las Chivas ranch. So that in a sense he does indeed become the landscape, the 'background' into which Lou retreats.

'*This is the place*,' she says to herself on reaching the ranch (160:33). What is most striking about the depiction that follows (and where Lawrence differs from other writers – including Dante himself – who do venture beyond the gates of paradise) is its complete absence of any suggestion of harmonious tranquillity, let alone conventional beauty. On the contrary, this paradise is presented in terms of unremitting struggle between the various living things that have inhabited it over the generations, each trying to assert its own consciousness, or raise the banner of its own particular form of existence. Drawing on ideas he had begun to formulate in essays such as 'Pan in America' (written 1924), Lawrence invokes a very specifically non-Christian, even anti-Christian idea of paradise. With its pack rats and black ants and lethal lightning storms and weeds forever 'strangling and choking' the alfalfa crop (168:38), the ranch – as its previous owner and his religious-minded New England woman, has discovered – is a living mockery of any Christian notion of a merciful god or universal love. 'There was no love on this ranch,' she has been forced to observe. Instead, there is 'life, intense, bristling life, full of energy, but also, with an undertone of sordid savageness' (168:8–10). There is the numinous beauty of the landscape itself, with its 'pale blue crests of mountains looking over the horizon ... as if peering in from another world altogether' ((165:16–18); an echo of St. Mawr's head, looking 'out of another world'). But there is also the 'mysterious malevolence' of the place (163:14); the 'seething cauldron of lower life, seething on the very tissue of the higher life, seething the soul away' (170:19–20).

The New England woman, whose lofty idea was to create a 'paradise of the spirit' in these mountains (166:39), has no real capacity, in her over-spiritualized vision of things, for coming to terms with 'the everlasting bristling tussle of the wild life' (170:11), and finally it defeats her. Disenchantment, however, has prepared Lou more thoroughly (and this device of giving the ranch a kind of evolutionary succession of owners is another fine touch). She is something like the unillusioned initiates in Yeats's sonnet *Meru* (1935): ready to come at last 'Into the desolation of reality'. She arrives at the ranch willing to embrace all aspects of the place; its savageness as well as its beauty. She is aware that it 'will hurt me sometimes and will wear me down sometimes' (175:20–21), but this wildness, with its gods both 'huger than man, and lower than man' is what she craves (170:323).

'It is very much easier to shatter prison bars than to open un-discovered doors to life,' Lawrence wrote elsewhere.⁴ 'The Woman Who Rode Away' and 'The Princess' are each effective enough at the shattering of bars – the dramatizing of their heroines' acts of repudia-tion; less so at the opening of 'undiscovered doors'. In *St. Mawr* both are accomplished consummately. Lou's grand processional journey from London to New Mexico takes her through a series of shatterings or disavowals: friendships, love, marriage, England, St. Mawr himself, even Phoenix, who for a time seems poised to play Romero to her Dollie Urquhart. These function as the principle of growth in her psyche: she becomes steadily more capacious as a character with everything she relinquishes. And they also propel her toward what is surely one of the great revelatory climaxes of modern literature. To read this sustained descriptive coda with the attention it merits is to experience something like what Rico, in brief reprieve from his own tensions, experiences while riding St. Mawr: 'that luxurious heavy ripple of life which is like nothing else on earth' (70:7–8).

Lawrence more than once expressed a desire to have these related stories published together in a volume. They appear here together for the first time.

James Lasdun

NOTES

1. Letter from D. H. Lawrence to Arthur McLeod, [4 October 1912], *The Letters of D. H. Lawrence*, Volume. I, *September 1901–May 1913* (Cam-bridge: Cambridge University Press, 1979), p. 459.

2. Letter from D. H. Lawrence to Catherine Carswell, 14 July 1916, *The Letters of D. H. Lawrence*, Volume. II, *June 1913–October 1916*, ed. George J. Zytaruk and James T. Boulton (Cambridge: Cambridge University Press, 1981), p. 635.

3.   D. H. Lawrence, 'Morality and the Novel' (1925), in *Study of Thomas Hardy and Other Essays*, ed. Bruce Steele (Cambridge: Cambridge University Press, 1985), p. 171.

4.   D. H. Lawrence, 'The Virgin and the Gipsy', in *The Virgin and the Gypsy and Other Stories*, ed. Michael Herbert, Bethan Jones and Lindeth Vasey (Cambridge: Cambridge University Press, 2006), p. 17.

Further Reading

CRITICAL STUDIES OF LAWRENCE'S WORK

The following is a selection of some of the best Lawrence criticism published since 1985.

Michael Bell, *D. H. Lawrence: Language and Being* (Cambridge University Press, 1992). Philosophically-based analysis of Lawrence's work.

Michael Black, *D. H. Lawrence: The Early Fiction* (Macmillan, 1986). Very close analytical approach to Lawrence's fiction up to and including *Sons and Lovers*.

James C. Cowan, *D. H. Lawrence: Self and Sexuality* (Ohio State University Press, 2002). Sensitive and intelligent psychoanalytical study.

Keith Cushman and Earl G. Ingersoll, eds., *D. H. Lawrence: New Worlds* (Fairleigh Dickinson, 2003). Gathers essays about Lawrence and America.

Paul Eggert and John Worthen, eds., *Lawrence and Comedy* (Cambridge University Press, 1996). Collects essays concerning Lawrence's uses of satire and comedy.

David Ellis, ed., *Casebook on 'Women in Love'* (Oxford University Press, 2006). Essays of modern criticism.

David Ellis and Howard Mills, *D. H. Lawrence's Non-Fiction: Art, Thought and Genre* (Cambridge University Press, 1988). Collection which examines in particular Lawrence's writing of the 1920s.

Anne Fernihough, *D. H. Lawrence: Aesthetics and Ideology* (Oxford University Press, 1993). Wide-ranging enquiry into the intellectual context of Lawrence's writing.

Anne Fernihough, ed., *The Cambridge Companion to D. H. Lawrence* (Cambridge University Press, 2001). Usefully wide-ranging collection.

Louis K. Greiff, *D. H. Lawrence: Fifty Years on Film* (Southern Illinois University Press, 2001). Detailed account and analysis of screen adaptations.

G. M. Hyde, *D. H. Lawrence* (Palgrave Macmillan, 1990). Brief but provocative account of all Lawrence's writing.

Earl G. Ingersoll, *D. H. Lawrence, Desire and Narrative* (University Press of Florida, 2001). Postmodern approach to the major fiction.

Paul Poplawski, ed., *Writing the Body in D. H. Lawrence: Essays on Language, Representation, and Sexuality* (Greenwood Press, 2001). Gathers modern essays.

N. H. Reeve, *Reading Late Lawrence* (Palgrave Macmillan, 2004). Especially finely written account of Lawrence's late fiction.

Neil Roberts, *D. H. Lawrence, Travel and Cultural Difference* (Palgrave Macmillan, 2004). Valuable post-colonial study of Lawrence's travel-related writings 1921-5.

Carol Siegel, *Lawrence Among the Women: Wavering Boundaries in Women's Literary Traditions* (University Press of Virginia, 1991). Important and wide-ranging feminist reassessment of Lawrence.

Jack Stewart, *The Vital Art of D. H. Lawrence* (Southern Illinois University Press, 1999). Insightful study of Lawrence and the visual arts.

Linda Ruth Williams, *Sex in the Head: Visions of Femininity and Film in D. H. Lawrence* (Harvester Wheatsheaf, 1993). Feminist approach to selected works of Lawrence.

John Worthen and Andrew Harrison, eds., *Casebook on 'Sons and Lovers'* (Oxford University Press, 2005). Essays of modern criticism.

Peter Widdowson, ed., *D. H. Lawrence* (London and New York: Longman, 1992). Useful collection surveying contemporary theoretical approaches to Lawrence.

REFERENCE, EDITIONS, LETTERS AND BIOGRAPHY

The standard bibliography of Lawrence's work is *A Bibliography of D. H. Lawrence*, 3rd edn., ed. Warren Roberts and Paul Poplawski (Cambridge University Press, 2001). A useful reference work is Paul Poplawski's *D. H. Lawrence: A Reference Companion* (Greenwood Press, 1996) which gathers material up to 1994 and includes comprehensive bibliographies for most of Lawrence's works; Poplawski's 'Guide to further reading' in the *Cambridge Companion to D. H. Lawrence* goes up to 2000.

Lawrence's letters – arguably including some of his very best writing – have been published in an eight-volume complete edition, edited by James T. Boulton and published by Cambridge University Press.

Lawrence's work has now been almost completely published in the Cambridge Edition; thirty-three volumes have appeared and are variously available in paperback and hardback. The edited texts from a number of the volumes have also been published by Penguin.

A biographical work on Lawrence still worth consulting is the magnificent three-volume *D. H. Lawrence: A Composite Biography*, ed. Edward Nehls (University of Wisconsin Press, 1957–9). Between 1991 and 1998, Cambridge University Press published a three-volume biography which remains the standard work: John Worthen, *D. H. Lawrence: The Early Years 1885–1912* (1991), Mark Kinkead-Weekes, *D. H. Lawrence: Triumph to Exile 1912–1922* (1996) and David Ellis, *D. H. Lawrence: Dying Game 1922–1930* (1998). The most recent single-volume modern biography is that by John Worthen, *D. H. Lawrence: The Life of an Outsider* (Penguin Books, 2005).

A Note on the Texts

The texts in this edition are those established for *The Woman Who Rode Away and Other Stories*, ed. Dieter Mehl and Christa Jansohn (Cambridge University Press, 1995) and *St. Mawr and Other Stories*, ed. Brian Finney (Cambridge University Press, 1983) (although *St. Mawr* itself has been slightly emended, as explained below). Each of these editions contains an apparatus of all the changes made to the base-texts, a full discussion of the editorial decisions taken, and an account of the complex history of textual transmission, including detailed information on manuscript and typescript sources.

The Woman Who Rode Away

Lawrence's manuscript (now unlocated) was written at Kiowa Ranch, New Mexico, in June 1924. It was typed by his friend Dorothy Brett (see explanatory note 179:2) in two copies and revised by Lawrence; one copy (Yale University) was used in America for the *Dial* publication in two numbers (July and August 1925); proofs for the *Dial* with some corrections by Lawrence also survive (Yale University). The other copy of the typescript (unlocated) was the source, in England, for publication in the *Criterion* (July 1925 and January 1926), the *Best British Short Stories of 1926* (November 1926) and Martin Secker's *The Woman Who Rode Away and Other Stories* (May 1928). The base-text here is the corrected typescript, emended from the corrections in the *Dial*.

St. Mawr

Lawrence's two manuscripts (destroyed in a fire in 1961) were written at Kiowa Ranch, June–September 1924. The first version of the story (which may have overlapped with the writing of 'The Woman Who Rode Away') was probably completed by mid-June; he then wrote a much longer second version which he completed by 13 September. This was typed by Brett in two copies and revised by Lawrence; the surviving typescript (University of Nottingham) was the setting-copy for Secker's *St. Mawr Together with The Princess* (May 1925), for which Lawrence corrected two sets of proofs. One set was returned to Secker on 23 March 1925, but that set is now unlocated.

The other set of proofs survives at Eton College Library, but this set was *not* returned to Secker and therefore did not contribute to the final corrections for his edition. It was instead given as a present to one of Lawrence's friends in Mexico City, Mrs Anne Conway, who had helped him while he was seriously ill there during February and March 1925. The proofs are inscribed to Mrs Conway in Lawrence's hand and were probably presented to her before he left Mexico City on 25 March 1925. They came to light only in 1985 and this is the first time they have been systematically collated with other states of the text in order to consider further textual emendation. They contain thirty-nine, mostly very minor, corrections (e.g., Lawrence corrected 'cottages' to 'cottagers' (63:19), 'Flena' to 'Elena' (69:8), 'at the that' to 'at that' (167:40)). Six of the corrections (three involving changes in wording) did not appear in Secker's text and therefore demonstrate that these proofs were not seen by Secker and that his set was corrected differently to some extent. The remaining thirty-three corrections, however, did appear in Secker's text, so it seems likely that Lawrence made at least some of the same corrections in the partner set of proofs.

Alfred Knopf's first American edition of *St. Mawr* (on its own) was almost certainly derived from Secker's uncorrected proofs and was published in June 1925. For this edition, Lawrence corrected yet another set of proofs (unlocated), probably some time in April 1925; twenty-seven of the corrections Lawrence had made in the Eton proofs are also found in Knopf's edition.

The base-text is the typescript, emended where the English and American first editions can reasonably be thought to include Lawrence's proof changes. By collation with the first editions, the Eton proofs can be seen to confirm a small number of such changes and the following five emendations to the Cambridge text are made here on that basis:[1]

44:35 'worked in' here emended to 'worked with'

51:29 'his big slightly prominent' here emended to 'his big, slightly prominent'

60:35 'someday' here emended to 'some day'

67:19 'came out' here emended to 'came out,'

106:7 '*Pino real*' here emended to '*Pino-real*'

See also explanatory notes for 55:29 and 61:36 for two unadopted substantive variants from the Eton proofs.[2]

The following additional emendations and corrections to the Cambridge text have been made for this edition (see corresponding explanatory notes for further comment):

42:36 'Cezanne' emended to 'Cézanne'

47:34 two single inverted commas ('') corrected to a set of double ones (")

60:40 'Sevres' emended to 'Sèvres' (from the American first edition)

61:33 'lets-be-happy' emended to 'let's-be-happy' (from the American first edition)

64:17–18 'one mother's meeting' emended to 'one mothers' meeting'

68:39 'its my duty' emended to 'it's my duty' (from the American first edition)

83:18 'Women's clothing take up' corrected to 'Women's clothing takes up' (from the base-text typescript)

83:30 'è' changed to the correct Italian 'è' (such accents appear in the typescript as a vertical mark)

100:38 'young Edward's teeth' emended to 'young Edwards' teeth'

The Princess

Lawrence's manuscript (University of Texas at Austin) was written at Kiowa Ranch, September–October 1924. Of the typescripts (unlocated) prepared by Brett in October 1924, one was used by the English magazine the *Calendar of Modern Letters* (March, April and May 1925) and its proofs, probably not corrected by Lawrence, were used by Secker for *St. Mawr Together with The Princess*, for which Lawrence did correct proofs. The base-text adopted here is the manuscript, emended where Secker's edition can reasonably be thought to include revisions made by Lawrence in the typescript and in proof. One typographical error in the Cambridge text is corrected here: 215:23 'cooly' corrected to 'coolly'.

Paul Poplawski

NOTES

1. Note that the pagination here differs from the original Cambridge edition: 'The Woman Who Rode Away' is 34 pages behind and the other two novellas 20 pages ahead of the pagination in the respective Cambridge volumes.

A Note on the Texts

2. For his kindness in making the Eton proofs of *St. Mawr* available to me for this edition, I would like to thank the librarian of Eton College Library, Michael Meredith. I am also grateful to the Department of Manuscripts and Special Collections at the University of Nottingham for access to the typescript of *St. Mawr*, and to Lindeth Vasey and John Worthen for much invaluable advice and guidance on relevant textual matters.

THE WOMAN WHO
RODE AWAY

ST. MAWR

THE PRINCESS

The Woman Who Rode Away

She had thought that this marriage, of all marriages, would be an adventure. Not that the man himself was exactly magical to her. A little, wiry, twisted fellow, twenty years older than herself, with brown eyes and greying hair, who had come to America a scrap of a wastrel, from Holland, years ago, as a tiny boy, and from the gold mines of the West had been kicked south into Mexico, and now was more or less rich, owning silver mines in the wilds of the Sierra Madre: it was obvious that the adventure lay in his circumstances, rather than his person. But he was still a little dynamo of energy, in spite of accidents survived, and what he had accomplished he had accomplished alone. One óf those human oddments there is no accounting for.

When she actually *saw* what he had accomplished, her heart quailed. Great green-covered, unbroken mountain-hills, and in the midst of the lifeless isolation, the sharp pinkish mounds of the dried mud from the silver-works. Under the nakedness of the works, the walled-in, one-storey adobe house, with its garden inside, and its deep inner verandah with tropical climbers on the sides. And when you looked up from this shut-in flowered patio, you saw the huge pink cone of the silver-mud refuse, and the machinery of the extracting plant, against heaven above. No more.

To be sure, the great wooden doors were often open. And then she could stand outside, in the vast open world. And see great, void, tree-clad hills piling behind one another, from nowhere into nowhere. They were green in autumn time. For the rest, pinkish stark dry and abstract.

And in his battered Ford car her husband would take her into the dead, thrice-dead little Spanish town forgotten among the mountains. The great, sun-dried dead church, the dead portales, the hopeless covered market-place, where, the first time she went, she saw a dead dog lying between the meat stalls and the vegetable array, stretched out as if for ever, nobody troubling to throw it away. Deadness within deadness.

Everybody feebly talking silver, and showing bits of ore. But silver was at a standstill. The great war came and went. Silver was a dead market. Her husband's mines were closed down. But she and he lived on in the adobe house under the works, among the flowers that were never very flowery to her.

She had two children, a boy and a girl. And her eldest, the boy, was nearly ten years old before she aroused from her stupor of subjected amazement. She was now thirty-three, a large, blue-eyed, dazed woman, beginning to grow stout. Her little, wiry, tough, twisted, brown-eyed husband was fifty-three, a man as tough as wire, tenacious as wire, still full of energy, but dimmed by the lapse of silver from the market, and by some curious inaccessibility on his wife's part.

He was a man of principles, and a good husband. In a way, he doted on her. He never quite got over his dazzled admiration of her. But essentially, he was still a bachelor. He had been thrown out on the world, a little bachelor, at the age of ten. When he married he was over forty, and had enough money to marry on. But his capital was all a bachelor's. He was boss of his own works, and marriage was the last and most intimate bit of his own works.

He admired his wife to extinction, he admired her body, all her points. And she was to him always the rather dazzling Californian girl from Berkeley, whom he had first known. Like any Sheik, he kept her guarded among those mountains of Chihuahua. He was jealous of her as he was of his silver mine: and that is saying a lot.

At thirty-three she really was still the girl from Berkeley, in all but physique. Her conscious development had stopped mysteriously with her marriage, completely arrested. Her husband had never become real to her, neither mentally nor physically. In spite of his late sort of passion for her, he never meant anything to her, physically. Only morally he swayed her, downed her, kept her in an invincible slavery.

So the years went by, in the adobe house strung round the sunny patio, with the silver-works overhead. Her husband was never still. When the silver went dead, he ran a ranch lower down, some twenty miles away, and raised pure-bred hogs, splendid creatures. At the same time, he hated pigs. He was a squeamish waif of an idealist, and really hated the physical side of life. He loved work, work, work, and making things. His marriage, his children, were something he was making, part of his business, but with a sentimental income this time.

Gradually her nerves began to go wrong: she must get out. She must get out. So he took her to El Paso for three months. And at least it was the United States.

But he kept his spell over her. The three months ended: back she was, just the same, in her adobe house among those eternal green or pinky-brown hills, void as only the undiscovered is void. She taught her children, she supervised the Mexican boys who were her servants. And sometimes her husband brought visitors, Spaniards or Mexicans or occasionally white men.

He really loved to have white men staying on the place. Yet he had not a moment's peace when they were there. It was as if his wife were some peculiar secret vein of ore in his mines, which no one must be aware of except himself. And she was fascinated by the young gentlemen, mining engineers, who were his guests at times. He too was fascinated by a real gentleman. But he was an old-timer bachelor with a wife, and if a gentleman looked at his wife, he felt as if his mine were being looted, the secrets of it pried out.

It was one of these young gentlemen who put the idea into her mind. They were all standing outside the great wooden doors of the patio, looking at the outer world. The eternal, motionless hills were all green, it was September, after the rains. There was no sign of anything, save the deserted mine, the deserted works, and a bunch of half-deserted miners' dwellings.

"I wonder," said the young man, "what there is behind those great blank hills."

"More hills," said Lederman. "If you go that way, Sonora and the coast. This way is the desert—you came from there—And the other way, hills and mountains."

"Yes, but what *lives* in the hills and the mountains? *Surely* there is something wonderful! It looks *so* like nowhere on earth: like being on the moon."

"There's plenty of game, if you want to shoot. And Indians, if you call *them* wonderful."

"Wild ones?"

"Wild enough."

"But friendly?"

"It depends. Some of them are quite wild, and they don't let anybody near. They kill a missionary at sight. And where a missionary can't get, nobody can."

"But what does the government say?"

"They're so far from everywhere, the government leaves 'em alone. And they're wily, if they think there'll be trouble, they send a delegation to Chihuahua and make a formal submission. The government is glad to leave it at that."

"And do they live quite wild, with their own savage customs and religion?"

"Oh yes. They use nothing but bows and arrows. I've seen them in town, in the Plaza, with funny sort of hats with flowers round them, and a bow in one hand, quite naked except for a sort of shirt, even in cold weather—striding round with their savages' bare legs."

"But don't you suppose it's wonderful, up there in their secret villages?"

"No. What would there be wonderful about it? Savages are savages, and all savages behave more or less alike: rather low down and dirty, unsanitary, with a few cunning tricks, and struggling to get enough to eat."

"But surely they have old, old religions and mysteries—it *must* be wonderful, surely it must."

"I don't know about mysteries—howling and heathen practices, more or less indecent. No, I see nothing wonderful in that kind of stuff. And I wonder that you should, when you have lived in London or Paris or New York—"

"Ah, *everybody* lives in London or Paris or New York—" said the young man, as if this were an argument.

And his peculiar vague enthusiasm for unknown Indians found a full echo in the woman's heart. She was overcome by a foolish romanticism more unreal than a girl's. She felt it was her destiny to wander into the secret haunts of these timeless, mysterious, marvellous Indians of the mountains.

She kept her secret. The young man was departing, her husband was going with him down to Torreón, on business: would be away for some days. But before the departure, she made her husband talk about the Indians: about the wandering tribes, resembling the Navajo, who were still wandering free; and the Yaquis of Sonora: and the different groups in the different valleys of Chihuahua State.

There was supposed to be one tribe, the Chilchuis, living in a high valley to the south, who were the sacred tribe of all the Indians. The descendants of Montezuma and of the old Aztec or Totonac kings still lived among them, and the old priests still kept up the ancient religion, and offered human sacrifices—so it was said. Some scientists had been to the Chilchui country, and had come back gaunt and exhausted with hunger and bitter privation, bringing various curious, barbaric objects of worship, but having seen nothing extraordinary in the hungry, stark village of savages.

Though Lederman talked in this off-hand way, it was obvious he was really touched by the vulgar marvel of mysterious savages.

"How far away are they?" she asked.

"Oh—three days on horseback—past Cuchitee and a little lake there is up there."

Her husband and the young man departed. The woman made her

crazy plans. Of late, to break the monotony of her life, she had harassed her husband into letting her go riding with him occasionally, on horseback. She was never allowed to go out alone. The country truly was not safe, lawless and crude.

But she had her own horse, and she dreamed of being free as she had been as a girl, among the hills of California.

Her daughter, nine years old, was now in a tiny convent in the little half-deserted Spanish mining-town five miles away.

"Manuel," said the woman to her house-servant, "I'm going to ride to the convent to see Margarita, and take her a few things. Perhaps I shall stay the night in the convent. You look after Freddy and see everything is all right till I come back."

"Shall I ride with you on the master's horse, or shall Juan?" asked the servant.

"Neither of you. I shall go alone."

The young man looked her in the eyes, in protest. Absolutely impossible that the woman should ride alone!

"I shall go alone." repeated the large, placid-seeming, fair-complexioned woman, with peculiar overbearing emphasis. And the man silently, unhappily yielded.

"Why are you going alone, Mother?" asked her son, as she made up parcels of food.

"Am I *never* to be let alone? Not one moment of my life?" she cried, with sudden explosion of energy. And the child, like the servant, shrank into silence.

She set off without a qualm, riding astride on her strong roan horse, and wearing a riding suit of coarse linen, a riding skirt over her linen breeches, a scarlet neck-tie over her white blouse, and a black felt hat on her head. She had food in her saddle-bags, an army canteen with water, and a large, native blanket tied on behind the saddle. Peering into the distance, she set off from her home. Manuel and the little boy stood in the gateway to watch her go. She did not even turn to wave them farewell.

But when she had ridden about a mile, she left the wild road and took a small trail to the right, that led into another valley, over steep places and past great trees, and through another deserted mining settlement. It was September, the water was running freely in the little stream that had fed the now-abandoned mine. She got down to drink, and let the horse drink too.

She saw natives coming through the trees, away up the slope. They

9

had seen her, and were watching her closely. She watched in turn. The three people, two women and a youth, were making a wide detour, so as not to come too close to her. She did not care. Mounting, she trotted ahead up the silent valley, beyond the silver-works, beyond any trace of mining. There was still a rough trail, that led over rocks and loose stones into the valley beyond. This trail she had already ridden, with her husband. Beyond that, she knew she must go south.

Curiously, she was not afraid, although it was a frightening country, the silent, fatal-seeming mountain slopes, the occasional distant, suspicious, elusive natives among the trees, the great carrion birds occasionally hovering, like great flies, in the distance, over some carrion or some ranch house or some group of huts.

As she climbed the trees shrank and the trail ran through a thorny scrub, that was trailed over with blue convolvulus and an occasional pink creeper. Then these flowers lapsed. She was nearing the pine-trees.

She was over the crest, and before her another silent, void, green-clad valley. It was past midday. Her horse turned to a little runlet of water, so she got down to eat her mid-day meal. She sat in silence looking at the motionless unliving valley, and at the sharp-peaked hills, rising higher to rock and pine-trees, southwards. She rested two hours in the heat of the day, while the horse cropped around her.

Curious that she was neither afraid nor lonely. Indeed the loneliness was like a drink of cold water to one who is very thirsty. And a strange elation sustained her from within.

She travelled on, and camped at night in a valley beside a stream, deep among the bushes. She had seen cattle and had crossed several trails. There must be a ranch not far off. She heard the strange wailing shriek of a mountain lion, and the answer of dogs. But she sat by her small camp fire in a secret hollow place and was not really afraid. She was buoyed up always by the curious, bubbling elation within her.

It was very cold before dawn. She lay wrapped in her blanket looking at the stars, listening to her horse shivering, and feeling like a woman who has died and passed beyond. She was not sure that she had not heard, during the night, a great crash at the centre of herself, which was the crash of her own death. Or else it was a crash at the centre of the earth, and meant something big and mysterious.

With the first peep of light she got up, numb with cold, and made a fire. She ate hastily, gave her horse some pieces of oil-seed cake, and set off again. She avoided any meeting— and since she met nobody, it was evident that she in turn was avoided. She came at last into sight of the village of Cuchitee, with its black houses with their reddish roofs, a sombre, dreary little cluster below another silent, long-abandoned mine. And beyond, a long, great mountain side, rising up green and light to the darker, shaggier green of pine-trees. And beyond the pine-trees stretches of naked rock against the sky, rock slashed already and brindled with white stripes of snow. High up, the new snow had already begun to fall.

And now, as she neared, more or less, her destination, she began to go vague and disheartened. She had passed the little lake among yellowing aspen trees whose white trunks were round and suave like the white round arms of some woman. What a lovely place! In California she would have raved about it. But here she looked and saw that it was lovely, but she didn't care. She was weary and spent with her two nights in the open, and afraid of the coming night. She didn't know where she was going, or what she was going for. Her horse plodded dejectedly on, towards that immense and forbidding mountain slope, following a stony little trail. And if she had had any will of her own left, she would have turned back, to the village, to be protected and sent home to her husband.

But she had no will of her own. Her horse splashed through a brook, and turned up a valley, under immense yellowing cotton-wood trees. She must have been near nine thousand feet above sea-level, and her head was light with the altitude and with weariness. Beyond the cotton-wood trees she could see, on each side, the steep sides of mountain-slopes hemming her in, sharp-plumaged with overlapping aspen, and higher up, with sprouting, pointed spruce and pine-trees. Her horse went on automatically. In this tight valley, on this slight trail, there was nowhere to go but ahead, climbing.

Suddenly her horse jumped, and three men in dark blankets were on the trail before her.

"Adios!" came the greeting, in the full, restrained Indian voice.

"Adios!" she replied, in her assured, American woman's voice.

"Where are you going?" came the quiet question, in Spanish.

The men in the dark serapes had come closer, and were looking up at her.

"On ahead," she replied coolly, in her hard, Saxon Spanish.

These were just natives to her: dark-faced, strongly-built men in dark serapes and straw hats. They would have been the same as the men who worked for her husband, except, strangely, for the long black hair that fell over their shoulders. She noted this long black hair with a certain distaste. These must be the wild Indians she had come to see.

"Where do you come from?" the same man asked. It was always the one man who spoke. He was young, with quick, large, bright black eyes that glanced sideways at her. He had a soft black moustache on his dark face, and a sparse tuft of beard, loose hairs on his chin. His long black hair, full of life, hung unrestrained on his shoulders. Dark as he was, he did not look as if he had washed lately.

His two companions were the same, but older men, powerful and silent. One had a thin black line of moustache, but was beardless. The other had the smooth cheeks and the sparse dark hairs marking the lines of his chin with the beard characteristic of the Indians.

"I come from far away," she replied, with half-jocular evasion.

This was received in silence.

"But where do you live?" asked the young man, with that same quiet insistence.

"In the north," she replied airily.

Again there was a moment's silence. The young man conversed quietly, in Indian, with his two companions.

"Where do you want to go, up this way?" he asked suddenly, with challenge and authority, pointing briefly up the trail.

"To the Chilchui Indians," answered the woman laconically.

The young man looked at her. His eyes were quick and black, and inhuman. He saw, in the full evening light, the faint sub-smile of assurance on her rather large, calm, fresh-complexioned face: the weary, bluish lines under her large blue eyes: and in her eyes, as she looked down at him, a half-childish, half-arrogant confidence in her own female power. But in her eyes also, a curious look of trance.

"*Usted es Señora?* You are a married lady?" the Indian said.

"Yes I am a married lady," she replied complacently.

"With a family?"

"With a husband and two children, boy and girl," she said.

The Indian turned to his companions and translated, in the low, gurgling speech, like hidden water running. They were evidently at a loss.

"Where is your husband?" asked the young man.

"Who knows?" she replied airily. "He has gone away on business for a week."

The black eyes watched her shrewdly. She, for all her weariness, smiled faintly in the pride of her own adventure and the assurance of her own womanhood, and the spell of the madness that was on her.

"And what do *you* want to do?" the Indian asked her.

"I want to visit the Chilchui Indians—to see their houses and to know their Gods," she replied.

The young man turned and translated quickly, and there was a silence almost of consternation. The grave elder men were glancing at her sideways, with strange looks, from under their decorated hats. And they said something to the young man, in deep chest voices.

The latter still hesitated. Then he turned to the woman.

"Good!" he said. "Let us go. But we cannot arrive until tomorrow. We shall have to make a camp tonight."

"Good!" she said. "I can make a camp."

Without more ado, they set off at a good speed up the stony trail. The young Indian ran alongside her horse's head, the other two ran behind. One of them had taken a thick stick, and occasionally he struck her horse a resounding blow on the haunch, to urge him forward. This made the horse jump, and threw her against the saddle horn, which, tired as she was, made her angry.

"Don't do that!" she cried, looking round angrily at the fellow. She met his black, large, bright eyes, and for the first time her spirit really quailed. The man's eyes were not human to her, and they did not see her as a beautiful white woman. He looked at her with a black, bright inhuman look, and saw no woman in her at all. As if she were some strange, unaccountable *thing*, incomprehensible to him, but inimical. She sat in her saddle in wonder, feeling once more as if she had died. And again he struck her horse, and jerked her badly in the saddle.

All the passionate anger of the spoilt white woman rose in her. She pulled her horse to a standstill, and turned with blazing eyes to the man at her bridle.

"Tell that fellow not to touch my horse again," she cried.

She met the eyes of the young man, and in their bright black inscrutability she saw a fine spark, as in a snake's eye, of derision. He spoke to his companion in the rear, in the low tones of the Indian. The man with the stick listened without looking. Then, giving a strange low cry to the horse, he struck it again on the rear, so that it leaped forward spasmodically up the stony trail, scattering the stones, pitching the weary woman in her seat.

The anger flew like a madness into her eyes, she went white at the gills. Fiercely she reined in her horse. But before she could turn, the young Indian had caught the reins under the horse's throat, jerked them forward, and was trotting ahead rapidly, leading the horse.

The woman was powerless. And along with her supreme anger there came a slight thrill of exultation. She knew she was dead.

The sun was setting, a great yellow light flooded the last of the aspens, flared on the trunks of the pine trees, the pine-needles bristled and stood out with dark lustre, the rocks glowed with unearthly glamour. And through this effulgence the Indian at her horse's head trotted unweariedly on, his dark blanket swinging, his bare legs glowing with a strange transfigured ruddiness, in the powerful light, and his straw hat with its half-absurd decorations of flowers and feathers shining showily above his river of long black hair. At times he would utter a low call to the horse, and then the other Indian, behind, would fetch the beast a whack with the stick.

The wonder-light faded off the mountains, the world began to grow dark, a cold air breathed down. In the sky, half a moon was struggling against the glow in the west. Huge shadows came down from steep rocky slopes. Water was rushing. The woman was conscious only of her fatigue, her unspeakable fatigue, and the cold wind from the heights. She was not aware how moonlight replaced daylight. It happened while she travelled unconscious with weariness.

For some hours they travelled by moonlight. Then suddenly they came to a standstill. The men conversed in low tones for a moment.

"We camp here," said the young man.

She waited for him to help her down. He merely stood holding the horse's bridle. She almost fell from the saddle, so fatigued.

They had chosen a place at the foot of rocks that still gave off a little warmth of the sun. One man cut pine-boughs, another erected little screens of pine-boughs against the rock, for shelter, and put boughs of balsam pine, for beds. The third made a small fire, to heat tortillas. They worked in silence.

The woman drank water. She did not want to eat—only to lie down.

"Where do I sleep?" she asked.

The young man pointed to one of the shelters. She crept in and lay inert. She did not care what happened to her, she was so weary, and so beyond everything. Through the twigs of spruce she could see the three men squatting round the fire on their hams, chewing the tortillas they picked from the ashes with their dark fingers, and drinking water from a gourd. They talked in low, muttering tones, with long intervals of silence. Her saddle and saddle-bags lay not far from the fire, unopened, untouched. The men were not interested in her nor her belongings. There they squatted with their hats on their heads, eating, eating mechanically, like animals, the dark serape with its fringe falling to the ground before and behind, the powerful dark legs naked and squatting like an animal's, showing the dirty white shirt and the sort of loin-cloth which was the only other garment, underneath. And they showed no more sign of interest in her than if she had been a piece of venison they were bringing home from the hunt, and had hung inside a shelter.

After a while they carefully extinguished the fire, and went inside their own shelter. Watching through the screen of boughs, she had a moment's thrill of fear and anxiety, seeing the dark forms cross and pass silently in the moonlight. Would they attack her now?

But no! They were as if oblivious of her. Her horse was hobbled: she could hear it hopping wearily. All was silent, mountain-silent, cold, deathly. She slept and woke, and slept in a semi-conscious numbness of cold and fatigue. A long, long night, icy and eternal, and she aware that she had died.

Yet when there was a stirring, and a clink of flint and steel, and the form of a man crouching like a dog over a bone, at a red splutter of fire, and she knew it was morning coming, it seemed to her the night had passed too soon.

When the fire was going, she came out of her shelter with one real desire left: for coffee. The men were warming more tortillas.

"Can we make coffee?" she asked.

The young man looked at her, and she imagined the same faint spark of derision in his eyes. He shook his head.

"We don't take it," he said. "There is no time."

And the elder men, squatting on their haunches, looked up at her in the terrible paling dawn, and there was not even derision in their eyes. Only that intense, yet remote, inhuman glitter which was terrible to her. They were inaccessible. They could not see her as a woman at all. As if she *were* not a woman. As if, perhaps, her whiteness took away all her womanhood, and left her as some giant, female white ant. That was all they could see in her.

Before the sun was up, she was in the saddle again, and they were climbing steeply, in the icy air. The sun came, and soon she was very hot, exposed to the glare in the bare places. It seemed to her they were climbing to the roof of the world. Beyond against heaven were slashes of snow.

During the course of the morning, they came to a place where the horse could not go further. They rested for a time with a great slant of living rock in front of them, like the glossy breast of some earth-beast. Across this rock, along a wavering crack, they had to go. It seemed to her that for hours she went in torment, on her hands and knees, from crack to crevice, along the slanting face of this pure rock-mountain. An Indian in front and an Indian behind walked slowly erect, shod with sandals of braided leather. But she in her riding-boots dared not stand erect.

Yet what she wondered, all the time, was why she persisted in clinging and crawling along these mile-long sheets of rock. Why she did not hurl herself down, and have done! The world was below her.

When they emerged at last on a stony slope, she looked back, and saw the third Indian coming carrying her saddle and saddle bags on his back, the whole hung from a band across his forehead. And he had his hat in his hand, as he stepped slowly, with the slow, soft, heavy tread of the Indian, unwavering in the chinks of rock, as if along a scratch in the mountain's iron shield.

The stony slope led downwards. The Indians seemed to grow excited. One ran ahead at a slow trot, disappearing round the curve of stones. And the track curved round and down, till at last in the full blaze of the mid-morning sun, they could see a valley below them, between walls of rock, as in a great wide chasm let in the mountains. A green valley, with a river, and trees, and clusters of low flat sparkling houses. It was all tiny and perfect, three thousand feet below. Even the flat bridge over the stream, and the square with the houses around it, the bigger buildings piled up at opposite ends of the square, the tall cotton-wood trees, the pastures and stretches of yellow-sere maize, the patches of brown sheep or goats in the distance, on the slopes, the railed enclosures by the stream-side. There it was, all small and perfect, looking magical, as any place will look magical, seen from the mountains above. The unusual thing was that the low houses glittered white, whitewashed, looking like crystals of salt, or silver. This frightened her.

They began the long, winding descent at the head of the barranca, following the stream that rushed and fell. At first it was all rocks: then the pine-trees began, and soon, the silver-limbed aspens. The flowers of autumn, big pink daisy-like flowers, and white ones, and many yellow flowers, were in profusion. But she had to sit down and rest, she was so weary. And she saw the bright flowers shadowily, as pale shadows hovering, as one who is dead must see them.

At length came grass and pasture-slopes between mingled aspen and pine-trees. A shepherd, naked in the sun save for his hat and his cotton loin-cloth, was driving his brown sheep away. In a grove of trees they sat and waited, she and the young Indian. The one with the saddle had also gone forward.

They heard a sound of someone coming. It was three men, in fine serapes of red and orange and yellow and black, and with brilliant feather head-dresses. The oldest had his grey hair braided with fur, and his red and orange-yellow serape was covered with curious black markings, like a leopard-skin. The other two were not grey-haired, but they were elders too. Their blankets were in stripes, and their head-dresses not so elaborate.

The young Indian addressed the elders in a few quiet words. They listened without answering or looking at him or at the woman, keeping their faces averted and their eyes turned to the ground, only listening. And at length they turned and looked at the woman.

The old chief, or medicine-man, whatever he was, had a deeply wrinkled and lined face of dark bronze, with a few sparse grey hairs round the mouth. Two long braids of grey hair, braided with fur and coloured feathers, hung on his shoulders. And yet, it was only his eyes that mattered. They were black and of extraordinary piercing strength, without a qualm of misgiving in their demonish, dauntless power. He looked into the eyes of the white woman with a long, piercing look, seeking she knew not what. She summoned all her strength to meet his eyes and keep up her guard. But it was no good. He was not looking at her as one human being looks at another. He never even perceived her resistance or her challenge, but looked past them both, into she knew not what.

She could see it was hopeless to expect any human communication with this old being.

He turned and said a few words to the young Indian.

"He asks, what do you seek here?" said the young man in Spanish.

"I? Nothing! I only came to see what it was like."

This was again translated, and the old man turned his eyes on her once more. Then he spoke again, in his low muttering tone, to the young Indian.

"He says, why does she leave her house with the white man? Does she want to bring the white man's God to the Chilchui?"

"No," she replied, foolhardy. "I came away from the white man's God myself. I came to look for the God of the Chilchui."

Profound silence followed, when this was translated. Then the old man spoke again, in a small voice almost of weariness.

"Does the white woman seek the gods of the Chilchui because she is weary of her own God?" came the question.

"Yes, she does. She is tired of the white man's God," she replied, thinking that was what they wanted her to say. "She would like to serve the gods of the Chilchui."

She was aware of an extraordinary thrill of triumph and exultance passing through the Indians, in the tense silence that followed when this was translated. Then they all looked at her with piercing black eyes, in which a steely covetous intent glittered incomprehensible. She was the more puzzled, as there was nothing sensual or sexual in the look. It had a terrible glittering purity that was beyond her. She was afraid, she would have been paralysed with fear, had not something died within her, leaving her with a cold, watchful wonder only.

The elders talked a little while, then the two went away, leaving her with the young man and the oldest chief. The old man now looked at her with a certain solicitude.

"He says, are you tired?" asked the young man.

"Very tired," she said.

"The men will bring you a carriage," said the young Indian.

The carriage, when it came, proved to be a litter consisting of a sort of hammock of dark woolen frieze, slung on to a pole which was borne on the shoulders of two long-haired Indians. The woolen hammock was spread on the ground, she sat down on it, and the two men raised the pole to their shoulders. Swinging rather as if she were in a sack, she was carried out of the grove of trees, following the old chief, whose leopard-spotted blanket moved curiously in the sunlight.

They had emerged in the valley-head. Just in front were the maize fields, with ripe ears of maize. The corn was not very tall in this high altitude. The well-worn path went between it, and all she could see was the erect form of the old chief, in the flame and black serape, stepping soft and heavy and swift, his head forward, looking neither to right nor left. Her bearers followed, stepping rhythmically, the long blue-black hair glistening like a river down the naked shoulders of the man in front.

They passed the maize, and came to a big wall or earthwork made of earth and adobe bricks. The wooden doors were open. Passing on, they were in a network of small gardens, full of flowers and herbs and fruit trees, each garden watered by a tiny ditch of running water. Among each cluster of trees and flowers was a small, glittering white house, windowless, and with closed door. The place was a network of little paths, small streams, and little bridges among square, flowering gardens.

Following the broadest path—a soft narrow track between leaves and grass, a path worn smooth by centuries of human feet, no hoof of horse nor any wheel to disfigure it—they came to the little river of swift bright water, and crossed on a log bridge. Everything was silent—there was no human being anywhere. The road went on under magnificent cotton-wood trees. It emerged suddenly outside the central plaza or square of the village.

This was a long oblong of low white houses with flat roofs, and two bigger buildings, having as it were little square huts piled on top of bigger long huts, stood at either end of the oblong, facing each other rather askew. Every little house was a dazzling white, save for the great round beam-ends which projected under the flat eaves, and for the flat roofs. Round each of the bigger buildings, on the outside of the square, was a stockyard fence, inside which was a garden with trees and flowers, and various small houses.

Not a soul was in sight. They passed silently between the houses into the central square. This was quite bare and arid, the earth trodden smooth by endless generations of passing feet, passing across from door to door. All the doors of the windowless houses gave on to this blank square, but all the doors were closed. The firewood lay near the threshold, a clay oven was still smoking, but there was no sign of moving life.

The old man walked straight across the square to the big house at the end, where the two upper storeys, as in a house of toy bricks, stood each one smaller than the lower one. A stone staircase, outside, led up to the roof of the first storey.

At the foot of this stair-case the litter-bearers stood still, and lowered the woman to the ground.

"You will come up," said the young Indian who spoke Spanish.

She mounted the stone stairs to the earthen roof of the first house, which formed a platform around the wall of the second storey. She followed around this platform to the back of the big house. There they descended again, into the garden at the rear.

So far they had seen no-one. But now two men appeared, bare-headed, with long braided hair, and wearing a sort of white shirt gathered into a loin-cloth. These went along with the three newcomers, across the garden where red flowers and yellow flowers were blooming, to a long, low white house. There they entered without knocking.

It was dark inside. There was a low murmur of men's voices. Several men were present, their white shirts showing in the gloom, their dark faces invisible. . . . They were sitting on a great log of smooth old wood, that lay along the far wall. And save for this log, the room seemed empty. But no, in the dark at one end was a couch, a sort of bed, and someone lying there, covered with furs.

The old Indian in the spotted serape, who had accompanied the woman, now took off his hat and his blanket and his sandals. Laying them aside, he approached the couch, and spoke in a low voice. For some moments there was no answer. Then an old man with the snow-white hair hanging round his darkly-visible face, roused himself like a vision, and leaned on one elbow, looking vaguely at the company, in tense silence.

The grey-haired Indian spoke again, and then the young Indian, taking the woman's hand, led her forward. In her linen riding habit, and black boots and hat, and her pathetic bit of a red tie, she stood there beside the fur-covered bed of the old, old man, who sat reared up, leaning on one elbow, remote as a ghost, his white hair streaming in disorder, his face almost black, yet with a far-off intentness, not of this world, leaning forward to look at her.

His face was so old, it was like dark glass, and the few curling hairs that sprang white from his lips and chin were quite incredible. The long white locks fell unbraided and disorderly on either side of the glassy, dark face. And under a faint powder of white eyebrows, the black eyes of the old chief looked at her as if from the far, far dead, seeing something that was never to be seen.

At last he spoke a few deep, hollow words, as if to the dark air.

"He says, do you bring your heart to the god of the Chilchui?" translated the young Indian.

"Tell him yes," she said, automatically.

There was a pause. The old Indian spoke again, as if to the air. One of the men present went out. There was a silence as if of eternity, in the dim room that was lighted only through the open door.

The woman looked round. Four old men with grey hair sat on the log by the wall facing the door. Two other men, powerful and impassive, stood near the door. They all had long hair, and wore white shirts gathered into a loin-cloth. Their powerful legs were naked and dark. There was a silence like eternity.

At length the man returned, with white and black clothing on his arm. The young Indian took them, and holding them in front of the woman, said:

"You must take off your clothes, and put these on."

"If all you men will go out," she said.

"No one will hurt you," he said quietly.

"Not while you men are here," she said.

He looked at the two men by the door. They came quickly forward, and suddenly gripped her arms as she stood, without hurting her, but with great power. Then two of the old men came, and with curious skill slit her boots down with keen knives, and drew them off, and slit her clothing so that it came away from her. In a few moments she stood there white and uncovered. The old man on the bed spoke, and they turned her round for him to see. He spoke again, and the young Indian deftly took the pins and comb from her fair hair, so that it fell over her shoulders in a bunchy tangle.

Then the old man spoke again. The Indian led her to the bedside. The white haired, glassy-dark old man moistened his finger-tips at his mouth, and most delicately touched her on the breasts and on the body, then on the back. And she winced strangely each time, as the finger-tips drew along her skin, as if Death itself were touching her.

And she wondered, almost sadly, why she did not feel ashamed in her nakedness. She only felt sad and lost. Because nobody felt ashamed. The elder men were all dark and tense with some other deep, gloomy, incomprehensible emotion, which suspended all her agitation, while the young Indian had a strange look of ecstasy on his face. And she, she was only utterly strange and beyond herself, as if her body were not her own.

They gave her the new clothing: a long white cotton shift, that came to her knees: then a tunic of thick blue woolen stuff, embroidered with scarlet and green flowers. It was fastened over one shoulder only, and belted with a braid sash of scarlet and black wool.

When she was thus dressed, they took her away, barefoot, to a little house in the stockaded garden. The young Indian told her she might have what she wanted. She asked for water to wash herself. He brought it in a jar, together with a long wooden bowl. Then he fastened the gate-door of her house, and left her a prisoner. She could see through the bars of the gate-door of her house, the red flowers of the garden, and a humming bird. Then from the roof of the big house she heard the long, heavy sound of a drum, unearthly to her in its summons, and an uplifted voice calling from the housetop in a strange language, with a far-away emotionless intonation, delivering some speech or message. And she listened as if from the dead.

But she was very tired. She lay down on a couch of skins, pulling over her the blanket of dark wool, and she slept, giving up everything.

When she woke it was late afternoon, and the young Indian was entering with a basket-tray containing food, tortillas and corn-mush with bits of meat, probably mutton, and a drink made of honey, and some fresh plums. He brought her also a long garland of red and yellow flowers with knots of blue buds at the end. He sprinkled the garland with water from a jar, then offered it to her, with a smile. He seemed very gentle and thoughtful, and on his face and in his dark eyes was a curious look of triumph and ecstasy, that frightened her a little. The glitter had gone from the black eyes, with their curving dark lashes, and he would look at her with this strange soft glow of ecstasy that was not quite human, and terribly impersonal, and which made her uneasy.

"Is there anything you want?" he said, in his low, slow, melodious voice, that always seemed withheld, as if he were speaking aside, to somebody else, or as if he did not want to let the sound come out to her.

"Am I going to be kept a prisoner here?" she asked.

"No, you can walk in the garden tomorrow," he said softly.

Always this curious solicitude.

"Do you like that drink?" he said, offering her a little earthenware cup. "It is very refreshing."

She sipped the liquor curiously. It was made with herbs and sweetened with honey, and had a strange, lingering flavour. The young man watched her with gratification.

"It has a peculiar taste," she said.

"It is very refreshing," he replied, his black eyes resting on her always with that look of gratified ecstasy. Then he went away. And presently she began to be sick, and to vomit violently, as if she had no control over herself.

Afterwards she felt a great soothing languor steal over her, her limbs felt strong and loose and full of languor, and she lay on her couch listening to the sounds of the village, watching the yellowing sky, smelling the scent of burning cedar-wood, or pine-wood. So distinctly she heard the yapping of tiny dogs, the shuffle of far-off feet, the murmur of voices, so keenly she detected the smell of smoke, and flowers, and evening falling, so vividly she saw the one bright star infinitely remote, stirring above the sunset, that she felt as if all her senses were diffused on the air, that she could distinguish the sound of evening flowers unfolding, and the actual crystal sound of the heavens, as the vast belts of the world-atmospheres slid past one another, and as if the moisture ascending and the moisture descending in the air resounded like some harp in the cosmos.

She was a prisoner in her house and in the stockaded garden, but she scarcely minded. And it was days before she realised that she never saw another woman. Only the men, the elderly men of the big house, that she imagined must be some sort of temple, and the men priests of some sort. For they always had the same colours, red, orange, yellow, and black, and the same grave, abstracted demeanour.

Sometimes an old man would come and sit in her room with her, in absolute silence. None spoke any language but Indian, save the one younger man. The older man would smile at her, and sit with her for an hour at a time, sometimes smiling at her, when she spoke in Spanish, but never answering save with this slow, benevolent-seeming smile. And they gave off a feeling of almost fatherly solicitude. Yet their dark eyes, brooding over her, had something away in their depths that was awesomely ferocious and relentless. They would cover it with a smile, at once, if they felt her looking. But she had seen it.

Always they treated her with this curious impersonal solicitude, this utterly impersonal gentleness, as an old man treats a child. But underneath it she felt there was something else, something terrible. When her old visitor had gone away, in his silent, insidious, fatherly fashion, a shock of fear would come over her; though of what she knew not.

The young Indian would sit and talk with her freely, as if with great candour. But with him too she felt that everything real was unsaid. Perhaps it was unspeakable. His big dark eyes would rest on her almost cherishingly, touched with ecstasy, and his beautiful, slow, languorous voice would trail out its simple, ungrammatical Spanish. He told her he was the grandson of the old, old man, son of the man in the spotted serape: and they were caciques, kings from the old days, before even the Spaniards came. But he himself had been in Mexico City, and also in the United States. He had worked as a laborer, building the roads in Los Angeles. He had travelled as far as Chicago.

"Don't you speak English, then?" she asked.

His eyes rested on her with a curious look of duplicity and conflict and he mutely shook his head.

"What did you do with your long hair, when you were in the United States?" she asked. "Did you cut it off?"

Again, with the look of torment in his eyes, he shook his head.

"No," he said, in the low, subdued voice, "I wore a hat, and a handkerchief tied round my head."

And he relapsed into silence, as if of tormented memories.

"Are you the only man of your people who has been to the United States?" she asked him.

"Yes. I am the only one who has been away from here for a long time. The others come back soon, in one week. They don't stay away. The old men don't let them."

"And why did you go?"

"The old men want me to go—because I shall be the Cacique—"

He talked always with the same naïveté, an almost childish candour. But she felt that this was perhaps just the effect of his Spanish. Or perhaps speech altogether was unreal to him. Anyhow, she felt that all the real things were kept back.

He came and sat with her a good deal—sometimes more than she wished—as if he wanted to be near her. She asked him if he was married. He said he was—with two children.

"I should like to see your children," she said.

But he answered only with that smile, a sweet, almost ecstatic smile, above which the dark eyes hardly changed from their enigmatic abstraction.

It was curious, he would sit with her by the hour, without ever making her self-conscious, or sex-conscious. He seemed to have no sex, as he sat there so still and gentle and apparently submissive, with his head bent a little forward, and the river of glistening black hair streaming maidenly over his shoulders.

Yet when she looked again, she saw his shoulders broad and powerful, his eyebrows black and level, the short, curved, obstinate black lashes over his lowered eyes, the small, fur-like line of moustache above his blackish, heavy lips, and the strong chin, and she knew that in some other mysterious way he was darkly and powerfully male. And he, feeling her watching him, would glance up at her swiftly with a dark, lurking look in his eyes, which immediately he veiled with that half-sad smile.

The days and the weeks went by, in a vague kind of contentment. She was uneasy sometimes, feeling she had lost the power over herself. She was not in her own power, she was under the spell of some other power. And at times she had moments of terror and horror. But then these Indians would come and sit with her, casting their insidious spell over her by their very silent presence, their silent, sexless, powerful physical presence. As they sat they seemed to take her will away, leaving her will-less and victim to her own indifference. And the young man would bring her a sweetened drink, often the same emetic drink, but sometimes other kinds. And after drinking, the languor filled her heavy limbs, her senses seemed to float in the air, listening, hearing. They had brought her a little female dog, which she called Flora. And once, in the trance of her senses, she felt she *heard* the little dog conceive, in her tiny womb, and begin to be complex, with young. And another day she could hear the vast sound of the earth going round, like some immense arrow-string booming.

But as the days grew shorter and colder, when she was cold, she would get a sudden revival of her will, and a desire to go out, to go away. And she insisted to the young man, she wanted to go out.

So one day, they let her climb to the topmost roof of the big house where she was, and look down the square. It was the day of the big dance, but not everybody was dancing. Women with babies in their arms stood in their doorways, watching. Opposite, at the other end of the square, there was a throng before the other big house, and a small, brilliant group on the terrace-roof of the first storey, in front of wide open doors of the upper storey. Through these wide open doors she could see fire glinting in darkness, and priests in headdresses of black and yellow and scarlet feathers, wearing robe-like blankets of black and red and yellow, with long green fringe, were moving about. A big drum was beating slowly and regularly, in the dense, Indian silence. The crowd below waited—

Then a drum started on a high beat, and there came the deep, powerful burst of men singing a heavy, savage music, like a wind roaring in some timeless forest, many mature men singing in one breath, like the wind; and long lines of dancers walked out from under the big house. Men with naked, golden-bronze bodies and streaming black hair, tufts of red and yellow feathers on their arms, and kilts of white frieze with a bar of heavy red and black and green embroidery round their waists, bending slightly forward and stamping the earth in their absorbed, monotonous stamp of the dance, a fox-fur, hung by the nose from their belt behind, swaying with the sumptuous swaying of a beautiful fox-fur, the tip of the tail writhing above the dancer's heels. And after each man, a woman with a strange elaborate headdress of feathers and seashells, and wearing a short black tunic, moving erect, holding up tufts of feathers in each hand, swaying her wrists rhythmically, and subtly beating the earth with her bare feet.

So, the long line of the dance unfurling from the big house opposite.

And from the big house beneath her, strange scent of incense, strange tense silence, then the answering burst of inhuman male singing, and the long line of the dance unfurling.

It went on all day, the insistence of the drum, the cavernous, roaring, storm-like sound of male singing, the incessant swinging of the fox-skins behind the powerful, gold-bronze, stamping legs of the men, the autumn sun from a perfect blue heaven pouring on the rivers of black hair, men's and women's, the valley all still, the walls of rock beyond, the awful huge bulking of the mountain against the pure sky, its snow seething with sheer whiteness.

For hours and hours she watched, spell-bound, and as if drugged. And in all the terrible persistence of the drumming and the primeval, rushing deep singing, and the endless stamping of the dance of fox-tailed men, the tread of heavy, bird-erect women in their black tunics, she seemed at last to feel her own death, her own obliteration. As if she were to be obliterated from the field of life again. In the strange towering symbols on the heads of the changeless, absorbed women she seemed to read once more the *Mene Mene Tekel Upharsin*. Her kind of womanhood, intensely personal and individual, was to be obliterated again, and the great primeval symbols were to tower once more over the fallen individual independence of woman. The sharpness and the quivering nervous consciousness of the highly-bred white woman was to be destroyed again, womanhood was to be cast once more into the great stream of impersonal sex and impersonal passion. Strangely, as if clairvoyant, she saw the immense sacrifice prepared. And she went back to her little house in a trance of agony.

After this, there was always a certain agony when she heard the drums at evening, and the strange uplifted savage sound of men singing round the drum, like wild creatures howling to the invisible gods of the moon and the vanished sun. Something of the chuckling sobbing cry of the coyote, something of the exultant bark of the fox, the far-off wild melancholy exultance of the howling wolf, the torment of the puma's scream, and the insistence of the ancient fierce human male, with his lapses of tenderness and his abiding ferocity.

Sometimes she would climb the high roof after nightfall, and listen to the dim cluster of young men round the drum on the bridge just beyond the square, singing by the hour. Sometimes there would be a fire, and in the fire-glow, dark men wearing white shirts or naked save for a loin-cloth, would be dancing and stamping like spectres, hour after hour in the dark cold air, within the fire-glow, forever dancing and stamping like turkeys, or dropping squatting by the fire to rest, throwing their blankets round them.

"Why do you all have the same colours?" she asked the young Indian. "Why do you all have red and yellow and black, over your white shirts? And the women have black tunics?"

He looked into her eyes, curiously, and the faint, evasive smile came on to his face. Behind the smile lay a soft, strange malignancy.

"Because our men are the fire and the daytime, and our women are the spaces between the stars at night," he said.

"Aren't the women even stars?" she said.

"No. We say they are the spaces between the stars, that keep the stars apart."

He looked at her oddly, and again the touch of derision came into his eyes.

"White people," he said, "they know nothing. They are like children, always with toys. We know the sun, and we know the moon. And we say, when a white woman give herself to our gods, then our gods will begin to make the world again, and the white man's gods will fall to pieces."

"How give herself?" she asked quickly.

And he, as quickly covered, covered himself with a subtle smile.

"She leave her own gods and come to our gods, I mean that," he said, soothingly.

But she was not reassured. An icy pang of fear and certainty was at her heart.

"The sun he is alive at one end of the sky," he continued, "and the moon lives at the other end. And the man all the time have to keep the sun happy in his side of the sky, and the woman have to keep the moon quiet at her side of the sky. All the time she have to work at this. And the sun can't ever go into the house of the moon, and the moon can't ever go into the house of the sun, in the sky. So the woman, she asks the moon to come into her cave, inside her. And the man, he draws the sun down till he has the power of the sun. All the time he do this. Then when the man gets a woman, the sun goes into the cave of the moon, and that is how everything in the world starts."

She listened watching him closely, as one enemy watches another, when he is speaking with double meanings.

"Then," she said, "why aren't you Indians masters of the white men?"

"Because," he said, "the Indian got weak, and lost his power with the sun, so the white men stole the sun. But they can't keep him—they don't know how. They got him, but they don't know what to do with him, like a boy who catch a big grizzly bear, and can't kill him, and can't run away from him. The grizzly bear eats the boy that catch him, when he want to run away from him. White men don't know what they are doing with the sun, and white women don't know what they do with the moon. The moon she got angry with white women, like a puma when someone kills her little ones. The moon, she bites white women—here inside—" and he pressed his side. "The moon, she is angry in a white woman's cave. The Indian can see it—And soon," he added, "the Indian women get the moon back and keep her quiet in their house. And the Indian men get the sun, and the power over all the world. White men don't know what the sun is. They never know."

He subsided into a curious exultant silence.

"But," she faltered, "why do you hate us so? Why do you hate me?"

He looked up suddenly with a light on his face, and a startling flame of a smile.

"No, we don't hate," he said softly, looking with a curious glitter into her face.

"You do," she said, forlorn and hopeless.

And after a moment's silence, he rose and went away.

Winter had now come, in the high valley, with snow that melted in the day's sun, and nights that were bitter cold. She lived on, in a kind of daze, feeling her power ebbing more and more away from her, as if her will were leaving her. She felt always in the same relaxed, confused victimised state, unless the sweetened herb drinks would numb her mind altogether, and release her senses into a sort of heightened, mystic acuteness and a feeling as if she were diffusing out deliciously into the harmony of things. This at length became the only state of consciousness she really recognised: this exquisite sense of bleeding out into the higher beauty and harmony of things. Then she could actually hear the great stars in heaven, which she saw through her door, speaking from their motion and brightness, saying things perfectly to the cosmos, as they trod in perfect ripples, like bells on the floor of heaven, passing one another and grouping in the timeless dance, with spaces of dark between. And she could hear the snow on a cold, cloudy day twittering and faintly whistling in the sky, like birds that flock and fly away in autumn, suddenly calling farewell to the invisible moon, and slipping out of the plains of the air, releasing peaceful warmth. She herself would call to the arrested snow to fall from the upper air. She would call to the unseen moon to cease to be angry, to make peace again with the unseen sun like a woman who ceases to be angry in her house. And she would smell the sweetness of the moon relaxing to the sun in the wintry heaven, when the snow fell in a faint, cold-perfumed relaxation, as the peace of the sun mingled again in a sort of unison with the peace of the moon.

She was aware too of the sort of shadow that was on the Indians of the valley, a deep, stoical disconsolation, almost religious in its depth.

"We have lost our power over the sun, and we are trying to get him back. But he is wild with us, and shy like a horse that has got away. We have to go through a lot."

So the young Indian said to her, looking into her eyes with a strained meaning. And she, as if bewitched, replied:

"I hope you will get him back."

The smile of triumph flew over his face.

"Do you hope it?" he said.

"I do," she answered, fatally.

"Then all right," he said. "We shall get him."

And he went away in exultance.

She felt she was drifting on some consummation, which she had no will to avoid, yet which seemed heavy and finally terrible to her.

It must have been almost December, for the days were short, when she was taken again before the aged man, and stripped of her clothing, and touched with the old finger-tips.

The aged cacique looked her in the eyes, with his eyes of lonely, far-off, black intentness, and murmured something to her.

"He wants you to make the sign of peace," the young man translated, showing her the gesture. "Peace and farewell to him."

She was fascinated by the black, glass-like, intent eyes of the old cacique, that watched her without blinking, like a basilisk's, overpowering her. In their depths also she saw a certain fatherly compassion, and pleading. She put her hand before her face, in the required manner, making the sign of peace and farewell. He made the sign of peace back again to her, then sank among his furs. She thought he was going to die, and that he knew it.

There followed a day of ceremonial, when she was brought out before all the people, in a blue cloak with white fringe, and holding blue feathers in her hands. Before an altar of one house, she was perfumed with incense and sprinkled with ash. Before the altar of the opposite house she was fumigated again with incense by the gorgeous, terrifying priests in yellow and scarlet and black, their faces painted with scarlet paint. And then they threw water on her. Meanwhile she was faintly aware of the fire on the altar, the heavy, heavy sound of a drum, the heavy sound of men beginning powerfully, deeply, savagely to sing, the swaying of the crowd of faces in the plaza below, and the formation for a sacred dance.

But at this time her commonplace consciousness was numb, she was aware of her immediate surroundings as shadows, almost immaterial. With refined and heightened senses she could hear the sound of the earth winging on its journey, like a shot arrow, the ripple-rustling of the air, and the boom of the great arrow-string. And it seemed to her there were two great influences in the upper air, one golden towards the sun, and one invisible silver; the first travelling like rain ascending to the gold presence sunwards, the second like rain descending silverily the ladders of space towards the hovering, lurking clouds over the snowy mountain-top. Then between them, another presence, waiting to shake himself free of moisture, or of heavy white snow that had mysteriously collected about him. And in summer, like a scorched eagle, he would wait to shake himself clear of the weight of heavy sunbeams. And he was coloured like fire. And he was always shaking himself clear, of snow or of heavy heat, like an eagle rustling.

Then there was a still stranger presence, standing watching from the blue distance: always watching. Sometimes running in upon the wind, or shimmering in the heat-waves. The blue wind itself, rushing as it were out of the holes of the earth into the sky, rushing out of the sky down upon the earth. The blue wind, the go-between, the invisible ghost that belonged to two worlds, playing upon the ascending and the descending chords of the rains.

More and more her ordinary personal consciousness had left her, she had gone into that other state of passional cosmic consciousness, like one who is drugged. The Indians, with their heavily religious natures, had made her succumb to their vision.

Only one personal question she asked the young Indian:

"Why am I the only one that wears blue?"

"It is the colour of the wind. It is the colour of what goes away and is never coming back, but which is always here, waiting like death among us. It is the colour of the dead. And it is the colour that stands away off, looking at us from the distance, that cannot be near to us. When we go near, it goes further. It can't come near. We are all brown and yellow and black hair, and white teeth and red blood. We are the ones that are here. You with blue eyes, you are the messengers from the far-away, you cannot stay, and now it is time for you to go back."

"Where to?" she asked.

"To the way-off things like the sun and the blue mother of rain, and tell them that we are the people on the world again, and we can bring the sun to the moon again, like a red horse to a blue mare; we are the people. The white women have stayed too long on the earth, the moon and the sun are waiting for her to go. Everything stands still. The moon is like a white she-goat, all the time shut up in a corral, and angry and butting. She want to get out. The white woman got to let her out."

"How?" she said.

"The white woman got to die and go like a wind to the sun, tell him the Indians will open the gate to him. And the Indian women will open the gate to the moon. The white woman don't let the moon come down out of the blue corral. The moon used to come down among the Indian women, like a white goat among iris flowers. And the sun want to come down to the Indian men, like an eagle to the pine-trees. The sun, he is shut out behind the white man, and the moon, she is shut out behind the white woman, and they can't get away. They are angry, everything in the world gets angrier. The Indian says, he will give the white woman to the sun, so the sun will leap over the white men and come to the Indian again. And the moon will be surprised; she will see the gate open, and she not know which way to go. But the Indian woman will call to the moon, *Come! Come! Come back into my grass-lands. The wicked white woman can't harm you any more.* Then the sun will look over the heads of the white men, and see the moon in the pastures of our women, with the Red Men standing around like pine-trees. Then he will leap over the heads of the white men, and come running fast to the Indians, through the spruce trees. And we, who are red and black and yellow, we who stay, we shall have the sun on our right hand and the moon on our left. So we can bring the rain down out of the blue meadows, and up out of the black. And we can call the wind that tells the corn to grow, when we ask him, and we shall make the clouds to break, and the sheep to have twin lambs. And we shall be full of power, like a spring day. But the white people will be a hard winter, without snow—"

"But," said the white woman, "I don't shut out the moon—how can I?"

"Yes," he said, "You shut the gate, and then laugh, think you have it all your own way."

She could never quite understand the way he looked at her. He was always so curiously gentle, and his smile was so soft. Yet there was such a glitter in his eyes, and an unrelenting sort of hate came out of his words, a strange, profound, impersonal hate. Personally he liked her, she was sure. He was gentle with her, attracted by her in some strange, soft, passionless way. But impersonally he hated her with a mystic hatred. He would smile at her winningly. Yet if, the next moment, she glanced round at him unawares, she would catch that gleam of pure after-hate in his eyes.

"Have I got to die and be given to the sun?" she asked.

"Sometime," he said, laughing evasively.—"Sometime we all die."

They were gentle with her, and very considerate with her. Strange men, the old priests and the young cacique alike, they watched over her and cared for her like women. In their soft, insidious understanding, there was something womanly. Yet their eyes, with that strange glitter, and their dark, shut mouths that would open to the broad jaw, the small, strong, white teeth, had something very primitively male, and cruel.

One wintry day, when snow was falling, they took her to a great dark chamber in the big House. The fire was burning in a corner on a high raised dais under a sort of hood or canopy of adobe-work. She saw in the fire-glow, the glowing bodies of the almost naked priests, and strange symbols on the roof and walls of the chamber. There was no door or window in the chamber, they had descended by a ladder from the roof. And the fire of pine-wood danced continually, showing walls painted with strange devices, which she could not understand, and a ceiling of poles making a curious pattern of black and red and yellow, and alcoves or niches in which were curious objects she could not discern.

The older priests were going through some ceremony near the fire, in silence, intense Indian silence. She was seated on a low projection of the wall, opposite the fire, two men seated beside her. Presently they gave her a drink from a cup, which she took gladly, because of the semi-trance it would induce.

In the darkness and in the silence she was accurately aware of everything that happened to her, how they took off her clothes, and standing her before a great, weird device on the wall, coloured blue and white and black, washed her all over with water and the amole infusion, washed even her hair, softly, carefully, and dried it on white cloths, till it was soft and glistening. Then they laid her on a couch under another great indecipherable image of red and black and yellow, and now rubbed all her body with sweet-scented oil, and massaged all her limbs, and her back, and her sides, with a long, strange, hypnotic massage. Their dark hands were incredibly powerful, yet soft with a watery softness she could not understand. And the dark faces, leaning near her white body, she saw were darkened with red pigment, with lines of yellow round the cheeks. And the dark eyes glittered absorbed, as the hands worked upon the soft white body of the woman.

They were so impersonal, absorbed in something that was beyond her. They never saw her as a personal woman: she could tell that. She was some mystic object to them, some vehicle of passions too remote for her to grasp. Herself in a state of trance, she watched their faces bending over her, dark, strangely glistening with the transparent red paint, and lined with bars of yellow. And in this weird, luminous-dark mask of living face, the eyes were fixed with an unchanging steadfast gleam, and the purplish-pigmented lips were closed in a full, sinister, sad grimness. The immense fundamental sadness, the grimness of ultimate decision, the fixity of revenge, and the nascent exultance of those that are going to triumph—these things she could read in their faces, as she lay and was rubbed into a misty glow by their uncanny dark hands. Her limbs, her flesh, her very bones at last seemed to be diffusing into a roseate sort of mist, in which her consciousness hovered like some sun-gleam in a flushed cloud.

She knew the gleam would fade, the cloud would go grey. But at present she did not believe it. She knew she was a victim: that all this elaborate work upon her was the work of victimising her. But she did not mind. She wanted it.

Later, they put a short blue tunic on her and took her to the upper terrace, and presented her to the people. She saw the plaza below her full of dark faces and of glittering eyes. There was no pity: only the curious hard exultance. The people gave a subdued cry when they saw her, and she shuddered. But she hardly cared.

Next day was the last. She slept in a chamber of the big house. At dawn they put on her a big blue blanket with a fringe, and led her out into the plaza, among the throng of silent, dark-blanketed people. There was pure white snow on the ground, and the dark people in their dark-brown blankets looked like inhabitants of another world.

A large drum was slowly pounding, and an old priest was declaiming from a housetop. But it was not till noon that a litter came forth, and the people gave that low, animal cry which was so moving. In the sack-like litter sat the old, old cacique, his white hair braided with black braid and large turquoise stones. His face was like a piece of obsidian. He lifted his hand in token, and the litter stopped in front of her. Fixing her with his old eyes, he spoke to her for a few moments, in his hollow voice. No-one translated.

Another litter came, and she was placed in it. Four priests moved ahead, in their scarlet and yellow and black, with plumed head-dresses. Then came the litter of the old cacique. Then the light drums began, and two groups of singers burst simultaneously into song, male and wild. And the golden-red, almost naked men, adorned with ceremonial feathers and kilts, the rivers of black hair down their backs, formed into two files and began to tread the dance. So they threaded out of the snowy plaza, in two long, sumptuous lines of dark red-gold and black and fur, swaying with a faint tinkle of bits of shell and flint, winding over the snow between the two bee-clusters of men who sang around the drum.

Slowly they moved out, and her litter, with its attendance of feathered, lurid, dancing priests, moved after. Everybody danced the tread of the dance-step, even, subtly, the litter-bearers. And out of the plaza they went, past smoking ovens, on the trail to the great cotton-wood trees, that stood like grey-silver lace against the blue sky, bare and exquisite above the snow. The river, diminished, rushed among fangs of ice. The chequer-squares of gardens within fences were all snowy, and the white houses now looked yellowish.

The whole valley glittered intolerably with pure snow, away to the walls of the standing rock. And across the flat cradle of snow-bed wound the long thread of the dance, shaking slowly and sumptuously in its orange and black motion. The high drums thudded quickly, and on the crystalline frozen air the swell and roar of the chant of savages was like an obsession.

She sat looking out of her litter with big, transfixed blue eyes, under which were the wan markings of her drugged weariness. She knew she was going to die, among the glisten of this snow, at the hands of this savage, sumptuous people. And as she stared at the blaze of blue sky above the slashed and ponderous mountain, she thought: "I am dead already. What difference does it make, the transition from the dead I am, to the dead I shall be, very soon!" Yet her soul sickened and felt wan.

The strange procession trailed on, in perpetual dance, slowly across the plain of snow, and then entered the slopes between the pine-trees.

She saw the copper-dark men dancing the dance-tread, onwards, between the copper-pale tree-trunks. And at last she too, in her swaying litter, entered the pine-trees.

They were travelling on and on, upwards, across the snow under the trees, past the superb shafts of pale, flaked copper, the rustle and shake and tread of the threading dance, penetrating into the forest, into the mountain. They were following a stream-bed: but the stream was dry, like summer, dried up by the frozenness of the head-waters. There were dark, red-bronze willow bushes with osiers like wild hair, and pallid aspen trees looking like cold flesh against the snow. Then jutting dark rocks.

At last she could tell that the dancers were moving forward no more. Nearer and nearer she came upon the drums, as to a lair of mysterious animals. Then through the bushes she emerged into a strange amphitheatre. Facing was a great wall of hollow rock, down the front of which hung a great, dripping, fang-like spoke of ice. The ice came pouring over the rock from the precipice above, and then stood arrested, dripping out of high heaven, almost down to the hollow stones where the stream-pool should be below. But the pool was dry.

On either side the dry pool, the lines of dancers had formed, and the dance was continuing without intermission, against a background of bushes.

But what she felt was that fanged inverted pinnacle of ice, hanging from the lip of the dark precipice above. And behind the great rope of ice, she saw the leopard-like figures of priests climbing the hollow cliff face, to the cave that like a dark socket bored a cavity, an orifice, half way up the crag.

Before she could realise, her litter-bearers were staggering in the footholds, climbing the rock. She too was behind the ice. There it hung, like a curtain that is not spread, but hangs like a great fang. And near above her was the orifice of the cave sinking dark into the rock. She watched it as she swayed upwards.

On the platform of the cave stood the priests, waiting in all their gorgeousness of feathers and fringed robes, watching her ascent. Two of them stooped to help her litter-bearers. And at length she was on the platform of the cave, far in behind the shaft of ice, above the hollow amphitheatre among the bushes below, where men were dancing, and the whole populace of the village was clustered in silence.

The sun was sloping down the afternoon sky, on the left. She knew that this was the shortest day of the year, and the last day of her life.

They stood her facing the iridescent column of ice, which fell down marvellously arrested, away in front of her.

Some signal was given, and the dance below stopped. There was now absolute silence. She was given a little to drink, then two priests took off her mantle and her tunic, and in her strange pallor she stood there, between the lurid robes of the priests, beyond the pillar of ice, beyond and above the dark-faced people. The throng below gave the low, wild cry. Then the priests turned her round, so she stood with her back to the open world, her long blond hair to the people below. And they cried again.

She was facing the cave, inwards. A fire was burning and flickering in the depths. Four priests had taken off their robes, and were almost naked as she was. They were powerful men in the prime of life, and they kept their dark, painted faces lowered.

From the fire came the old, old priest, with an incense-pan. He was naked and in a state of barbaric ecstasy. He fumigated his victim, reciting at the same time in a hollow voice. Behind him came another robeless priest, with two flint knives.

When she was fumigated, they laid her on a large flat stone, the four powerful men holding her by the outstretched arms and legs. Behind stood the aged man, like a skeleton covered with dark glass, holding a knife and transfixedly watching the sun; and behind him again was another naked priest, with a knife.

She felt little sensation, though she knew all that was happening. Turning to the sky, she looked at the yellow sun. It was sinking. The shaft of ice was like a shadow between her and it. And she realised that the yellow rays were filling half the cave, though they had not reached the altar where the fire was, at the far end of the funnel-shaped cavity.

Yes, the rays were creeping round slowly. As they grew ruddier, they penetrated further. When the red sun was about to sink, he would shine full through the shaft of ice deep into the hollow of the cave, to the innermost.

She understood now that this was what the men were waiting for. Even those that held her down were bent and twisted round, their black eyes watching the sun with a glittering eagerness, and awe, and craving. The black eyes of the aged cacique were fixed like black mirrors on the sun, as if sightless, yet containing some terrible answer to the reddening winter planet. And all the eyes of the priests were fixed and glittering on the sinking orb, in the reddening, icy silence of the winter afternoon.

They were anxious, terribly anxious, and fierce. Their ferocity wanted something, and they were waiting the moment. And their ferocity was ready to leap out into a mystic exultance, of triumph. But still they were anxious.

Only the eyes of that oldest man were not anxious. Black, and fixed, and as if sightless, they watched the sun, seeing beyond the sun. And in their black, empty concentration there was power, power intensely abstract and remote, but deep, deep to the heart of the earth, and the heart of the sun. In absolute motionlessness he watched till the red sun should send his ray through the column of ice. Then the old man would strike, and strike home, accomplish the sacrifice and achieve the power.

The mastery that man must hold, and that passes from race to race.

St. Mawr

Lou Witt had had her own way so long, that by the age of twenty-five she didn't know where she was. Having one's own way landed one completely at sea.

To be sure for a while she had failed in her grand love affair with Rico. And then she had had something really to despair about. But even that had worked out as she wanted. Rico had come back to her, and was dutifully married to her. And now, when she was twenty-five and he was three months older, they were a charming married couple. He flirted with other women still, to be sure. He wouldn't be the handsome Rico if he didn't. But she had "got" him. Oh yes! You had only to see the uneasy backward glance at her, from his big blue eyes: just like a horse that is edging away from its master: to know how completely he was mastered.

She, with her odd little *museau*, not exactly pretty, but very attractive; and her quaint air of playing at being well-bred, in a sort of charade game; and her queer familiarity with foreign cities and foreign languages; and the lurking sense of being an outsider everywhere, like a sort of gipsy, who is at home anywhere and nowhere: all this made up her charm and her failure. She didn't quite belong.

Of course she was American: Louisiana family, moved down to Texas. And she was moderately rich, with no close relation except her mother. But she had been sent to school in France when she was twelve, and since she had finished school, she had drifted from Paris to Palermo, Biarritz to Vienna and back via Munich to London, then down again to Rome. Only fleeting trips to her America.

So what sort of American was she, after all?

And what sort of European was she either? She didn't "belong" anywhere. Perhaps most of all in Rome, among the artists and the Embassy people.

It was in Rome she had met Rico. He was an Australian, son of a government official in Melbourne, who had been made a baronet. So one day Rico would be Sir Henry, as he was the only son. Meanwhile he floated round Europe on a very small allowance—his father wasn't rich in capital—and was being an artist.

They met in Rome when they were twenty-two, and had a love affair in Capri. Rico was handsome, elegant, but mostly he had spots of paint

41

on his trousers and he ruined a necktie pulling it off. He behaved in a most floridly elegant fashion, fascinating to the Italians. But at the same time he was canny and shrewd and sensible as any young poser could be, and on principle, good-hearted, anxious. He was anxious for his future, and anxious for his place in the world, he was poor, and suddenly wasteful in spite of all his tension of economy, and suddenly spiteful in spite of all his ingratiating efforts, and suddenly ungrateful in spite of all his burden of gratitude, and suddenly rude in spite of all his good manners, and suddenly detestable in spite of all his suave, courtier-like amiability.

He was fascinated by Lou's quaint aplomb, her experiences, her "knowledge," her *gamine* knowingness, her aloneness, her pretty clothes that were sometimes an utter failure, and her southern "drawl" that was sometimes so irritating. That sing-song which was so American. Yet she used no Americanisms at all, except when she lapsed into her odd spasms of acid irony, when she was very American indeed!

And she was fascinated by Rico. They played to each other like two butterflies at one flower. They pretended to be very poor in Rome—he *was* poor: and very rich in Naples. Everybody stared their eyes out at them. And they had that love affair in Capri.

But they reacted badly on each other's nerves. She became ill. Her mother appeared. He couldn't stand Mrs Witt, and Mrs Witt couldn't stand him. There was a terrible fortnight. Then Lou was popped into a convent nursing-home in Umbria, and Rico dashed off to Paris. Nothing would stop him. He must go back to Australia.

He went to Melbourne, and while there, his father died, leaving him a baronet's title and an income still very moderate. Lou visited America once more, as the strangest of strange lands to her. She came away disheartened, panting for Europe, and of course, doomed to meet Rico again.

They couldn't get away from one another, even though in the course of their rather restrained correspondence, he informed her that he was "probably" marrying a very dear girl, friend of his childhood, only daughter of one of the oldest families in Victoria. Not saying much.

He didn't commit the probability, but reappeared in Paris, wanting to paint his head off, terribly inspired by Cézanne and by old Renoir. He dined at the Rotonde with Lou and Mrs Witt, who, with her queer democratic New Orleans sort of conceit looked round the drinking-hall with savage contempt, and at Rico as part of the show. "Certainly," she said, "when these people here have got any money, they fall in love on a full stomach. And when they've got no money, they fall in love with a full pocket. I never was in a more disgusting place. They take their love like some people take after-dinner pills."

She would watch with her arching, full, strong grey eyes, sitting there erect and silent in her well-bought American clothes. And then she would deliver some such charge of grape-shot. Rico always writhed.

Mrs Witt hated Paris: "this sordid, unlucky city," she called it. "Something unlucky is bound to happen to me in this sinister, unclean town," she said. "I feel it in the air. I feel *contagion* in the air of this place. For heaven's sake, Louise, let us go to Morocco or somewhere."

"No mother dear, I can't now. Rico has proposed to me, and I have accepted him. Let us think about a wedding, shall we?"

"There!" said Mrs Witt. "I said it was an unlucky city!"

And the peculiar look of extreme New Orleans annoyance came round her sharp nose. But Lou and Rico were both twenty-four years old, and beyond management. And anyhow, Lou would be Lady Carrington. But Mrs Witt was exasperated beyond exasperation. She would almost rather have preferred Lou to elope with one of the great, evil porters at Les Halles. Mrs Witt was at the age when the malevolent male in man, the old Adam, begins to loom above all the social tailoring. And yet—and yet—it was better to have Lady Carrington for a daughter, seeing Lou was that sort.

There was a marriage, after which Mrs Witt departed to America, Lou and Rico leased a little old house in Westminster, and began to settle into a certain layer of English society. Rico was becoming an almost fashionable portrait painter. At least, *he* was almost fashionable, whether his portraits were or not. And Lou too was almost fashionable: almost a hit. There was some flaw somewhere. In spite of their appearances, both Rico and she would never quite go down, in any society. They were the drifting artist sort. Yet neither of them was content to be of the drifting artist sort. They wanted to fit in, to make good.

Hence the little house in Westminster, the portraits, the dinners, the friends, and the visits. Mrs Witt came and sardonically established herself in a suite in a quiet but good-class hotel not far off. Being on the spot. And her terrible grey eyes with the touch of a leer looked on at the hollow mockery of things. As if *she* knew of anything better!

Lou and Rico had a curious exhausting effect on one another:

neither knew why. They were fond of one another. Some inscrutable
bond held them together. But it was a strange vibration of the nerves,
rather than of the blood. A nervous attachment, rather than a sexual
love. A curious tension of will, rather than a spontaneous passion. Each
was curiously under the domination of the other. They were a
pair—they had to be together. Yet quite soon they shrank from one
another. This attachment of the will and the nerves was destructive.
As soon as one felt strong, the other felt ill. As soon as the ill one
recovered strength, down went the one who had been well.

And soon, tacitly, the marriage became more like a friendship,
Platonic. It was a marriage, but without sex. Sex was shattering and
exhausting, they shrank from it, and became like brother and sister.
But still they were husband and wife. And the lack of physical relation
was a secret source of uneasiness and chagrin to both of them. They
would neither of them accept it. Rico looked with contemplative,
anxious eyes at other women.

Mrs Witt kept track of everything, watching as it were from outside
the fence, like a potent well-dressed demon, full of uncanny energy
and a shattering sort of sense. She said little: but her small, occasionally
biting remarks revealed her attitude of contempt for the ménage.

Rico entertained clever and well-known people. Mrs Witt would
appear, in her New York gowns and few good jewels. She was
handsome, with her vigorous grey hair. But her heavy-lidded grey eyes
were the despair of any hostess. They looked too many shattering
things. And it was but too obvious that these clever, well-known
English people got on her nerves terribly, with their finickiness and
their fine-drawn discriminations. She wanted to put her foot through
all these fine-drawn distinctions. She thought continually of the house
of her girlhood, the plantation, the negroes, the planters: the sardonic
grimness that underlay all the big, shiftless life. And she wanted to
cleave with some of this grimness of the big, dangerous America, into
the safe, finicky drawing-rooms of London. So naturally she was not
popular.

But being a woman of energy, she had to do *something*. During the
latter part of the war, she had worked with the American Red Cross in
France, nursing. She loved men—real men. But, on close contact, it was
difficult to define what she meant by "real" men. She never met any.

Out of the débâcle of the war she had emerged with an odd piece
of débris, in the shape of Geronimo Trujillo. He was an American,
son of a Mexican father and a Navajo Indian mother, from Arizona.

When you knew him well, you recognised the real half-breed, though at a glance he might pass as a sunburnt citizen of any nation, particularly of France. He looked like a certain sort of Frenchman, with his curiously-set dark eyes, his straight black hair, his thin black moustache, his rather long cheeks, and his almost slouching, diffident, sardonic bearing. Only when you knew him, and looked right into his eyes, you saw that unforgettable glint of the Indian.

He had been badly shell-shocked, and was for a time a wreck. Mrs Witt, having nursed him into convalescence, asked him where he was going next. He didn't know. His father and mother were dead, and he had nothing to take him back to Phoenix, Arizona. Having had an education in one of the Indian high-schools, the unhappy fellow had now no place in life at all. Another of the many misfits.

There was something of the Paris *Apache* in his appearance: but he was all the time withheld, and nervously shut inside himself. Mrs Witt was intrigued by him.

"Very well, Phoenix," she said, refusing to adopt his Spanish name, "I'll see what I can do."

What she did was to get him a place on a sort of manor farm, with some acquaintances of hers. He was very good with horses, and had a curious success with turkeys and geese and fowls.

Some time after Lou's marriage, Mrs Witt reappeared in London, from the country, with Phoenix in tow, and a couple of horses. She had decided that she would ride in the Park in the morning, and see the world that way. Phoenix was to be her groom.

So, to the great misgiving of Rico, behold Mrs Witt in splendidly tailored habit and perfect boots, a smart black hat on her smart grey hair, riding a grey gelding as smart as she was, and looking down her conceited, inquisitive, scornful, aristocratic-democratic Louisiana nose at the people in Piccadilly, as she crossed to the Row, followed by the taciturn shadow of Phoenix, who sat on a chestnut with three white feet as if he had grown there.

Mrs Witt, like many other people, always expected to find the real *beau monde* and the real *grand monde* somewhere or other. She didn't quite give in to what she saw in the Bois de Boulogne, or in Monte Carlo, or on the Pincio: all a bit shoddy, and not very *beau* and not at all *grand*. There she was, with her grey eagle eye, her splendid complexion and her weapon-like health of a woman of fifty, dropping her eyelids a little, very slightly nervous, but completely prepared to despise the *monde* she was entering in Rotten Row.

In she sailed, and up and down that regatta-canal of horsemen and horsewomen under the trees of the Park.—And yes, there were lovely girls with fair hair down their backs, on happy ponies. And awfully well-groomed papas, and tight mamas who looked as if they were going to pour tea between the ears of their horses, and converse with banal skill, one eye on the teapot, one on the visitor with whom she was talking, and all the rest of her hostess' argus-eyes upon everybody in sight. That alert argus capability of the English matron was startling and a bit horrifying. Mrs Witt would at once think of the old negro mammies, away in Louisiana. And her eyes became dagger-like as she watched the clipped, shorn, mincing young Englishmen. She refused to look at the prosperous Jews.

It was still the days before motor-cars were allowed in the Park, but Rico and Lou, sliding round Hyde Park Corner and up Park Lane in their car would watch the steely horsewoman and the saturnine groom with a sort of dismay. Mrs Witt seemed to be pointing a pistol at the bosom of every other horseman or horsewoman, and announcing: *Your virility or your life!—Your femininity or your life!* She didn't know herself what she really wanted them to be: but it was something as democratic as Abraham Lincoln and as aristocratic as a Russian Czar, as highbrow as Arthur Balfour, and as taciturn and unideal as Phoenix. Everything at once.

There was nothing for it: Lou had to buy herself a horse and ride at her mother's side, for very decency's sake. Mrs Witt was *so* like a smooth, levelled, gun-metal pistol, Lou had to be a sort of sheath. And she really looked pretty, with her clusters of dark, curly, New Orleans hair, like grapes, and her quaint brown eyes that didn't quite match, and that looked a bit sleepy and vague, and at the same time quick as a squirrel's. She was slight and elegant, and a tiny bit rakish, and somebody suggested she might be on the movies.

Nevertheless, they were in the society columns next morning—*two new and striking figures in the Row this morning were Lady Henry Carrington and her mother Mrs Witt* etc: And Mrs Witt liked it, let her say what she might. So did Lou. Lou liked it immensely. She simply luxuriated in the sun of publicity.

"Rico dear, you must get a horse."

The tone was soft and southern and drawling, but the overtone had a decisive finality. In vain Rico squirmed—he had a way of writhing and squirming which perhaps he had caught at Oxford. In vain he protested that he couldn't ride, and that he didn't care for riding. He got quite angry, and his handsome arched nose tilted and his upper lip lifted from his teeth, like a dog that is going to bite. Yet daren't quite bite.

And that was Rico. He daren't quite bite. Not that he was really afraid of the others. He was afraid of himself, once he let himself go. He might rip up in an eruption of life-long anger all this pretty-pretty picture of a charming young wife and a delightful little home and a fascinating success as a painter of fashionable, and at the same time "great" portraits: with colour, wonderful colour, and at the same time, form, marvellous form. He had composed this little *tableau vivant* with great effort. He didn't want to erupt like some suddenly wicked horse—Rico was really more like a horse than a dog, a horse that might go nasty any moment. For the time, he was good, very good, dangerously good.

"Why, Rico dear, I thought you used to ride so much, in Australia, when you were young? Didn't you tell me all about it, hm?"—and as she ended on that slow, singing *hm?*, which acted on him like an irritant and a drug, he knew he was beaten.

Lou kept the sorrel mare in a mews just behind the house in Westminster, and she was always slipping round to the stables. She had a funny little nostalgia for the place: something that really surprised her. She had never had the faintest notion that she cared for horses and stables and grooms. But she did. She was fascinated. Perhaps it was her childhood's Texas associations come back. Whatever it was, her life with Rico in the elegant little house, and all her social engagements seemed like a dream, the substantial reality of which was those mews in Westminster, her sorrel mare, the owner of the mews, Mr Saintsbury, and the grooms he employed. Mr Saintsbury was a horsey elderly man like an old maid, and he loved the sound of titles.

"Lady Carrington!—well I never! You've come to us for a bit of company again, I see. I don't know whatever we shall do if you go away, we shall be that lonely!" and he flashed his old-maid's smile at her. "No matter how grey the morning, your Ladyship would make a beam of sunshine. Poppy is all right, I think . . ."

Poppy was the sorrel mare with the no white feet and the startled eye, and she was all right. And Mr Saintsbury was smiling with his old-maid's mouth, and showing all his teeth.

"Come across with me, Lady Carrington, and look at a new horse just up from the country? I think he's worth a look, and I believe you have a moment to spare, your Ladyship."

Her Ladyship had too many moments to spare. She followed the sprightly, elderly, cleanshaven man across the yard to a loose box, and waited while he opened the door.

In the inner dark she saw a handsome bay horse with his clean ears pricked like daggers from his naked head as he swung handsomely round to stare at the open doorway. He had big, black, brilliant eyes, with a sharp questioning glint, and that air of tense, alert quietness which betrays an animal that can be dangerous.

"Is he quiet?" Lou asked.

"Why—yes—my Lady! He's quiet, with those that know how to handle him. *Cup! my boy! Cup my beauty! Cup then! St. Mawr!*"

Loquacious even with the animals, he went softly forward and laid his hand on the horse's shoulder, soft and quiet as a fly settling. Lou saw the brilliant skin of the horse crinkle a little in apprehensive anticipation, like the shadow of the descending hand on a bright red-gold liquid. But then the animal relaxed again.

"Quiet with those that know how to handle him, and a bit of a ruffian with those that don't. Isn't that the ticket, eh, St. Mawr?"

"What is his name?" Lou asked.

The man repeated it, with a slight Welsh twist—"He's from the Welsh borders, belonging to a Welsh gentleman, Mr Griffith Edwards. But they're wanting to sell him."

"How old is he?" asked Lou.

"About seven years—seven years and five months," said Mr Saintsbury, dropping his voice as if it were a secret.

"Could one ride him in the Park—"

"Well—yes! I should say a gentleman who knew how to handle him could ride him very well and make a very handsome figure in the Park—"

Lou at once decided that this handsome figure should be Rico's. For she was already half in love with St. Mawr. He was of such a lovely red-gold colour, and a dark, invisible fire seemed to come out of him. But in his big black eyes there was a lurking afterthought. Something told her that the horse was not quite happy: that somewhere deep in his animal consciousness lived a dangerous, half-revealed resentment, a diffused sense of hostility. She realised that he was sensitive, in spite of his flaming, healthy strength, and nervous with a touchy uneasiness that might make him vindictive.

"Has he got any tricks?" she asked.

"Not that I know of, my Lady: not tricks exactly. But he's one of these temperamental creatures, as they say. Though *I* say, every horse is temperamental, when you come down to it.—But this one, it is as if he was a trifle raw somewhere. Touch this raw spot, and there's no answering for him."

"Where is he raw?" asked Lou, somewhat mystified. She thought he might really have some physical sore.

"Why, that's hard to say, my Lady. If he was a human being, you'd say something had gone wrong in his life. But with a horse, it's not that, exactly. A high-bred animal like St. Mawr needs understanding, and I don't know as anybody has quite got the hang of him. I confess I haven't myself. But I do realise that he is a special animal and needs a special sort of touch, and I'm willing he should have it, did I but know exactly what it is."

She looked at the glowing bay horse, that stood there with his ears back, his face averted, but attending as if he were some lightning conductor. He was a stallion. When she realised this, she became more afraid of him.

"Why does Mr Griffith Edwards want to sell him?" she asked.

"Well—my Lady—They raised him for stud purposes—but he didn't answer. There are horses like that: don't seem to fancy the mares, for some reason.—Well anyway, they couldn't keep him for the stud. And as you see, he's a powerful, beautiful hackney, clean as a whistle, and eaten up with his own power. But there's no putting him between the shafts. He won't stand it. He's a fine saddle-horse, beautiful action, and lovely to ride.—But he's got to be handled, and there you are."

Lou felt there was something behind the man's reticence.

"Has he ever made a break?" she asked, apprehensive.

"Made a break?" replied the man. "Well, if I must admit it, he's had two accidents. Mr Griffith Edwards' son rode him a bit wild, away there in the forest of Dean, and the young fellow had his skull smashed in, against a low oak bough. Last Autumn, that was. And some time back, he crushed a groom against the side of the stall—injured him fatally.—But they were both accidents, my Lady. Things will happen."

The man spoke in a melancholy, fatalistic way. The horse, with his ears laid back, seemed to be listening tensely, his face averted. He looked like something finely bred and passionate, that has been judged and condemned.

"May I say *how do you do*?" she said to the horse, drawing a little nearer in her white, summery dress, and lifting her hand, that glittered with emeralds and diamonds.

He drifted away from her, as if some wind blew him. Then he ducked his head, and looked sideways at her, from his black, full eye.

"I think I'm all right," she said, edging nearer, while he watched her.

She laid her hand on his side, and gently stroked him. Then she stroked his shoulder, and then the hard, tense arch of his neck. And she was startled to feel the vivid heat of his life come through to her, through the lacquer of red-gold gloss. So slippery with vivid, hot life!

She paused, as if thinking, while her hand rested on the horse's sun-arched neck. Dimly, in her weary young-woman's soul, an ancient understanding seemed to flood in.

She wanted to buy St. Mawr.

"I think," she said to Saintsbury, "if I can, I will buy him."

The man looked at her long and shrewdly.

"Well my Lady," he said at last. "There shall be nothing kept from you. But what would your Ladyship do with him, if I may make so bold?"

"I don't know," she replied, vaguely. "I might take him to America."

The man paused once more, then said:

"They say it's been the making of some horses, to take them over the water, to Australia or such places. It might repay you—you never know."

She wanted to buy St. Mawr. She wanted him to belong to her. For some reason the sight of him, his power, his alive, alert intensity, his unyieldingness, made her want to cry.

She never did cry: except sometimes with vexation, or to get her own way. As far as weeping went, her heart felt as dry as a Christmas walnut. What was the good of tears, anyhow? You had to keep on holding on, in this life, never give way, and never give in. Tears only left one weakened and ragged.

But now, as if that mysterious fire of the horse's body had split some rock in her, she went home and hid herself in her room, and just cried. The wild, brilliant, alert head of St. Mawr seemed to look at her out of another world. It was as if she had had a vision, as if the walls of her own world had suddenly melted away, leaving her in a great darkness, in the midst of which the large, brilliant eyes of that horse looked at her with demonish question, while his naked ears stood up like daggers from the naked lines of his inhuman head, and his great body glowed red with power.

What was it? Almost like a god looking at her terribly out of the everlasting dark, she had felt the eyes of that horse; great, glowing, fearsome eyes, arched with a question, and containing a white blade of light like a threat. What was his non-human question, and his uncanny threat? She didn't know. He was some splendid demon, and she must worship him.

She hid herself away from Rico. She could not bear the triviality and superficiality of her human relationships. Looming like some god out of the darkness was the head of that horse, with the wide, terrible, questioning eyes. And she felt that it forbade her to be her ordinary, commonplace self. It forbade her to be just Rico's wife, young Lady Carrington, and all that.

It haunted her, the horse. It had looked at her as she had never been looked at before: terrible, gleaming, questioning eyes arching out of darkness, and backed by all the fire of that great ruddy body. What did it mean, and what ban did it put upon her? She felt it put a ban on her heart: wielded some uncanny authority over her, that she dared not, could not understand.

No matter where she was, what she was doing, at the back of her consciousness loomed a great, over-aweing figure out of a dark background: St. Mawr, looking at her without really seeing her, yet gleaming a question at her, from his wide terrible eyes, and gleaming a sort of menace, doom. Master of doom, he seemed to be!

"You are thinking about something, Lou dear!" Rico said to her that evening.

He was so quick and sensitive to detect her moods—so exciting in this respect. And his big, slightly prominent blue eyes, with the whites a little bloodshot, glanced at her quickly, with searching, and anxiety, and a touch of fear. As if his conscience were always uneasy.—He too was rather like a horse—but forever quivering with a sort of cold, dangerous mistrust, which he covered with anxious love.

At the middle of his eyes was a central powerlessness, that left him anxious. It used to touch her to pity, that central look of powerlessness in him. But now, since she had seen the full, dark, passionate blaze of power and of different life, in the eyes of the thwarted horse, the anxious powerlessness of the man drove her mad. Rico was so handsome, and he was so self-controlled, he had a gallant sort of kindness and a real worldly shrewdness. One had to admire him: at least *she* had to.

But after all, and after all, it was a bluff, an attitude. He kept it all working in himself, deliberately. It was an attitude. She read psychologists who said that everything was an attitude. Even the best of everything.—But now she realised that, with men and women, everything is an attitude only when something else is lacking. Something is lacking and they are thrown back on their own devices. That black fiery flow in the eyes of the horse was not "attitude." It was something much more terrifying, and real, the only thing that was real. Gushing from the darkness in menace and question, and blazing out in the splendid body of the horse.

"Was I thinking about something?" she replied, in her slow, amused, casual fashion. As if everything was so casual and easy to her. And so it was, from the hard, polished side of herself. But that wasn't the whole story.

"I think you were, Loulina. May we offer the penny?"

"Don't trouble," she said. "I was thinking, if I was thinking of anything, about a bay horse called St. Mawr."—Her secret *almost* crept into her eyes.

"The name is awfully attractive," he said with a laugh.

"Not so attractive as the creature himself. I'm going to buy him."

"Not really!" he said. "But why?"

"He *is* so attractive. I'm going to buy him for you."

"For *me*! *Darling*! how you do take me for granted. He may not be in the least attractive to me. As you know, I have hardly any feeling for horses at all.—Besides, how much does he cost?"

"That I don't know, Rico dear. But I'm sure you'll love him, for my sake."—She felt, now, she was merely playing for her own ends.

"Lou dearest, *don't* spend a fortune on a horse for me, which I *don't* want. Honestly, I prefer a car."

"Won't you ride with me in the Park, Rico?"

"Honestly, dear Lou, I don't want to."

"Why not, dear boy? You'd look so beautiful. I wish you would.—And anyhow, come with me to look at St. Mawr."

Rico was divided. He had a certain uneasy feeling about horses. At the same time, he *would* like to cut a handsome figure in the Park.

They went across to the mews. A little Welsh groom was watering the brilliant horse.

"Yes dear, he certainly *is* beautiful: such a marvellous colour! Almost orange! But rather large, I should say, to ride in the Park."

"No, for you he's perfect. You are so tall."

"He'd be marvellous in a composition. That colour!"

And all Rico could do was to gaze with the artist's eye at the horse, with a glance at the groom.

"Don't you think the man is rather fascinating too?" he said, nursing his chin artistically and penetratingly.

The groom, Lewis, was a little, quick, rather bow-legged, loosely-built fellow of indeterminate age, with a mop of black hair and a little black beard. He was grooming the brilliant St. Mawr, out in the open. The horse was really glorious: like a marigold, with a pure golden sheen, a shimmer of green-gold lacquer, upon a burning red-orange. There on the shoulder you saw the yellow lacquer glisten. Lewis, a little scrub of a fellow, worked absorbedly, unheedingly at the horse, with an absorption that was almost ritualistic. He seemed the attendant shadow of the ruddy animal.

"He goes with the horse," said Lou. "If we buy St. Mawr we get the man thrown in."

"They'd be *so* amusing to paint: such an extraordinary contrast! But darling, I *hope* you won't insist on buying the horse. It's so frightfully expensive."

"Mother will help me.—You'd look so well on him, Rico."

"If ever I dared take the liberty of getting on his back—!"

"Why not?" She went quickly across the cobbled yard.

"Good morning Lewis. How is St. Mawr?"

Lewis straightened himself and looked at her from under the falling mop of his black hair.

"All right," he said.

He peered straight at her from under his overhanging black hair. He had pale grey eyes, that looked phosphorescent, and suggested the eyes of a wild cat peering intent from under the darkness of some bush where it lies unseen. Lou, with her brown, unmatched, oddly perplexed eyes, felt herself found out.—"He's a common little fellow," she thought to herself. "But he knows a woman and a horse, at sight."—Aloud she said, in her southern drawl:

"How do you think he'd be with Sir Henry?"

Lewis turned his remote, coldly watchful eyes on the young baronet. Rico was tall and handsome and balanced on his hips. His face was long and well-defined, and with the hair taken straight back from the brow. It seemed as well-made as his clothing, and as perpetually presentable. You could not imagine his face dirty, or scrubby and unshaven, or bearded, or even moustached. It was perfectly prepared for social purposes. If his head had been cut off, like John the Baptist's, it would have been a thing complete in itself, would not have missed the body in the least. The body was perfectly tailored. The head was one of the famous "talking heads" of modern youth, with eyebrows a trifle Mephistophelian, large blue eyes a trifle bold, and curved mouth thrilling to death to kiss.

Lewis, the groom, staring from between his bush of hair and his beard, watched like an animal from the underbrush. And Rico was still sufficiently a colonial to be uneasily aware of the underbrush, uneasy under the watchfulness of the pale grey eyes, and uneasy in that man-to-man exposure which is characteristic of the democratic colonies and of America. He knew he must ultimately be judged on his merits as a man, alone without a background: an ungarnished colonial.

This lack of background, this defenceless man-to-man business which left him at the mercy of every servant, was bad for his nerves. For he was *also* an artist. He bore up against it in a kind of desperation, and was easily moved to rancorous resentment. At the same time he was free of the Englishman's water-tight *suffisance*. He really was aware that he would have to hold his own all alone, thrown alone on his own defences in the universe. The extreme democracy of the Colonies had taught him this.

And this, the little aboriginal Lewis recognised in him. He recognised also Rico's curious hollow misgiving, fear of some deficiency in himself, beneath all his handsome, young-hero appearance.

"He'd be all right with anybody as would meet him half way," said Lewis, in the quick Welsh manner of speech, impersonal.

"You hear, Rico!" said Lou in her sing-song, turning to her husband.

"Perfectly, darling!"

"Would you be willing to meet St. Mawr half way, hmm?"

"All the way, darling! Mahomet would go *all* the way, to that mountain. Who would dare do otherwise?"

He spoke with a laughing, yet piqued sarcasm.

"Why, I think St. Mawr would understand perfectly," she said in the soft voice of a woman haunted by love. And she went and laid her hand on the slippery, life-smooth shoulder of the horse. He, with his strange equine head lowered, its exquisite fine lines reaching a little snake-like forward, and his ears a little back, was watching her sideways, from the corner of his eye. He was in a state of absolute mistrust, like a cat crouching to spring.

"St. Mawr!" she said. "St. Mawr! What is the matter? Surely you and I are all right!"

And she spoke softly, dreamily stroked the animal's neck. She could feel a response gradually coming from him. But he would not lift up his head. And when Rico suddenly moved nearer, he sprang with a sudden jerk backwards, as if lightning exploded in his four hoofs.

The groom spoke a few low words in Welsh. Lou, frightened, stood with lifted hand arrested. She had been going to stroke him.

"Why did he do that?" she said.

"They gave him a beating once or twice," said the groom in a neutral voice, "and he doesn't forget."

She could hear a neutral sort of judgement in Lewis' voice. And she thought of the "raw spot."

Not any raw spot at all. A battle between two worlds. She realised that St. Mawr drew his hot breaths in another world from Rico's, from our world. Perhaps the old Greek horses had lived in St. Mawr's world. And the old Greek heroes, even Hippolytus, had known it.

With their strangely naked equine heads, and something of a snake in their way of looking round, and lifting their sensitive, dangerous muzzles, they moved in a prehistoric twilight where all things loomed phantasmagoric, all on one plane, sudden presences suddenly jutting out of the matrix. It was another world, an older, heavily potent world. And in this world the horse was swift and fierce and supreme, undominated and unsurpassed.—"Meet him half way," Lewis said. But half way across from our human world to that terrific equine twilight was not a small step. It was a step, she knew, that Rico could never take. She knew it. But she was prepared to sacrifice Rico.

St. Mawr was bought, and Lewis was hired along with him. At first, Lewis rode him behind Lou, in the Row, to get him going. He behaved perfectly.

Phoenix, the half-Indian, was very jealous when he saw the black-bearded Welsh groom on St. Mawr.

"What horse you got there?" he asked, looking at the other man with the curious unseeing stare in his hard, Navajo eyes, in which the Indian glint moved like a spark upon a dark chaos. In Phoenix's high-boned face there was all the race-misery of the dispossessed Indian, with an added blankness left by shell-shock. But at the same time, there was that unyielding, save to death, which is characteristic of his tribe; his mother's tribe. Difficult to say what subtle thread bound him to the Navajo, and made his destiny a Red Man's destiny still.

They were a curious pair of grooms, following the correct, and yet extraordinary, pair of American mistresses. Mrs Witt and Phoenix both rode with long stirrups and straight leg, sitting close to the saddle, without posting. Phoenix looked as if he and the horse were all one piece, he never seemed to rise in the saddle at all, neither trotting nor galloping, but sat like a man riding bareback. And all the time he stared around, at the riders in the Row, at the people grouped outside the rail, chatting, at the children walking with their nurses, as if he were looking at a mirage, in whose actuality he never believed for a moment. London was all a sort of dark mirage to him. His wide, nervous-looking brown eyes, with a smallish brown pupil that showed the white all round, seemed to be focussed on the far distance, as if he could not see things too near. He was watching the pale deserts of Arizona shimmer with moving light, the long mirage of a shallow lake ripple, the great pallid concave of earth and sky expanding with interchanged light. And a horse-shape loom large and portentous in the mirage, like some pre-historic beast.

That was real to him: the phantasm of Arizona. But this London was something his eye passed over, as a false mirage.

He looked too smart in his well-tailored groom's clothes, so smart, he might have been one of the satirised new-rich. Perhaps it was a sort of half-breed physical assertion that came through his clothing, the savage's physical assertion of himself. Anyhow, he looked "common," rather horsey and loud.

Except his face. In the golden suavity of his high-boned Indian face, that was hairless, with hardly any eyebrows, there was a blank, lost look that was almost touching. The same startled blank look was in his eyes. But in the smallish dark pupils the dagger-point of light still gleamed unbroken.

He was a good groom, watchful, quick, and on the spot in an instant, if anything went wrong. He had a curious quiet power over the horses, unemotional, unsympathetic, but silently potent. In the same way, watching the traffic of Piccadilly with his blank, glinting eye, he would calculate everything instinctively, as if it were an enemy, and pilot Mrs Witt by the strength of his silent will. He threw around her the tense watchfulness of her own America, and made her feel at home.

"Phoenix," she said, turning abruptly in her saddle as they walked the horses past the sheltering policeman at Hyde Park Corner, "I can't tell you how glad I am to have something a hundred per-cent American at the back of me, when I go through these gates."

She looked at him from dangerous grey eyes as if she meant it indeed, in vindictive earnest. A ghost of a smile went up to his high cheek-bones, but he did not answer.

"Why mother?" said Lou, sing-song. "It feels to me so friendly—!"

"Yes Louise, it does. *So* friendly! That's why I mistrust it so entirely—"

And she set off at a canter up the Row, under the green trees, her face like the face of Medusa at fifty, a weapon in itself. She stared at everything and everybody, with that stare of cold dynamite waiting to explode them all. Lou posted trotting at her side, graceful and elegant, and faintly amused. Behind came Phoenix, like a shadow, with his yellowish, high-boned face still looking sick. And at his side, on the big brilliant bay horse, the smallish, black-bearded Welshman.

Between Phoenix and Lewis there was a latent, but unspoken and wary sympathy. Phoenix was terribly impressed by St. Mawr, he could not leave off staring at him. And Lewis rode the brilliant, handsome-moving stallion so very quietly, like an insinuation.

Of the two men, Lewis looked the darker, with his black beard coming up to his thick black eyebrows. He was swarthy, with a rather short nose, and the uncanny pale-grey eyes that watched everything and cared about nothing. He cared about nothing in the world, except, at the present, St. Mawr. People did not matter to him. He rode his horse and watched the world from the vantage ground of St. Mawr, with a final indifference.

"You been with that horse long?" asked Phoenix.

"Since he was born."

Phoenix watched the action of St. Mawr as they went. The bay moved proud and springy, but with perfect good sense, among the stream of riders. It was a beautiful June morning, the leaves overhead were thick and green, there came the first whiff of lime-tree scent. To Phoenix, however, the city was a sort of nightmare mirage, and to Lewis, it was a sort of prison. The presence of people he felt as a prison around him.

Mrs Witt and Lou were turning, at the end of the Row, bowing to some acquaintances. The grooms pulled aside. Mrs Witt looked at Lewis with a cold eye.

"It seems an extraordinary thing to me, Louise," she said, "to see a groom with a beard."

"It isn't usual, mother," said Lou. "Do you mind?"

"Not at all. At least, I think I don't. I get very tired of modern bare-faced young men, *very*! The clean, pure boy, don't you know! Doesn't it make you tired?—No, I think a groom with a beard is quite attractive."

She gazed into the crowd defiantly, perching her finely shod toe with warlike firmness on the stirrup-iron. Then suddenly she reined in, and turned her horse towards the grooms.

"Lewis!" she said. "I want to ask you a question. Supposing, now, that Lady Carrington wanted you to shave off that beard, what should you say?"

Lewis instinctively put up his hand to the said beard.

"They've wanted me to shave it off, Mam," he said. "But I've never done it."

"But why? Tell me why?"

"It's part of me, Mam."

Mrs Witt pulled on again.

"Isn't that extraordinary, Louise?" she said. "Don't you like the way he says *Mam*? It sounds so impossible to me. Could any woman think of herself as Mam? Never!—Since Queen Victoria. But, do you know it hadn't occurred to me that a man's beard was really part of him. It always seemed to me that men wore their beards, like they wear their neckties, for show. I shall always remember Lewis for saying his beard was part of him. Isn't it curious, the way he rides? He seems to sink himself in the horse. When I speak to him, I'm not sure whether I'm speaking to a man or to a horse."

A few days later, Rico himself appeared on St. Mawr, for the morning ride. He rode self-consciously, as he did everything, and he was just a little nervous. But his mother-in-law was benevolent. She made him ride between her and Lou, like three ships slowly sailing abreast.

And that very day, who should come driving in an open carriage through the Park, but the Queen Mother! Dear old Queen Alexandra, there was a flutter everywhere. And she bowed expressly to Rico, mistaking him, no doubt, for somebody else.

"Do you know," said Rico as they sat at lunch, he and Lou and Mrs Witt, in Mrs Witt's sitting-room in the dark, quiet hotel in Mayfair; "I really like riding St. Mawr *so* much. He really is a noble animal.—If ever I am made a Lord—which heaven forbid!—I shall be Lord St. Mawr."

"You mean," said Mrs Witt, "his real lordship would be the horse?"

"Very possible, I admit," said Rico, with a curl of his long upper lip.

"Don't you think mother," said Lou, "there *is* something quite noble about St. Mawr? He strikes me as the first noble thing I have ever seen."

"Certainly I've not seen any *man* that could compare with him. Because these English noblemen—well! I'd rather look at a negro Pullman-boy, if I was looking for what *I* call nobility."

Poor Rico was getting crosser and crosser. There was a devil in Mrs Witt. She had a hard, bright devil inside her, that she seemed to be able to let loose at will.

She let it loose the next day, when Rico and Lou joined her in the Row. She was silent but deadly with the horses, balking them in every way. She suddenly crowded over against the rail, in front of St. Mawr, so that the stallion had to rear, to pull himself up. Then, having a clear track, she suddenly set off at a gallop, like an explosion, and the stallion, all on edge, set off after her.

It seemed as if the whole Park, that morning, were in a state of nervous tension. Perhaps there was thunder in the air. But St. Mawr kept on dancing and pulling at the bit, and wheeling sideways up against the railing, to the terror of the children and the onlookers, who squealed and jumped back suddenly, sending the nerves of the stallion into a rush like rockets. He reared and fought as Rico pulled him round.

Then he went on: dancing, pulling, springily progressing sideways, possessed with all the demons of perversity. Poor Rico's face grew longer and angrier. A fury rose in him, which he could hardly control. He hated his horse, and viciously tried to force him to a quiet, straight trot. Up went St. Mawr on his hind legs, to the terror of the Row. He got the bit in his teeth, and began to fight.

But Phoenix, cleverly, was in front of him.

"You get off, Rico!" called Mrs Witt's voice, with all the calm of her wicked exultance.

And almost before he knew what he was doing, Rico had sprung lightly to the ground, and was hanging on to the bridle of the rearing stallion.

Phoenix also lightly jumped down, and ran to St. Mawr, handing his bridle to Rico. Then began a dancing and a splashing, a rearing and a plunging. St. Mawr was being wicked. But Phoenix, the indifference of conflict in his face, sat tight and immovable, without any emotion, only the heaviness of his impersonal will settling down like a weight, all the time, on the horse. There was, perhaps, a curious barbaric exultance in bare, dark will, devoid of emotion or personal feeling.

So they had a little display in the Row for almost five minutes, the brilliant horse rearing and fighting. Rico, with a stiff long face, scrambled on to Phoenix's horse, and withdrew to a safe distance. Policemen came, and an officious mounted police rode up to save the situation. But it was obvious that Phoenix, detached and apparently unconcerned, but barbarically potent in his will, would bring the horse to order.

Which he did, and rode the creature home. Rico was requested not to ride St. Mawr in the Row any more, as the stallion was dangerous to public safety. The authorities knew all about him.

Where ended the first fiasco of St. Mawr.

"We didn't get on very well with his lordship this morning," said Mrs Witt triumphantly.

"No, he didn't like his company *at all*!" Rico snarled back.

He wanted Lou to sell the horse again.

"I doubt if anyone would buy him, dear," she said. "He's a known character."

"Then make a gift of him—to your mother," said Rico with venom.

"Why to mother?" asked Lou innocently.

"She might be able to cope with him—or he with her!" The last phrase was deadly. Having delivered it, Rico departed.

Lou remained at a loss. She felt almost always a little bit dazed, as if she could not see clear nor feel clear. A curious deadness upon her, like the first touch of death. And through this cloud of numbness, or deadness, came all her muted experiences.

Why was it? She did not know. But she felt that in some way it came from a battle of wills. Her mother, Rico, herself, it was always an unspoken, unconscious battle of wills, which was gradually numbing and paralysing her. She knew Rico meant nothing but kindness by her. She knew her mother only wanted to watch over her. Yet always there was this tension of will, that was so numbing. As if at the depths of him, Rico were always angry, though he seemed so "happy" on top. And Mrs Witt was organically angry. So they were like a couple of bombs, timed to explode some day, but ticking on like two ordinary timepieces, in the meanwhile.

She had come definitely to realise this: that Rico's anger was wound up tight at the bottom of him, like a steel spring that kept his works going, while he himself was "charming," like a bomb-clock with Sèvres paintings or Dresden figures on the outside. But his very charm was a sort of anger, and his love was a destruction in itself. He just couldn't help it.

And she? Perhaps she was a good deal the same herself. Wound up tight inside, and enjoying herself being "lovely." But wound up tight on some tension that, she realised now with wonder, was really a sort of anger. This, the main-spring that drove her on the round of "joys."

She used really to enjoy the tension, and the *élan* it gave her. While she knew nothing about it. So long as she felt it really was life and happiness, this *élan*, this tension and excitement of "enjoying oneself."

Now suddenly she doubted the whole show. She attributed to it the curious numbness that was overcoming her, as if she couldn't feel any more.

She wanted to come unwound. She wanted to escape this battle of wills.

Only St. Mawr gave her some hint of the possibility. He was so powerful, and so dangerous. But in his dark eye, that looked, with its cloudy brown pupil, a cloud within a dark fire, like a world beyond our world, there was a dark vitality glowing, and within the fire, another sort of wisdom. She felt sure of it: even when he put his ears back, and bared his teeth, and his great eyes came bolting out of his naked horse's head, and she saw demons upon demons in the chaos of his horrid eyes.

Why did he seem to her like some living background, into which she wanted to retreat? When he reared his head and neighed from his deep chest, like deep wind-bells resounding, she seemed to hear the echoes of another, darker, more spacious, more dangerous, more splendid world than ours, that was beyond her. And there she wanted to go.

She kept it utterly a secret, to herself. Because Rico would just have lifted his long upper lip, in his bare face, in a condescending sort of "understanding." And her mother would, as usual, have suspected her of side-stepping. People, all the people she knew, seemed so entirely contained within their cardboard let's-be-happy world. Their wills were fixed like machines on happiness, or fun, or the-best-ever. This ghastly cheery-o! touch, that made all her blood go numb.

Since she had really seen St. Mawr looming fiery and terrible in an outer darkness, she could not believe the world she lived in. She could not believe it was actually happening, when she was dancing in the afternoon at Claridge's, or in the evening at the Carlton, sliding about with some suave young man who wasn't like a man at all to her. Or down in Sussex for the weekend with the Enderley's:—the talk, the eating and drinking, the flirtation, the endless dancing: it all seemed far more bodiless and, in a strange way, wraith-like, than any fairy story. She seemed to be eating Barmecide food, that had been conjured up out of thin air, by the power of words. She seemed to be talking to handsome young bare-faced unrealities, not men at all: as she slid about with them, in the perpetual dance, they too seemed to have been conjured up out of air, merely for this soaring, slithering dance-business. And she could not believe that, when the lights went out, they wouldn't melt back into thin air again, and complete nonentity. The strange nonentity of it all! Everything just conjured up, and nothing real. "*Isn't this the best ever!*" they would beamingly assert, like the wraiths of enjoyment, without any genuine substance. And she would beam back: "*Lots of fun!*"

She was thankful the season was over, and everybody was leaving London. She and Rico were due to go to Scotland, but not till August. In the meantime they would go to her mother.

Mrs Witt had taken a cottage in Shropshire, on the Welsh border, and had moved down there with Phoenix and her horses. The open, heather-and-bilberry-covered hills were splendid for riding.

Rico consented to spend the month in Shropshire, because for near neighbours Mrs Witt had the Manbys, at Corrabach Hall. The Manbys were rich Australians returned to the old country and set up as Squires, all in full blow. Rico had known them in Victoria: they were of good family: and the girls made a great fuss of him.

So down went Lou and Rico, Lewis, Poppy and St. Mawr, to Shrewsbury, then out into the country. Mrs Witt's "cottage" was a tall red-brick Georgian house looking straight on to the churchyard, and the dark, looming, big Church..

"I never knew what a comfort it would be," said Mrs Witt, "to have grave-stones under my drawing-room windows, and funerals for lunch."

She really did take a strange pleasure in sitting in her panelled room, that was painted grey, and watching the Dean or one of the curates officiating at the graveside, among a group of black country mourners with black-bordered handkerchiefs luxuriantly in use.

"Mother!" said Lou. "I think it's gruesome!"

She had a room at the back, looking over the walled garden and the stables. Nevertheless there was the *boom!* *boom!* of the passing-bell, and the chiming and pealing on Sundays. The shadow of the

Church, indeed! A very audible shadow, making itself heard insistently.

The Dean was a big, burly, fat man with a pleasant manner. He was a gentleman, and a man of learning in his own line. But he let Mrs Witt know that he looked down on her just a trifle—as a parvenu American, a Yankee—though she never was a Yankee: and at the same time he had a sincere respect for her, as a rich woman. Yes, a sincere respect for her, as a rich woman.

Lou knew that every Englishman, especially of the upper classes, has a wholesome respect for riches. But then, who hasn't?

The Dean was more *impressed* by Mrs Witt than by little Lou. But to Lady Carrington he was charming: she was *almost* "one of us," you know. And he was very gracious to Rico: "your father's splendid colonial service."

Mrs Witt had now a new pantomime to amuse her: the Georgian house, her own pew in Church—it went with the old house: a village of thatched cottages—some of them with corrugated iron over the thatch: the cottage people, farm laborers and their families, with a few, very few outsiders: the wicked little group of cottagers down at Mile End, famous for ill-living. The Mile-Enders were all Allisons and Jephsons, and in-bred, the Dean said: result of working through the centuries at the Quarry, and living isolated there at Mile End.

Isolated! Imagine it! A mile and a half from the railway station, ten miles from Shrewsbury. Mrs Witt thought of Texas, and said:

"Yes they are *very* isolated, away down there!"

And the Dean never for a moment suspected sarcasm.

But there she had the whole thing staged complete for her: English village life. Even miners breaking in to shatter the rather stuffy, unwholesome harmony.—All the men touched their caps to her, all the women did a bit of a reverence, the children stood aside for her, if she appeared in the Street.

They were all poor again: the laborers could no longer afford even a glass of beer in the evenings, since the Glorious war.

"Now I think that *is* terrible." said Mrs Witt. "Not to be able to get away from those stuffy, squalid, picturesque cottages for an hour in the evening, to drink a glass of beer."

"It's a pity, I do agree with you, Mrs Witt. But Mr Watson has organised a men's reading-room, where the men can smoke and play dominoes, and read if they wish."

"But that" said Mrs Witt, "is not the same as that cosy parlour in the *Moon and Stars.*"

"I quite agree," said the Dean. "It isn't."

Mrs Witt marched to the landlord of the *Moon and Stars*, and asked for a glass of cider.

"I want," she said, in her American accent, "these poor laborers to have their glass of beer in the evenings."

"They want it themselves," said Harvey.

"Then they must have it—"

The upshot was, she decided to supply one large barrel of beer per week and the landlord was to sell it to the laborers at a penny a glass.

"My own country has gone dry," she asserted. "But not because we can't *afford* it."

By the time Lou and Rico appeared, she was deep in. She actually interfered very little: the barrel of beer was her one public act. But she *did* know everybody by sight, already, and she *did* know everybody's circumstances. And she had attended one prayer-meeting, one mothers' meeting, one sewing-bee, one "social," one Sunday School meeting, one Band of Hope meeting, and one Sunday School treat. She ignored the poky little Wesleyan and Baptist chapels, and was true-blue episcopalian.

"How strange these picturesque old villages are, Louise!" she said, with a duskiness around her sharp, well-bred nose. "How *easy* it all seems, all on a definite pattern. And how false! And underneath, *how corrupt*!"

She gave that queer, triumphant leer from her grey eyes, and queer demonish wrinkles seemed to twitter on her face.

Lou shrank away. She was beginning to be afraid of her mother's insatiable curiosity, that always looked for the snake under the flowers. Or rather, for the maggots.

Always this same morbid interest in other people and their doings, their privacies, their dirty linen. Always this air of alertness for personal happenings, personalities, personalities, personalities. Always this subtle criticism and appraisal of other people, this analysis of other people's motives. If anatomy pre-supposes a corpse, then psychology pre-supposes a world of corpses. Personalities, which means personal criticism and analysis, pre-supposes a whole world-laboratory of human psyches waiting to be vivisected. If you cut a thing up, of course it will smell. Hence, nothing raises such an infernal stink, at last, as human psychology.

Mrs Witt was a pure psychologist, a fiendish psychologist. And Rico, in his way, was a psychologist too. But he had a formula. "Let's *know* the worst, dear! But let's look on the bright side, and believe the best."

"Isn't the Dean a priceless old darling!" said Rico at breakfast.

And it had begun. Work had started in the psychic vivisection laboratory.

"Isn't he wonderful!" said Lou vaguely.

"So delightfully worldly!—*Some of us are not born to make money, dear boy. Luckily for us, we can marry it.*"—Rico made a priceless face.

"Is Mrs Vyner so rich?" asked Lou.

"She is, quite a wealthy woman—in coal," replied Mrs Witt. "But the Dean is surely worth his weight, even in gold. And he's a massive figure. I can imagine there would be great satisfaction in having him for a husband."

"Why, mother?" asked Lou.

"Oh, such a presence! One of these old Englishmen, that nobody can put in their pocket. You can't imagine his wife asking him to thread her needle. Something after all so *robust*! So different from *young* Englishmen, who all seem to me like ladies, perfect ladies."

"*Somebody* has to keep up the tradition of the perfect lady," said Rico.

"I know it," said Mrs Witt. "And if the women won't do it, the young gentlemen take on the burden. They bear it very well."

It was in full swing, the cut and thrust. And poor Lou, who had reached the point of stupefaction in the game, felt she did not know what to do with herself.

Rico and Mrs Witt were deadly enemies, yet neither could keep clear of the other. It might have been they who were married to one another, their duel and their duet were so relentless.

But Rico immediately started the social round: first the Manbys: then motor twenty miles to luncheon at Lady Tewkesbury's: then young Mr Burns came flying down in his aeroplane from Chester: then they must motor to the sea, to Sir Edward Edwards' place, where there was a moonlight bathing party. Everything intensely thrilling, and so innerly wearisome, Lou felt.

But back of it all was St. Mawr, looming like a bonfire in the dark. He really was a tiresome horse to own. He worried the mares, if they were in the same paddock with him, always driving them round. And with any other horse he just fought with definite intent to kill. So he had to stay alone.

"That St. Mawr, he's a bad horse," said Phoenix.

"Maybe!" said Lewis.

"You don' like quiet horses?" said Phoenix.

"Most horses *is* quiet," said Lewis. "St. Mawr, he's different."

"Why don't he never get any foals?"

"Doesn't want to, I should think. Same as me."

"What good is a horse like that? Better shoot him, before he kill somebody."

"What good'll they get, shooting St. Mawr?" said Lewis.

"If he kills somebody!—" said Phoenix.

But there was no answer.

The two grooms both lived over the stables, and Lou, from her window, saw a good deal of them. They were two quiet men, yet she was very much aware of their presence, aware of Phoenix's rather high square shoulders and his fine, straight, vigorous black hair that tended to stand up assertively on his head, as he went quietly, drifting about his various jobs. He was not lazy, but he did everything with a sort of diffidence, as if from a distance, and handled his horses carefully, cautiously, and cleverly, but without sympathy. He seemed to be holding something back, all the time, unconsciously, as if in his very being there was some secret. But it was a secret of *will*. His quiet, reluctant movements, as if he never really wanted to do anything; his long flat-stepping stride; the permanent challenge in his high cheek-bones, the Indian glint in his eyes, and his peculiar stare, watchful and yet unseeing, made him unpopular with the women servants.

Nevertheless, women had a certain fascination for him: he would stare at the pretty young maids with an intent blank stare, when they were not looking. Yet he was rather overbearing, domineering with them, and they resented him. It was evident to Lou that he looked upon himself as belonging to the master, not to the servant class. When he flirted with the maids, as he very often did, for he had a certain crude ostentatiousness, he seemed to let them feel that he despised them as inferiors, servants, while he admired their pretty charms, as fresh, country maids.

"I'm fair nervous of that Phoenix," said Fanny, the fair-haired maid. "He makes you feel what he'd do to you if he could."

"He'd better not try with me," said Mabel. "I'd scratch his cheeky eyes out. Cheek!—for it's nothing else! He's nobody—Common as they're made!"

"He makes you feel you was there for him to trample on," said Fanny.

"Mercy, you *are* soft! If anybody's that it's him. Oh my, Fanny, you've no right to let a fellow make you feel like *that*! Make *them* feel that *they're* dirt, for you to trample on: which they are!"

Fanny, however, being a shy little blonde thing, wasn't good at assuming the trampling rôle. She was definitely nervous of Phoenix. And he enjoyed it. An invisible smile seemed to creep up his cheek-bones, and the glint moved in his eyes as he teased her. He tormented her by his very presence, as he knew.

He would come silently up when she was busy, and stand behind her perfectly still, so that she was unaware of his presence. Then, silently, he would *make* her aware. Till she glanced nervously round, and with a scream, saw him.

One day Lou watched this little play. Fanny had been picking over a bowl of black currants, sitting on the bench under the maple tree in a corner of the yard. She didn't look round till she had picked up her bowl to go to the kitchen. Then there was a scream and a crash.

When Lou came out, Phoenix was crouching down silently gathering up the currants, which the little maid, scarlet and trembling, was collecting into another bowl. Phoenix seemed to be smiling down his back.

"Phoenix!" said Lou. "I wish you wouldn't startle Fanny!"

He looked up, and she saw the glint of ridicule in his eyes.

"Who, me?" he said.

"Yes, you. You go up behind Fanny, to startle her. You're not to do it."

He slowly stood erect, and lapsed into his peculiar invisible silence. Only for a second his eyes glanced at Lou's, and then she saw the cold anger, the gleam of malevolence and contempt. He could not bear being commanded, or reprimanded, by a woman.

Yet it was even worse with a man.

"What's that, Lou?" said Rico, appearing all handsome and in the picture, in white flannels with an apricot silk shirt.

"I'm telling Phoenix he's not to torment Fanny!"

"Oh!"—and Rico's voice immediately became his father's, the important government official's. "Certainly *not*! Most certainly *not*!" He looked at the scattered currants and the broken bowl. Fanny melted into tears.—"This, I suppose, is some of the results!—Now look here, Phoenix, you're to leave the maids strictly alone. I shall ask them to report to me whenever, or *if* ever, you interfere with them. But I hope you *won't* interfere with them—in any way. You understand?"

As Rico became more and more Sir Henry and the Government Official, Lou's bones melted more and more into discomfort. Phoenix stood in his peculiar silence, the invisible smile on his cheek-bones.

"You understand what I'm saying to you?" Rico demanded, in intensified acid tones.

But Phoenix only stood there, as it were behind a cover of his own will, and looked back at Rico with a faint smile on his face and the glint moving in his eyes.

"Do you intend to answer?" Rico's upper lip lifted nastily.

"Mrs Witt is my boss," came from Phoenix.

The scarlet flew up Rico's throat and flushed his face, his eyes went glaucous. Then quickly his face turned yellow.

Lou looked at the two men: her husband, whose rages, over-controlled, were organically terrible: the half-breed, whose dark-coloured lips were widened in a faint smile of derision, but in whose eyes caution and hate were playing against one another. She realised that Phoenix would accept *her* reprimand, or her mother's, because he could despise the two of them as mere women. But Rico's bossiness aroused murder pure and simple.

She took her husband's arm.

"Come dear!" she said, in her half plaintive way. "I'm sure Phoenix understands. We all understand.—Go to the kitchen, Fanny, never mind the currants There are plenty more in the garden."

Rico was always thankful to be drawn quickly, submissively away from his own rage. He was afraid of it. He was afraid lest he should fly at the groom in some horrible fashion. The very thought horrified him. But in actuality he came very near to it.

He walked stiffly, feeling paralysed by his own fury. And those words, *Mrs Witt is my boss*, were like hot acid in his brain. An insult!

"By the way, Belle-Mère!" he said when they joined Mrs Witt—she hated being called Belle-Mère, and once said: "If I'm the bell-mare, are you one of the colts?"—She also hated his voice of smothered fury—"I had to speak to Phoenix about persecuting the maids. He took the liberty of informing me that you were his boss, so perhaps you had better speak to him."

"I certainly will. I believe they're my maids, and nobody else's, so it's my duty to look after them. Who was he persecuting?"

"I'm the responsible one, mother," said Lou———

Rico disappeared in a moment. He must get out: get away from the house. How? Something was wrong with the car. Yet he must get away, away. He would go over to Corrabach. He would ride St. Mawr. He had been talking about the horse, and Flora Manby was dying to see him. She had said: "Oh, I can't *wait* to see that marvellous horse of yours."

He would ride him over. It was only seven miles. He found Lou's maid Elena, and sent her to tell Lewis. Meanwhile, to soothe himself, he dressed himself most carefully in white riding-breeches and a shirt of purple silk crape, with a flowing black tie spotted red like a ladybird, and black riding-boots. Then he took a *chic* little white hat with a black band.

St. Mawr was saddled and waiting, and Lewis had saddled a second horse.

"Thanks, Lewis, I'm going alone!" said Rico.

This was the first time he had ridden St. Mawr in the country, and he was nervous. But he was also in the hell of a smothered fury. All his careful dressing had not really soothed him. So his fury consumed his nervousness.

He mounted with a swing, blind and rough. St. Mawr reared.

"Stop that!" snarled Rico, and put him to the gate.

Once out in the village street, the horse went dancing sideways. He insisted on dancing at the sidewalk, to the exaggerated terror of the children. Rico, exasperated, pulled him across. But no, he wouldn't go down the centre of the village street. He began dancing and edging on to the other sidewalk, so the foot-passengers fled into the shops in terror.

The devil was in him. He would turn down every turning where he was not meant to go. He reared with panic at a furniture van. He *insisted* on going down the wrong side of the road. Rico was riding him with a martingale, and he could see the rolling, bloodshot eye.

"Damn you, *go!*" said Rico, giving him a dig with the spurs.

And away they went, down the high-road, in a thunderbolt. It was a hot day, with thunder threatening, so Rico was soon in a flame of heat. He held on tight, with fixed eyes, trying all the time to rein in the horse. What he really was afraid of was that the brute would shy suddenly, as he galloped. Watching for this, he didn't care when they sailed past the turning to Corrabach.

St. Mawr flew on, in a sort of *élan*. Marvellous the power and life in the creature. There was really a great joy in the motion. If only

he wouldn't take the corners at a gallop, nearly swerving Rico off!
Luckily the road was clear. To ride to ride at this terrific gallop, on
into eternity!

After several miles, the horse slowed down, and Rico managed to
pull him into a lane that might lead to Corrabach. When all was said
and done, it was a wonderful ride. St. Mawr could go like the wind,
but with that luxurious heavy ripple of life which is like nothing else
on earth. It seemed to carry one at once into another world, away from
the life of the nerves.

So Rico arrived after all something of a conqueror, at Corrabach.
To be sure, he was perspiring, and so was his horse. But he was a hero
from another, heroic world.

"Oh, such a hot ride!" he said, as he walked on to the lawn at
Corrabach Hall. "Between the sun and the horse, really!—between
two fires!"

"Don't you trouble, you're looking dandy, a bit hot and flushed-
like!" said Flora Manby. "Let's go and see your horse."

And her exclamation was: "Oh, he's *lovely*! He's *fine*! I'd love to
try him once—"

Rico decided to accept the invitation to stay overnight at Corrabach.
Usually he was very careful, and refused to stay, unless Lou was with
him. But they telephoned to the post office at Chomesbury, would Mr
Jones please send a message to Lady Carrington that Sir Henry was
staying the night at Corrabach Hall, but would be home next day. Mr
Jones received the request with unction, and said he would go over
himself to give the message to Lady Carrington.

Lady Carrington was in the walled garden. The peculiarity of Mrs
Witt's house was that, for grounds proper, it had the churchyard.

"I never thought, Louise, that one day I should have an old English
church-yard for my lawns and shrubbery and park, and funeral
mourners for my herds of deer. It's curious. For the first time in my
life, a funeral has become a real thing to me. I feel I could write a
book on them."

But Louise only felt intimidated.

At the back of the house was a flagged courtyard, with stables and
a maple tree in a corner, and big doors opening on to the village street.
But at the side was a walled garden, with fruit trees and currant bushes
and a great bed of rhubarb, and some tufts of flowers, peonies, pink
roses, sweet williams. Phoenix, who had a certain taste for gardening,
would be out there thinning the carrots or tying up the lettuce. He

was not lazy. Only he would not take work seriously, as a job. He would be quite amused, tying up lettuces, and would tie up head after head, quite prettily. Then, becoming bored, he would abandon his task, light a cigarette, and go and stand on the threshold of the big doors, in full view of the street, watching, and yet completely indifferent.

After Rico's departure on St. Mawr, Lou went into the garden. And there she saw Phoenix working in the onion bed. He was bending over, in his own silence, busy with nimble, amused fingers among the grassy young onions. She thought he had not seen her, so she went down another path, to where a swing bed hung under the apple trees. There she sat with a book and a bundle of magazines. But she did not read.

She was musing vaguely. Vaguely, she was glad that Rico was away for a while. Vaguely, she felt a sense of bitterness, of complete futility: the complete futility of her living. This left her drifting in a sea of utter chagrin. And Rico seemed to her the symbol of the futility. Vaguely, she was aware that something else existed, but she didn't know where it was or what it was.

In the distance she could see Phoenix's dark, rather tall-built head, with its black, fine, intensely-living hair tending to stand on end, like a brush with long, very fine black bristles. His hair, she thought, betrayed him as an animal of a different species. He was growing a little bored by weeding onions: that also she could tell. Soon he would want some other amusement.

Presently Lewis appeared. He was small, energetic, a little bit bow-legged, and he walked with a slight strut. He wore khaki riding-breeches, leather gaiters, and a blue shirt. And like Phoenix, he rarely had any cap or hat on his head. His thick black hair was parted at the side and brushed over heavily sideways, dropping on his forehead at the right. It was very long, a real mop, under which his eyebrows were dark and steady.

"Seen Lady Carrington?" he asked of Phoenix.

"Yes, she's sitting on that swing over there—she's been there quite a while."

The wretch—he had seen her from the very first!

Lewis came striding over, looking towards her with his pale grey eyes, from under his mop of hair.

"Mr Jones from the post office wants to see you, my Lady, with a message from Sir Henry."

Instantly alarm took possession of Lou's soul.

"Oh!—Does he want to see me personally?—What message? Is

71

anything wrong?—" And her voice trailed out over the last word, with a sort of anxious nonchalance.

"I don't think it's anything amiss," said Lewis reassuringly.

"Oh! You don't!" the relief came into her voice. The she looked at Lewis with a slight, winning smile in her unmatched eyes. "I'm so afraid of St. Mawr, you know." Her voice was soft and cajoling. Phoenix was listening in the distance.

"St. Mawr's all right, if you don't do nothing to him," Lewis replied.

"I'm sure he is!—But how is one to know when one is doing something to him—?—Tell Mr Jones to come here, please," she concluded, on a changed tone.

Mr Jones, a man of forty-five, thick-set, with a fresh complexion and rather foolish brown eyes, and a big brown moustache, came prancing down the path, smiling rather fatuously, and doffing his straw hat with a gorgeous bow the moment he saw Lou sitting in her slim white frock on the coloured swing bed under the trees with their hard green apples.

"Good morning Mr Jones!"

"Good morning Lady Carrington—If I may say so, what a picture you make—a beautiful picture—"

He beamed under his big brown moustache like the greatest lady-killer.

"Do I!—Did Sir Henry say he was all right?"

"He didn't *say* exactly, but I should expect he is all right— — —" and Mr Jones delivered his message, in the mayonnaise of his own unction.

"Thank you so much, Mr Jones. It's awfully good of you to come and tell me. Now I shan't worry about Sir Henry *at all*."

"It's a great pleasure to come and deliver a satisfactory message to Lady Carrington.—But it won't be kind to Sir Henry if you don't worry about him *at all* in his absence. We all enjoy being worried about by those we love—so long as there is nothing to worry about of course!—"

"Quite!" said Lou. "Now won't you take a glass of port and a biscuit—or a whisky and soda? And thank you ever so much."

"Thank *you*, my Lady.—I might drink a whisky and soda, since you are so good."

And he beamed fatuously.

"Let Mr Jones mix himself a whisky and soda, Lewis," said Lou.

"Heavens!" she thought, as the postmaster retreated a little uncomfortably down the garden path, his bald spot passing in and out of the sun, under the trees: "How ridiculous everything is, how ridiculous, ridiculous!" Yet she didn't really dislike Mr Jones and his interlude.

Phoenix was melting away out of the garden. He had to follow the fun.

"Phoenix!" Lou called. "Bring me a glass of water, will you? Or send somebody with it."

He stood in the path looking round at her.

"All right!" he said.

And he turned away again.

She did not like being alone in the garden. She liked to have the men working somewhere near. Curious how pleasant it was to sit there in the garden when Phoenix was about, or Lewis. It made her feel she could never be lonely or jumpy. But when Rico was there, she was all aching nerve.

Phoenix came back with a glass of water, lemon juice, sugar, and a small bottle of brandy. He knew Lou liked a spoonful of brandy in her iced lemonade.

"How thoughtful of you Phoenix!" she said. "Did Mr Jones get his whisky?"

"He was just getting it."

"That's right.—By the way, Phoenix, I wish you wouldn't get mad, if Sir Henry speaks to you. He is *really* so kind."—

She looked up at the man. He stood there watching her in silence, the invisible smile on this face, and the inscrutable Indian glint moving in his eyes. What was he thinking? There was something passive and almost submissive about him, but underneath this, an unyielding resistance and cruelty: yes, even cruelty. She felt that, on top, he was submissive and attentive, bringing her her lemonade as she liked it, without being told: thinking for her quite subtly. But underneath, there was an unchanging hatred. He submitted circumstantially, he worked for a wage. And even circumstantially, he *liked* his mistress—*la patrona*—and her daughter. But much deeper than any circumstance or any circumstantial liking, was the categorical hatred upon which he was founded, and with which he was powerless. His liking for Lou and for Mrs Witt, his serving them and working for a wage, was all side-tracking his own nature, which was grounded on hatred of their very existence. But what was he to do? He had to live. Therefore he had to serve, to work for a wage, and even to be faithful.

And yet *their* existence made his own existence negative. If he was to exist, positively, they would have to cease to exist. At the same time, a fatal sort of tolerance made him serve these women, and go on serving.

"Sir Henry is *so* kind to everybody," Lou insisted.

The half-breed met her eyes, and smiled uncomfortably.

"Yes, he's a kind man," he replied, as if sincerely.

"Then why do you mind, if he speaks to you?"

"I don't mind," said Phoenix glibly.

"But you do. Or else you wouldn't make him so angry."

"Was he angry?—I don't know," said Phoenix.

"He was very angry. And you *do* know."

"No I don't know if he's angry. I don't know," the fellow persisted. And there was a glib sort of satisfaction in his tone.

"That's awfully unkind of you, Phoenix," she said, growing offended in her turn.

"No, I don't know if he's angry. I don't want to make him angry. I don't know"—

He had taken on a tone of naive ignorance, which at once gratified her pride as a woman, and deceived her.

"Well, you believe me when I tell you you *did* make him angry, don't you?"

"Yes, I believe when you tell me."

"And you promise me, won't you, not to do it again? It's *so* bad for him—so bad for his nerves, and for his eyes. It makes them inflamed, and injures his eyesight. And you know, as an artist, it's terrible if anything happens to his eyesight—"

Phoenix was watching her closely, to take it in. He still was not good at understanding continuous, logical statement. Logical connection in speech seemed to stupefy him, make him stupid. He understood in disconnected assertions of fact. But he had gathered what she said. "He gets mad at you. When he gets mad, it hurts his eyes. His eyes hurt him. He can't see, because his eyes hurt him. He want to paint a picture, he can't. He can't paint a picture, he can't see clear—"

Yes, he had understood. She saw he had understood. The bright glint of satisfaction moved in his eyes.

"So now promise me, won't you, you won't make him mad again: you won't make him angry?"

"No, I won't make him angry. I don't do anything to make him angry," Phoenix answered, rather glibly.

"And you do understand, don't you? You do know how kind he is: how he'd do a good turn to anybody?"

"Yes, he's a kind man," said Phoenix.

"I'm so glad you realise.—There, that's luncheon! How nice it is to sit here in the garden, when everybody is nice to you! No, I can carry the tray, don't you bother."

But he took the tray from her hand, and followed her to the house. And as he walked behind her, he watched the slim white nape of her neck, beneath the clustering of her bobbed hair, something as a stoat watches a rabbit he is following.

In the afternoon Lou retreated once more to her place in the garden. There she lay, sitting with a bunch of pillows behind her, neither reading nor working, just musing. She had learned the new joy: to do absolutely nothing, but to lie and let the sunshine filter through the leaves, to see the bunch of red-hot-poker flowers pierce scarlet into the afternoon, beside the comparative neutrality of some fox gloves. The mere colour of hard red, like the big oriental poppies that had fallen, and these poker flowers, lingered in her consciousness like a communication.

Into this peaceful indolence, when even the big, dark-grey tower of the church beyond the wall and the yew-trees, was keeping its bells in silence, advanced Mrs Witt, in a broad panama hat and a white dress.

"Don't you want to ride, or do something, Louise?" she asked ominously.

"Don't you want to be peaceful, Mother?" retorted Louise.

"Yes—an *active* peace.—I can't *believe* that my daughter can be content to lie on a hammock and do *nothing*, not even read or improve her mind, the greater part of the day."

"Well, your daughter *is* content to do that. It's her greatest pleasure."

"I know it. I can see it. And it surprises me *very* much. When I was your age, I was never still. I had so much go—"

"'*Those maids thank God
    Are 'neath the sod,
    And all their generation*.'—No but, mother, I only take life differently. Perhaps you used up that sort of *go*. I'm the harem type, mother: only I never want the men inside the lattice."

"Are you really my daughter?—Well! A woman never knows what will happen to her.—I'm an *American* woman, and I suppose I've got to remain one, no matter where I am.—What did you want, Lewis?"

The groom had approached down the path.

"If I am to saddle Poppy?" said Lewis.

"No, apparently *not*!" replied Mrs Witt. "Your mistress prefers the hammock to the saddle."

"Thank you, Lewis. What mother says is true this afternoon, at least." And she gave him a peculiar little cross-eyed smile.

"Who," said Mrs Witt to the man, "has been cutting at your hair?"

There was a moment of silent resentment.

"I did it myself, Mam! Sir Henry said it was too long."

"He certainly spoke the truth.—But I believe there's a barber in the village on Saturdays—or you could ride over to Shrewsbury.—Just turn round, and let me look at the back. Is it the money?"

"No Mam. I don't like these fellows touching my head."

He spoke coldly, with a certain hostile reserve that at once piqued Mrs Witt.

"Don't you really!" she said. "But it's quite *impossible* for you to go about as you are. It gives you a half-witted appearance. Go now into the yard, and get a chair and a dust-sheet. I'll cut your hair."

The man hesitated, hostile.

"Don't be afraid, I know how it's done. I've cut the hair of many a poor wounded boy in hospital: and shaved them too. *You've got such a touch, nurse!* Poor fellow, he was dying, though none of us knew it.—Those are the compliments I value, Louise.—Get that chair now, and a dust-sheet. I'll borrow your hair-scissors from Elena, Louise."

Mrs Witt, happily on the war-path, was herself again. She didn't care for work, actual work. But she loved trimming. She loved arranging unnatural and pretty salads, devising new and piquant-looking ice-creams, having a turkey stuffed exactly as she knew a stuffed turkey in Louisiana, with chestnuts and butter and stuff, or showing a servant how to turn waffles on a waffle-iron, or to bake a ham with brown sugar and cloves and a moistening of rum. She liked pruning rose-trees, or beginning to cut a yew hedge into shape. She liked ordering her own and Louise's shoes, with an exactitude and a knowledge of shoe-making that sent the salesmen crazy. She was a demon in shoes. Reappearing from America, she would pounce on her daughter. "Louise, throw those shoes away. Give them to one of the maids."—"But mother, they are some of the best French shoes. I like them."—"Throw them away. A shoe has only two excuses for existing: perfect comfort or perfect appearance. Those have neither.

I have brought you some shoes. "—Yes, she had brought ten pairs of shoes from New York. She knew her daughter's foot as she knew her own.

So now she was in her element, looming behind Lewis as he sat in the middle of the yard swathed in a dust-sheet. She had on an overall and a pair of wash-leather gloves, and she poised a pair of long scissors like one of the fates. In her big hat she looked curiously young, but with the youth of a by-gone generation. Her heavy-lidded, laconic grey eyes were alert, studying the groom's black mop of hair. Her eyebrows made thin, uptilting black arches on her brow. Her fresh skin was slightly powdered, and she was really handsome, in a bold, by-gone, eighteenth-century style. Some of the curious, adventurous stoicism of the eighteenth-century: and then a certain blatant American efficiency.

Lou, who had strayed into the yard to see, looked so much younger and so many thousand of years older than her mother, as she stood in her wisp-like diffidence, the clusters of grape-like bobbed hair hanging beside her face, with its fresh colouring and its ancient weariness, her slightly squinting eyes, that were so disillusioned they were becoming faun-like.

"Not too short, mother, not too short!" she remonstrated, as Mrs Witt, with a terrific flourish of efficiency, darted at the man's black hair, and the thick flakes fell like black snow.

"Now Louise, I'm right in this job, please don't interfere.—Two things I hate to see: a man with his wool in his neck and ears and a bare-faced young man who looks as if he'd bought his face as well as his hair from a men's beauty-specialist."

And efficiently she bent down, clip—clip—clipping! while Lewis sat utterly immobile, with sunken head, in a sort of despair.

Phoenix stood against the stable door, with his restless, eternal cigarette. And in the kitchen doorway the maids appeared and fled, appeared and fled in delight. The old gardener, a fixture who went with the house, creaked in and stood with his legs apart, silent in intense condemnation.

"First time I ever see such a thing!" he muttered to himself, as he creaked on into the garden. He was a bad-tempered old soul, who thoroughly disapproved of the household, and would have given notice, but that he knew which side his bread was buttered: and there was butter unstinted on his bread, in Mrs Witt's kitchen.

Mrs Witt stood back to survey her handywork, holding those

terrifying shears with their beak erect. Lewis lifted his head and looked stealthily round, like a creature in a trap.

"Keep still!" she said. "I haven't finished."

And she went for his front hair, with vigour, lifting up long layers and snipping off the ends artistically: till at last he sat with a black aureole upon the floor, and his ears standing out with curious new alertness from the sides of his clean-clipped head.

"Stand up," she said, "and let me look."

He stood up, looking absurdly young, with the hair all cut away from his neck and ears, left thick only on top. She surveyed her work with satisfaction.

"You look so much younger," she said; "you would be surprised.— Sit down again."

She clipped the back of his neck with the shears, and then, with a very slight hesitation, she said:

"Now about the beard!"

But the man rose suddenly from the chair, pulling the dust-cloth from his neck with desperation.

"No, I'll do that myself," he said, looking her in the eyes with a cold light in his pale grey, uncanny eyes.

She hesitated in a kind of wonder at his queer male rebellion.

"Now listen, I shall do it much better than you—and besides—" she added hurriedly, snatching at the dust-cloth he was flinging on the chair—"I haven't quite finished round the ears."

"I think I shall do," he said, again looking her in the eyes, with a cold white gleam of finality. "Thank you for what you've done."

And he walked away to the stable.

"You'd better sweep up here," Mrs Witt called.

"Yes Mam," he replied, looking round at her again with an odd resentment, but continuing to walk away.

"However!" said Mrs Witt. "I suppose he'll do."

And she divested herself of gloves and overall, and walked indoors to wash and to change. Lou went indoors too.

"It is extraordinary, what hair that man has!" said Mrs Witt. "Did I tell you when I was in Paris, I saw a woman's face in the hotel, that I thought I knew? I couldn't place her, till she was coming towards me. *Aren't you Rachel Fannière?* she said. *Aren't you Janette Leroy?* We hadn't seen each other since we were girls of twelve and thirteen, at school in New Orleans. *Oh!* she said to me. *Is every illusion doomed to perish? You had such wonderful golden curls! All my life I've said,*

78

Oh, if only I had such lovely hair as Rachel Fannière! I've seen those beautiful golden curls of yours all my life. And now I meet you, you're grey! Wasn't that terrible, Louise? Well, that man's hair made me think of it—so thick and curious. It's strange, what a difference there is in hair. I suppose it's because he's just an animal—no mind! There's nothing I admire in a man like a good *mind*. Your father was a very clever man, and all the men I've admired have been clever. But isn't it curious, now, I've never cared much to touch their hair. How strange life is! If it gives one thing, it takes away another.—And even those poor boys in hospital: I have shaved them, or cut their hair, like a mother, never thinking anything of it. Lovely, intelligent, clean boys, most of them were. Yet it never did anything to me. I never knew before that something could happen to one from a person's *hair*! Like to Janette Leroy from my curls when I was a child. And now I'm grey, as she says.—I wonder how old a man Lewis is, Louise! Didn't he look absurdly young with his ears pricking up?"

"I think Rico said he was forty or forty-one."

"And never been married?"

"No—not as far as I know."

"Isn't that curious now!—just an animal! no mind! A man with no mind! I've always thought that the *most* despicable thing. Yet such wonderful hair to touch. Your Henry has quite a good mind, yet I would simply shrink from touching his hair.—I suppose one likes stroking a cat's fur, just the same. Just the animal in man. Curious that I never seem to have met it, Louise. Now I come to think of it, he has the eyes of a human cat: a human tom-cat. Would you call him stupid? Yes, he's very stupid."

"No mother, he's not stupid. He only doesn't care about our sort of things."

"Like an animal! But what a strange look he has in his eyes! a strange sort of intelligence! and a confidence in himself. Isn't that curious, Louise, in a man with as little mind as he has? Do you know, I should say he could see through a woman pretty well."

"Why mother!" said Lou impatiently. "I think one gets so tired of your men with mind, as you call it. There are so many of that sort of clever men. And there are lots of men who aren't very clever, but are rather nice: and lots are stupid. It seems to me there's something else besides mind and cleverness, or niceness or cleanness. Perhaps it is the animal. Just think of St. Mawr! I've thought so much about him. We call him an animal, but we never know what it means. He seems a far greater mystery to me, than a clever man. He's a horse. Why can't one say in the same way, of a man: *He's a man?* There seems no mystery in being a man. But there's a terrible mystery in St. Mawr. "

Mrs Witt watched her daughter quizzically.

"Louise," she said. "You won't tell me that the mere animal is all that counts in a man. I will never believe it. Man is wonderful because he is able to *think*. "

"But is he?" cried Lou, with sudden exasperation. "Their thinking seems to me all so childish: like stringing the same beads over and over again. Ah, Men! They and their thinking are all so *paltry*. How can you be impressed?"

Mrs Witt raised her eyebrows sardonically.

"Perhaps I'm not—any more," she said with a grim smile.

"But," she added, "I still can't see that I am to be impressed by the mere animal in man. The animals are the same as we are. It seems to me they have the same feelings and wants as we do, in a commonplace way. The only difference is that they have no minds: no human minds, at least. And no matter what you say, Louise, lack of mind makes the commonplace. "

Lou knitted her brows nervously.

" I suppose it does, mother.—But men's minds *are* so commonplace: look at Dean Vyner and his mind! Or look at Arthur Balfour, as a shining example. Isn't *that* commonplace, that cleverness? I would hate St. Mawr to be spoilt by such a mind. "

"Yes Louise, so would I. Because the men you mention are really old women, knitting the same pattern over and over again. Nevertheless, I shall never alter my belief, that real mind is all that matters in a man, and it's *that* that we women love. "

"Yes mother!—But what *is* real mind? The old woman who knits the most complicated pattern? Oh, I can hear all their needles clicking, the clever men! As a matter of fact, mother, I believe Lewis has far more real mind than Dean Vyner or any of the clever ones. He has a good intuitive mind, he knows things without thinking them. "

"That may be, Louise! But he is a servant. He is *under*. A real man should never be under.—And then you could never be intimate with a man like Lewis. "

"I don't want intimacy, mother. I'm too tired of it all. I love St. Mawr because he isn't intimate. He stands where one can't get at him. And he burns with life. And where does his life come from, to him? That's the mystery. That great burning life in him, which never is dead. Most men have a deadness in them, that frightens me so, because of my own deadness. Why can't men get their life straight, like St. Mawr, and then think? Why can't they think quick, mother: quick as a woman: only farther than we do? Why isn't men's thinking quick like fire, mother? Why is it so slow, so dead, so deadly dull?"

"I can't tell you, Louise. My own opinion of the men of today has grown very small. But I can live in spite of it."

"No mother. We seem to be living off old fuel, like the camel when he lives off his hump. Life doesn't rush into us, as it does even into St. Mawr, and he's a dependent animal. I can't live, mother. I just can't."

"I don't see why not? *I'm* full of life."

"I know you are, mother. But I'm not, and I'm your daughter.—And don't misunderstand me, mother. I don't want to be an animal like a horse or a cat or a lioness, though they all fascinate me, the way they get their life *straight*, not from a lot of old tanks, as we do. I don't admire the cave man, and that sort of thing. But think mother, if we could get our lives straight from the source, as the animals do, and still be ourselves. You don't like men, yourself. But you've no idea how men just tire me out: even the very thought of them. You say they are too animal. But they're not, mother. It's the animal in them has gone perverse, or cringing, or humble, or domesticated, like dogs. I don't know one single man who is a proud living animal. I know they've left off really thinking. But then men always do leave off really thinking, when the last bit of wild animal dies in them."

"Because we have minds—"

"We have no minds once we are tame, mother. Men are all women, knitting and crochetting words together."

"I can't altogether agree, you know, Louise."

"I know you don't.—You like clever men. But clever men are mostly such unpleasant *animals*. As animals, so very unpleasant. And in men like Rico, the animal has gone queer and wrong. And in those nice clean boys you liked so much in the war, there is no wild animal left in them. They're all tame dogs, even when they're brave and well-bred. They're all tame dogs, mother, with human masters. There's no mystery in them."

"What do you want, Louise? You *do* want the cave man, who'll knock you on the head with a club."

"Don't be silly, mother. That's much more your subconscious line, you admirer of Mind.—I don't consider the cave man is a real human animal at all. He's a brute, a degenerate. A pure animal man would be as lovely as a deer or a leopard, burning like a flame fed straight from underneath. And he'd be part of the unseen, like a mouse is, even. And he'd never cease to wonder, he'd breathe silence and unseen wonder, as the partridges do, running in the stubble. He'd be all the animals in turn, instead of one, fixed, automatic thing, which he is now, grinding on the nerves.—Ah no, mother, I want the wonder back again, or I shall die. I don't want to be like you, just criticizing and annihilating these dreary people, and enjoying it."

"My dear daughter, whatever else the human animal might be, he'd be a dangerous commodity."

"I wish he would, mother. I'm dying of these empty, dangerless men, who are only sentimental and spiteful."

"Nonsense, you're not dying."

"I am, mother. And I should be dead, if there weren't St. Mawr and Phoenix and Lewis in the world."

"St. Mawr and Phoenix and Lewis, I thought you said they were servants!"

"That's the worst of it. If only they were masters! If only there were some men with as much natural life as they have, and then brave quick minds that commanded instead of serving!"

"There are no such men," said Mrs Witt, with a certain grim satisfaction.

"I know it. But I'm young, and I've got to live. And the thing that is offered me as life just starves me, starves me to death, mother. What am I to do? You enjoy shattering people like Dean Vyner. But I am young, I can't live that way."

"That may be."

It had long ago struck Lou, how much more her mother realised and understood, than ever Rico did. Rico was afraid, always afraid of realising. Rico, with his good manners and his habitual kindness, and that peculiar imprisoned sneer of his.

He arrived home next morning on St. Mawr, rather flushed and gaudy, and over-kind, with an *empressé* anxiety about Lou's welfare which spoke too many volumes. Especially as he was accompanied by Flora Manby, and by Flora's sister Elsie, and Elsie's husband, Frederick Edwards. They all came on horseback.

"Such awful ages since I saw you!" said Flora to Lou. "Sorry if we burst in on you. We're only just saying *How do you do*! and going on to the inn. They've got rooms all ready for us there. We thought we'd stay just one night over here, and ride tomorrow to the Devil's Chair. Won't you come? Lots of fun! Isn't Mrs Witt at home?"

Mrs Witt was out for the moment. When she returned, she had on her curious stiff face, yet she greeted the newcomers with a certain cordiality: she felt it would be diplomatic, no doubt.

"There *are* two rooms here," she said, "and if you care to poke into them, why we shall be *delighted* to have you. But I'll show them to you first, because they are poor, inconvenient rooms, with no running water and *miles* from the baths."

Flora and Elsie declared that they were "perfectly darling sweet rooms—not overcrowded."—

"Well," said Mrs Witt. "The conveniences certainly don't fill up much space. But if you like to take them for what they are—"

"Why we feel absolutely overwhelmed, don't we Elsie!—But we've no clothes—!"

Suddenly the silence had turned into a house-party. The Manby girls appeared to lunch in fine muslin dresses, bought in Paris, fresh as daisies. Women's clothing takes up so little space, especially in summer! Fred Edwards was one of those blond Englishmen with a little brush moustache and those strong blue eyes which were always attempting the sentimental, but which Lou, in her prejudice, considered cruel: upon what grounds, she never analysed. However, he took a gallant tone with her at once, and she had to seem to simper. Rico, watching her, was so relieved when he saw the simper coming.

It had begun again, the whole clockwork of "lots of fun!"

"Isn't Fred flirting perfectly outrageously with Lady Carrington—! She looks so *sweet*!" cried Flora, over her coffee-cup. "Don't you mind, Harry!"

They called Rico "Harry"! His boy-name.

"Only a very little," said Harry, "*L'uomo è cacciatore.*"

"Oh now, what does that mean?" cried Flora, who always thrilled to Rico's bits of affectation.

"It means," said Mrs Witt, leaning forward and speaking in her most suave voice, "that man is a hunter."

Even Flora shrank under the smooth acid of the irony.

"Oh well now!" she cried. "If he is, then what is woman?"

"The hunted," said Mrs Witt, in a still smoother acid.

"At least," said Rico, "she is always *game*!"

"Ah, is she though!" came Fred's manly, well-bred tones. "I'm not so sure."

Mrs Witt looked from one man to the other, as if she were dropping them down the bottomless pit.

Lou escaped to look at St. Mawr. He was still moist where the saddle had been. And he seemed a little bit extinguished, as if virtue had gone out of him.

But when he lifted his lovely naked head, like a bunch of flames, to see who it was had entered, she saw he was still himself. Forever sensitive and alert, his head lifted like the summit of a fountain. And within him the clean bones striking to the earth, his hoofs intervening between him and the ground like lesser jewels.

He knew her and did not resent her. But he took no notice of her. He would never "respond." At first she had resented it. Now she was glad. He would never be intimate, thank heaven.

She hid herself away till teatime: but she could not hide from the sound of voices. Dinner was early, at seven. Dean Vyner came—Mrs Vyner was an invalid—and also an artist who had a studio in the village and did etchings. He was a man of about thirty-eight, and poor, just beginning to accept himself as a failure, as far as making money goes. But he worked at his etchings and studied esoteric matters like astrology and alchemy. Rico patronised him, and was a little afraid of him. Lou could not quite make him out. After knocking about Paris and London and Munich, he was trying to become staid, and to persuade himself that English village life, with squire and dean in the background, humble artist in the middle, and laborer in the common foreground, was a genuine life. His self-persuasion was only moderately successful. This was betrayed by the curious arrest in his body: he seemed to have to force himself into movement: and by the curious duplicity in his yellow-grey, twinkling eyes, that twinkled and expanded like a goat's, with mockery, irony, and frustration.

"Your face is curiously like Pan's," said Lou to him at dinner.

It was true, in a commonplace sense. He had the tilted eyebrows, the twinkling goaty look, and the pointed ears of a goat-Pan.

"People have said so," he replied. "But I'm afraid it's not the face of the Great God Pan. Isn't it rather the Great Goat Pan!"

"I say, that's good!" cried Rico. "The Great Goat Pan!"

"I have always found it difficult," said the Dean, "to see the Great God Pan in that goat-legged old father of satyrs. He may have a good deal of influence—the world will always be full of goaty old satyrs. But we find them somewhat vulgar. Even our late King Edward. The goaty old satyrs are too comprehensible to me, to be venerable, and I fail to see a Great God in the father of them all."

"Your ears should be getting red," said Lou to Cartwright.—She too had an odd squinting smile that suggested nymphs, so irresponsible and unbelieving.

"Oh no, nothing personal!" cried the Dean.

"I am not sure," said Cartwright, with a small smile. "But don't you imagine Pan once *was* a great god, before the anthropomorphic Greeks turned him into half a man?"

"Ah!—maybe. That is very possible. But—I have noticed the limitation in myself—my mind has no grasp whatsoever of Europe before the Greeks arose. Mr Wells' Outline does not help me there, either," the Dean added with a smile.

"But what was Pan before he was a man with goat legs?" asked Lou.

"Before he looked like me?" said Cartwright with a faint grin. "I should say he was the God that is hidden in everything. In those days you saw the thing, you never saw the God in it: I mean in the tree or the fountain or the animal. If you ever saw the God instead of the thing, you died. If you saw it with the naked eye, that is. But in the night you might see the God. And you knew it was there."

"The modern pantheist not only sees the God in everything, he takes photographs of it," said the Dean.

"Oh, and the divine pictures he paints!" cried Rico.

"Quite!" said Cartwright.

"But if they never *saw* the God in the thing, the old ones, how did they know he was there? How did they have any Pan at all?" said Lou.

"Pan was the hidden mystery—the hidden cause. That's how it was a great God. Pan wasn't *he* at all: not even a great God. He was Pan, All: what you see when you see in full. In the daytime you see the thing. But if your third eye is open, which sees only the things that can't be seen, you may see Pan within the thing, hidden: you may see with your third eye, which is darkness."

"Do you think I might see Pan in a horse, for example?"

"Easily. In St. Mawr!"—Cartwright gave her a knowing look.

"But," said Mrs Witt, "it would be difficult, I should say, to open the third eye and see Pan in a man."

"Probably," said Cartwright smiling. "In man he is over-visible: the old satyr: the fallen Pan."

"Exactly!" said Mrs Witt. And she fell into a muse. "The fallen

Pan!" she re-echoed. "Wouldn't a man be wonderful, in whom Pan hadn't fallen!"

Over the coffee in the grey drawing-room, she suddenly asked:

"Supposing, Mr Cartwright, one *did* open the third eye and see Pan in an actual man—I wonder what it would be like?"

She half lowered her eyelids and tilted her face in a strange way, as if she were tasting something, and not quite sure.

"I wonder!" he said, smiling his enigmatic smile. But she could see he did not understand.

"Louise!" said Mrs Witt at bedtime. "Come into my room for a moment, I want to ask you something."

"What is it, mother?"

"You, you *get* something from what Mr Cartwright said, about seeing Pan with the third eye? Seeing Pan in something?"

Mrs Witt came rather close, and tilted her face with strange insinuating question, at her daughter.

"I think I do, mother."

"In what?"—The question came as a pistol-shot.

"I think, mother," said Lou reluctantly, "in St. Mawr."

"In a horse!"—Mrs Witt contracted her eyes slightly. "Yes, I can see that. I know what you mean. It *is* in St. Mawr. It *is*! But in St. Mawr it makes me *afraid*—" she dragged out the word. Then she came a step closer. "But Louise, did you ever see it in a man?"

"What, mother?"

"Pan. Did you ever see Pan in a man, as you see Pan in St. Mawr?"

Louise hesitated.

"No mother, I don't think I did. When I look at men with my third eye, as you call it—I think I see—mostly—a sort of—pan-cake." She uttered the last word with a despairing grin, not knowing quite what to say.

"Oh Louise, isn't that it! Doesn't one always see a pancake!—Now listen, Louise. Have you ever been in love?"

"Yes, as far as I understand it."

"Listen now. Did you ever see Pan in the man you loved? Tell me if you did?"

"As I see Pan in St. Mawr?—no mother." And suddenly her lips began to tremble and the tears came to her eyes.

"Listen Louise.—I've been in love innumerable times—and *really* in love twice. Twice!—yet for fifteen years I've left off wanting to have anything to do with a man, really. For fifteen years! And why?—Do you know?—Because I couldn't see that peculiar hidden Pan in any of them. And I became that I needed to. I needed it. But it wasn't there. Not in any man. Even when I was in love with a man, it was for other things: because I *understood* him so well, or he understood me, or we had such sympathy. Never the hidden Pan.—Do you understand what I mean? Unfallen Pan!"

"More or less, mother."

"But now my third eye is coming open, I believe. I am tired of all these men like breakfast cakes, with a tea-spoonful of mind or a tea-spoonful of spirit in them, for baking powder. Isn't it extra-ordinary, that young man Cartwright talks about Pan, but he knows nothing of it all. He knows nothing of the unfallen Pan: only the fallen Pan with goat legs and a leer—and that sort of power, don't you know—"

"But what do you know of the unfallen Pan, mother?"

"Don't ask me, Louise! I feel all of a tremble, as if I was just on the verge."

She flashed a little look of incipient triumph, and said goodnight.

An excursion on horseback had been arranged for the next day, to two old groups of rocks, called the Angel's Chair and the Devil's Chair, which crowned the moor-like hills looking into Wales, ten miles away. Everybody was going—they were to start early in the morning, and Lewis would be the guide, since no-one exactly knew the way.

Lou got up soon after sunrise. There was a summer scent in the trees of early morning, and monkshood flowers stood up dark and tall, with shadows. She dressed in the green linen riding-skirt her maid had put ready for her, with a close bluish smock.

"Are you going out already, dear?" called Rico from his room.

"Just to smell the roses before we start, Rico."

He appeared in the doorway in his yellow silk pyjamas. His large blue eyes had that rolling irritable look and the slightly bloodshot whites which made her want to escape.

"Booted and spurred!—the *energy*!" he cried.

"It's a lovely day to ride," she said.

"A lovely day to do anything *except* ride!" he said. "Why spoil the day riding!"—A curious bitter-acid escaped into his tone. It was evident he hated the excursion.

"Why, we needn't go if you don't want to, Rico."

"Oh, I'm sure I shall love it, once I get started. It's all this business of *starting*, with horses and paraphernalia—"

Lou went into the yard. The horses were drinking at the trough under the pump, their colours strong and rich in the shadow of the tree.

"You're not coming with us, Phoenix?" she said.

"Lewis, he's riding my horse."

She could tell Phoenix did not like being left behind.

By half-past seven, everybody was ready. The sun was in the yard, the horses were saddled. They came swishing their tails. Lewis brought out St. Mawr from his separate box, speaking to him very quietly, in Welsh: a murmuring, soothing little speech. Lou, alert, could see that he was uneasy.

"How is St. Mawr this morning?" she asked.

"He's all right. He doesn't like so many people. He'll be all right once he's started."

The strangers were in the saddle: they moved out to the deep shade of the village road outside. Rico came to his horse, to mount. St. Mawr jumped away as if he had seen the devil.

"Steady, fool!" cried Rico.

The bay stood with his four feet spread, his neck arched, his big dark eye glancing sideways with that watchful, frightening look.

"You shouldn't be irritable with him, Rico!" said Lou. "Steady then, St. Mawr! Be steady."

But a certain anger rose also in her. The creature was so big, so brilliant, and so stupid, standing there with his hind legs spread, ready to jump aside or to rear terrifically, and his great eye glancing with a sort of suspicious frenzy. What was there to be suspicious of, after all?—Rico would do him no harm.

"No-one will harm you, St. Mawr," she reasoned, a bit exasperated.

The groom was talking quietly, murmuringly, in Welsh. Rico slowly advancing again, to put his foot in the stirrup. The stallion was watching from the corner of his eye, a strange glare of suspicious frenzy burning stupidly. Any moment, his immense physical force might be let loose in a frenzy of panic—or malice. He was really very irritating.

"Probably he doesn't like that apricot shirt," said Mrs Witt, "although it tones into him wonderfully well."

She pronounced it *ap*—ricot, and it irritated Rico terribly.

"Ought we to have *asked* him, before we put it on?" he flashed, his upper lip lifting venomously.

"I should say you should," replied Mrs Witt coolly.

88

Rico turned with a sudden rush to the horse. Back went the great animal, with a sudden splashing crash of hoofs on the cobble-stones, and Lewis hanging on like a shadow. Up went the fore-feet, showing the belly.

"The thing is accursed," said Rico, who had dropped the reins in sudden shock, and stood marooned. His rage overwhelmed him like a black flood.

"Nothing in the world is so irritating as a horse that is acting up," thought Lou.

"Say Harry!" called Flora from the road. "Come out here into the road to mount him."

Lewis looked at Rico and nodded. Then soothing the big, quivering animal, he led him springily out to the road under the trees, where the three friends were waiting. Lou and her mother got quickly into the saddle, to follow. And in another moment Rico was mounted and bouncing down the road in the wrong direction, Lewis following on the chestnut. It was some time before Rico could get St. Mawr round. Watching him from behind, those waiting could judge how the young Baronet hated it.

But at last they set off—Rico ahead, unevenly but quietly, with the two Manby girls, Lou following with the fair young man, who had been in a cavalry regiment, and who kept looking round for Mrs Witt.

"Don't look round for me," she called. "I'm riding behind, out of the dust."

Just behind Mrs Witt came Lewis. It was a whole cavalcade trotting in the morning sun past the cottages and the cottage gardens, round the field that was the recreation ground, into the deep hedges of the lane.

"Why is St. Mawr so bad at starting? Can't you get him into better shape?" she asked over her shoulder.

"Beg your pardon Mam!"

Lewis trotted a little nearer. She glanced over her shoulder at him, at his dark, unmoved face, his cool little figure.

"I think *Mam*! is so ugly. Why not leave it out!" she said. Then she repeated her question.

"St. Mawr doesn't trust anybody," Lewis replied.

"Not you?"

"Yes, he trusts me—mostly."

"Then why not other people?"

"They're different."

"All of them?"

"About all of them."

"How are they different?"

He looked at her with his remote, uncanny grey eyes.

"Different," he said, not knowing how else to put it.

They rode on slowly, up the steep rise of the wood, then down into a glade where ran a little railway built for hauling some mysterious mineral out of the hill, in war-time, and now already abandoned. Even on this countryside, the dead hand of the war lay like a corpse decomposing.

They rode up again, past the fox gloves under the trees. Ahead, the brilliant St. Mawr, and the sorrel and grey horses were swimming like butterflies through the sea of bracken, glittering from sun to shade, shade to sun. Then once more they were on a crest, and through the thinning trees could see the slopes of the moors beyond the next dip.

Soon they were in the open, rolling hills, golden in the morning and empty save for a couple of distant bilberry-pickers, whitish figures pick—pick—picking with curious, rather disgusting assiduity. The horses were on an old trail, which climbed through the pinky tips of heather and ling, across patches of green bilberry. Here and there were tufts of hare-bells blue as bubbles.

They were out, high on the hills. And there to west lay Wales, folded in crumpled folds, goldish in the morning light, with its moor-like slopes and patches of corn uncannily distinct. Between was a hollow wide valley of summer haze, showing white farms among trees, and grey slate roofs.

"Ride beside me," she said to Lewis. "Nothing makes me want to go back to America like the old look of these little villages.—You have never been to America?"

"No Mam."

"Don't you ever want to go?"

"I wouldn't mind going."

"But you're not just crazy to go?"

"No Mam."

"Quite content as you are?"

He looked at her, and his pale, remote eyes met hers.

"I don't fret myself." he replied.

"Not about anything at all—ever?"

His eyes glanced ahead, at the other riders.

"No Mam!" he replied, without looking at her.

She rode a few moments in silence.

"What is that over there?" she asked, pointing across the valley. "What is it called?"

"Yon's Montgomery."

"Montgomery! And is that *Wales*—?" she trailed the ending curiously.

"Yes Mam."

"Where you come from?"

"No Mam! I come from Merioneth."

"Not from Wales? I thought you were Welsh?"

"Yes Mam. Merioneth *is* Wales."

"And you are Welsh?"

"Yes Mam."

"I had a Welsh grandmother. But I come from Louisiana, and when I go back home, the negroes still call me Miss Rachel. *Oh, my, it's little Miss Rachel come back home! Why, ain't I mighty glad to see you—u, Miss Rachel!* That gives me such a strange feeling, you know."

The man glanced at her curiously, especially when she imitated the negroes.

"Do you feel strange when you go home?" she asked.

"I was brought up by an aunt and uncle," he said. "I never go to see them."

"And you don't have any home?"

"No Mam."

"No wife nor anything?"

"No Mam."

"But what do you do with your life?"

"I keep to myself."

"And care about nothing?"

"I mind St. Mawr."

"But you've not always had St. Mawr—and you won't always have him.—Were you in the war?"

"Yes Mam."

"At the front?"

"Yes Mam—but I was a groom."

"And you came out all right?"

"I lost my little finger from a bullet."

He held up his small, dark left hand, from which the little finger was missing.

"And did you like the war—or didn't you?"

"I didn't like it."

Again his pale grey eyes met hers, and they looked so non-human and uncommunicative, so without connection, and inaccessible, she was troubled.

"Tell me," she said. "Did you never want a wife and a home and children, like other men?"

"No Mam. I never wanted a home of my own."

"Nor a wife of your own?"

"No Mam."

"Nor children of your own?"

"No Mam."

She reined in her horse.

"Now wait a minute," she said. "Now tell me why."

His horse came to standstill, and the two riders faced one another.

"Tell me why—I must know why you never wanted a wife and children and a home. I must know why you're not like other men."

"I never felt like it," he said. "I made my life with horses."

"Did you hate people very much? Did you have a very unhappy time as a child?"

"My aunt and uncle didn't like me, and I didn't like them."

"So you've never liked anybody?"

"Maybe not," he said. "Not to get as far as marrying them."

She touched her horse and moved on.

"Isn't that curious!" she said. "I've loved people, at various times. But I don't believe *I've* ever liked anybody, except a few of our negroes. I don't like Louise, though she's my daughter and I love her. But I don't really *like* her.—I think you're the first person I've ever liked since I was on our plantation, and we had some *very fine* negroes.—And I think that's very curious.—Now I want to know if you like *me*."

She looked at him searchingly, but he did not answer.

"Tell me," she said. "I don't mind if you say no. But tell me if you like me. I feel I must know."

The flicker of a smile went over his face—a very rare thing with him.

"Maybe I do," he said. He was thinking that she put him on a level with a negro slave on a plantation: in his idea, negroes were still slaves. But he did not care where she put him.

"Well, I'm glad—I'm glad if you like me. Because you *don't* like most people, I know that."

They had passed the hollow where the old Aldecar Chapel hid in damp isolation, beside the ruined mill, over the stream that came down from the moors. Climbing the sharp slope, they saw the folded hills like great shut fingers, with steep, deep clefts between. On the near sky-line was a bunch of rocks: and away to the right, another bunch.

"Yon's the Angel's Chair," said Lewis, pointing to the nearer rocks. "And yon's the Devil's Chair, where we're going."

"Oh!" said Mrs Witt. "And aren't we going to the Angel's Chair?"

"No Mam!"

"Why not?"

"There's nothing to see there. The other's higher, and bigger, and that's where folks mostly go."

"Is that so!—They give the Devil the higher seat in this country, do they? I think they're right.—" And as she got no answer, she added: "You believe in the Devil, don't you?"

"I never met him," he answered, evasively.

Ahead, they could see the other horses twinkling in a cavalcade up the slope, the black, the bay, the two greys and the sorrel, sometimes bunching, sometimes straggling. At a gate all waited for Mrs Witt. The fair young man fell in beside her, and talked hunting at her. He had hunted the fox over these hills, and was vigorously excited locating the spot where the hounds first gave cry, etc.

"Really!" said Mrs Witt, "*Really*! Is that so!"

If irony could have been condensed to prussic acid, the fair young man would have ended his life's history with his reminiscences.

They came at last, trotting in file along a narrow track between heather, along the saddle of a hill, to where the knot of pale granite suddenly cropped out. It was one of those places where the spirit of aboriginal England still lingers, the old savage England, whose last blood flows still in a few Englishmen, Welshmen, Cornishmen. The rocks, whitish with weather of all the ages, jutted against the blue August sky, heavy with age-moulded roundnesses.

Lewis stayed below with the horses, the party scrambled rather awkwardly, in their riding-boots, up the foot-worn boulders. At length they stood in the place called the Chair, looking west, west towards Wales, that rolled in golden folds upwards. It was neither impressive nor a very picturesque landscape: the hollow valley with farms, and then the rather bare upheaval of hills, slopes with corn and moor and pasture, rising like a barricade, seemingly high, slantingly. Yet it had a strange effect on the imagination.

"Oh mother," said Lou, "doesn't it make you feel old, old, older than anything ever was?"

"It certainly does seem aged," said Mrs Witt.

"It makes me want to die," said Lou. "I feel we've lasted almost too long."

"Don't say that, Lady Carrington. Why you're a spring chicken yet: or shall I say an unopened rosebud," remarked the fair young man.

"No," said Lou. "All these millions of ancestors have used all the life up. We're not really alive, in the sense that they were alive."

"But who?" said Rico. "Who are *they*?"

"The people who lived on these hills, in the days gone by."

"But the same people still live on the hills, darling. It's just the same stock."

"No Rico. That old fighting stock that worshipped devils among these stones—I'm sure they did—"

"But look here, do you mean they were any better than we are?" asked the fair young man.

Lou looked at him quizzically.

"We don't exist," she said, squinting at him oddly.

"I jolly well know *I* do," said the fair young man.

"I consider these days are the best ever, especially for girls," said Flora Manby. "And anyhow they're our own days, so I don't jolly well see the use of crying them down."

They were all silent, with the last echoes of emphatic *joie de vivre* trumpeting on the air, across the hills of Wales.

"Spoken like a brick, Flora," said Rico. "Say it again, we may not have the Devil's Chair for a pulpit next time."

"I do," reiterated Flora. "I think this is the best age there ever was, for a girl to have a good time in. I read all through H. G. Wells' history, and I shut it up and thanked my stars I live in nineteen-twenty odd, not in some other beastly date when a woman had to cringe before mouldy domineering men."

After this, they turned to scramble to another part of the rocks, to the famous Needle's Eye.

"Thank you so much, I am really better without help," said Mrs Witt to the fair young man, as she slid downwards till a piece of grey silk stocking showed above her tall boot. But she got her toe in a safe place, and in a moment stood beside him, while he caught her arm protectingly. He might as well have caught the paw of a mountain lion protectingly.

"I should like *so* much to know," she said suavely, looking into his eyes with a demonish straight look, "what makes you so certain that you exist?"

He looked back at her, and his jaunty blue eyes went baffled. Then a slow, hot, salmon-coloured flush stole over his face, and he turned abruptly round.

The Needle's Eye was a hole in the ancient grey rock, like a window, looking to England; England at the moment in shadow. A stream wound and glinted in the flat shadow, and beyond that, the flat, insignificant hills heaped in mounds of shade. Cloud was coming—the English side was in shadow. Wales was still in the sun, but the shadow was spreading. The day was going to disappoint them. Lou was a tiny bit chilled, already.

Luncheon was still several miles away. The party hastened down to the horses. Lou picked a few sprigs of ling, and some hare-bells, and some straggling yellow flowers: not because she wanted them, but to distract herself. The atmosphere of "enjoying ourselves" was becoming cruel to her: it sapped all the life out of her. "Oh, if only I needn't enjoy myself," she moaned inwardly. But the Manby girls were enjoying themselves so much. "I think it's frantically lovely up here," said the other one—not Flora—Elsie.

"It *is* beautiful, isn't it! I'm *so* glad you like it," replied Rico. And he was really relieved and gratified, because the other one said she was enjoying it so frightfully. He dared not say to Lou, as he wanted to: "I'm afraid, Lou darling, you don't love it as much as we do."—He was afraid of her answer: "No dear, I don't love it at all! I want to be away from these people."

Slightly piqued, he rode on with the Manby group, and Lou came behind with her mother. Cloud was covering the sky with grey. There was a cold wind. Everybody was anxious to get to the farm for luncheon, and be safely home before rain came.

They were riding along one of the narrow little foot-tracks, mere grooves of grass between heather and bright green bilberry. The blond young man was ahead, then his wife, then Flora, then Rico. Lou, from a little distance, watched the glossy, powerful haunches of St. Mawr swaying with life, always too much life, like a menace. The fair young man was whistling a new dance tune.

"That's an awfully attractive tune," Rico called. "Do whistle it again, Fred, I should like to memorise it."

Fred began to whistle it again.

At that moment St. Mawr exploded again, shied sideways as if a bomb had gone off, and kept backing through the heather.

"Fool!" cried Rico, thoroughly unnerved: he had been terribly sideways in the saddle, Lou had feared he was going to fall. But he got his seat, and pulled the reins viciously, to bring the horse to order, and put him on the track again. St. Mawr began to rear: his favourite trick. Rico got him forward a few yards, when up he went again.

"Fool!" yelled Rico, hanging in the air.

He pulled the horse over backwards, on top of him.

Lou gave a loud, unnatural, horrible scream: she heard it herself, at the same time as she heard the crash of the falling horse. Then she saw a pale gold belly, and hoofs that worked and flashed in the air, and St. Mawr writhing, straining his head terrifically upwards, his great eyes starting from the naked lines of his nose. With a great neck arching cruelly from the ground, he was pulling frantically at the reins, which Rico still held tight.—Yes, Rico, lying strangely sideways, his eyes also starting from his yellow-white face, among the heather, still clutched the reins.

Young Edwards was rushing forward, and circling round the writhing, immense horse, whose pale-gold inverted bulk seemed to fill the universe.

"Let him get up, Carrington! Let him get up!" he was yelling, darting warily near, to get the reins.—Another spasmodic convulsion of the horse.

Horror! The young man reeled backwards with his face in his hands. He had got a kick in the face. Red blood running down his chin!

Lewis was there, on the ground, getting the reins out of Rico's hands. St. Mawr gave a great curve like a fish, spread his fore-feet on the earth and reared his head, looking round in a ghastly fashion. His eyes were arched, his nostrils wide, his face ghastly in a sort of panic. He rested thus, seated with his fore-feet planted and his face in panic, almost like some terrible lizard, for several moments. Then he heaved sickeningly to his feet, and stood convulsed, trembling.

There lay Rico, crumpled and rather sideways, staring at the heavens from a yellow, dead-looking face. Lewis, glancing round in a sort of horror, looked in dread at St. Mawr again. Flora had been hovering.— She now rushed screeching to the prostrate Rico:

"Harry! Harry! you're not dead! Oh Harry! Harry! Harry!"

Lou had dismounted—She didn't know when. She stood a little way off, as if spell-bound, while Flora cried *Harry! Harry! Harry!*

Suddenly Rico sat up.

"Where is the horse?" he said.

At the same time an added whiteness came on his face, and he bit his lip with pain, and he fell prostrate again in a faint. Flora rushed to put her arm round him.

Where was the horse? He had backed slowly away, in an agony of suspicion, while Lewis murmured to him in vain. His head was raised again, the eyes still starting from their sockets, and a terrible guilty, ghost-like look on his face. When Lewis drew a little nearer he twitched and shrank like a shaken steel spring, away—not to be touched. He seemed to be seeing legions of ghosts, down the dark avenues of all the centuries that have lapsed since the horse became subject to man.

And the other young man? He was still standing, at a little distance, with his face in his hands, motionless, the blood falling on his white shirt, and his wife at his side, pleading distracted.

Mrs Witt too was there, as if cast in steel, watching. She made no sound and did not move, only, from a fixed, impassive face, watched each thing.

"Do tell me what you think is the matter?" Lou pleaded, distracted, to Flora, who was supporting Rico and weeping torrents of unknown tears.

Then Mrs Witt came forward and began in a very practical manner to unclose the shirt-neck and feel the young man's heart. Rico opened his eyes again, said "*Really!*" and closed his eyes once more.

"It's fainting!" said Mrs Witt. "We have no brandy."

Lou, too weary to be able to feel anything, said:

"I'll go and get some."

She went to her alarmed horse, who stood among the others with her head down, in suspense. Almost unconsciously Lou mounted, set her face ahead, and was riding away.

Then Poppy shied too, with a sudden start, and Lou pulled up. "Why?" she said to her horse. "Why did you do that?"

She looked round, and saw in the heather a glimpse of yellow and black.

"A snake!" she said wonderingly.

And she looked closer.

It was a dead adder that had been drinking at a reedy pool in a little depression just off the road, and had been killed with stones. There it lay, also crumpled, its head crushed, its gold-and-yellow back still glittering dully, and a bit of pale-blue belly showing, killed that morning!

Lou rode on, her face set towards the farm. An unspeakable weariness had overcome her. She could not even suffer. Weariness of spirit left her in a sort of apathy.

And she had a vision, a vision of evil. Or not strictly a vision. She became aware of evil, evil, evil, rolling in great waves over the earth. Always she had thought there was no such thing—only a mere negation of good. Now, like an ocean to whose surface she had risen, she saw the dark-grey waves of evil rearing in a great tide.

And it had swept mankind away without mankind's knowing. It had caught up the nations as the rising ocean might lift the fishes, and was sweeping them on in a great tide of evil. They did not know. The people did not know. They did not even wish it. They wanted to be good and to have everything joyful and enjoyable. Everything joyful and enjoyable: for everybody. This was what they wanted, if you asked them.

But at the same time, they had fallen under the spell of evil. It was a soft, subtle thing, soft as water, and its motion was soft and imperceptible, as the running of a tide is invisible to one who is out on the ocean. And they were all out on the ocean, being borne along in the current of the mysterious evil, creatures of the evil principle, as fishes are creatures of the sea.

There was no relief. The whole world was enveloped in one great flood. All the nations, the white, the brown, the black, the yellow, all were immersed in the strange tide of evil that was subtly, irresistibly rising. No-one, perhaps, deliberately wished it. Nearly every individual wanted peace and a good time all round: everybody to have a good time.

But some strange thing had happened, and the vast, mysterious force of positive evil was let loose. She felt that from the core of Asia the evil welled up, as from some strange pole, and slowly was drowning earth.

It was something horrifying, something you could not escape from. It had come to her as in a vision, when she saw the pale gold belly of the stallion upturned, the hoofs working wildly, the wicked curved hams of the horse, and then the evil straining of that arched, fish-like neck, with the dilated eyes of the head. Thrown backwards, and working its hoofs in the air. Reversed, and purely evil.

She saw the same in people. They were thrown backwards, and

writhing with evil. And the rider, crushed, was still reining them down.

What did it mean? Evil, evil, and a rapid return to the sordid chaos. Which was wrong, the horse or the rider? Or both?

She thought with horror of St. Mawr, and of the look on his face. But she thought with horror, a colder horror, of Rico's face as he snarled *Fool*! His fear, his impotence as a master, as a rider, his presumption. And she thought with horror of those other people, so glib, so glibly evil.

What did they want to do, those Manby girls? Undermine, undermine, undermine. They wanted to undermine Rico, just as that fair young man would have liked to undermine her. Believe in nothing, care about nothing: but keep the surface easy, and have a good time. *Let us undermine one another. There is nothing to believe in, so let us undermine everything. But look out! No scenes, no spoiling the game. Stick to the rules of the game. Be sporting, and don't do anything that would make a commotion. Keep the game going smooth and jolly, and bear your bit like a sport. Never, by any chance, injure your fellow man openly. But always injure him secretly. Make a fool of him, and undermine his nature. Break him up by undermining him, if you can. It's good sport.*

The evil! The mysterious potency of evil. She could see it all the time, in individuals, in society, in the press. There it was in socialism and bolshevism: the same evil. But bolshevism made a mess of the outside of life, so turn it down. Try fascism. Fascism would keep the surface of life intact, and carry on the undermining business all the better. All the better sport. Never draw blood. Keep the hemorrhage internal, invisible.

And as soon as fascism makes a break—which it is bound to, because all evil works up to a break—then turn it down. With gusto, turn it down.

Mankind, like a horse, ridden by a stranger, smooth-faced, evil rider. Evil himself, smooth-faced and pseudo-handsome, riding mankind past the dead snake, to the last break.

Mankind no longer its own master. Ridden by this pseudo-handsome ghoul of outward loyalty, inward treachery, in a game of betrayal, betrayal, betrayal. The last of the gods of our era, Judas supreme!

People performing outward acts of loyalty, piety, self-sacrifice. But inwardly bent on undermining, betraying. Directing all their subtle evil will against any positive living thing. Masquerading as the ideal, in order to poison the real.

Creation destroys as it goes, throws down one tree for the rise of another. But ideal mankind would abolish death, multiply itself million upon million, rear up city upon city, save every parasite alive, until the accumulation of mere existence is swollen to a horror. But go on saving life, the ghastly salvation army of ideal mankind. At the same time secretly, viciously, potently undermine the natural creation, betray it with kiss after kiss, destroy it from the inside, till you have the swollen rottenness of our teeming existences.—But keep the game going. Nobody's going to make another bad break, such as Germany and Russia made.

Two bad breaks the secret evil has made: in Germany and in Russia. Watch it! Let evil keep a policeman's eye on evil! The surface of life must remain unruptured. Production must be heaped upon production. And the natural creation must be betrayed by many more kisses, yet. Judas is the last God, and by heaven, the most potent.

But even Judas made a break: hanged himself, and his bowels gushed out. Not long after his triumph.

Man must destroy as he goes, as trees fall for trees to rise. The accumulation of life and things means rottenness. Life must destroy life, in the unfolding of creation. We save up life at the expense of the unfolding, till all is full of rottenness. Then at last, we make a break.

What's to be done? Generally speaking, nothing. The dead will have to bury their dead, while the earth stinks of corpses. The individual can but depart from the mass, and try to cleanse himself. Try to hold fast to the living thing, which destroys as it goes, but remains sweet. And in his soul fight, fight, fight to preserve that which is life in him from the ghastly kisses and poison-bites of the myriad evil ones. Retreat to the desert, and fight. But in his soul adhere to that which is life itself, creatively destroying as it goes: destroying the stiff old thing to let the new bud come through. The one passionate principle of creative being, which recognises the natural good, and has a sword for the swarms of evil. Fights, fights, fights to protect itself. But with itself, is strong and at peace.

Lou came to the farm, and got brandy, and asked the men to come out to carry in the injured.

It turned out that the kick in the face had knocked a couple of young Edwards' teeth out, and would disfigure him a little.

"To go through the war, and then get this!" he mumbled, with a vindictive glance at St. Mawr.

And it turned out that Rico had two broken ribs and a crushed ankle. Poor Rico, he would limp for life.

"I want St. Mawr *shot*!" was almost his first word, when he was in bed at the farm and Lou was sitting beside him.

"What good would that do, dear?" she said.

"The brute is evil. I want him *shot*!"

Rico could make the last word sound like the spitting of a bullet.

"Do you want to shoot him yourself?"

"No. But I want to have him shot. I shall never be easy till I know he has a bullet through him. He's got a wicked character. I don't feel you are safe, with him down there. I shall get one of the Manbys' game-keepers to shoot him. You might tell Flora—or I'll tell her myself, when she comes."

"Don't talk about it now, dear. You've got a temperature."

Was it true, St. Mawr was evil? She would never forget him writhing and lunging on the ground, nor his awful face when he reared up. But then that noble look of his: surely he was not mean? Whereas all evil had an inner meanness, mean! Was he mean! Was he meanly treacherous? Did he know he could kill, and meanly wait his opportunity?

She was afraid. And if this were true, then he *should* be shot. Perhaps he ought to be shot.

This thought haunted her. Was there something mean and treacherous in St. Mawr's spirit, the vulgar evil? If so, then have him shot. At moments, an anger would rise in her, as she thought of his frenzied rearing, and his mad, hideous writhing on the ground, and in the heat of her anger she would want to hurry down to her mother's house, and have the creature shot at once. It would be a satisfaction, and a vindication of human rights. Because after all, Rico was so considerate of the brutal horse. But not a spark of consideration did the stallion have for Rico. No, it was the slavish malevolence of a domesticated creature that kept cropping up in St. Mawr. The slave, taking his slavish vengeance, then dropping back into subservience.

All the slaves of this world, accumulating their preparations for slavish vengeance, and then, when they have taken it, ready to drop back into servility. Freedom! Most slaves can't be freed, no matter how you let them loose. Like domestic animals, they are, in the long run, more afraid of freedom than of masters: and freed by some generous master, they will at last crawl back to some mean boss, who will have no scruples about kicking them. Because, for them, far better kicks and servility than the hard, lonely responsibility of real freedom.

The wild animal is at every moment intensely self-disciplined, poised in the tension of self-defence, self-preservation, and self-assertion. The moments of relaxation are rare and most carefully chosen. Even sleep is watchful, guarded, unrelaxing, the wild courage pitched one degree higher than the wild fear. Courage, the wild thing's courage to maintain itself alone and living in the midst of a diverse universe.

Did St. Mawr have this courage?

And did Rico?

Ah Rico! He was one of mankind's myriad conspirators, who conspire to live in absolute physical safety, whilst willing the minor disintegration of all positive living.

But St. Mawr? Was it the natural wild thing in him which caused these disasters? Or was it the slave, asserting himself for vengeance?

If the latter, let him be shot. It would be a great satisfaction to see him dead.

But if the former—

When she could leave Rico with the nurse, she motored down to her mother for a couple of days. Rico lay in bed at the farm.

Everything seemed curiously changed. There was a new silence about the place, a new coolness. Summer had passed with several thunderstorms, and the blue, cool touch of autumn was about the house. Dahlias and perennial yellow sunflowers were out, the yellow of ending summer, the red coals of early autumn. First mauve tips of michaelmas daisies were showing. Something suddenly carried her away to the great bare spaces of Texas, the blue sky, the flat, burnt earth, the miles of sunflowers. Another sky, another silence, towards the setting sun.

And suddenly, she craved again for the more absolute silence of America. English stillness was so soft, like an inaudible murmur of voices, of presences. But the silence in the empty spaces of America was still unutterable, almost cruel.

St. Mawr was in a small field by himself: she could not bear that he should be always in stable. Slowly she went through the gate towards him. And he stood there looking at her, the bright bay creature.

She could tell he was feeling somewhat subdued, after his late escapade. He was aware of the general human condemnation: the human damning. But something obstinate and uncanny in him made him not relent.

"Hello! St. Mawr!" she said, as she drew near, and he stood watching her, his ears pricked, his big eyes glancing sideways at her.

But he moved away when she wanted to touch him.

"Don't trouble," she said, "I don't want to catch you or do anything to you."

He stood still, listening to the sound of her voice, and giving quick, small glances at her. His underlip trembled. But he did not blink. His eyes remained wide and unrelenting. There was a curious malicious obstinacy in him which roused her anger.

"I don't want to touch you," she said. "I only want to look at you, and even you can't prevent that."

She stood gazing hard at him, wanting to know, to settle the question of his meanness or his spirit. A thing with a brave spirit is not mean.

He was uneasy, as she watched him. He pretended to hear something, the mares two fields away, and he lifted his head and neighed. She knew the powerful, splendid sound so well: like bells made of living membrane. And he looked so noble again, with his head tilted up, listening, and his male eyes looking proudly over the distance, eagerly.

But it was all a bluff.

He knew, and became silent again. And as he stood there a few yards away from her, his head lifted and wary, his body full of power and tension, his face slightly averted from her, she felt a great animal sadness come from him. A strange animal atmosphere of sadness, that was vague and disseminated through the air, and made her feel as though she breathed grief. She breathed it into her breast, as if it were a great sigh down the ages, that passed into her breast. And she felt a great woe: the woe of human unworthiness. The race of men judged in the consciousness of the animals they have subdued, and there found unworthy, ignoble.

Ignoble men, unworthy of the animals they have subjugated, bred the woe in the spirit of their creatures. St. Mawr, that bright horse, one of the kings of creation in the order below man, it had been a fulfilment for him to serve the brave, reckless, perhaps cruel men of the past, who had a flickering, rising flame of nobility in them. To serve that flame of mysterious further nobility. Nothing matters, but that strange flame, of inborn nobility that obliges men to be brave, and onward plunging. And the horse will bear him on.

But now where is the flame of dangerous, forward-pressing nobility in men? Dead, dead, guttering out in a stink of self-sacrifice whose feeble light is a light of exhaustion and *laisser-faire*.

And the horse, is he to go on carrying man forward into this?—this gutter?

No! Man wisely invents motor-cars and other machines, automobile and locomotive. The horse is superannuated, for man.

But alas, man is even more superannuated, for the horse.

Dimly in a woman's muse, Lou realised this, as she breathed the horse's sadness, his accumulated vague woe from the generations of latter-day ignobility. And a grief and a sympathy flooded her, for the horse. She realised now how his sadness recoiled into these frenzies of obstinacy and malevolence. Underneath it all was grief, an unconscious, vague, pervading animal grief, which perhaps only Lewis understood, because he felt the same. The grief of the generous creature which sees all ends turning to the morass of ignoble living.

She did not want to say any more to the horse: she did not want to look at him any more. The grief flooded her soul, that made her want to be alone. She knew now what it all amounted to. She knew that the horse, born to serve nobly, had waited in vain for some one noble to serve. His spirit knew that nobility had gone out of men. And this left him high and dry, in a sort of despair.

As she walked away from him, towards the gate, slowly he began to walk after her.

Phoenix came striding through the gate towards her.

"You not afraid of that horse?" he asked sardonically, in his quiet, subtle voice.

"Not at the present moment," she replied, even more quietly, looking direct at him. She was not in any mood to be jeered at.

And instantly the sardonic grimace left his face, followed by the sudden blankness, and the look of race-misery in the keen eyes.

"Do you want me to be afraid?" she said, continuing to the gate.

"No, I don't want it," he replied, dejected.

"Are you afraid of him yourself?" she said, glancing round. St. Mawr had stopped, seeing Phoenix, and had turned away again.

"I'm not afraid of no horses," said Phoenix.

Lou went on quietly. At the gate, she asked him:

"Don't you like St. Mawr, Phoenix?"

"I like him. He's a very good horse."

"Even after what he's done to Sir Henry?"

"That don't make no difference to him being a good horse."

"But suppose he'd done it to you?"

"I don't care. I say it my own fault."

"Don't you think he is wicked?"

"I don't think so. He don't kick anybody. He don't bite anybody. He don't pitch, he don't buck, he don't do nothing."

"He rears," said Lou.

"Well, what is rearing!" said the man, with a slow, contemptuous smile.

"A good deal, when a horse falls back on you."

"That horse don't want to fall back on you, if you don't make him. If you know how to ride him.—That horse want his own way sometime. If you don't let him, you got to fight him. Then look out!"

"Look out he doesn't kill you, you mean!"

"Look out you don't let him," said Phoenix, with his slow, grim, sardonic smile.

Lou watched the smooth, golden face with its thin line of moustache and its sad eyes with the glint in them. Cruel—there was something cruel in him, right down in the abyss of him. But at the same time, there was an aloneness, and a grim little satisfaction in a fight, and the peculiar courage of an inherited despair. People who inherit despair may at last turn it into greater heroism. It was almost so with Phoenix. Three-quarters of his blood was probably Indian and the remaining quarter, that came through the Mexican father, had the Spanish-American despair to add to the Indian. It was almost complete enough to leave him free to be heroic.

"What are we going to do with him, though?" she asked.

"Why don't you and Mrs Witt go back to America—you never been west. You go west."

"Where, to California?"

"No. To Arizona or New Mexico or Colorado or Wyoming, anywhere. Not to California."

Phoenix looked at her keenly, and she saw the desire dark in him. He wanted to go back. But he was afraid to go back alone, empty-handed, as it were. He had suffered too much, and in that country his sufferings would overcome him, unless he had some other background. He had been too much in contact with the white world, and his own world was too dejected, in a sense, too hopeless for his own hopelessness. He needed an alien contact to give him relief.

But he wanted to go back. His necessity to go back was becoming too strong for him.

"What is it like in Arizona?" she asked. "Isn't it all pale-coloured sand and alkali, and a few cactuses, and terribly hot and deathly?"

"No!" he cried. "I don't take you there. I take you to the mountains,—Trees—" he lifted up his hand and looked at the sky—"big trees—Pine! *Pino-real* and *pinavete*, smell good. And then you come down, *piñón*, not very tall, and *cedro*, cedar, smell good in the fire. And then you see the desert, away below, go miles and miles, and where the canyon go, the crack where it look red! I know, I been there, working a cattle ranch."

He looked at her with a haunted glow in his dark eyes. The poor fellow was suffering from nostalgia. And as he glowed at her in that queer mystical way, she too seemed to see that country, with its dark, heavy mountains holding in their lap the great stretches of pale, creased, silent desert that still is virgin of idea, its word unspoken.

Phoenix was watching her closely and subtly. He wanted something of her. He wanted it intensely, heavily, and he watched her as if he could force her to give it him. He wanted her to take him back to America, because, rudderless, he was afraid to go back alone. He wanted her to take him back: avidly he wanted it. She was to be the means to his end.

Why shouldn't he go back by himself? Why should he crave for her to go too? Why should he want her there?

There was no answer, except that he did.

"Why, Phoenix," she said. "I might possibly go back to America. But you know, Sir Henry would never go there. He doesn't like America, though he's never been. But I'm sure he'd never go there to live."

"Let him stay here," said Phoenix abruptly, the sardonic look on his face as he watched her face. "You come, and let him stay here."

"Ah, that's a whole story!" she said, and moved away.

As she went, he looked after her, standing silent and arrested and watching as an Indian watches.—It was not love. Personal love counts so little when the greater griefs, the greater hopes, the great despairs and the great resolutions come upon us.

She found Mrs Witt rather more silent, more firmly closed within herself, than usual. Her mouth was shut tight, her brows were arched rather more imperiously than ever, she was revolving some inward problem about which Lou was far too wise to enquire.

In the afternoon Dean Vyner and Mrs Vyner came to call on Lady Carrington.

"What bad luck this is, Lady Carrington!" said the Dean. "Knocks Scotland on the head for you this year, I'm afraid. How did you leave your husband?"

"He seems to be doing as well as he could do!" said Lou.

"But how *very* unfortunate!" murmured the invalid Mrs Vyner. "Such a handsome young man, in the bloom of youth! Does he suffer much pain?"

"Chiefly his foot," said Lou.

"Oh, I *do* so hope they'll be able to restore the ankle. Oh how dreadful, to be lamed at his age!"

"The doctor doesn't know. There *may* be a limp," said Lou.

"That horse has certainly left his mark on two good-looking young fellows," said the Dean. "If you don't mind my saying so, Lady Carrington, I think he's a bad egg."

"Who, St. Mawr?" said Lou, in her American sing-song.

"Yes, Lady Carrington," murmured Mrs Vyner, in her invalid's low tone. "Don't you think he ought to be put away? He seems to me the incarnation of cruelty. His neigh! It goes through me like knives. Cruel! Cruel! Oh, I think he should be put away."

"How put away?" murmured Lou, taking on an invalid's low tone herself.

"Shot, I suppose," said the Dean.

"It is quite painless. He'll know nothing," murmured Mrs Vyner hastily. "And think of the harm he has done already! Horrible! Horrible!" she shuddered. "Poor Sir Henry lame for life, and Eddy Edwards disfigured. Besides all that has gone before. Ah no, such a creature ought not to live!"

"To live, and have a groom to look after him and feed him," said the Dean. "It's a bit thick, while he's smashing up the very people that give him bread—or oats, since he's a horse.—But I suppose you'll be wanting to get rid of him?"

"Rico does," murmured Lou.

"Very naturally. So should I. A vicious horse is worse than a vicious man—except that you are free to put him six feet underground, and end his vice finally, by your own act."

"Do you think St. Mawr is vicious?" said Lou.

"Well, of course—if we're driven to definitions—! I *know* he's dangerous."

"And do you think we ought to shoot everything that is dangerous?" asked Lou, her colour rising.

"But Lady Carrington, have you consulted your husband? Surely his wish should be law, in a matter of this sort! And on such an occasion! For *you*, who are a woman, it is enough that the horse is cruel, cruel, evil! I felt it long before anything happened. That evil male cruelty! Ah!" and she clasped her hands convulsively.

"I suppose," said Lou slowly, "that St. Mawr is really Rico's horse: I gave him to him, I suppose. But I don't believe I could let him shoot him, for all that."

"Ah Lady Carrington," said the Dean breezily. "You can shift the responsibility. The horse is a public menace, put it at that. We can get an order to have him done away with, at the public expense. And among ourselves we can find some suitable compensation for you, as a mark of sympathy. Which, believe me, is very sincere! One hates to have to destroy a fine looking animal. But I would sacrifice a dozen rather than have our Rico limping."

"Yes indeed!" murmured Mrs Vyner.

"Will you excuse me one moment, while I see about tea," said Lou, rising and leaving the room. Her colour was high, and there was a glint in her eye. These people almost roused her to hatred. Oh, these awful, house-bred, house-inbred human-beings, how repulsive they were!

She hurried to her mother's dressing room. Mrs Witt was very carefully putting a touch of red on her lips.

"Mother, they want to shoot St. Mawr," she said.

"I know," said Mrs Witt, as calmly as if Lou had said tea was ready.

"Well—" stammered Lou, rather put out. "Don't you think it cheek?"

"It depends, I suppose, on the point of view," said Mrs Witt dispassionately, looking closely at her lips. "I don't think the English climate agrees with me. I need something to stand up against, no matter whether it's great heat or great cold. This climate, like the food and the people, is most always lukewarm or tepid, one or the other. And the tepid and the lukewarm are not really my line." She spoke with a slow drawl.

"But they're in the drawing-room, mother, trying to force me to have St. Mawr killed."

"What about tea?" said Mrs Witt.

"I don't care," said Lou.

Mrs Witt worked the bell-handle.

"I suppose, Louise," she said, in her most beaming eighteenth-century manner, "that these are your guests, so you will preside over the ceremony of pouring out."

"No mother, you do it. I can't smile today."

"I can," said Mrs Witt.

And she bowed her head slowly, with a faint, ceremoniously-effusive smile, as if handing a cup of tea.

Lou's face flickered to a smile.

"Then you pour out for them. You can stand them better than I can."

"Yes," said Mrs Witt. "I saw Mrs Vyner's hat coming across the churchyard. It looks so like a crumpled cup and saucer, that I have been saying to myself ever since: *Dear Mrs Vyner, can't I fill your cup!*—and then pouring tea into that hat. And I hear the Dean responding: *My head is covered with cream, my cup runneth over*—That is the way they make *me* feel."

They marched downstairs, and Mrs Witt poured tea with that devastating correctness which made Mrs Vyner, who was utterly impervious to sarcasm, pronounce her "indecipherably vulgar."

But the Dean was the old bull-dog, and he had set his teeth in a subject.

"I was talking to Lady Carrington about that stallion, Mrs Witt."

"Did you say stallion?" asked Mrs Witt, with perfect neutrality.

"Why, yes, I presume that's what he is."

"I presume so," said Mrs Witt colourlessly.

"I'm afraid Lady Carrington is a little sensitive on the wrong score," said the Dean.

"I beg your pardon," said Mrs Witt, leaning forward in her most colourless polite manner. "You mean the stallion's score?"

"Yes," said the Dean testily. "The horse St. Mawr."

"The stallion St. Mawr," echoed Mrs Witt, with utmost mild vagueness. She completely ignored Mrs Vyner, who felt plunged like a specimen into methylated spirit. There was a moment's full stop.

"Yes?" said Mrs Witt naively.

"You agree that we can't have any more of these accidents to your young men?" said the Dean rather hastily.

"I certainly do!" Mrs Witt spoke very slowly, and the Dean's lady began to look up. She might find a loop-hole through which to wriggle into the contest. "You know, Dean, that my son-in-law calls me, for preference, *belle mère*! It sounds so awfully English when he says it,

I always see myself as an old grey mare with a bell round her neck, leading a bunch of horses." She smiled a prim little smile, *very* conversationally. "Well!" and she pulled herself up from the aside. "Now as the bell-mare of the bunch of horses, I shall see to it that my son-in-law doesn't go too near that stallion again. That stallion won't stand mischief."

She spoke so earnestly, that the Dean looked at her with round wide eyes, completely taken aback.

"We all know, Mrs Witt, that the author of the mischief is St. Mawr himself." he said, in a loud tone.

"Really! you think *that*?" Her voice went up in American surprise. "Why how *strange*—!" and she lingered over the last word.

"Strange, eh?—After what's just happened?" said the Dean, with a deadly little smile.

"Why yes! Most strange! I saw with my own eyes my son-in-law pull that stallion over backwards, and hold him down with the reins as tight as he could hold them; pull St. Mawr's head backwards on to the ground, till the groom had to crawl up and force the reins out of my son-in-law's hands. Don't you think that was mischievous on Sir Henry's part?"

The Dean was growing purple. He made an apoplectic movement with his hand. Mrs Vyner was turned to a seated pillar of salt, strangely dressed up.

"Mrs Witt, you are playing on words."

"No Dean Vyner, I am not. My son-in-law pulled that horse over backwards and pinned him down with the reins."

"I am sorry for the horse." said the Dean, with heavy sarcasm.

"I am *very*," said Mrs Witt, "sorry for that stallion: *very*!"

Here Mrs Vyner rose as if a chair-spring had suddenly propelled her to her feet. She was streaky pink in the face.

"Mrs Witt," she panted, "you misdirect your sympathies. That poor young man—in the beauty of youth—"

"Isn't he *beautiful*—" murmured Mrs Witt, extravagantly in sympathy. "He's my daughter's husband!" And she looked at the petrified Lou.

"Certainly!" panted the Dean's wife. "And you can defend that—that—"

"That stallion," said Mrs Witt. "But you see, Mrs Vyner," she added, leaning forward female and confidential, "if the old grey mare doesn't defend the stallion, who will? All the blooming young ladies will defend my beautiful son-in-law. You feel so *warmly* for him yourself! I'm an American woman, and I always have to stand up for the accused. And I stand up for that stallion. I say it is not right. He was pulled over backwards and then pinned down by my son-in-law—who may have meant to do it, or may not. And now people abuse him.—Just tell everybody, Mrs Vyner and Dean Vyner—" She looked round at the Dean—"that the belle-mère's sympathies are with the stallion."

She looked from one to the other with a faint and gracious little bow, her black eyebrows arching in her eighteenth-century face like black rainbows, and her full, bold grey eyes absolutely incomprehensible.

"Well, it's a peculiar message to have to hand round, Mrs Witt," the Dean began to boom, when she interrupted him by laying her hand on his arm and leaning forward, looking up into his face like a clinging pleading female:

"Oh, but *do* hand it, Dean, *do* hand it," she pleaded, gazing intently into his face.

He backed uncomfortably from that gaze.

"Since you wish it," he said, in a chest voice.

"I most certainly *do*—" she said, as if she were wishing the sweetest wish on earth. Then turning to Mrs Vyner:

"Goodbye Mrs Vyner. We *do* appreciate your coming, my daughter and I."

"I came out of kindness—" said Mrs Vyner.

"Oh, I know it, I know it," said Mrs Witt. "Thank you *so* much. Goodbye! Goodbye Dean! Who is taking the morning service on Sunday. I hope it is you, because I want to come."

"It *is* me," said the Dean. "Goodbye! Well, goodbye Lady Carrington. I shall be going over to see our young man tomorrow, and will gladly take you or anything you have to send."

"Perhaps Mother would like to go," said Lou, softly, plaintively.

"Well, we shall see," said the Dean. "Goodbye for the present!"

Mother and daughter stood at the window watching the two cross the churchyard. Dean and wife knew it, but daren't look round, and daren't admit the fact to one another.

Lou was grinning with a complete grin that gave her an odd, dryad or faun look, intensified.

"It was almost as good as pouring tea into her hat," said Mrs Witt serenely. "People like that tire me out. I shall take a glass of sherry."

"So will I, mother.—It was even better than pouring tea in her hat.—You meant, didn't you, if you poured tea in her hat, to put cream and sugar in first?"

"I did," said Mrs Witt.

But after the excitement of the encounter had passed away, Lou felt as if her life had passed away too. She went to bed, feeling she could stand no more.

In the morning she found her mother sitting at a window watching a funeral. It was raining heavily, so that some of the mourners even wore mackintosh coats. The funeral was in the poorer corner of the churchyard, where another new grave was covered with wreaths of sodden, shrivelling flowers.—The yellowish coffin stood on the wet earth, in the rain: the curate held his hat, in a sort of permanent salute, above his head, like a little umbrella, as he hastened on with the service. The people seemed too wet to weep more wet.

It was a long coffin.

"Mother, do you really *like* watching?" asked Lou irritably, as Mrs Witt sat in complete absorption.

"I do, Louise, I really enjoy it."

"Enjoy, mother!"—Lou was almost disgusted.

"I'll tell you why. I imagine I'm the one in the coffin—this is a girl of eighteen, who died of consumption—and those are my relatives, and I'm watching them put me away. And you know, Louise, I've come to the conclusion that hardly anybody in the world really lives, and so hardly anybody really dies. They may well say *Oh Death where is thy sting-a-ling-a-ling?* Even Death can't sting those that have never really lived.—I always used to want that—to die without death stinging me.—And I'm sure the girl in the coffin is saying to herself: *Fancy Aunt Emma putting on a drab slicker, and wearing it while they bury me. Doesn't show much respect. But then my mother's family always were common!* I feel there should be a solemn burial of a roll of newspapers containing the account of the death and funeral, next week. It would be just as serious: the grave of all the world's remarks—"

"I don't want to think about it, mother. One ought to be able to laugh at it. I want to laugh at it."

"Well, Louise, I think it's just as great a mistake to laugh at everything as to cry at everything. Laughter's not the one panacea, either. I should *really* like, before I do come to be buried in a box, to know where I am. That young girl in that coffin never was anywhere—any more than the newspaper remarks on her death and burial. And I begin to wonder if I've ever been anywhere. I seem to have been a daily sequence of newspaper remarks, myself. I'm sure I never really conceived you and gave you birth. It all happened in newspaper notices. It's a newspaper fact that you are my child, and that's about all there is to it."

Lou smiled as she listened.

"I always knew you were philosophic, mother. But I never dreamed it would come to elegies in a country churchyard, written to your motherhood."

"*Exactly*, Louise! Here I sit and sing the elegy to my own motherhood. I never had any motherhood, except in newspaper fact. I never was a wife, except in newspaper notices. I never was a young girl, except in newspaper remarks. Bury everything I ever said or that was said about me, and you've buried *me*. But since Kind Words Can Never Die, I can't be buried, and death has no sting-aling-aling for *me*!—Now listen to me, Louise: I want death to be real to me—not as it was to that young girl. I *want* it to hurt me, Louise. If it hurts me enough, I shall know I was alive."

She set her face and gazed under half-dropped lids at the funeral, stoic, fate-like, and yet, for the first time, with a certain pure wistfulness of a young, virgin girl. This frightened Lou very much. She was so used to the matchless Amazon in her mother, that when she saw her sit there, still, wistful, virginal, tender as a girl who has never taken armour, wistful at the window that only looked on graves, a serious terror took hold of the young woman. The terror of *too late*!

Lou felt years, centuries older than her mother, at that moment, with the tiresome responsibility of youth to protect and guide their elders.

"What can we do about it, mother?" she asked protectively.

"Do nothing, Louise. I'm not going to have anybody wisely steering my canoe, now I feel the rapids are near. I shall go with the river. Don't you pretend to do anything for me. I've done enough mischief myself, that way. I'm going down the stream, at last."

There was a pause.

"But in actuality, what?" asked Lou a little ironically.

"I don't quite know. Wait a while."

"Go back to America?"

"That is possible."

"I may come too."

"I've always waited for you to go back of your own will."

Lou went away, wandering round the house. She was so unutterably tired of everything—weary of the house, the graveyard, weary of the thought of Rico. She would have to go back to him tomorrow, to nurse him. Poor old Rico, going on like an amiable machine from day to day. It wasn't his fault. But his life was a rattling nullity, and her life rattled in null correspondence. She had hardly strength enough to stop rattling and be still. Perhaps she had not strength enough.

She did not know. She felt so weak, that unless something carried her away, she would go on rattling her bit in the great machine of human life, till she collapsed, and her rattle rattled itself out, and there was a sort of barren silence where the sound of her had been.

She wandered out in the rain, to the coach house where Lewis and Phoenix were sitting facing one another, one on a bin, the other on the inner doorstep.

"Well," she said, smiling oddly. "What's to be done?"

The two men stood up. Outside the rain fell steadily on the flagstones of the yard, past the leaves of trees. Lou sat down on the little iron step of the dogcart.

"That's cold," said Phoenix. "You sit here." And he threw a yellow horse-blanket on the box where he had been sitting.

"I don't want to take your seat," she said.

"All right, you take it."

He moved across and sat gingerly on the shaft of the dogcart.—Lou seated herself, and loosened her soft tartan shawl. Her face was pink and fresh, and her dark hair curled almost merrily in the damp. But under her eyes were the finger-prints of deadly weariness.

She looked up at the two men, again smiling in her odd fashion.

"What are we going to do?" she asked.

They looked at her closely, seeking her meaning.

"What about?" said Phoenix, a faint smile reflecting on his face, merely because she smiled.

"Oh, everything," she said, hugging her shawl again. "You know what they want? They want to shoot St. Mawr."

The two men exchanged glances.

"Who want it?" said Phoenix.

"Why—all our *friends*!" she made a little *moue*. "Dean Vyner does."

Again the men exchanged glances. There was a pause. Then Phoenix said, looking aside:

"The boss is selling him."

"Who?"

"Sir Henry."—The half-breed always spoke the title with difficulty, and with a sort of sneer. "He sell him to Miss Manby."

"How do you know?"

"The man from Corrabach told me last night. Flora, she say it."

Lou's eyes met the sardonic, empty-seeing eyes of Phoenix direct. There was too much sarcastic understanding. She looked aside.

"What else did he say?" she asked.

"I don't know," said Phoenix, evasively. "He say they cut him—else shoot him. Think they cut him—and if he die, he die."

Lou understood. He meant they would geld St. Mawr—at his age.

She looked at Lewis. He sat with his head down, so she could not see his face.

"Do you think it is true?" she asked. "Lewis? Do you think they would try to geld St. Mawr—to make him a gelding?"

Lewis looked up at her. There was a faint deadly glimmer of contempt on his face.

"Very likely, Mam," he said.

She was afraid of his cold, uncanny pale eyes, with their uneasy grey dawn of contempt. These two men, with their silent, deadly inner purpose, were not like other men. They seemed like two silent enemies of all the other men she knew. Enemies in the great white camp, disguised as servants, waiting the incalculable opportunity. What the opportunity might be, none knew.

"Sir Henry hasn't mentioned anything to me, about selling St. Mawr to Miss Manby," she said.

The derisive flicker of a smile came on Phoenix's face.

"He sell him first, and tell you then," he said, with his deadly impassive manner.

"But do you really think so?" she asked.

It was extraordinary, how much corrosive contempt Phoenix could convey, saying nothing. She felt it almost as an insult. Yet it was a relief to her.

"You know, I can't believe it. I can't believe Sir Henry would want to have St. Mawr mutilated. I believe he'd rather shoot him."

"You think so?" said Phoenix, with a faint grin.

Lou turned to Lewis.

"Lewis, will you tell me what you truly think."

Lewis looked at her with a hard, straight, fearless British stare.

"That man Philips was in the *Moon and Stars* last night. He said Miss Manby told him, she was buying St. Mawr, and she asked him, if he thought it would be safe to cut him, and make a horse of him. He said it would be better, take some of the nonsense out of him. He's no good for a sire, anyhow—"

Lewis dropped his head again, and tapped a tattoo with the toe of his rather small foot.

"And what do you think?" said Lou.—It occurred to her how sensible and practical Miss Manby was, so much more so than the Dean.

Lewis looked up at her with his pale eyes.

"It won't have anything to do with me," he said. "I shan't go to Corrabach Hall."

"What will you do, then?"

Lewis did not answer. He looked at Phoenix.

"Maybe him and me go to America," said Phoenix, looking at the void.

"Can he get in?" said Lou.

"Yes, he can. I know how," said Phoenix.

"And the money?" she said.

"We got money."

There was a silence, after which she asked of Lewis:

"You'd leave St. Mawr to his fate?"

"I can't help his fate," said Lewis. "There's too many people in the world, for me to help anything."

"Poor St. Mawr!"

She went indoors again, and up to her room: then higher, to the top rooms of the tall Georgian house. From one window she could see the fields in the rain. She could see St. Mawr himself, alone as usual, standing with his head up looking across the fences. He was streaked dark with rain. Beautiful, with his poised head and massive neck, and his supple hindquarters. He was neighing to Poppy. Clear on the wet wind came the sound of his bell-like, stallion's calling, that Mrs Vyner called cruel. It was a strange noise, with a splendour that belonged to another world-age. The mean cruelty of Mrs Vyner's humanitarianism, the barren cruelty of Flora Manby, the eunuch cruelty of Rico. Our whole eunuch civilisation, nasty-minded as eunuchs are, with their kind of sneaking, sterilising cruelty.

Yet even she herself, seeing St. Mawr's conceited march along the fence, could not help addressing him:

"Yes my boy! If you knew what Miss Flora Manby was preparing for you! *She'll* sharpen a knife that will settle you."

And Lou called her mother.

The two American women stood high at the window, overlooking the wet, close, hedged-and-fenced English landscape. Everything enclosed, enclosed, to stifling. The very apples on the trees looked so shut in, it was impossible to imagine any speck of "Knowledge" lurking inside them. Good to eat, good to cook, good even for show. But the wild sap of untameable and inexhaustible knowledge—no! Bred out of them. Geldings, even the apples.

Mrs Witt listened to Lou's half-humorous statements.

"You must admit, mother, Flora is a sensible girl," she said.

"I admit it, Louise."

"She goes straight to the root of the matter."

"And eradicates the root. Wise girl! And what is your answer?"

"I don't know, mother. What would you say?"

"I know what *I* should say."

"Tell me."

"I should say: *Miss Manby, you may have my husband, but not my horse. My husband won't need emasculating, and my horse I won't have you meddle with. I'll preserve one last male thing in the museum of this world, if I can.*"

Lou listened, smiling faintly.

"That's what I will say," she replied at length. "The funny thing is, mother, they think all their men with their bare faces or their little quotation-mark's moustaches *are* so tremendously male. That fox-hunting one!"

"I know it. Like little male motor-cars. Give him a little gas, and start him on the low gear, and away he goes: all his male gear rattling, like a cheap motor-car."

"I'm afraid I dislike men altogether, mother."

"You may, Louise. Think of Flora Manby, and how you love the fair sex."

"After all, St. Mawr is better. And I'm glad if he gives them a kick in the face."

"Ah Louise!" Mrs Witt suddenly clasped her hands with wicked passion. "*Ay, qué gozo!* as our Juan used to say, on your father's ranch in Texas." She gazed in a sort of wicked ecstasy out of the window.

They heard Lou's maid softly calling Lady Carrington from below. Lou went to the stairs.

"What is it?"

"Lewis wants to speak to you, my Lady."

"Send him into the sitting-room."

The two women went down.

"What is it, Lewis?" asked Lou.

"Am I to bring in St. Mawr, in case they send for him from Corrabach?"

"No," said Lou swiftly.

"Wait a minute," put in Mrs Witt. "What makes you think they will send for St. Mawr from Corrabach, Lewis?" she asked, suave as a grey leopard cat.

"Miss Manby went up to Flints Farm with Dean Vyner this morning, and they've just come back. They stopped the car, and Miss Manby got out at the field gate, to look at St. Mawr. I'm thinking, if she made the bargain with Sir Henry, she'll be sending a man over this afternoon, and if I'd better brush St. Mawr down a bit, in case."

The man stood strangely still, and the words came like shadows of his real meaning. It was a challenge.

"I see," said Mrs Witt slowly.

Lou's face darkened. She too saw.

"So that is her game," she said. "That is why they got me down here."

"Never mind, Louise," said Mrs Witt. Then to Lewis: "Yes, please bring in St. Mawr. You wish it, don't you, Louise?"

"Yes," hesitated Lou. She saw by Mrs Witt's closed face that a counter-move was prepared.

"And Lewis," said Mrs Witt. "My daughter may wish you to ride St. Mawr this afternoon—not to Corrabach Hall."

"Very good, Mam."

Mrs Witt sat silent for some time, after Lewis had gone, gathering inspiration from the wet, grisly gravestones.

"Don't you think it's time we made a move, daughter?" she asked.

"Any move," said Lou desperately.

"Very well then.—My dearest friends, and my *only* friends, in this country, are in Oxfordshire. I will set off to *ride* to Merriton this afternoon, and Lewis will ride with me on St. Mawr."

"But you can't ride to Merriton in an afternoon." said Lou.

"I know it. I shall ride across country. I shall *enjoy* it, Louise.—Yes.—I shall consider I am on my way back to America. I am most deadly tired of this country. From Merriton I shall make my arrangements to go to America, and take Lewis and Phoenix and St.

Mawr along with me. I think they want to go.—You will decide for yourself."

"Yes, I'll come too," said Lou casually.

"Very well. I'll start immediately after lunch, for I can't *breathe* in this place any longer. Where are Henry's automobile maps?"

Afternoon saw Mrs Witt, in a large waterproof cape, mounted on her horse, Lewis, in another cape, mounted on St. Mawr, trotting through the rain, splashing in the puddles, moving slowly southwards. They took the open country, and would pass quite near to Flints Farm. But Mrs Witt did not care. With great difficulty she had managed to fasten a small waterproof roll behind her, containing her night things. She seemed to breathe the first breath of freedom.

And sure enough, an hour or so after Mrs Witt's departure, arrived Flora Manby in a splashed up motor-car, accompanied by her sister, and bringing a groom and a saddle.

"Do you know, Harry sold me St. Mawr," she said. "I'm just wild to get that horse in hand."

"How?" said Lou.

"Oh, I don't know. There are ways. Do you mind if Philips rides him over now, to Corrabach?—Oh, I forgot, Harry sent you a note."

"*Dearest Loulina: Have you been gone from here two days or two years. It seems the latter. You are terribly missed. Flora wanted so much to buy St. Mawr, to save us further trouble, that I have sold him to her. She is giving me what we paid: rather, what you paid; so of course the money is yours. I am thankful we are rid of the animal, and that he falls into competent hands—I asked her please to remove him from your charge today. And I can't tell how much easier I am in my mind, to think of him gone. You are coming back to me tomorrow aren't you? I shall think of nothing else but you, till I see you. A rivederci, darling dear! R.*"

"I'm so sorry," said Lou. "Mother went on horseback to see some friends, and Lewis went with her on St. Mawr. He knows the road."

"She'll be back this evening?" said Flora.

"I don't know. Mother is so uncertain. She may be away a day or two."

"Well, here's the cheque for St. Mawr."

"No, I won't take it now—No thank you—not till mother comes back with the goods."

Flora was chagrined. The two women knew they hated one another. The visit was a brief one.

Mrs Witt rode on in the rain, which abated as the afternoon wore down, and the evening came without rain, and with a suffusion of pale yellow light. All the time she had trotted in silence, with Lewis just behind her. And she scarcely saw the heather-covered hill with the deep clefts between them, nor the oak-woods, nor the lingering fox gloves, nor the earth at all. Inside herself she felt a profound repugnance for the English country: she preferred even the crudeness of Central Park in New York.

And she felt an almost savage desire to get away from Europe, from everything European. Now she was really *en route*, she cared not a straw for St. Mawr or for Lewis or anything. Something just writhed inside her, all the time, against Europe. That closeness, that sense of cohesion, that sense of being fused into a lump with all the rest—no matter how much distance you kept—this drove her mad. In America the cohesion was a matter of choice and will. But in Europe it was organic, like the helpless particles of one sprawling body. And the great body in a state of incipient decay.

She was a woman of fifty-one: and she seemed hardly to have lived a day. She looked behind her—the thin trees and swamps of Louisiana, the sultry, sub-tropical excitement of decaying New Orleans, the vast bare dryness of Texas, with mobs of cattle in an illumined dust! The half-European thrills of New York! The false stability of Boston! A clever husband, who was a brilliant lawyer, but who was far more thrilled by his cattle ranch than by his law: and who drank heavily, and died. The years of first widowhood in Boston, consoled by a self-satisfied sort of intellectual courtship from clever men.—For curiously enough, while she wanted it, she had always been able to compel men to pay court to her. All kinds of men.—Then a rather dashing time in New York—when she was in her early forties. Then the long *visual* philandering in Europe. She left off "loving," save through the eye, when she came to Europe. And when she made her trips to America, she found it was finished there also, her "loving."

What was the matter? Examining herself, she had long ago decided that her nature was a destructive force. But then, she justified herself, she had only destroyed that which was destructible. If she could have found something indestructible, especially in men, though she would have fought against it, she would have been glad at last to be defeated by it.

That was the point. She really wanted to be defeated, in her own eyes. And nobody had ever defeated her. Men were never really her match. A woman of terrible strong health, she felt even that in her strong limbs there was far more electric power than in the limbs of any man she had met. That curious fluid electric force, that could make any man kiss her hand, if she so willed it. A queen, as far as she wished. And not having been very clever at school, she always had the greatest respect for the mental powers. Her own were not mental powers. Rather electric, as of some strange physical dynamo within her. So she had been ready to bow before Mind.

But alas! After a brief time, she had found Mind, at least the man who was supposed to have the mind, bowing before her. Her own peculiar dynamic force was stronger than the force of Mind. She could make Mind kiss her hand.

And not by any sensual tricks. She did not really care about sensualities, especially as a younger woman. Sex was a mere adjunct. She cared about the mysterious, intense, dynamic sympathy that could flow between her and some "live" man—a man who was highly conscious, a real live wire. That she cared about.

But she had never rested until she had made the man she admired: and admiration was the root of her attraction to any man: made him kiss her hand. In both senses, actual and metaphorical. Physical and metaphysical. Conquered his country.

She had always succeeded. And she believed that, if she cared, she always *would* succeed. In the world of living men. Because of the power that was in her, in her arms, in her strong shapely, but terrible hands, in all the great dynamo of her body.

For this reason she had been so terribly contemptuous of Rico, and of Lou's infatuation. Ye Gods! what was Rico in the scale of men!

Perhaps she despised the younger generation too easily. Because she did not see its sources of power, she concluded it was powerless. Whereas perhaps the power of accommodating oneself to any circumstance and committing oneself to no circumstance is the last triumph of mankind.

Her generation had had its day. She had had her day. The world of her men had sunk into a sort of insignificance. And with a great contempt she despised the world that had come into place instead: the world of Rico and Flora Manby, the world represented, to her, by the Prince of Wales.

In such a world, there was nothing even to conquer. It gave everything and gave nothing to everybody and anybody all the time. *Dio benedetto!* as Rico would say. A great complicated tangle of nonentities ravelled in nothingness. So it seemed to her.

Great God! This was the generation she had helped to bring into the world.

She had had her day. And, as far as the mysterious battle of life went, she had won all the way. Just as Cleopatra, in the mysterious business of a woman's life, won all the way.

Though that bald tough Caesar had drawn his iron from the fire without losing much of its temper. And he had gone his way. And Antony surely was splendid to die with.

In her life there had been no tough Caesar to go his way in cold blood, away from her. Her men had gone from her like dogs on three legs, into the crowd. And certainly there was no gorgeous Antony to die for and with.

Almost she was tempted in her heart to cry: "Conquer me, Oh God, before I die!"—But then she had a terrible contempt for the God that was supposed to rule this universe. She felt she could make *him* kiss her hand. Here she was a woman of fifty-one, past the change of life. And her great dread was to die an empty, barren death. Oh, if only Death might open dark wings of mystery and consolation. To die an easy, barren death. To pass out as she had passed in, without mystery or the rustling of darkness! That was her last, final, ashy dread.

"Old!" she said to herself. "I am not *old*! I have lived many years, that is all. But I am as timeless as an hourglass that turns morning and night, and spills the hours of sleep one way, the hours of consciousness the other way, without itself being affected. Nothing in all my life has ever truly affected me.—I believe Cleopatra only tried the asp, as she tried her pearls in wine, to see if it would really, really have any effect on her. Nothing had ever really had any effect on her, neither Caesar nor Antony nor any of them. Never once had she really been lost, lost to herself. Then try death, see if that trick would work. If she would lose herself to herself that way.—Ah death—!"

But Mrs Witt mistrusted death too. She felt she might pass out as a bed of asters passes out in autumn, to mere nothingness.—And something in her longed to die, at least, *positively*: to be folded then at last into throbbing wings of mystery, like a hawk that goes to sleep. Not like a thing made into a parcel and put into the last rubbish-heap.

So she rode trotting across the hills, mile after mile, in silence. Avoiding the roads, avoiding everything, avoiding everybody, just trotting forwards, towards night.

And by nightfall they had travelled twenty-five miles. She had motored around this country, and knew the little towns and the inns. She knew where she would sleep.

The morning came beautiful and sunny. A woman so strong in health, why should she ride with the face of death before her eyes? But she did.

Yet in sunny morning she must do something about it.

"Lewis!" she said. "Come here and tell me something, please! Tell me," she said, "do you believe in God?"

"In God!" he said, wondering. "I never think about it."

"But do you say your prayers?"

"No Mam!"

"Why don't you?"

He thought about it for some minutes.

"I don't like religion. My aunt and uncle were religious."

"You don't like religion," she repeated. "And you don't believe in God.—Well then—"

"Nay!" he hesitated. "I never said I didn't believe in God.—Only I'm sure I'm not a Methodist. And I feel a fool in a proper church.—And I feel a fool saying my prayers.—And I feel a fool when ministers and parsons come getting at me.—I never think about God, if folks don't try to make me." He had a small, sly smile, almost gay.

"And you don't like feeling a fool?" She smiled rather patronisingly.

"No Mam."

"Do I make you feel a fool?" she asked, drily.

He looked at her without answering.

"Why don't you answer?" she said, pressing.

"I think you'd like to make a fool of me sometimes," he said.

"Now?" she pressed.

He looked at her with that slow, distant look.

"Maybe!" he said, rather unconcernedly.

Curiously, she couldn't touch him. He always seemed to be watching her from a distance, as if from another country. Even if she made a fool of him, something in him would all the time be far away from her, not implicated.

She caught herself up in the personal game, and returned to her own isolated question. A vicious habit made her start the personal tricks. She didn't want to really.

There was something about this little man—sometimes, to herself, she called him *Little Jack Horner, Sat in a corner*—that irritated her and made her want to taunt him. His peculiar little inaccessibility, that was so tight and easy.

Then again, there was something, his way of looking at her as if he looked from out of another country, a country of which he was an inhabitant, and where she had never been: this touched her strangely. Perhaps behind this little man was the mystery. In spite of the fact that in actual life, in her world, he was only a groom, almost chétif, with his legs a little bit horsey and bowed; and of no education, saying *Yes Mam*! and *No Mam*! and accomplishing nothing, simply nothing at all on the face of the earth. Strictly a nonentity.

And yet, what made him perhaps the only real entity to her, his seeming to inhabit another world than hers. A world dark and still, where language never ruffled the growing leaves, and seared their edges like a bad wind.

Was it an illusion, however? Sometimes she thought it was. Just bunkum, which she had faked up, in order to have something to mystify about.

But then, when she saw Phoenix and Lewis silently together, she knew there *was* another communion, silent, excluding her. And sometimes when Lewis was alone with St. Mawr: and once, when she saw him pick up a bird that had stunned itself against a wire: she had realised another world, silent, where each creature is alone in its own aura of silence, the mystery of power: as Lewis had power with St. Mawr, and even with Phoenix.

The visible world, and the invisible. Or rather, the audible and the inaudible. She had lived so long, and so completely, in the visible, audible world. She would not easily admit that other, inaudible. She always wanted to jeer, as she approached the brink of it.

Even now, she wanted to jeer at the little fellow, because of his holding himself inaccessible within the inaudible, silent world. And she knew he knew it.

"Did you never want to be rich, and be a gentleman, like Sir Henry?" she asked.

"I would many times have liked to be rich. But I never exactly wanted to be a gentleman," he said.

"Why not?"

"I can't exactly say. I should be uncomfortable if I was like they are."

"And are you comfortable now?"

"When I'm let alone."

"And do they let you alone? Does the world let you alone?"

"No, they don't."

"Well then—!"

"I keep to myself all I can."

"And are you comfortable, as you call it, when you keep to yourself?"

"Yes, I am."

"But when you keep to yourself, what do you keep to? What precious treasure have you to keep to?"

He looked, and saw she was jeering.

"None," he said. "I've got nothing of that sort."

She rode impatiently on ahead.

And the moment she had done so, she regretted it. She might put the little fellow, with contempt, out of her reckoning. But no, she would not do it.

She had put so much out of her reckoning: soon she would be left in an empty circle, with her empty self at the centre.

She reined in again.

"Lewis!" she said. "I don't want you to take offence at anything I say."

"No Mam."

"I don't want you to say just *No Mam*! all the time!" she cried impulsively. "Promise me."

"Yes Mam!"

"But really! Promise me you won't be offended at whatever I say."

"Yes Mam!"

She looked at him searchingly. To her surprise, she was almost in tears. A woman of her years! And with a servant!

But his face was blank and stony, with a stony, distant look of pride that made him inaccessible to her emotions.

He met her eyes again: with that cold, distant look, looking straight into her hot, confused, pained self. So cold and as if merely refuting her. He didn't believe her, nor trust her, nor like her even. She was an attacking enemy to him. Only he stayed really far away from her, looking down at her from a sort of distant hill where her weapons could not reach: not quite.

And at the same time, it hurt him in a dumb, living way, that she made these attacks on him. She could see the cloud of hurt in his eyes, no matter how distantly he looked at her.

They bought food in a village shop, and sat under a tree near a field where men were already cutting oats, in a warm valley. Lewis had stabled the horses for a couple of hours, to feed and rest. But he came to join her under the tree, to eat.—He sat at a little distance from her, with the bread and cheese in his small brown hands, eating silently, and watching the harvesters. She was cross with him, and therefore she was stingy, would give him nothing to eat but dry bread and cheese. Herself, she was not hungry.—So all the time he kept his face a little averted from her. As a matter of fact, he kept his whole being averted from her, away from her. He did not want to touch her, nor to be touched by her. He kept his spirit there, alert, on its guard, but out of contact. It was as if he had unconsciously accepted the battle, the old battle. He was her target, the old object of her deadly weapons. But he refused to shoot back. It was as if he caught all her missiles in full flight, before they touched him, and silently threw them on the ground behind him. And in some essential part of himself he ignored her, staying in another world.

That other world! Mere male armour of artificial imperviousness! It angered her.

Yet she knew, by the way he watched the harvesters, and the grasshoppers popping into notice, that it was another world. And when a girl went by, carrying food to the field, it was at him she glanced. And he gave that quick, animal little smile that came from him unawares. Another world!

Yet also, there was a sort of meanness about him: a *suffisance*! A keep-yourself-for-yourself, and don't give yourself away.

Well!—she rose impatiently.

It was hot in the afternoon, and she was rather tired. She went to the inn and slept, and did not start again till teatime.

Then they had to ride rather late. The sun sank, among a smell of cornfields, clear and yellow-red behind motionless dark trees. Pale smoke rose from cottage chimneys. Not a cloud was in the sky, which held the upward-floating light like a bowl inverted on purpose. A new moon sparkled and was gone. It was beginning of night.

Away in the distance, they saw a curious pinkish glare of fire, probably furnaces. And Mrs Witt thought she could detect the scent of furnace smoke, or factory smoke. But then she always said that of the English air: it was never quite free of the smell of smoke, coal-smoke.

They were riding slowly on a path through fields, down a long slope. Away below was a puther of lights. All the darkness seemed full of half-spent crossing lights, a curious uneasiness. High in the sky a star seemed to be walking. It was an aeroplane with a light. Its buzz rattled above. Not a space, not a speck of this country that wasn't humanised, occupied by the human claim. Not even the sky.

They descended slowly through a dark wood, which they had entered through a gate. Lewis was all the time dismounting and opening gates, letting her pass, shutting the gate and mounting again.

So, in a while she came to the edge of the wood's darkness, and saw the open pale concave of the world beyond. The darkness was never dark. It shook with the concussion of many invisible lights, lights of towns, villages, mines, factories, furnaces, squatting in the valleys and behind all the hills.

Yet, as Rachel Witt drew rein at the gate emerging from the wood, a very big, soft star fell in heaven, cleaving the hubbub of this human night with a gleam from the greater world.

"See! a star falling!" said Lewis, as he opened the gate.

"I saw it," said Mrs Witt, walking her horse past him.

There was a curious excitement of wonder, or magic, in the little man's voice. Even in this night something strange had stirred awake in him.

"You ask me about God," he said to her, walking his horse alongside in the shadow of the wood's-edge, the darkness of the old Pan, that kept our artificially-lit world at bay. "I don't know about God. But when I see a star fall like that out of long-distance places in the sky: and the moon sinking saying Goodbye! Goodbye! Goodbye! and nobody listening: I think I hear something, though I wouldn't call it God."

"What then?" said Rachel Witt.

"And you smell the smell of oak-leaves now," he said, "now the air is cold. They smell to me more alive than people. The trees hold their bodies hard and still, but they watch and listen with their leaves. And I think they say to me: *Is that you passing there, Morgan Lewis? All right, you pass quickly, we shan't do anything to you. You are like a holly-bush.*"

"Yes," said Rachel Witt, drily. "*Why?*"

"All the time, the trees grow, and listen. And if you cut a tree down without asking pardon, trees will hurt you some time in your life, in the night time."

"I suppose," said Rachel Witt, "that's an old superstition."

"They say that ash-trees don't like people. When the other people were most in the country—I mean like what they call fairies, that have all gone now—they liked ash-trees best. And you know the little green things with little small nuts in them, that come flying down from ash-trees—*pigeons*, we call them—they're the seeds—the other people used to catch them and eat them before they fell to the ground. And that made the people so they could hear trees living and feeling things.—But when all these people that there are now came to England, they liked the oak-trees best, because their pigs ate the acorns. So now you can tell the ash-trees are mad, they want to kill all these people. But the oak-trees are many more than the ash-trees."

"And do you eat the ash-tree seeds?" she asked.

"I always ate them, when I was little. Then I wasn't frightened of ash-trees, like most of the others. And I wasn't frightened of the moon. If you didn't go near the fire all day, and if you didn't eat any cooked food nor anything that had been in the sun, but only things like turnips or radishes or pig-nuts, and then went without any clothes on, in the full moon, then you could see the people in the moon, and go with them. They never have fire, and they never speak, and their bodies are clear almost like jelly. They die in a minute if there's a bit of fire near them. But they know more than we. Because unless fire touches them, they never die. They see people live and they see people perish, and they say, people are only like twigs on a tree, you break them off the tree, and kindle fire with them. You make a fire of them, and they are gone, the fire is gone, everything is gone. But the people of the moon don't die, and fire is nothing to them. They look at it from the distance of the sky, and see it burning things up, people all appearing and disappearing like twigs that come in spring and you cut them in autumn and make a fire of them and they are gone. And they say: what do people matter? If you want to matter, you must become a moon-boy. Then all your life, fire can't blind you and people can't hurt you. Because at full moon you can join the moon people, and go through the air and pass any cool places, pass through rocks and through the trunks of trees, and when you come to people lying warm in bed, you punish them."

"How?"

"You sit on the pillow where they breathe, and you put a web across their mouth, so they can't breathe the fresh air that comes from the moon. So they go on breathing the same air again and again, and that makes them more and more stupefied. The sun gives out heat, but the moon gives out fresh air. That's what the moon people do: they wash the air clean with moonlight."

He was talking with a strange eager naïveté that amused Rachel Witt, and made her a little uncomfortable in her skin. Was he after all no more than a sort of imbecile?

"Who told you all this stuff?" she asked abruptly.

And, as abruptly, he pulled himself up.

"We used to say it, when we were children."

"But you don't believe it? It *is* only childishness, after all."

He paused a moment or two.

"No," he said, in his ironical little day-voice. "I know I shan't make anything but a fool of myself, with that talk. But all sorts of things go through our heads, and some seem to linger, and some don't. But you asking me about God put it into my mind, I suppose. I don't know what sort of things I believe in: only I know it's not what the chapel-folks believe in. We none of us believe in them when it comes to earning a living, or, with you people, when it comes to spending your fortune. Then we know that bread costs money, and even your sleep you have to pay for.—That's work. Or, with you people, it's just owning property and seeing you get your value for your money.—But a man's mind is always full of things. And some people's minds, like my aunt and uncle, are full of religion and hell for everybody except themselves. And some people's minds are all money, money, money, and how to get hold of something they haven't got hold of yet. And some people, like you, are always curious about what everybody else in the world is after. And some people are all for enjoying themselves and being thought much of, and some, like Lady Carrington, don't know what to do with themselves. Myself, I don't want to have in my mind the things other people have in their minds. I'm one that likes my own things best. And if, when I see a bright star fall, like tonight, I think to myself: *There's movement in the sky. The world is going to change again. They're throwing something to us from the distance, and we've got to have it, whether we want it or not. Tomorrow there will be a difference for everybody, thrown out of the sky upon us, whether we want it or not*: then that's how I want to think, so let me please myself."

"You know what a shooting star actually is, I suppose?—and that there are always many in August, because we pass through a region of them?"

"Yes Mam, I've been told. But stones don't come at us from the sky for nothing. Either it's like when a man tosses an apple to you out of his orchard, as you go by. Or it's like when somebody shies a stone at you, to cut your head open. You'll never make me believe the sky is like an empty house with a slate falling from the roof. The world has its own life, the sky has a life of its own, and never is it like stones rolling down a rubbish heap and falling into a pond. Many things twitch and twitter within the sky, and many things happen beyond us. My own way of thinking is my own way."

"I never knew you talk so much."

"No Mam. It's your asking me that about God. Or else it's the night-time.—I don't believe in God and being good and going to Heaven. Neither do I worship idols, so I'm not a heathen as my aunt called me. Never from a boy did I want to believe the things they kept grinding in their guts at home, and at Sunday School, and at school. A man's mind has to be full of something, so I keep to what we used to think as lads. It's childish nonsense, I know it. But it suits me. Better than other people's stuff. Your man Phoenix is about the same, when he lets on.—Anyhow, it's my own stuff, that we believed as lads, and I like it better than other people's stuff.—You asking about God made me let on. But I would never belong to any club, or trades-union, and God's the same to my mind."

With this he gave a little kick to his horse, and St. Mawr went dancing excitedly along the highway they now entered, leaving Mrs Witt to trot after as rapidly as she could.

When she came to the hotel, to which she had telegraphed for rooms, Lewis disappeared, and she was left thinking hard.

It was not till they were twenty miles from Merriton, riding through a slow morning mist, and she had a rather far-away, wistful look on her face, unusual for her, that she turned to him in the saddle and said:

"Now don't be surprised, Lewis, at what I am going to say. I am going to ask you, now, supposing I wanted to marry you, what should you say?"

He looked at her quickly, and was at once on his guard.

"That you didn't mean it," he replied hastily.

"Yes"—she hesitated, and her face looked wistful and tired.—"Supposing I *did* mean it. Supposing I did *really*, from my heart, want to marry you and be a wife to you—" she looked away across the fields—"then what should you say?"

Her voice sounded sad, a little broken.

"Why Mam!" he replied, knitting his brow and shaking his head a little. "I should say you didn't mean it, you know. Something would have come over you."

"But supposing I *wanted* something to come over me?"

He shook his head.

"It would never do, Mam! Some people's flesh and blood is kneaded like bread: and that's me. And some are rolled like fine pastry, like Lady Carrington. And some are mixed with gunpowder. They're like a cartridge you put in a gun, Mam."

She listened impatiently.

"Don't talk," she said, "about bread and cakes and pastry, it all means nothing. You used to answer short enough, *Yes Mam! No Mam!* That will do now. Do you mean *Yes!* or *No?*"

His eyes met hers. She was again hectoring.

"No Mam!" he said, quite neutral.

"Why?"

As she waited for his answer, she saw the foundations of his loquacity dry up, his face go distant and mute again, as it always used to be, till these last two days, when it had had a funny touch of inconsequential merriness.

He looked steadily into her eyes, and his look was neutral, sombre, and hurt. He looked at her as if infinite seas, infinite spaces divided him and her. And his eyes seemed to put her away beyond some sort of fence. An anger congealed cold like lava, set impassive against her, and all her sort.

"No Mam. I couldn't give my body to any woman who didn't respect it."

"But I do respect it, I do!"—she flushed hot like a girl.

"No Mam. Not as *I* mean it," he replied.

There was a touch of anger against her in his voice, and a distance of distaste.

"And how do *you* mean it?" she replied, the full sarcasm coming back into her tones. She could see that, as a woman to touch and fondle, he saw her as repellant: only repellant.

"I have to be a servant to women now," he said, "even to earn my wage. I could never touch with my body a woman whose servant I was."

"You're not my servant: my daughter pays your wages.—And all that is beside the point, between a man and a woman."

"No woman who I touched with my body should ever speak to me as you speak to me, or think of me as you think of me," he said.

"But!—" she stammered. "I think of you—with love. And can you be so unkind as to notice the way I speak? You know it's only my way."

"You, as a woman," he said, "you have no respect for a man."

"Respect! Respect!" she cried. "I'm likely to lose what respect I have left. I know I can *love* a man. But whether a man can love a woman—"

"No," said Lewis. "I never could, and I think I never shall. Because I don't want to. The thought of it makes me feel shame."

"What do you mean?" she cried.

"Nothing in the world," he said, "would make me feel such shame as to have a woman shouting at me, or mocking at me, as I see women mocking and despising the men they marry. No woman shall touch my body, and mock me or despise me. No woman."

"But men must be mocked, or despised even, sometimes."

"No. Not this man. Not by the woman I touch with my body."

"Are you perfect?"

"I don't know. But if I touch a woman with my body, it must put a lock on her, to respect what I will never have despised: never!"

"What will you never have despised?"

"My body! And my touch upon the woman."

"Why insist so on your body?"—And she looked at him with a touch of contemptuous mockery, raillery.

He looked her in the eyes, steadily, and coldly, putting her away from him, and himself far away from her.

"Do you expect that any woman will stay your humble slave, today?" she asked cuttingly.

But he only watched her, coldly, distant, refusing any connection.

"Between men and women, it's a question of give and take. A man can't expect *always* to be humbly adored."

He watched her still, cold, rather pale, putting her far from him. Then he turned his horse and set off rapidly along the road, leaving her to follow.

She walked her horse and let him go, thinking to herself:

"There's a little bantam cock. And a groom! Imagine it! Thinking he can dictate to a woman!"

She was in love with him. And he, in an odd way, was in love with her. She had known it by the odd, uncanny merriment in him, and his unexpected loquacity. But he would not have her come physically near him. Unapproachable there as a cactus, guarding his "body" from her contact. As if contact with her would be mortal insult and fatal injury to his marvellous "body."

What a little cock-sparrow!

Let him ride ahead. He would have to wait for her somewhere.

She found him at the entrance to the next village. His face was pallid and set. She could tell he felt he had been insulted, so he had congealed into stiff insentience.

"At the bottom of all men is the same," she said to herself: "an empty, male conceit of themselves."

She too rode up with a face like a mask, and straight on to the hotel.

"Can you serve dinner to myself and my servant?" she asked at the inn: which, fortunately for her, accommodated motorists, otherwise they would have said *No*!

"I think," said Lewis as they came in sight of Merriton, "I'd better give Lady Carrington a week's notice."

A complete little stranger! And an impudent one.

"Exactly as you please," she said.

She found several letters from her daughter at Marshal Place.

"Dear Mother: No sooner had you gone off than Flora appeared, not at all in the bud, but rather in full blow. She demanded her victim; Shylock demanding the pound of flesh: and wanted to hand over the shekels.

"Joyfully I refused them. She said 'Harry' was much better, and invited him and me to stay at Corrabach Hall till he was quite well: it would be less strain on your household, while he was still in bed and helpless. So the plan is, that he shall be brought down on Friday, if he is really fit for the journey, and we drive straight to Corrabach. I am packing his bags and mine, clearing up our traces: his trunks to go to Corrabach, mine to stay here and make up their minds.—I am going to Flints Farm again tomorrow, dutifully, though I am no flower for the bedside.—I do so want to know if Rico has already called her Fiorita: or perhaps Florecita. It reminds me of old William's joke: *Now yuh tell me, little Missy: which is the best posey that grow?* And the hushed whisper in which he said the answer: *The Collyposy*! Oh dear, I am so tired of feeling spiteful, but how else is one to feel.

"You looked most prosaically romantic, setting off in a rubber cape, followed by Lewis. Hope the roads were not very slippery, and that you had a good time, à la *Mademoiselle de Maupin*. Do remember, dear, not to devour little Lewis before you have got half way—"

"Dear Mother: I half expected word from you before I left, but nothing came. Forrester drove me up here just before lunch. Rico seems much better: almost himself, and a little more than that. He broached our staying at Corrabach very tactfully. I told him Flora had asked me, and it seemed a good plan. Then I told him about St. Mawr. He was a little piqued, and there was a pause of very disapproving silence. Then he said: *Very well, darling. If you wish to keep the animal, do so by all means. I make a present of him again.* Me: *That's so good of you, Rico. Because I know revenge is sweet.* Rico: *Revenge, Loulina! I don't think I was selling him for vengeance! Merely to get rid of him to Flora, who can keep better hold over him.*—Me: *But you know, dear, she was going to geld him!* Rico: *I don't think anybody knew it. We only wondered if it were possible, to make him more amenable. Did she tell you?* Me: *No—Phoenix did. He had it from a groom.* Rico: *Dear me! A concatenation of grooms! So your mother rode off with Lewis, and carried St. Mawr out of danger! I understand! Let us hope worse won't befall.* Me: *Whom?* Rico: *Never mind, dear! It's so lovely to see you. You are looking rested. I thought those Countess of Witton roses the most marvellous things in the world, till you came, now they're quite in the background.* He had some very lovely red roses, in a crystal bowl: the room smelled of roses. Me: *Where did they come from?* Rico: *Oh Flora brought them!* Me: *Bowl and all?* Rico: *Bowl and all! Wasn't it dear of her?* Me: *Why yes! But then she's the goddess of flowers, isn't she?* Poor darling, he was offended that I should twit him while he is ill, so I relented. He has had a couple of marvellous invalid's bed-jackets sent from London: one a pinkish yellow, with rose-arabesque facings: this one in fine cloth. But unfortunately he has already dropped soup on it. The other is a lovely silvery and blue and green soft brocade. He had that one on to receive me, and I at once complimented him on it. He has got a new ring too: sent by Aspasia Weingartner: a rather lovely intaglio of Priapus under an apple bough, at least, so he says it is. He made a naughty face, and said: *The Priapus stage is rather advanced for poor me.* I asked what the Priapus stage was, but he said *Oh nothing!* Then nurse said: *There's a big classical dictionary that Miss Manby brought up, if you wish to see it.* So I have been studying the Classical Gods. The world always was a queer place. It's a very queer one when Rico is the god Priapus. He would go round the orchard painting life-like apples on the trees, and inviting nymphs to come and eat them. And the nymphs would pretend they were real: *Why, Sir Prippy, what stunningly naughty apples!* There's nothing so artificial as sinning nowadays. I suppose it once was real.

"I'm bored here: wish I had my horse."

"Dear Mother: I'm so glad you are enjoying your ride. I'm sure it is like riding into history, like the Yankee at the Court of King

Arthur, in those old bye-lanes and Roman roads. They still fascinate me: at least, more before I get there than when I am actually there. I begin to feel real American and to resent the past. Why doesn't the past decently bury itself, instead of sitting waiting to be admired by the present?

"Phoenix brought Poppy. I am so fond of her: rode for five hours yesterday. I was glad to get away from this farm. The doctor came, and said Rico would be able to go down to Corrabach tomorrow. Flora came to hear the bulletin, and sailed back full of zest. Apparently Rico is going to do a portrait of her, sitting up in bed. What a mercy the bedclothes won't be mine, when Priapus wields his palette from the pillow.

"Phoenix thinks you intend to go to America with St. Mawr, and that I am coming too, leaving Rico this side.—I wonder. I feel so unreal, nowadays, as if I too were nothing more than a painting by Rico on a millboard. I feel almost too unreal even to make up my mind to anything. It is terrible when the life-flow dies out of one, and everything is like cardboard, and oneself is like cardboard. I'm sure it is worse than being dead. I realised it yesterday when Phoenix and I had a picnic lunch by a stream. You see I must imitate you in all things. He found me some water-cresses, and they tasted so damp and *alive*, I knew how deadened I was. Phoenix wants us to go and have a ranch in Arizona, and raise horses, with St. Mawr, if willing, for Father Abraham. I wonder if it matters what one does: if it isn't all the same thing over again? Only Phoenix, his funny blank face, makes my heart melt and go sad. But I believe he'd be cruel too. I saw it in his face when he didn't know I was looking. Anything, though, rather than this deadness and this paint-Priapus business. Au revoir, mother dear! Keep on having a good time—"

"Dear Mother—I had your letter from Merriton: am so glad you arrived safe and sound in body and temper. There was such a funny letter from Lewis, too: I enclose it. What makes him take this extraordinary line? But I'm writing to tell him to take St. Mawr to London, and wait for me there. I have telegraphed Mrs Squire to get the house ready for me. I shall go straight there.

"Things developed here, as they were bound to. I just couldn't bear it. No sooner was Rico put in the automobile than a self-conscious importance came over him, like when the wounded hero is carried into the middle of the stage. *Why so solemn, Rico dear?* I asked him, trying to laugh him out of it. *Not solemn, dear, only feeling a little transient.*

I don't think he knew himself what he meant. Flora was on the steps
as the car drew up, dressed in severe white. She only needed an apron,
to become a nurse: or a veil, to become a bride. Between the two, she
had an unbearable air of a woman in seduced circumstances, as the
Times said. She ordered two menservants about in subdued, you would
have said hushed, but competent tones. And then I saw there was a
touch of the priestess about her as well: Cassandra preparing for her
violation: Iphigenia, with Rico for Orestes, on a stretcher: he looking
like Adonis, fully prepared to be an unconscionable time in dying.
They had given him a lovely room, downstairs, with doors opening
on to a little garden all of its own. I believe it was Flora's boudoir.
I left nurse and the men to put him to bed. Flora was hovering
anxiously in the passage outside. *Oh what a marvellous room! Oh how
colourful, how beautiful!* came Rico's tones, the hero behind the scenes.
I must say, it was like a harvest festival, with roses and gaillardias in
the shadow, and cornflowers in the light, and a bowl of grapes, and
nectarines among leaves. *I'm so anxious that he should be happy*, Flora
said to me in the passage. *You know him best. Is there anything else I
could do for him?* Me: *Why, if you went to the piano and sang, I'm sure
he'd love it. Couldn't you sing: Oh my love is like a rred rred rrose!*—You
know how Rico imitates Scotch!

"Thank goodness I have a bedroom upstairs: nurse sleeps in a little
ante-chamber to Rico's room. The Edwards are still here, the blonde
young man with some very futuristic plaster on his face. *Awfully good
of you to come!* he said to me, looking at me out of one eye, and holding
my hand fervently. How's that for cheek? *It's awfully good of Miss
Manby to let me come*, said I. He: *Ah, but Flora is always a sport, a
topping good sport!*

"I don't know what's the matter, but it just all put me into a fiendish
temper. I felt I couldn't sit there at luncheon with that bright youthful
company, and hear about their tennis and their polo and their hunting
and their flirtatiousness making me sick. So I asked for a tray
in my room. Do as I might, I couldn't help being horrid.

"Oh, and Rico! He really is too awful. Lying there in bed with every
ear open, like Adonis waiting to be persuaded not to die. Seizing a
hushed moment to take Flora's hand and press it to his lips,
murmuring: *How awfully good you are to me, dear Flora!* And Flora:
I'd be better, if I knew how, Harry! So cheerful with it all! No, it's
too much. My sense of humour is leaving me: which means, I'm
getting into too bad a temper to be able to ridicule it all. I suppose

I feel in the minority. It's an awful thought, to think that most all the young people in the world are like this: so bright and cheerful, and *sporting*, and so brimming with libido. How awful!

"I said to Rico: *You're very comfortable here, aren't you?* He: *Comfortable! It's comparative heaven.* Me: *Would you mind if I went away?* A deadly pause. He is deadly afraid of being left alone with Flora. He feels safe so long as I am about, and he can take refuge in his marriage ties. He: *Where do you want to go, dear?* Me: *To Mother. To London. Mother is planning to go to America, and she wants me to go.* Rico: *But you don't want to go t-h-e-e-re-e!* You know, Mother, how Rico can put a venomous emphasis on a word, till it suggests pure poison. It nettled me. *I'm not sure*, I said. Rico: *Oh, but you can't stand that awful America.* Me: *I want to try again.* Rico: *But Lou dear, it will be winter before you get there. And this is absolutely the wrong moment for me to go over there. I am only just making headway over here. When I am absolutely sure of a position in England, then we can nip across the Atlantic and scoop in a few dollars, if you like. Just now, even when I am well, would be fatal. I've only just sketched in the outline of my success in London, and one ought to arrive in New York ready-made as a famous and important Artist.* Me: *But Mother and I didn't think of going to New York. We thought we'd sail straight to New Orleans—if we could: or to Havana. And then go west to Arizona.* The poor boy looked at me in such distress. *But Loulina darling, do you mean you want to leave me in the lurch for the winter season? You can't mean it. We're just getting on so splendidly, really!*—I was surprised at the depth of feeling in his voice: how tremendously his career as an artist—a popular artist— matters to him. I can never believe it.—You know, Mother, you and I feel alike about daubing paint on canvas: every possible daub that can be daubed has already been done, so people ought to leave off. Rico is so shrewd. I always think he's got his tongue in his cheek, and I'm always staggered once more to find that he takes it absolutely seriously. His career! The Modern British Society of Painters: perhaps even the Royal Academy! Those people we see in London, and those portraits Rico does! He may even be a second László, or a thirteenth Orpen, and die happy! Oh! Mother! How can it really matter to *anybody*!

"But I was really rather upset, when I realised how his heart was fixed on his career, and that I might be spoiling everything for him. So I went away to think about it. And then I realised how unpopular you are, and how unpopular I shall be myself, in a little while. A sort of hatred for people has come over me. I hate their ways and their bunk, and I feel like kicking them in the face, as St. Mawr did that young man. Not that I should ever do it. And I don't think I should ever have made my final announcement to Rico, if he hadn't been such a beautiful pig in clover, here at Corrabach Hall. He has known the Manbys all his life, they and he are sections of one engine. He would be far happier with Flora: or I won't say happier, because there is something in him which rebels: but he would on the whole fit much better. I myself am at the end of my limit, and beyond it. I can't 'mix' any more, and I refuse to. I feel like a bit of eggshell in the mayonnaise: the only thing is to take it out, you can't beat it in. I *know* I shall cause a fiasco, even in Rico's career, if I stay. I shall go on being rude and hateful to people as I am at Corrabach, and Rico will lose all his nerve.

"So I have told him. I said this evening, when no-one was about: *Rico dear, listen to me seriously. I can't stand these people. If you ask me to endure another week of them, I shall either become ill, or insult them, as mother does. And I don't want to do either.* Rico: *But darling, isn't everybody perfect to you!* Me: *I tell you, I shall just make a break, like St. Mawr, if I don't get out. I simply can't stand people.*—The poor darling, his face goes so blank and anxious. He knows what I mean, because, except that they tickle his vanity all the time, he hates them as much as I do. But his vanity is the chief thing to him. He: *Lou darling, can't you wait till I get up, and we can go away to the Tyrol or somewhere for a spell?* Me: *Won't you come with me to America, to the South-West? I believe it's marvellous country.*—I saw his face switch into hostility; quite vicious. He: *Are you so keen on spoiling everything for me? Is that what I married you for? Do you do it deliberately?* Me: *Everything is already spoilt for me. I tell you I can't stand people, your Floras and your Aspasias, and your forthcoming young Englishmen. After all, I am an American, like mother, and I've got to go back.* He: *Really! And am I to come along as part of the luggage? Labelled Cabin!* Me: *You do as you wish, Rico.* He: *I wish to God you did as you wished, Lou dear. I'm afraid you do as Mrs Witt wishes. I always heard that the holiest thing in the world was a mother.* Me: *No dear, it's just that I can't stand people.* He (with a snarl): *And I suppose I'm lumped in as* PEOPLE! And when he'd said it, it was true. We neither of us said anything for a time. Then he said, calculating: *Very well, dear! You take a trip to the land of stars and stripes, and I'll stay here and go on with my work. And when you've seen enough of their stars and tasted enough of their stripes, you can come back and take your place again with me.*—We left it at that.

"You and I are supposed to have important business connected with our estates in Texas—it sounds so well—so we are making a hurried trip to the States, as they call them. I shall leave for London early next week—"

Mrs Witt read this long letter with satisfaction. She herself had one strange craving: to get back to America. It was not that she idealised her native country: she was a tartar of restlessness there, quite as much as in Europe. It was not that she expected to arrive at any blessed abiding place. No, in America she would go on fuming and chafing the same. But at least she would be in America, in her own country. And that was what she wanted.

She picked up the sheet of poor paper, that had been folded in Lou's letter. It was the letter from Lewis, quite nicely written. "Lady Carrington, I write to tell you and Sir Henry that I think I better quit your service, as it would be more comfortable all round. If you will write and tell me what you want me to do with St. Mawr, I will do whatever you tell me. With kind regards to Lady Carrington and Sir Henry, I remain, Your obedient servant, Morgan Lewis."

Mrs Witt put the letter aside, and sat looking out of the window. She felt, strangely, as if already her soul had gone away from her actual surroundings. She was there, in Oxfordshire, in the body, but her spirit had departed elsewhere. A listlessness was upon her. It was with an effort she roused herself, to write to her lawyer in London, to get her release from her English obligations. Then she wrote to the London hotel.

For the first time in her life, she wished she had a maid, to do little things for her. All her life, she had had too much energy to endure anyone hanging round her, personally. Now she gave up. Her wrists seemed numb, as if the power in her were switched off.

When she went down, they said Lewis had asked to speak to her. She had hardly seen him since they had arrived at Merriton.

"I've had a letter from Lady Carrington, Mam. She says will I take St. Mawr to London and wait for her there. But she says I am to come to you, Mam, for definite orders."

"Very well, Lewis. I shall be going to London in a few days' time. You arrange for St. Mawr to go up one day this week, and you will take him to the Mews. Come to me for anything you want. And don't talk of leaving my daughter. We want you to go with St. Mawr to America, with us and Phoenix."

"And your horse, Mam?"

"I shall leave him here at Merriton. I shall give him to Miss Atherton."

"Very good Mam!"

"Dear Daughter: I shall be in my old quarters in Mayfair next Saturday, calling the same day at your house to see if everything is ready for you. Lewis has fixed up with the railway: he goes to town tomorrow. The reason of his letter was that I had asked him if he would care to marry me, and he turned me down with emphasis. But I will tell you about it. You and I are the scribe and the Pharisee; I never could write a letter, and you could never leave off—"

"Dearest Mother: I smelt something rash, but I know it's no use saying: How *could* you? I only wonder, though, that you should think of marriage. You know, dear, I ache in every fibre to be left alone, from all that sort of thing. I feel all bruises, like one who has been assassinated. I do so understand why Jesus said: *Noli me tangere*. Touch me not, I am not yet ascended unto the Father. Everything had hurt him so much, wearied him so beyond endurance, he felt he could not bear one little human touch on his body. I am like that. I can hardly bear even Elena to hand me a dress. As for a man—and marriage—ah no! *Noli me tangere, homine*! I am not yet ascended unto the Father. Oh, leave me alone, leave me alone! That is all my cry to all the world.

"Curiously, I feel that Phoenix understands what I feel. He leaves me so understandingly alone, he almost gives me my sheath of aloneness: or at least, he protects me in my sheath. I am grateful for him.

"Whereas Rico feels my aloneness as a sort of shame to himself. He wants at least a blinding *pretence* of intimacy. Ah intimacy! The thought of it fills me with aches, and the pretence of it exhausts me beyond myself.

"Yes, I long to go away to the west, to be away from the world like one dead and in another life, in a valley that life has not yet entered.

"Rico asked me: What are you doing with St. Mawr? When I said we were taking him with us, he said: *Oh, the Corpus delicti*! Whether that means anything I don't know. But he has grown sarcastic beyond my depth.

"I shall see you tomorrow—"

Lou arrived in town, at the dead end of August, with her maid and Phoenix. How wonderful it seemed, to have London empty of all her set: her own little house to herself, with just the housekeeper and her own maid. The fact of being alone in those surroundings was so wonderful. It made the surroundings themselves seem all the more ghostly. Everything that had been actual to her was turning ghostly: even her little drawing-room was the ghost of a room, belonging to the dead people who had known it, or to all the dead generations that had brought such a room into being, evolved it out of their quaint domestic desires. And now, in herself, those desires were suddenly spent: gone out like a lamp that suddenly dies. And then she saw her pale, delicate room with its little green agate bowl and its two little porcelain birds and its soft, roundish chairs, turned into something ghostly, like a room set out in a museum. She felt like fastening little labels on the furniture: *Lady Louise Carrington Lounge Chair, Last used August 1923*. Not for the benefit of posterity: but to remove her own self into another world, another realm of existence.

"My house, my house, my house, how can I ever have taken so much pains about it!" she kept saying to herself. It was like one of her old hats, suddenly discovered neatly put away in an old hatbox. And what a horror: an old "fashionable" hat!

Lewis came to see her, and he sat there in one of her delicate mauve chairs, with his feet on a delicate old carpet from Turkestan, and she just wondered. He wore his leather gaiters and khaki breeches as usual, and a faded blue shirt. But his beard and hair were trimmed, he was tidy. There was a certain fineness of contour about him, a certain subtle gleam, which made him seem, apart from his rough boots, not at all gross, or coarse, in that setting of rather silky, oriental furnishings. Rather he made the Asiatic, sensuous exquisiteness of her old rugs and her old white Chinese figures seem a weariness. Beauty! What was beauty, she asked herself? The Oriental exquisiteness seemed to her all like dead flowers whose hour had come, to be thrown away.

Lou could understand her mother's wanting, for a moment, to marry him. His detachedness and his acceptance of something in destiny which people cannot accept. Right in the middle of him he accepted something from destiny, that gave him a quality of eternity. He did not care about persons, people, even events. In his own odd way, he was an aristocrat, inaccessible in his aristocracy. But it was the aristocracy of the invisible powers, the greater influences, nothing to do with human society.

"You don't really want to leave St. Mawr, do you?" Lou asked him. "You don't really want to quit, as you said?"

He looked at her steadily, from his pale grey eyes, without answering, not knowing what to say.

"Mother told me what she said to you.—But she doesn't mind, she says you are entirely within your rights. She has a real regard for you. But we mustn't let our regards run us into actions which are beyond our scope, must we? That makes everything unreal. But you will come with us to America with St. Mawr, won't you? We depend on you."

"I don't want to be uncomfortable," he said.

"Don't be," she smiled. "I myself hate unreal situations—I feel I can't stand them anymore. And most marriages are unreal situations. But apart from anything exaggerated, you like being with mother and me, don't you?"

"Yes, I do. I like Mrs Witt as well. But not—"

"I know. There won't be any more of that—"

"You see, Lady Carrington," he said, with a little heat, "I'm not by nature a marrying man. And I should feel I was selling myself."

"Quite!—Why do you think you are not a marrying man, though?"

"Me! I don't feel myself after I've been with women." He spoke in a low tone looking down at his hands. "I feel messed up. I'm better to keep to myself.—Because—" and here he looked up with a flare in his eyes: "women—they only want to make you give in to them, so that they feel almighty, and you feel small."

"Don't you like feeling small?" Lou smiled. "And don't you want to make them give in to you?"

"Not me," he said. "I don't want nothing. Nothing, I want."

"Poor mother!" said Lou. "She thinks if she feels moved by a man, it must result in marriage—or that kind of thing. Surely she makes a mistake. I think you and Phoenix and mother and I might live somewhere in a far-away wild place, and make a good life: so long as we didn't begin to mix up marriage, or love or that sort of thing into it. It seems to me men and women have really hurt one another so much, nowadays, that they had better stay apart till they have learned to be gentle with one another again. Not all this forced passion and destructive philandering. Men and women should stay apart, till their hearts grow gentle towards one another again. Now, it's only each one fighting for his own—or her own—underneath the cover of tenderness."

"*Dear*!—*darling*!—*Yes my love*!" mocked Lewis, with a faint smile of amused contempt.

"Exactly. People always say *dearest*! when they hate each other most."

Lewis nodded, looking at her with a sudden sombre gloom in his eyes. A queer bitterness showed on his mouth. But even then, he was so still and remote.

The housekeeper came and announced The Honorable Laura Ridley. This was like a blow in the face to Lou. She rose hurriedly—and Lewis rose, moving to the door.

"Don't go please, Lewis," said Lou—and then Laura Ridley appeared in the doorway. She was a woman a few years older than Lou, but she looked younger. She might have been a shy girl of twenty-two, with her fresh complexion, her hesitant manner, her round, startled brown eyes, her bobbed hair.

"Hello!" said the newcomer. "Imagine your being back! I saw you in Paddington."

Those sharp eyes would see everything.

"I thought everyone was out of town," said Lou. "This is Mr Lewis."

Laura gave him a little nod, then sat on the edge of her chair.

"No," she said. "I did go to Ireland to my people, but I came back. I prefer London when I can be more or less alone in it. I thought I'd just run in for a moment, before you're gone again.—Scotland, isn't it?"

"No, Mother and I are going to America."

"America! Oh, I thought it was Scotland."

"It was. But we have suddenly to go to America."

"I see!—And what about Rico?"

"He is staying on in Shropshire. Didn't you hear of his accident?"
Lou told about it briefly.

"But how awful!" said Laura. "But there! I knew it! I had a premonition, when I saw that horse. We had a horse that killed a man. Then my father got rid of it. But ours was a mare, that one. Yours is a boy."

"A full grown man I'm afraid."

"Yes of course, I remember.—But how awful! I suppose you won't ride in the Row. The awful people that ride there nowadays, anyhow! Oh, aren't they awful! Aren't people monstrous, really! My word, when I see the horses crossing Hyde Park Corner, on a wet day, and coming down smash on those slippery stones, giving their riders a fractured skull!—No joke!"

She enquired details of Rico.

"Oh, I suppose I shall see him when he gets back," she said. "But I'm sorry you are going. I shall miss you, I'm afraid. Though you won't be staying long in America. No one stays there longer than they can help."

"I think the winter through, at least," said Lou.

"Oh, all the winter! So long? I'm sorry to hear *that*. You're one of the few, very few people one can talk *really* simply with. Extraordinary, isn't it, how few really simple people there are! And they get fewer and fewer. I stayed a fortnight with my people, and a week of that I was in bed. It was really horrible. They really try to take the life out of one, *really*! Just because one won't be as they are, and play their game. I simply refused, and came away."

"But you can't cut yourself off altogether," said Lou.

"No, I suppose not. One has to see somebody. Luckily one has a few artists for friends. They're the only real People, anyhow—" She glanced round inquisitively at Lewis, and said, with a slight, impertinent elvish smile on her virgin face:

"Are you an artist?"

"No Mam!" he said. "I'm a groom."

"Oh, I see!" she looked him up and down.

"Lewis is St. Mawr's master," said Lou.

"Oh, the horse! the terrible horse!" She paused a moment. Then again she turned to Lewis with that faint smile, slightly condescending, slightly impertinent, slightly flirtatious.

"Aren't you afraid of him?" she asked.

"No Mam."

"Aren't you *really*!—And can you always master him?"

"Mostly. He knows me."

"Yes! I suppose that's it."—She looked him up and down again, then turned away to Lou.

"What have you been painting lately?" said Lou. Laura was not a bad painter.

"Oh, hardly anything. I haven't been able to get on at all. This is one of my bad intervals."

Here Lewis rose, and looked at Lou.

"All right," she said. "Come in after lunch, and we'll finish those arrangements."

Laura gazed after the man, as he dived out of the room, as if her eyes were gimlets that could bore into his secret.

In the course of the conversation she said:

"What a curious little man that was!"

"Which?"

"The groom who was here just now. *Very* curious! Such peculiar eyes. I shouldn't wonder if he had psychic powers."

"What sort of psychic powers?" said Lou.

"Could *see* things.—And hypnotic too. He might have hypnotic powers."

"What makes you think so?"

"He gives me that sort of feeling. Very curious! Probably he hypnotises the horse.—Are you leaving the horse here, by the way, in stable?"

"No, taking him to America."

"Taking him to America! How extraordinary!"

"It's mother's idea. She thinks he might be valuable as a stock horse on a ranch. You know we still have interest in a ranch in Texas."

"Oh, I see! Yes, probably he'd be very valuable, to improve the breed of the horses over there.—My father has some very lovely hunters. Isn't it disgraceful, he would never let me ride!"

"Why?"

"Because we girls weren't important, in his opinion.—So you're taking the horse to America! With the little man?"

"Yes, St. Mawr will hardly behave without him."

"I see!—I see—ee—ee! Just you and Mrs Witt and the little man. I'm sure you'll find he has psychic powers."

"I'm afraid I'm not so good at finding things out," said Lou.

"Aren't you? No, I suppose not. I am. I have a flair. I sort of *smell* things.—Then the horse is already here, is he? When do you think you'll sail?"

"Mother is finding a merchant boat that will go to Galveston, Texas, and take us along with the horse. She knows people who will find the right thing. But it takes time."

"What a much nicer way to travel, than on one of those great liners! Oh, how awful they are! So vulgar! Floating palaces they call them! My word, the people inside the palaces!—Yes, I should say that would be a much pleasanter way of travelling: on a cargo boat."

Laura wanted to go down to the Mews to see St. Mawr. The two women went together.

St. Mawr stood in his box, bright and tense as usual.

"Yes!" said Laura Ridley, with a slight hiss, "Yes! Isn't he beautiful. Such very perfect legs!"—She eyed him round with those gimlet-sharp eyes of hers. "Almost a pity to let him go out of

145

England. We need some of his perfect *bone*, I feel.—But his eye! Hasn't he got a look in it, my word!"

"I can never see that he looks wicked," said Lou.

"Can't you!"—Laura had a slight hiss in her speech, a sort of aristocratic decision in her enunciation, that got on Lou's nerves.—"He looks wicked to me!"

"He's not *mean*," said Lou. "He'd never do anything mean to you."

"Oh, mean! I daresay not. No! I'll grant him that, he gives fair warning. His eye says *Beware*!—But isn't he a beauty, *isn't* he!" Lou could feel the peculiar reverence for St. Mawr's breeding, his show qualities. Herself, all she cared about was the horse himself, his real nature. "Isn't it extraordinary," Laura continued, "that you never get a *really*, perfectly satisfactory animal! There's always something wrong. And in men too. Isn't it curious? there's always something—something wrong—or something missing. Why is it?"

"I don't know," said Lou. She felt unable to cope with any more. And she was glad when Laura left her.

The days passed slowly, quietly, London almost empty of Lou's acquaintances. Mrs Witt was busy getting all sorts of papers and permits: such a fuss! The battle light was still in her eye. But about her nose was a dusky, pinched look that made Lou wonder.

Both women wanted to be gone: they felt they had already flown in spirit, and it was weary, having the body left behind.

At last all was ready: they only awaited the telegram to say when their cargo-boat would sail. Trunks stood there packed, like great stones locked for ever. The Westminster house seemed already a shell. Rico wrote and telegraphed, tenderly, but there was a sense of relentless effort in it all, rather than of any real tenderness. He had taken his position.

Then the telegram came, the boat was ready to sail.

"There now!" said Mrs Witt, as if it had been a sentence of death.

"Why do you look like that, mother?"

"I feel I haven't an ounce of energy left in my body."

"But how queer, for you, mother. Do you think you are ill?"

"No Louise. I just feel that way: as if I hadn't an ounce of energy left in my body."

"You'll feel yourself again, once you are away."

"Maybe I shall."

After all, it was only a matter of telephoning. The hotel and the railway porters and taxi-men would do the rest.

It was a grey, cloudy day, cold even. Mother and daughter sat in a cold first-class carriage and watched the little, Hampshire country-side go past: little, old, unreal it seemed to them both, and passing away like a dream whose edges only are in consciousness. Autumn! Was this autumn? Were these trees, fields, villages? It seemed but the dim, dissolving edges of a dream, without inward substance.

At Southampton it was raining: and just a chaos, till they stepped on to a clean boat, and were received by a clean young captain, quite sympathetic, and quite a gentleman. Mrs Witt, however, hardly looked at him, but went down to her cabin and lay down in her bunk.

There, lying concealed, she felt the engines start, she knew the voyage had begun. But she lay still. She saw the clouds and the rain, and refused to be disturbed.

Lou had lunch with the young captain, and she felt she ought to be flirty. The young man was so polite and attentive. And she wished so much she were alone.

Afterwards, she sat on deck and saw the Isle of Wight pass shadowily, in a misty rain. She didn't know it was the Isle of Wight. To her, it was just the lowest bit of the British Isles. She saw it fading away: and with it, her life, going like a clot of shadow in a mist of nothingness. She had no feelings about it, none: neither about Rico, nor her London house, nor anything. All passing in a grey curtain of rainy drizzle, like a death, and she, with not a feeling left.

They entered the Channel, and felt the slow heave of the sea. And soon, the clouds broke in a little wind. The sky began to clear. By mid-afternoon it was blue summer, on the blue, running waters of the Channel. And soon, the ship steering for Santander, there was the coast of France, the rocks twinkling like some magic world.

The magic world! And back of it, that post-war Paris, which Lou knew only too well, and which depressed her so thoroughly. Or that post-war Monte Carlo, the Riviera still more depressing even than Paris. No no, one must not land, even on magic coasts. Else you found yourself in a railway station and a "centre of civilisation" in five minutes.

Mrs Witt hated the sea, and stayed, as a rule, practically the whole time of the crossing, in her bunk. There she was now, silent, shut up like a steel trap, as in her tomb. She did not even read. Just lay and stared at the passing sky. And the only thing to do was to leave her alone.

Lewis and Phoenix hung on the rail, and watched everything. Or they went down to see St. Mawr. Or they stood talking in the doorway of the wireless operator's cabin. Lou begged the Captain to give them jobs to do.

The queer, transitory, unreal feeling, as the ship crossed the great, heavy Atlantic. It was rather bad weather. And Lou felt, as she had felt before, that this grey, wolf-like, cold-blooded Ocean hated men and their ships and their smoky passage. Heavy grey waves, a low-sagging sky: rain: yellow, weird evenings with snatches of sun: so it went on. Till they got way south, into the westward-running stream. Then they began to get blue weather and blue water.

To go south! Always to go south, away from the arctic horror as far as possible! That was Lou's instinct. To go out of the clutch of greyness and low skies, of seeping rain, and of slow, blanketing snow. Never again to see the mud and rain and snow of a northern winter, nor to feel the idealistic, Christianised tension of the now irreligious north.

As they neared Havana, and the water sparkled at night with phosphorus, and the flying-fishes came like drops of bright water, sailing out of the massive-slippery waves, Mrs Witt emerged once more. She still had that shut-up, deathly look on her face. But she prowled round the deck, and manifested at least a little interest in affairs not her own. Here at sea, she hardly remembered the existence of St. Mawr or Lewis or Phoenix. She was not very deeply aware even of Lou's existence.—But of course, it would all come back, once they were on land.

They sailed in hot sunshine out of a blue, blue sea, past the castle into the harbour at Havana. There was a lot of shipping: and this was already America. Mrs Witt had herself and Lou put ashore immediately. They took a motor-car and drove at once to the great boulevard that is the centre of Havana. Here they saw a long rank of motor-cars, all drawn up ready to take a couple of hundred American tourists for one more tour. There were the tourists, all with badges in their coats, lest they should get lost.

"They get so drunk by night," said the driver in Spanish, "that the policemen find them lying in the road—turn them over, see the badge—and, hup!—carry them to their hotel." He grinned sardonically.

Lou and her mother lunched at the Hotel d'Angleterre, and Mrs Witt watched transfixed while a couple of her countrymen, a stout successful man and his wife, lunched abroad. They had cocktails—then lobster—and a bottle of hock—then a bottle of champagne—then a half-bottle of port—And Mrs Witt rose in haste as the liqueurs came. For that successful man and his wife had gone on imbibing with a sort of fixed and deliberate will, apparently tasting nothing, but saying to themselves: Now we're drinking Rhine wine! Now we're drinking 1912 champagne. Yah, Prohibition! Thou canst not put it over me.—Their complexions became more and more lurid. Mrs Witt fled, fearing a Havana débâcle. But she said nothing.

In the afternoon, they motored into the country, to see the great brewery gardens, the new villa suburb, and through the lanes past the old, decaying plantations with palm-trees. In one lane they met the fifty motor-cars with the two hundred tourists all with badges on their chests and self-satisfaction on their faces. Mrs Witt watched in grim silence.

"Plus ça change, plus c'est la même chose," said Lou, with a wicked little smile. "On n'est pas mieux ici, mother."

"I know it," said Mrs Witt.

The hotels by the sea were all shut up: it was not yet the "season." Not till November. And then!—Why then Havana would be an American city, in full leaf of green dollar bills. The green leaf of American prosperity shedding itself recklessly, from every roaming sprig of a tourist, over this city of sunshine and alcohol. Green leaves unfolded in Pittsburgh and Chicago, showering in winter downfall in Havana.

Mother and daughter drank tea in a corner of the Hotel d'Angleterre once more, and returned to the ferry.

The Gulf of Mexico was blue and rippling, with the phantom of islands on the south. Great porpoises rolled and leaped, running in front of the ship in the clear water, diving, travelling in perfect motion, straight, with the tip of the ship touching the tip of their tails, then rolling over, cork-screwing and showing their bellies as they went. Marvellous! The marvellous beauty and fascination of natural wild things! The horror of man's unnatural life, his heaped-up civilisation!

The flying-fishes burst out of the sea in clouds of silvery, transparent motion. Blue above and below, the Gulf seemed a silent, empty, timeless place where man did not really reach. And Lou was again fascinated by the glamour of the universe.

But bump! She and her mother were in a first-class hotel again, calling down the telephone for the bell-boy and ice-water. And soon they were in a Pullman, off towards San Antonio.

It was America, it was Texas. They were at their ranch, on the great level of yellow autumn, with the vast sky above. And after all, from the hot wide sky, and the hot, wide, red earth, there *did* come something new, something not used-up. Lou *did* feel exhilarated.

The Texans were there, tall blonde people, ingenuously cheerful, ingenuously, childishly intimate, as if the fact that you had never seen them before was as nothing compared to the fact that you'd all been living in one room together all your lives, so that nothing was hidden from either of you. The one room being the mere shanty of the world in which we all live. Strange, uninspired cheerfulness, filling, as it were, the blank of complete incomprehension.

And off they set in their motor-cars, chiefly high-legged Fords, rattling away down the red trails between yellow sunflowers or sere grass or dry cotton, away, away into great distances, cheerfully raising the dust of haste. It left Lou in a sort of blank amazement. But it left her amused, not depressed. The old screws of emotion and intimacy that had been screwed down so tightly upon her fell out of their holes, here. The Texan intimacy weighed no more on her than a postage stamp, even if, for the moment, it stuck as close. And there was a certain underneath recklessness, even a stoicism in all the apparently childish people, which left one free. They might appear childish: but they stoically depended on themselves alone, in reality. Not as in England, where every man waited to pour the burden of himself upon you.

St. Mawr arrived safely, a bit bewildered. The Texans eyed him closely, struck silent, as ever, by anything pure-bred and beautiful. He was somehow too beautiful, too perfected, in this great open country. The long-legged Texan horses, with their elaborate saddles, seemed somehow more natural.

Even St. Mawr felt himself strange, as it were naked and singled out, in this rough place. Like a jewel among stones, a pearl before swine, maybe. But the swine were no fools. They knew a pearl from a grain of maize, and a grain of maize from a pearl. And they knew what they wanted. When it was pearls, it was pearls: though chiefly, it was maize. Which shows good sense. They could see St. Mawr's points. Only he needn't draw the point too fine, or it would just not pierce the tough skin of this country.

The ranch-man mounted him—just threw a soft skin over his back, jumped on, and away down the red trail, raising the dust among the tall wild yellow of sunflowers, in the hot wild sun. Then back again in a fume, and the man slipped off.

"He's got the stuff in him, he sure has," said the man.

And the horse seemed pleased with this rough handling. Lewis looked on in wonder, and a little envy.

Lou and her mother stayed a fortnight on the ranch. It was all so queer: so crude, so rough, so easy, so artificially civilised, and so meaningless. Lou could not get over the feeling that it all meant nothing. There were no roots of reality at all. No consciousness below the surface, no meaning in anything save the obvious, the blatantly obvious. It was like life enacted in a mirror. Visually, it was wildly vital. But there was nothing behind it. Or like a cinematograph: flat shapes, exactly like men, but without any substance of reality, rapidly rattling away with talk, emotions, activity, all in the flat, nothing behind it. No deeper consciousness at all.—So it seemed to her.

One moved from dream to dream, from phantasm to phantasm.

But at least, this Texan life, if it had no bowels, no vitals, at least it could not prey on one's own vitals. It was this much better than Europe.

Lewis was silent, and rather piqued. St. Mawr had already made advances to the boss' long-legged, arched-necked, glossy-maned Texan mare. And the boss was pleased.

What a world!

Mrs Witt eyed it all shrewdly. But she failed to participate. Lou was a bit scared at the emptiness of it all, and the queer, phantasmal self-consciousness. Cowboys just as self-conscious as Rico, far more sentimental, inwardly vague and unreal. Cowboys that went after their cows in black Ford motor-cars: and who self-consciously saw Lady Carrington falling to them, as elegant young ladies from the East fall to the noble cowboy of the films, or in Zane Grey. It was all film-psychology.

And at the same time, these boys led a hard, hard life, often dangerous and gruesome. Nevertheless, inwardly they were self-conscious film-heroes. The boss himself, a man over forty, long and lean and with a great deal of stringy energy, showed off before her in a strong silent manner, existing for the time being purely in his imagination of the sort of picture he made to her, the sort of impression he made on her.

So they all were, coloured up like a Zane Grey book-jacket, all of them living in the mirror. The kind of picture they made to somebody else.

And at the same time, with energy, courage, and a stoical grit getting their work done, and putting through what they had to put through.

It left Lou blank with wonder. And in the face of this strange cheerful living in the mirror—a rather cheap mirror at that—England began to seem real to her again.

Then she had to remember herself back in England. And no, oh God, England was not real either, except poisonously.

What was real? What under heaven was real?

Her mother had gone dumb and, as it were, out of range. Phoenix was a bit assured and bouncy, back more or less in his own conditions. Lewis was a bit impressed by the emptiness of everything, the *lack* of concentration. And St. Mawr followed at the heels of the boss' long-legged black Texan mare, almost slavishly.

What, in heaven's name, was one to make of it all?

Soon, she could not stand this sort of living in a film-setting, with the mechanical energy of "making good," that is, making money, to keep the show going. The mystic duty to "make good," meaning to make the ranch pay a laudable interest on the "owners'" investment. Lou herself being one of the owners. And the interest that came to her, from her father's will, being the money she spent to buy St. Mawr and to fit up that house in Westminster. Then also the mystic duty to "feel good." Everybody had to *feel good, fine*! "How are you this morning, Mr Latham?"—"*Fine*! Eh! Don't you feel good out here, eh? Lady Carrington?"—"*Fine*!"—Lou pronounced it with the same ringing conviction. It was Coué all the time!

"Shall we stay here long, mother?" she asked.

"Not a day longer than you want to, Louise. I stay entirely for your sake."

"Then let us go, mother."

They left St. Mawr and Lewis. But Phoenix wanted to come along. So they motored to San Antonio, got into the Pullman, and travelled as far as El Paso. Then they changed to go north. Santa Fe would be at least "easy." And Mrs Witt had acquaintances there.

They found the fiesta over in Santa Fe: Indians, Mexicans, artists had finished their great effort to amuse and attract the tourists. *Welcome Mr Tourist* said a great board on one side of the high-road. And on the other side, a little nearer to town: *Thank You, Mr Tourist*.

"Plus ça change—" Lou began.

"Ça ne change jamais—except for the worse!" said Mrs Witt, like a pistol going off. And Lou held her peace, after she had sighed to herself, and said in her own mind: "*Welcome Also Mrs and Miss Tourist!*"

There was no getting a word out of Mrs Witt, these days. Whereas Phoenix was becoming almost loquacious.

They stayed a while in Santa Fe, in the clean, comfortable, "homely" hotel, where "every room had its bath": a spotless white bath, with very hot water night and day. The tourists and commercial travellers sat in the big hall down below, everybody living in the mirror! And of course, they knew Lady Carrington down to her shoe-soles. And they all expected her to know them down to their shoe-soles. For the only object of the mirror is to reflect images.

For two days mother and daughter ate in the mayonnaise intimacy of the dining-room. Then Mrs Witt struck, and telephoned down every meal-time, for her meal in her room. She got to staying in bed later and later, as on the ship. Lou became uneasy. This was worse than Europe.

Phoenix was still there, as a sort of half-friend, half-servant retainer. He was perfectly happy, roving round among the Mexicans and Indians, talking Spanish all day, and telling about England and his two mistresses, rolling the ball of his own importance.

"I'm afraid we've got Phoenix for life," said Lou.

"Not unless we wish," said Mrs Witt indifferently. And she picked up a novel which she didn't want to read, but which she was going to read.

"What shall we do next, mother?" Lou asked.

"As far as I am concerned, there is no next," said Mrs Witt.

"Come mother! Let's go back to Italy or somewhere, if it's as bad as that."

"Never again, Louise, shall I cross that water. I have come home to die."

"I don't see much home about it—the Gonzalez Hotel in Santa Fe."

"Indeed not! But as good as anywhere else, to die in."

"Oh mother, don't be silly! Shall we look for somewhere where we can be by ourselves?"

"I leave it to you, Louise. I have made my last decision."

"What is that, mother."

"Never, never to make another decision."

"Not even to decide to die?"

"No, not even that."

"Or *not* to die?"

"Not that either."

Mrs Witt shut up like a trap. She refused to rise from her bed that day.

Lou went to consult Phoenix. The result was, the two set out to look at a little ranch that was for sale.

It was autumn, and the loveliest time in the South-West, where there is no spring, snow blowing into the hot lap of summer: and no real summer, hail falling in thick ice, from the thunderstorms: and even no very definite winter, hot sun melting the snow and giving an impression of spring at any time. But autumn there is, when the winds of the desert are almost still, and the mountains fume no clouds. But morning comes cold and delicate, upon the wild sunflowers and the puffing, yellow-flowered greasewood. For the desert blooms in autumn. In spring it is grey ash all the time, and only the strong breath of the summer sun, and the heavy splashing of thunder rain succeed at last, by September, in blowing it into soft, puffy yellow fire.

It was such a delicate morning when Lou drove out with Phoenix towards the mountains, to look at this ranch that a Mexican wanted to sell. For the brief moment, the high mountains had lost their snow: it would be back again in a fortnight: and stood dim and delicate with autumn haze. The desert stretched away pale, as pale as the sky, but silvery and sere, with hummock-mounds of shadow, and long wings of shadow, like the reflection of some great bird. The same eagle-shadows came like rude paintings of the outstretched bird, upon the mountains, where the aspens were turning yellow. For the moment, the brief moment, the great desert-and-mountain landscape had lost its certain cruelty, and looked tender, dreamy. And many, many birds were flickering around.

Lou and Phoenix bumped and hesitated over a long trail: then wound down into a deep canyon: and then the car began to climb, climb, climb, in steep rushes, and in long heart-breaking, uneven pulls. The road was bad, and driving was no joke. But it was the sort of road Phoenix was used to. He sat impassive and watchful, and kept on, till his engine boiled. He was *himself* in this country: impassive, detached, self-satisfied and silently assertive. Guarding himself at every moment, but, on his guard, sure of himself. Seeing no difference at all between Lou or Mrs Witt and himself, except that they had money and he had none, while he had a native importance which they lacked. He depended on them for money, they on him for the power to live out here in the West. Intimately, he was as good as they. Money was their only advantage.

As Lou sat beside him in the front seat of the car, where it bumped less than behind, she felt this. She felt a peculiar tough-necked arrogance in him, as if he were asserting himself to put something over her. He wanted her to allow him to make advances to her, to allow him to suggest that he should be her lover. And then, finally, she would marry him, and he would be on the same footing as she and her mother.

In return, he would look after her, and give her his support and countenance, as a man, and stand between her and the world. In this sense, he would be faithful to her, and loyal. But as far as other women went, Mexican women or Indian women: why, that was none of her business. His marrying her would be a pact between two aliens, on behalf of one another, and he would keep his part of it all right. But himself, as a private man and a predative alien-blooded male, this had nothing to do with her. It didn't enter into her scope and count. She was one of these nervous white women with lots of money. She was very nice too. But as a *squaw*—as a real woman in a shawl whom a man went after for the pleasure of the night—why, she hardly counted. One of these white women who talk clever and know things like a man. She could hardly expect a half-savage male to acknowledge her as his female counterpart.—No! She had the bucks! And she had all the paraphernalia of the white man's civilisation, which a savage can play with and so escape his own hollow boredom. But his own real female counterpart?—Phoenix would just have shrugged his shoulders, and thought the question not worth answering. How could there be any answer in *her*, to the phallic male in him? Couldn't! Yet it would flatter his vanity and his self-esteem immensely, to possess her. That would be possessing the very clue to the white man's overwhelming world. And if she would let him possess her, he would be absolutely loyal to her, as far as affairs and appearances went. Only, the aboriginal phallic male in him simply couldn't recognise her as a woman at all. In this respect, she didn't exist. It needed the shawled Indian or Mexican women, with their squeaky, plaintive voices, their shuffling, watery humility, and the dark glances of their big, knowing eyes. When an Indian woman looked at him from under her black fringe, with dark, half-secretive suggestion in her big eyes: and when she stood before him hugged in her shawl, in such apparently complete quiescent humility: and when she spoke to him in her mousey squeak of a high, plaintive voice, as if it were difficult for her female bashfulness even to emit so much sound: and when she shuffled away with her legs wide apart, because of her wide-topped, white, high buckskin boots with tiny white feet, and her dark-knotted hair so full of hard, yet subtle lure: and when he remembered the almost watery softness of the Indian woman's dark, warm flesh: then he was a male, an old, secretive, rat-like male. But before Lou's straightforwardness and utter sexual incompetence, he just stood in contempt. And to him, even a French cocotte was utterly devoid of the right sort of sex. She couldn't really move him. She couldn't satisfy the furtiveness in him. He needed this plaintive, squeaky, dark-fringed Indian quality. Something furtive and soft and rat-like, really to rouse him.

Nevertheless he was ready to trade his sex, which, in his opinion, every white woman was secretly pining for, for the white woman's money and social privileges. In the daytime, all the thrill and excitement of the white man's motor-cars and moving-pictures and ice-cream sodas and so forth. In the night, the soft, watery-soft warmth of an Indian or half-Indian woman. This was Phoenix's idea of life for himself.

Meanwhile, if a white woman gave him the privileges of the white man's world, he would do his duty by her as far as all that went.

Lou, sitting very very still beside him as he drove the car: he was not a very good driver, not quick and marvellous as some white men are, particularly some French chauffeurs she had known, but usually a little behind-hand in his movements: she knew more or less all that he felt. More or less she divined as a woman does. Even from a certain rather assured stupidity of his shoulders, and a certain rather stupid assertiveness of his knees, she knew him.

But she did not judge him too harshly. Somewhere deep, deep in herself she knew she too was at fault. And this made her sometimes inclined to humble herself, as a woman, before the furtive assertiveness of this underground, "knowing" savage. He was so different from Rico.

Yet, after all, *was* he? In his rootlessness, his drifting, his real meaninglessness, was he different from Rico? And his childish, spellbound absorption in the motor-car, or in the moving-pictures, or in an ice-cream soda—was it very different from Rico? Anyhow, was it really any better? Pleasanter, perhaps, to a woman, because of the childishness of it.

The same with his opinion of himself as a sexual male! So childish, really, it was almost thrilling to a woman. But then, so stupid also, with that furtive lurking in holes and imagining it could not be detected. He imagined he kept himself dark, in his sexual rat-holes. He imagined he was not detected!

No no, Lou was not such a fool as she looked, in his eyes anyhow. She knew what she wanted. She wanted relief from the nervous tension and irritation of her life, she wanted to escape from the friction which is the whole stimulus in modern social life. She wanted to be still: only that, to be very, very still, and recover her own soul.

When Phoenix presumed she was looking for some secretly sexual male such as himself, he was ridiculously mistaken. Even the illusion of the beautiful St. Mawr was gone. And Phoenix, roaming round like a sexual rat in promiscuous back yards!—*Merci, mon cher*! For that was all he was: a sexual rat in the great barn-yard of man's habitat, looking for female rats!

Merci, mon cher! You are had.

Nevertheless, in his very mistakenness, he was a relief to her. His mistake was amusing rather than impressive. And the fact that one half of his intelligence was a complete dark blank, that too was a relief.

Strictly, and perhaps in the best sense, he was a servant. His very unconsciousness and his very limitation served as a shelter, as one shelters within the limitations of four walls. The very decided limits to his intelligence were a shelter to her. They made her feel safe.

But that feeling of safety did not deceive her. It was the feeling one derived from having a *true* servant attached to one, a man whose psychic limitations left him incapable of anything but service, and whose strong flow of natural life, at the same time, made him *need* to serve.

And Lou, sitting there so very still and frail, yet self-contained, had not lived for nothing. She no longer wanted to fool herself. She had no desire at all to fool herself into thinking that a Phoenix might be a husband and a mate. No desire that way at all. His obtuseness was a servant's obtuseness. She was grateful to him for serving, and she paid him a wage. Moreover, she provided him with something to do, to occupy his life. In a sense, she gave him his life, and rescued him from his own boredom. It was a balance.

He did not know what she was thinking. There was a certain physical sympathy between them. His obtuseness made him think it was also a sexual sympathy.

"It's a nice trip, you and me!" he said suddenly, turning and looking her in the eyes with an excited look, and ending on a foolish little laugh.

She realised that she should have sat in the back seat.

"But it's a bad road," she said. "Hadn't you better stop and put the sides of the hood up, your engine is boiling."

He looked away with a quick switch of interest to the red thermometer in front of his machine.

"She's boiling," he said, stopping, and getting out with a quick alacrity to go to look at the engine.

Lou got out also, and went to the back seat, shutting the door decisively.

"I think I'll ride at the back," she said, "it gets so frightfully hot in front, when the engine heats up.—Do you think she needs some water? Have you got some in the canteen?"

"She's full," he said, peering into the steaming valve.

"You can run a bit out, if you think there's any need. I wonder if it's much further!"

"*Quién sabe*!" said he, slightly impertinent.

She relapsed into her own stillness. She realised how careful, how very careful she must be of relaxing into sympathy, and reposing, as it were, on Phoenix. He would read it as a sexual appeal. Perhaps he couldn't help it. She had only herself to blame. He was obtuse, as a man and a savage. He had only one interpretation, sex, for any woman's approach to him.

And she knew, with the last clear knowledge of weary disillusion, that she did not want to be mixed up in Phoenix's sexual promiscuities. The very thought was an insult to her. The crude, clumsy servant-male: no no, not that. He was a good fellow, a very good fellow, as far as he went. But he fell far short of physical intimacy.

"No no," she said to herself, "I was wrong to ride in the front seat with him. I must sit alone, just alone. Because sex, mere sex, is repellant to me. I will never prostitute myself again. Unless something touches my very spirit, the very quick of me, I will stay alone, just alone. Alone, and give myself only to the unseen presences, serve only the other, unseen presences."

She understood now the meaning of the Vestal Virgins, the Virgins of the holy fire in the old temples. They were symbolic of herself, of woman weary of the embrace of incompetent men, weary, weary, weary of all that, turning to the unseen gods, the unseen spirits, the hidden fire, and devoting herself to that, and that alone. Receiving thence her pacification and her fulfilment.

Not these little, incompetent, childish self-opinionated men! Not these to touch her. She watched Phoenix's rather stupid shoulders, as he drove the car on between the piñon trees and the cedars of the narrow mesa ridge, to the mountain foot. He was a good fellow. But let him run among women of his own sort. Something was beyond him. And this something must remain beyond him, never allow itself to come within his reach. Otherwise he would paw it and mess it up, and be as miserable as a child that has broken its father's watch.

No no! She had loved an American, and lived with him for a fortnight. She had had a long, intimate friendship with an Italian. Perhaps it was love on his part. And she had yielded to him. Then her love and marriage to Rico.

And what of it all? Nothing. It was almost nothing. It was as if only the outside of herself, her top layers, were human. This inveigled her into intimacies. As soon as the intimacy penetrated, or attempted to penetrate inside her, it was a disaster. Just a humiliation and a breaking down.

Within these outer layers of herself lay the successive inner sanctuaries of herself. And these were inviolable. She accepted it.

"I am not a marrying woman," she said to herself. "I am not a lover nor a mistress nor a wife. It is no good. Love can't really come into me from the outside, and I can never, never mate with any man, since the mystic new man will never come to me. No no, let me know myself and my rôle. I am one of the eternal Virgins, serving the eternal fire. My dealings with men have only broken my stillness and messed up my doorways. It has been my own fault. I ought to stay virgin and still, very, very still, and serve the most perfect service. I want my temple and my loneliness and my Apollo mystery of the inner fire. And with men, only the delicate, subtler, more remote relations. No coming near. A coming near only breaks the delicate veils, and broken veils, like broken flowers, only lead to rottenness."

She felt a great peace inside herself as she made this realisation. And a thankfulness. Because, after all, it seemed to her that the hidden fire was alive and burning in this sky, over the desert, in the mountains. She felt a certain latent holiness in the very atmosphere, a young, spring-fire of latent holiness, such as she had never felt in Europe, or in the East. "For me," she said, as she looked away at the mountains in shadow and the pale-warm desert beneath, with wings of shadow upon it: "For me, this place is sacred. It is blessed."

But as she watched Phoenix: as she remembered the motor-cars and tourists, and the rather dreary Mexicans of Santa Fe, and the lurking, invidious Indians, with something of a rat-like secretiveness and defeatedness in their bearing, she realised that the latent fire of the vast landscape struggled under a great weight of dirt-like inertia. She had to mind the dirt, most carefully and vividly avoid it and keep it away from her, here in this place that at last seemed sacred to her.

The motor-car climbed up, past the tall pine-trees, to the foot of the mountains, and came at last to a wire gate, where nothing was to be expected. Phoenix opened the gate, and they drove on, through more trees, into a clearing where dried up bean-plants were yellow.

"This man got no water for his beans," said Phoenix. "Not got much beans this year."

They climbed slowly up the incline, through more pine-trees, and out into another clearing, where a couple of horses were grazing. And there they saw the ranch itself, little low cabins with patched roofs, under a few pine-trees, and facing the long twelve-acre clearing, or field, where the michaelmas daisies were purple mist, and spangled with clumps of yellow flowers.

"Not got no alfalfa here neither!" said Phoenix, as the car waded past the flowers. "Must be a dry place, up here. Got no water, sure they haven't."

Yet it was the place Lou wanted. In an instant, her heart sprang to it. The instant the car stopped, and she saw the two cabins inside the rickety fence, the rather broken corral beyond, and behind all, tall, blue balsam pines, the round hills, the solid uprise of the mountain flank: and getting down, she looked across the purple and gold of the clearing, downwards at the ring of pine-trees standing so still, so crude and untameable, the motionless desert beyond the bristles of the pine crests, a thousand feet below: and beyond the desert, blue mountains, and far, far-off blue mountains in Arizona: "*This is the place,*" she said to herself.

This little tumble-down ranch, only a homestead of a hundred-and-sixty acres, was, as it were, man's last effort towards the wild heart of the Rockies, at this point. Sixty years before, a restless schoolmaster had wandered out from the East, looking for gold among the mountains. He found a very little, then no more. But the mountains had got hold of him, he could not go back.

There was a little trickling spring of pure water, a thread of treasure perhaps better than gold. So the schoolmaster took up a homestead on the lot where this little spring arose. He struggled, and got himself his log cabin erected, his fence put up, sloping at the mountain-side through the pine-trees and dropping into the hollows where the ghost-white mariposa lilies stood leafless and naked in flower, in spring, on tall invisible stems. He made the long clearing for alfalfa.

And fell so into debt, that he had to trade his homestead away, to clear his debt. Then he made a tiny living teaching the children of the few American prospectors who had squatted in the valleys, beside the Mexicans.

The trader who got the ranch tackled it with a will. He built another log cabin, and a big corral, and brought water from the canyon two miles and more across the mountain slope, in a little runnel ditch, and more water, piped a mile or more down the little canyon immediately above the cabins. He got a flow of water for his houses: for being a true American, he felt he could not *really* say he had conquered his environment till he had got running water, taps, and wash-hand basins inside his house.

Taps, running water and wash-hand basins he accomplished. And, undaunted through the years, he prepared the basin for a fountain in the little fenced-in enclosure, and he built a little bath-house. After a number of years, he sent up the enamelled bath-tub to be put in the little log bath-house on the little wild ranch hung right against the savage Rockies, above the desert.

But here the mountains finished him. He was a trader down below, in the Mexican village. This little ranch was, as it were, his hobby, his ideal. He and his New England wife spent their summers there: and turned on the taps in the cabins and turned them off again, and felt really that civilisation had conquered.

All this plumbing from the savage ravines of the canyons—one of them nameless to this day—cost, however, money. In fact, the ranch cost a great deal of money. But it was all to be got back. The big clearing was to be irrigated for alfalfa, the little clearing for beans, and the third clearing, under the corral, for potatoes. All these things the trader could trade to the Mexicans, very advantageously.

And moreover, since somebody had started a praise of the famous goat's cheese made by Mexican peasants in New Mexico, goats there should be.

Goats there were: five hundred of them, eventually. And they fed chiefly in the wild mountain hollows, the no-man's-land. The Mexicans call them fire-mouths, because everything they nibble dies. Not because of their flaming mouths, really, but because they nibble a live plant down, down to the quick, till it can put forth no more.

So, the energetic trader, in the course of five or six years, had got the ranch ready. The long three-roomed cabin was for him and his New England wife. In the two-roomed cabin lived the Mexican family who really had charge of the ranch. For the trader was mostly fixed to his store, seventeen miles away, down in the Mexican village.

The ranch lay over eight thousand feet up, the snows of winter came deep and the white goats, looking dirty yellow, swam in snow with their poor curved horns poking out like dead sticks. But the corral had a long, cosy, shut-in goat-shed all down one side, and into this crowded the five-hundred, their acrid goat-smell rising like hot acid over the snow. And the thin, pock-marked Mexican threw them alfalfa out of the log barn. Until the hot sun sank the snow again, and froze the surface, when patter-patter went the two-thousand little goat-hoofs, over the silver-frozen snow, up at the mountain. Nibble, nibble, nibble, the fire-mouths, at every tender twig. And the goat-bell climbed, and the baa-ing came from among the dense and shaggy pine-trees. And sometimes, in a soft drift under the trees, a goat, or several goats went through, into the white depths, and some were lost thus, to reappear dead and frozen at the thaw.

By evening, they were driven down again, like a dirty yellowish-white stream carrying dark sticks on its yeasty surface, tripping and bleating over the frozen snow, past the bustling dark green pine-trees, down to the trampled mess of the corral. And everywhere, everywhere over the snow, yellow stains and dark pills of goat-droppings melting into the surface crystal. On still, glittering nights, when the frost was hard, the smell of goats came up like some uncanny acid fire, and great stars sitting on the mountain's edge seemed to be watching like the eyes of a mountain lion, brought by the scent. Then the coyotes in the near canyon howled and sobbed, and ran like shadows over the snow. But the goat corral had been built tight.

In the course of years, the goat-herd had grown from fifty to five hundred, and surely that was increase. The goat-milk cheeses sat drying on their little racks. In spring, there was a great flowing and skipping of kids. In summer and early autumn, there was a pest of flies, rising from all that goat-smell and that cast-out whey of goats-milk, after the cheese making. The rats came, and the pack-rats, swarming.

And after all, it was difficult to sell or trade the cheeses, and little profit to be made. And in dry summers, no water came down in the narrow ditch-channel, that straddled in wooden runnels over the deep clefts in the mountain-side. No water meant no alfalfa. In winter the goats scarcely drank at all. In summer they could be watered at the little spring. But the thirsty land was not so easy to accommodate.

Five hundred fine white angora goats, with their massive handsome padres! They were beautiful enough. And the trader made all he could of them. Come summer, they were run down into the narrow tank filled with the fiery dipping fluid. Then their lovely white wool was clipped. It was beautiful, and valuable, but comparatively little of it.

And it all cost, cost, cost. And a man was always let down. At one time no water. At another a poison-weed. Then a sickness. Always, some mysterious malevolence fighting, fighting against the will of man. A strange invisible influence coming out of the livid rock-fastnesses in the bowels of those uncreated Rocky Mountains, preying upon the will of man, and slowly wearing down his resistance, his onward-pushing spirit. The curious, subtle thing, like a mountain fever, got into the blood, so that the men at the ranch, and the animals with them, had bursts of queer, violent, half-frenzied energy, in which, however, they were wont to lose their wariness. And then, damage of some sort. The horses ripped and cut themselves, or they were struck by lightning, the men had great hurts, or sickness. A curious disintegration working all the time, a sort of malevolent breath, like a stupefying, irritant gas, coming out of the unfathomed mountains.

The pack-rats with their bushy tails and big ears, came down out of the hills, and were jumping and bouncing about: symbols of the curious debasing malevolence that was in the spirit of the place. The Mexicans in charge, good honest men, worked all they could. But they were like most of the Mexicans in the South-West, as if they had been pithed, to use one of Kipling's words. As if the invidious malevolence of the country itself had slowly taken all the pith of manhood from them, leaving a hopeless sort of corpus of a man.

And the same happened to the white men, exposed to the open country. Slowly, they were pithed. The energy went out of them. And more than that, the interest. An inertia of indifference invading the soul, leaving the body healthy and active, but wasting the soul, the living interest, quite away.

It was the New England wife of the trader who put most energy into the ranch. She looked on it as her home. She had a little white fence put all round the two cabins: the bright brass water-taps she kept shining in the two kitchens: outside the kitchen door she had a little kitchen garden and nasturtiums, after a great fight with invading animals, that nibbled everything away. And she got so far as the preparation of the round concrete basin which was to be a little pool, under the few enclosed pine-trees between the two cabins, a pool with a tiny fountain jet.

But this, with the bath-tub, was her limit, as the five hundred goats were her man's limit. Out of the mountains came two breaths of influence: the breath of the curious, frenzied energy, that took away one's intelligence as alcohol or any other stimulus does: and then the most strange invidiousness that ate away the soul. The woman loved her ranch, almost with passion. It was she who felt the stimulus, more than the men. It seemed to enter her like a sort of sex passion, intensifying her ego, making her full of violence and of blind female energy. The energy, and the blindness of it! A strange blind frenzy, like an intoxication while it lasted. And the sense of beauty that thrilled her New England woman's soul.

Her cabin faced the slow downslope of the clearing, the alfalfa field: her long, low cabin, crouching under the great pine-tree that threw up its trunk sheer in front of the house, in the yard. That pine-tree was the guardian of the place. But a bristling, almost demonish guardian, from the far-off crude ages of the world. Its great pillar of pale, flakey-ribbed copper rose there in strange callous indifference, and the grim permanence, which is in pine-trees. A passionless, non-phallic column, rising in the shadows of the pre-sexual world, before the hot-blooded ithyphallic column ever erected itself. A cold, blossomless, resinous sap surging and oozing gum, from that pallid brownish bark. And the wind hissing in the needles, like a vast nest of serpents. And the pine cones falling plumb as the hail hit them. Then lying all over the yard, open in the sun like wooden roses, but hard, sexless, rigid with a blind will.

Past the column of that pine-tree, the alfalfa field sloped gently down, to the circling guard of pine-trees, from which silent, living barrier isolated pines rose to ragged heights at intervals, in blind assertiveness. Strange, those pine-trees! In some lights all their needles glistened like polished steel, all subtly glittering with a whitish glitter among darkness, like real needles. Then again, at evening, the trunks would flare up orange red, and the tufts would be dark, alert tufts like a wolf's tail touching the air. Again, in the morning sunlight they would be soft and still, hardly noticeable. But all the same, present, and watchful. Never sympathetic, always watchfully on their guard, and resistant, they hedged one in with the aroma and the power and the slight horror of the pre-sexual primeval world. The world where each creature was crudely limited to its own ego, crude and bristling and cold, and then crowding in packs like pine-trees and wolves.

But beyond the pine-trees, ah, there beyond, there was beauty for the spirit to soar in. The circle of pines, with the loose trees rising high and ragged at intervals, this was the barrier, the fence to the foreground. Beyond was only distance, the desert a thousand feet below, and beyond.

The desert swept its great fawn-coloured circle around, away beyond and below like a beach, with a long mountain-side of pure blue shadow closing in the near corner, and strange bluish hummocks of mountains rising like wet rock from a vast strand, away in the middle distance, and beyond, in the farthest distance, pale blue crests of mountains looking over the horizon, from the west, as if peering in from another world altogether.

Ah, that was beauty!—perhaps the most beautiful thing in the world. It was pure beauty, *absolute* beauty! There! That was it. To the little woman from New England, with her tense fierce soul and her egoistic passion of service, this beauty was absolute, a *ne plus ultra*. From her doorway, from her porch, she could watch the vast, eagle-like wheeling of the daylight, that turned as the eagles which lived in the near rocks turned overhead in the blue, turning their luminous, dark-edged-patterned bellies and underwings upon the pure air, like winged orbs. So the daylight made the vast turn upon the desert, brushing the farthest outwatching mountains. And sometimes, the vast strand of the desert would float with curious undulations and exhalations amid the blue fragility of mountains, whose upper edges were harder than the floating bases. And sometimes she would see the little brown adobe houses of the village Mexicans, twenty miles away, like little cube crystals of insect-houses dotting upon the desert, very distinct, with a cotton-wood tree or two rising near. And sometimes she would see the far-off rocks, thirty miles away, where the canyon made a gateway between the mountains. Quite clear, like an open gateway out of a vast yard, she would see the cut-out bit of the canyon-passage. And on the desert itself, curious puckered folds of mesa-sides. And a blackish crack which in places revealed the otherwise invisible canyon of the Rio Grande. And beyond everything, the mountains like icebergs showing up from an outer sea. Then later, the sun would go down blazing above the shallow cauldron of simmering darkness, and the round mountain of Colorado would lump up into uncanny significance, northwards. That was always rather frightening. But morning came again, with the sun peeping over the mountain slopes and lighting the desert away in the distance long, long before it lighted on her yard. And then she would see another valley, like magic and very lovely, with green fields and long tufts of cotton-wood trees, and a few long-cubical adobe houses, lying floating in shallow light below, like a vision.

Ah: it was beauty, beauty absolute, at any hour of the day: whether the perfect clarity of morning, or the mountains beyond the simmering desert at noon, or the purple lumping of northern mounds under a red sun at night. Or whether the dust whirled in tall columns, travelling across the desert far away, like pillars of cloud by day, tall, leaning pillars of dust hastening with ghostly haste: or whether, in the early part of the year, suddenly in the morning a whole sea of solid white would rise rolling below, a solid mist from melted snow, ghost-white under the mountain sun, the world below blotted out: or whether the black rain and cloud streaked down, far across the desert, and lightning stung down with sharp white stings on the horizon: or the cloud travelled and burst overhead, with rivers of fluid blue fire running out of heaven and exploding on earth, and hail coming down like a world of ice shattered above: or the hot sun rode in again: or snow fell in heavy silence: or the world was blinding white under a blue sky, and one must hurry under the pine-trees for shelter against that vast, white, back-beating light which rushed up at one and made one almost unconscious, amid the snow.

It was always beauty, *always*! It was always great, and splendid, and, for some reason, natural. It was never grandiose or theatrical. Always, for some reason, perfect. And quite simple, in spite of it all.

So it was, when you watched the vast and living landscape. The landscape lived, and lived as the world of the gods, unsullied and unconcerned. The great circling landscape lived its own life, sumptuous and uncaring. Man did not exist for it.

And if it had been a question simply of living through the eyes, into the *distance*, then this would have been Paradise, and the little New England woman on her ranch would have found what she was always looking for, the earthly paradise of the spirit.

But even a woman cannot live only into the distance, the beyond.

Willy-nilly she finds herself juxtaposed to the near things, the thing in itself. And willy-nilly she is caught up into the fight with the immediate object.

The New England woman had fought to make the nearness as perfect as the distance: for the distance was absolute beauty. She had been confident of success. She had felt quite assured, when the water came running out of her bright brass taps, the wild water of the hills caught, tricked into the narrow iron pipes, and led tamely to her kitchen, to jump out over her sink, into her wash-basin, at her service. *There!* she said. I have tamed the waters of the mountain to my service.

So she had, for the moment.

At the same time, the invisible attack was being made upon her. While she revelled in the beauty of the luminous world that wheeled around and below her, the grey, rat-like spirit of the inner mountains was attacking her from behind. She could not keep her attention. And, curiously, she could not keep even her speech. When she was saying something, suddenly the next word would be gone out of her, as if a pack-rat had carried it off. And she sat blank, stuttering, staring in the empty cupboard of her mind, like Mother Hubbard, and seeing the cupboard bare. And this irritated her husband intensely.

Her chickens, of which she was so proud, were carried away. Or they strayed. Or they fell sick. At first she could cope with their circumstances. But after a while, she couldn't. She couldn't care. A drug like numbness possessed her spirit, and at the very middle of her, she couldn't care what happened to her chickens.

The same when a couple of horses were struck by lightning. It frightened her. The rivers of fluid fire that suddenly fell out of the sky and exploded on the earth near by, as if the whole earth had burst like a bomb, frightened her from the very core of her, and made her know, secretly and with cynical certainty, *that there was no merciful God in the heavens.* A very tall, elegant pine-tree just above her cabin took the lightning, and stood tall and elegant as before, but with a white seam spiralling from its crest, all down its tall trunk, to earth. The perfect scar, white and long as lightning itself. And every time she looked at it, she said to herself, in spite of herself: *There is no Almighty loving God. The God there is shaggy as the pine-trees, and horrible as the lightning.* Outwardly, she never confessed this. Openly, she thought of her dear New England Church as usual. But in the violent undercurrent of her woman's soul, after the storms, she would look at that living seamed tree, and the voice would say in her, almost savagely: *What nonsense about Jesus and a God of Love, in a place like this! This is more awful and more splendid. I like it better.* The very chipmunks, in their jerky helter-skelter, the blue jays wrangling in the pine-tree in the dawn, the grey squirrel undulating to the tree-trunk, then pausing to chatter at her and scold her, with a shrewd fearlessness, as if she were the alien, the outsider, the creature that should not be permitted among the trees, all destroyed the illusion she cherished, of love, universal love. There was no love on this ranch. There was life, intense, bristling life, full of energy, but also, with an undertone of savage sordidness.

The black ants in her cupboard, the pack-rats bouncing on her ceiling like hippopotamuses in the night, the two sick goats: there was a peculiar undercurrent of squalor, flowing under the curious *tussle* of wild life. That was it. The wild life, even the life of the trees and flowers, seemed one bristling, hair-raising tussle. The very flowers came up bristly, and many of them were fang-mouthed, like the dead-nettle: and none had any real scent. But they were very fascinating, too, in their very fierceness. In May, the curious columbines of the stream-beds, columbines scarlet outside and yellow in, like the red and yellow of a herald's uniform: farther from the dove nothing could be: then the beautiful rosy-blue of the great tufts of the flower they called blue-bell, but which was really a flower of the snap-dragon family: these grew in powerful beauty in the little clearing of the pine-trees, followed by the flower the settlers had mysteriously called herb honeysuckle: a tangle of long drops of pure fire-red, hanging from slim invisible stalks of smoke colour. The purest, most perfect vermilion scarlet, cleanest fire-colour, hanging in long drops like a shower of fire-rain that is just going to strike the earth. A little later, more in the open, there came another sheer fire-red flower, sparking, fierce red stars running up a bristly grey ladder, as if the earth's fire-centre had blown out some red sparks, white-speckled and deadly inside, puffing for a moment in the day air.

So it was! The alfalfa field was one raging, seething conflict of plants trying to get hold. One dry year, and the bristly wild things had got hold: the spiky, blue-leaved thistle-poppy with its moon-white flowers, the low clumps of blue nettle-flower, the later rush, after the sereness of June and July, the rush of red sparks and michaelmas daisies, and the tough wild sunflowers, strangling and choking the dark, tender green of the clover-like alfalfa! A battle, a battle, with banners of bright scarlet and yellow.

When a really defenceless flower did issue, like the moth-still, ghost-centred mariposa lily, with its inner moth-dust of yellow, it came invisible. There was nothing to be seen, but a hair of greyish grass near the oak-scrub. Behold, this invisible long stalk was balancing a white, ghostly, three-petalled flower, naked out of nothingness. A mariposa lily!

Only the pink wild roses smelled sweet, like the old world. They were sweet-briar roses. And the dark blue hare-bells among the oak-scrub, like the ice-dark bubbles of the mountain flowers in the Alps, the Alpenglocken.

The roses of the desert are the cactus flowers, crystal of translucent yellow or of rose-colour. But set among spines the devil himself must have conceived in a moment of sheer ecstasy.

Nay, it was a world before and after the God of Love. Even the very humming-birds hanging about the flowering squaw-berry bushes, when the snow had gone, in May, they were before and after the God of Love. And the blue jays were crested dark with challenge, and the yellow-and-dark woodpecker was fearless like a warrior in war-paint, as he struck the wood. While on the fence the hawks sat motionless, like dark fists clenched under heaven, ignoring man and his ways.

Summer, it was true, unfolded the tender cotton-wood leaves, and the tender aspen. But what a tangle and a ghostly aloofness in the aspen thickets high up on the mountains, the coldness that is in the eyes and the long cornelian talons of the bear.

Summer brought the little wild strawberries, with their savage aroma, and the late summer brought the rose-jewel raspberries in the valley cleft. But how lonely, how harsh-lonely and menacing it was, to be alone in that shadowy, steep cleft of a canyon just above the cabins, picking raspberries, while the thunder gathered thick and blue-purple at the mountain tops. The many wild raspberries hanging rose-red in the thickets. But the stream bed below all silent, water-less. And the trees all bristling in silence, and waiting like warriors at an out-post. And the berries waiting for the sharp-eyed, cold, long-snouted bear to come rambling and shaking his heavy sharp fur. The berries grew for the bears, and the little New England woman, with her uncanny sensitiveness to underlying influences, felt all the time she was stealing. Stealing the wild raspberries in the secret little canyon behind her home. And when she had made them into jam, she could almost taste the theft in her preserves.

She confessed nothing of this. She tried even to confess nothing of her dread. But she was afraid. Especially she was conscious of the prowling, intense aerial electricity all the summer, after June. The air was thick with wandering currents of fierce electric fluid, waiting to discharge themselves. And almost every day there was the rage and battle of thunder. But the air was never cleared. There was no relief. However the thunder raged, and spent itself, yet, afterwards, among the sunshine was the strange lurking and wandering of the electric currents, moving invisible, with strange menace, between the atoms of the air. She knew. Oh she knew!

And her love for her ranch turned sometimes into a certain repulsion. The underlying rat-dirt, the everlasting bristling tussle of the wild life, with the tangle and the bones strewing. Bones of horses struck by lightning, bones of dead cattle, skulls of goats with little horns: bleached, unburied bones. Then the cruel electricity of the mountains. And then, most mysterious but worst of all, the animosity of the spirit of place: the crude, half-created spirit of place, like some serpent-bird forever attacking man, in a hatred of man's onward-struggle towards further creation.

The seething caldron of lower life, seething on the very tissue of the higher life, seething the soul away, seething at the marrow. The vast and unrelenting will of the swarming lower life, working forever against man's attempt at a higher life, a further created being.

At last, after many years, the little woman admitted to herself that she was glad to go down from the ranch, when November came with snows. She was glad to come to a more human home, her house in the village. And as winter passed by, and spring came again, she knew she did not want to go up to the ranch again. It had broken something in her. It had hurt her terribly. It had maimed her for ever in her hope, her belief in paradise on earth. Now, she hid from herself her own corpse, the corpse of her New England belief in a world ultimately all for love. The belief, and herself with it, was a corpse. The gods of those inner mountains were grim and invidious and relentless, huger than man, and lower than man. Yet man could never master them.

The little woman in her flower-garden away below, by the stream-irrigated village, hid away from the thought of it all. She would not go to the ranch any more.

The Mexicans stayed in charge, looking after the goats. But the place didn't pay. It didn't pay, not quite. It had paid. It might pay. But the effort, the effort! And as the marrow is eaten out of a man's bones and the soul out of his belly, contending with the strange rapacity of savage life, the lower stage of creation, he cannot make the effort any more.

Then also, the war came, making many men give up their enterprises at civilisation.

Every new stroke of civilisation has cost the lives of countless brave men, who have fallen defeated by the "dragon," in their efforts to win the apples of the Hesperides, or the fleece of gold. Fallen in their efforts to overcome the old, half-sordid savagery of the lower stages of creation, and win to the next stage.

For all savagery is half-sordid. And man is only himself when he is fighting on and on, to overcome the sordidness.

And every civilisation, when it loses its inward vision and its cleaner energy, falls into a new sort of sordidness, more vast and more stupendous than the old savage sort. An Augean stables of metallic filth.

And all the time, man has to rouse himself afresh, to cleanse the new accumulations of refuse. To win from the crude wild nature the victory and the power to make another start, and to cleanse behind him the century-deep deposits of layer upon layer of refuse: even of tin cans.

The ranch dwindled. The flock of goats declined. The water ceased to flow. And at length the trader gave it up.

He rented the place to a Mexican, who lived on the handful of beans he raised, and who was being slowly driven out by the vermin.

And now arrived Lou, new blood to the attack. She went back to Santa Fe, saw the trader and a lawyer, and bought the ranch for twelve hundred dollars. She was so pleased with herself.

She went upstairs to tell her mother.

"Mother, I've bought a ranch."

"It is just as well, for I can't stand the noise of automobiles outside here another week."

"It is quiet on my ranch, mother: the stillness simply speaks."

"I had rather it held its tongue. I am simply drugged with all the bad novels I have read. I feel as if the sky was a big cracked bell and a million clappers were hammering human speech out of it."

"Aren't you interested in my ranch, mother?"

"I hope I may be, by and by."

Mrs Witt actually got up the next morning, and accompanied her daughter in the hired motor-car, driven by Phoenix, to the ranch: which was called Las Chivas. She sat like a pillar of salt, her face looking what the Indians call a False Face, meaning a mask. She seemed to have crystallised into neutrality. She watched the desert with its tufts of yellow greasewood go lurching past: she saw the fallen apples on the ground in the orchards near the adobe cottages: she looked down into the deep arroyo, and at the stream they forded in the car, and at the mountains blocking up the sky ahead, all with indifference. High on the mountains was snow: lower, blue-grey livid rock: and below the livid rock the aspens were expiring their daffodil yellow, this year, and the oak-scrub was dark and reddish, like gore. She saw it all with a sort of stony indifference.

"Don't you think it's lovely?" said Lou.

"I can *see* it is lovely," replied her mother.

The michaelmas daisies in the clearing as they drove up to the ranch were sharp-rayed with purple, like a coming night.

Mrs Witt eyed the two log cabins, one of which was delapidated and practically abandoned. She looked at the rather ricketty corral, whose long planks had silvered and warped in the fierce sun. On one of the roof-planks a pack-rat was sitting erect like an old Indian keeping watch on a pueblo roof. He showed his white belly, and folded his hands, and lifted his big ears, for all the world like an old immobile Indian.

"Isn't it for all the world as if *he* were the real boss of the place, Louise?" she said cynically.

And turning to the Mexican, who was a rag of a man but a pleasant courteous fellow, she asked him why he didn't shoot the rat.

"Not worth a shell!" said the Mexican, with a faint hopeless smile.

Mrs Witt paced round and saw everything: it did not take long. She gazed in silence at the water of the spring, trickling out of an iron pipe into a barrel, under the cotton-wood tree in an arroyo.

"Well Louise," she said. "I am glad you feel competent to cope with so much hopelessness and so many rats."

"But mother, you must admit it is beautiful."

"Yes, I suppose it is. But to use one of your Henry's phrases, beauty is a cold egg, as far as I am concerned."

"Rico never would have said that beauty was a cold egg to him."

"No, he wouldn't. He sits on it like a broody old hen on a china imitation.—Are you going to bring him here?"

"*Bring* him!—No. But he can come if he likes," stammered Lou.

"*Oh—h*! won't it be beau-ti-ful!" cried Mrs Witt, rolling her head and lifting her shoulders in savage imitation of her son-in-law.

"Perhaps he won't come, mother," said Lou, hurt.

"He will most certainly come, Louise, to see what's doing: unless you tell him you don't want him."

"Anyhow I needn't think about it till spring," said Lou, anxiously pushing the matter aside.

Mrs Witt climbed the steep slope above the cabins, to the mouth of the little canyon. There she sat on a fallen tree, and surveyed the world beyond: a world not of men. She could not fail to be roused.

"What is your idea in coming here, daughter?" she asked.

"I love it here, mother."

"But what do you expect to achieve by it?"

"I was rather hoping, mother, to escape achievement. I'll tell you—and you musn't get cross if it sounds silly. As far as people go, my heart is quite broken. As far as people go, I don't want any more. I can't stand any more. What heart I ever had for it—for life with people—is quite broken. I want to be alone, mother: with you here, and Phoenix perhaps to look after horses and drive a car. But I want to be by myself, really."

"With Phoenix in the background! Are you sure he won't be coming into the foreground before long?"

"No mother, no more of that. If I've got to say it, Phoenix is a servant: he's really placed, as far as I can see. Always the same, playing about in the old back-yard. I can't take those men seriously. I can't fool round with them, or fool myself about them. I can't and I won't fool myself any more, mother, especially about men. They don't count. So why should you want them to pay me out."

For the moment, this silenced Mrs Witt. Then she said:

"Why, *I* don't want it. Why should I! But after all you've got to live. You've never *lived* yet: not in my opinion."

"Neither, mother, in my opinion, have you," said Lou drily.

And this silenced Mrs Witt altogether. She had to be silent, or angrily on the defensive. And the latter she wouldn't be. She couldn't, really, in honesty.

"What do you call life?" Lou continued. "Wriggling half-naked at a public show, and going off in a taxi to sleep with some half-drunken fool who thinks he's a man because—Oh mother, I don't even want to think of it. I know you have a lurking idea that *that is life*. Let it be so then. But leave me out. Men in that aspect simply nauseate me: so grovelling and ratty. Life in that aspect simply drains all my life away. I tell you, for all that sort of thing, I'm broken, absolutely broken: if I wasn't broken to start with."

"Well Louise," said Mrs Witt after a pause. "I'm convinced that ever since men and women were men and women, people who took things seriously, and had time for it, got their hearts broken. Haven't I had mine broken! It's as sure as having your virginity broken: and it amounts to about as much. It's a beginning rather than an end."

"So it is, mother. It's the beginning of something else, and the end of something that's done with. I *know*, and there's no altering it, that I've got to live differently. It sounds silly, but I don't know how else to put it. I've got to live for something that matters, way, way down in me. And I think sex would matter, to my very soul, if it was really sacred. But cheap sex kills me."

"You have had a fancy for rather cheap men, perhaps."

"Perhaps I have. Perhaps I should always be a fool, where people are concerned. Now I want to leave off that kind of foolery. There's something else, mother, that I want to give myself to. I know it. I know it absolutely. Why should I let myself be shouted down any more!"

Mrs Witt sat staring at the distance, her face a cynical mask.

"What is the something bigger? And *pray*, what is it bigger than?" she asked, in that tone of honied suavity which was her deadliest poison. "I want to learn. I am out to know. I'm terribly intrigued by it—Something bigger! Girls in my generation occasionally entered convents, for *something bigger*. I always wondered if they found it. They seemed to me inclined in the imbecile direction, but perhaps that was because I was *something less*—"

There was a definite pause between the mother and daughter, a silence that was a pure breach. Then Lou said:

"You know quite well I'm not conventy, mother, whatever else I am—even a bit of an imbecile. But that kind of religion seems to me the other half of men. Instead of running after them you run away from them, and get the thrill that way. I don't hate men *because* they're men, as nuns do. I dislike them because they're not men enough: babies, and playboys, and poor things showing off all the time, even to themselves. I don't say I'm any better. I only wish, with all my soul, that some men *were* bigger and stronger and *deeper* than I am...."

"How do you know they're not—?" asked Mrs Witt.

"How *do* I know?—" said Lou mockingly.

And the pause that was a breach resumed itself. Mrs Witt was teasing with a little stick the bewildered black ants among the fir-needles.

"And no doubt you are right about men." she said at length. "But at your age, the only sensible thing is to try and keep up the illusion. After all, as you say, you may be no better."

"I may be no better. But keeping up the illusion means fooling myself. And I won't do it. When I see a man who is even a bit attractive to me—even as much as Phoenix—I say to myself: *Would you care for him afterwards? Does he really mean anything to you, except just a sensation?*—And I know he doesn't. No mother, of this I am convinced: either my taking a man shall have a meaning and a mystery that penetrates my very soul, or I will keep to myself.—And what I *know*, is that the time has come for me to keep to myself. No more messing about."

"Very well, daughter. You will probably spend your life keeping to yourself."

"Do you think I mind! There's something else for me, mother. There's something else even that loves me and wants me. I can't tell you what it is. It's a spirit. And it's here, on this ranch. It's here, in this landscape. It's something more real to me than men are, and it soothes me, and it holds me up. I don't know what it is, definitely. It's something wild, that will hurt me sometimes and will wear me down sometimes. I know it. But it's something big, bigger than men, bigger than people, bigger than religion. It's something to do with wild America. And it's something to do with me. It's a mission, if you like. I am imbecile enough for that!—But it's my mission to keep myself for the spirit that is wild, and has waited so long here: even waited for such as me. Now I've come! Now I'm here. Now I am where I want to be: with the spirit that wants me.—And that's how it is. And neither Rico nor Phoenix nor anybody else really matters to me. They are in the world's back-yard. And I am here, right deep in America, where there's a wild spirit wants me, a wild spirit more than men. And it doesn't want to save me either. It needs me. It craves for me. And to it, my sex is deep and sacred, deeper than I am, with a deep nature aware deep down of my sex. It saves me from cheapness, mother. And even you could never do that for me."

Mrs Witt rose to her feet, and stood looking far, far away, at the turquoise ridge of mountains half sunk under the horizon.

"How much did you say you paid for Las Chivas?" she asked.

"Twelve hundred dollars," said Lou, surprised.

"Then I call it cheap, considering all there is to it: even the name!"

The Princess

To her father, she was The Princess. To her Boston aunts and uncles she was just *Dollie Urquhart, poor little thing*.

Colin Urquhart was just a bit mad. He was of an old Scottish family, and he claimed royal blood. The blood of Scottish kings flowed in his veins. On this point, his American relatives said, he was just a bit "off." They could not bear any more to be told *which* royal blood of Scotland blued his veins. The whole thing was rather ridiculous, and a sore point. The only fact they remembered was that it was not Stuart.

He was a handsome man, with a wide-open blue eye that seemed sometimes to be looking at nothing, soft black hair brushed rather low on his low, broad brow, and a very attractive body. Add to this a most beautiful speaking voice, usually rather hushed and diffident, but sometimes resonant and powerful like bronze, and you have the sum of his charms. He looked like some old Celtic hero. He looked as if he should have worn a greyish kilt and a sporran, and shown his knees. His voice came direct out of the hushed Ossianic past.

For the rest, he was one of those gentlemen of sufficient but not excessive means, who fifty years ago wandered vaguely about, never arriving anywhere, never doing anything, and never definitely being anything, yet well received and familiar in the good society of more than one country.

He did not marry till he was nearly forty: and then it was a wealthy Miss Prescott from New England. Hannah Prescott at twenty-two was fascinated by the man with the soft black hair not yet touched by grey, and the wide, rather vague blue eyes. Many women had been fascinated before her. But Colin Urquhart, by his very vagueness, had avoided any decisive connection.

Mrs Urquhart lived three years in the mist and glamour of her husband's presence. And then it broke her. It was like living with a fascinating spectre. About most things he was completely, even ghostlily oblivious. He was always charming, courteous, perfectly gracious in that hushed, musical voice of his. But absent. When all came to all, he just wasn't there. Not all there, as the vulgar say.

He was the father of the little girl she bore at the end of the first year. But this did not substantiate him the more. His very beauty and his haunting musical quality became dreadful to her after the first few months. The strange echo: he was like a living echo! His very flesh, when you touched it, did not seem quite the flesh of a real man.

Perhaps it was that he was a little bit mad. She thought it definitely the night her baby was born.

"Ah, so my little princess has come at last!" he said, in his throaty, singing Celtic voice, like a glad chant, swaying absorbed.

It was a tiny frail baby, with wide, amazed blue eyes. They christened it Mary Henrietta. She called the little thing: *My Dollie.* He called it always: *My Princess.*

It was useless to fly at him. He just opened his wide blue eyes wider, and took a childlike silent dignity there was no getting past.

Hannah Prescott had never been robust. She had no great desire to live. So when the baby was two years old, she suddenly died.

The Prescotts felt a deep but unadmitted resentment against Colin Urquhart. They said he was selfish. Therefore they discontinued Hannah's income, a month after her burial in Florence, after they had urged the father to give the child over to them, and he had courteously, musically, but quite finally refused. He treated the Prescotts as if they were not of his world, not realities to him: just casual phenomena, or gramophones, talking-machines that had to be answered. He answered them. But of their actual existence he was never once aware.

They debated having him certified unsuitable to be guardian of his own child. But that would have created a scandal. So they did the simplest thing, after all: washed their hands of him. But they wrote scrupulously to the child, and sent her modest presents of money at Christmas, and on the anniversary of the death of her mother.

To The Princess her Boston relatives were for many years just a nominal reality. She lived with her father: and he travelled continually, though in a modest way, living on his moderate income. And never going to America. The child changed nurses all the time. In Italy it was a contadina: in India she had an ayah: in Germany she had a yellow-haired peasant girl.

Father and child were inseparable. He was not a recluse. Wherever he went, he was to be seen paying formal calls, going out to luncheon or to tea, rarely to dinner. And always with the child. People called her Princess Urquhart, as if that were her christened name.

She was a quick, dainty little thing with dark gold hair that went a soft brown, and wide, slightly prominent blue eyes that were at once so candid and so knowing. She was always grown-up: she never really grew up. Always strangely wise, and always childish.

It was her father's fault.

"My little Princess must never take too much notice of people and the things they say and do," he repeated to her. "People don't know what they are doing and saying. They chatter-chatter, and they hurt one another and they hurt themselves very often, till they cry. But don't take any notice, my little Princess. Because it is all nothing. Inside everybody there is another creature, a demon which doesn't care at all. You peel away all the things they say and do and feel, as cook peels away the outside of the onions. And in the middle of everybody, there is a green demon which you can't peel away. And this green demon never changes, and it doesn't care at all about all the things that happen to the outside leaves of the person, all the chatter-chatter, and all the husbands and wives and children, and troubles and fusses. You peel everything away from people, and there is a green, upright demon in every man and woman: and this demon is a man's real self, and a woman's real self. It doesn't really care about anybody, it belongs to the demons and the primitive fairies who never care—.—But even so, there are big demons and mean demons, and splendid demonish fairies and vulgar ones. But there are no royal fairy women left. Only you, my little Princess. You are the last of the royal race of the old people; the last, my Princess. There are no others. You and I are the last. When I am dead there will be only you.—And that is why, darling, you will never care for any of the people in the world very much. Because their demons are all dwindled and vulgar. They are not royal. Only you are royal, after me. Always remember that. And always remember, it is a *great secret*. If you tell people, they will try to kill you, because they will envy you for being a princess. It is our great secret, darling. I am a prince, and you a princess, of the old, old blood. And we keep our secret between us, all alone. And so, darling, you must treat all people very politely, because *noblesse oblige*. But you must never forget, that you alone are the last of princesses, and that all others are less than you are: less noble, more vulgar. Treat them politely and gently and kindly, darling. But you are the Princess, and they are commoners. Never try to think of them as if they were like you. They are not. You will find, always, that they are lacking, lacking in the royal touch, which only you have—"

The Princess learned her lesson early: the first lesson, of absolute reticence, the impossibility of intimacy with any other than her father: the second lesson, of naïve, slightly benevolent politeness. As a small child, something crystallised in her character, making her clear and finished, and as impervious as crystal.

"Dear child!" her hostesses said of her. "She is so quaint and old-fashioned: such a lady, poor little mite!"

She was erect, and very dainty. Always small, nearly tiny in physique, she seemed like a changeling beside her big, handsome, slightly mad father. She dressed very simply, usually in blues or delicate greys, with little collars of old Milan point, or very finely-worked linen. She had exquisite little hands, that made the piano sound like a spinet when she played. She was rather given to wearing cloaks and capes, instead of coats, out of doors, and little eighteenth-century sort of hats. Her complexion was pure apple-blossom.

She looked as if she had stepped out of a picture. But no-one, to her dying day, ever knew exactly the strange picture her father had framed her in, and from which she never stepped.

Her grandfather and grandmother and her Aunt Maud demanded twice to see her: once in Rome and once in Paris. Each time they were charmed, piqued, and annoyed. She was so exquisite and such a little virgin. At the same time, so knowing, and so oddly assured. That odd, assured touch of condescension, and the inward coldness, infuriated her American relations.

Only she really fascinated her grandfather. He was spellbound: in a way, in love with the little faultless thing. His wife would catch him brooding, musing over his grandchild, long months after the meeting, and craving to see her again. He cherished to the end the fond hope that she might come to live with him and her grandmother.

"Thank you so much, grandfather. You are so very kind. But Papa and I are such an odd couple, you see, such a crochetty old couple, living in a world of our own."

Her father let her see the world, from the outside. And he let her read. When she was in her teens she read Zola and Maupassant, and with the eyes of Zola and Maupassant she looked on Paris. A little later, she read Tolstoi and Dostoevsky. The latter confused her. The others, she seemed to understand with a very shrewd, canny understanding, just as she understood the Decameron stories as she read them in their old Italian, or the Nibelung poems. Strange and *uncanny*, she seemed to understand things in a cold light perfectly, with all the flush of fire absent. She was something like a changeling, not quite human.

This earned her, also, strange antipathies. Cabmen and railway-porters, especially in Paris and Rome, would suddenly treat her with brutal rudeness, when she was alone. They seemed to look on her with sudden violent antipathy. They sensed in her a curious impertinence, an easy, sterile impertinence towards the things *they* felt most. She was so assured, and her flower of maidenhood was so scentless. She could look at a lusty, sensual Roman cabman as if he were a sort of grotesque to make her smile. She knew all about him, in Zola. And the peculiar condescension with which she would give him her order, as if she, frail beautiful thing, were the only reality, and he, coarse monster, were a sort of Caliban floundering in the mud on the margin of the pool of the perfect lotus, would suddenly enrage the fellow, the real Mediterranean, who prided himself on his *beauté mâle*, and to whom the phallic mystery was still the only mystery. And he would turn a terrible face on her, bully her in a brutal, coarse fashion, hideous. For to him, she had only the blasphemous impertinence of her own sterility.

Encounters like these made her tremble, and made her know she must have support from the outside. The power of her spirit did not extend to these low people: and they had all the physical power. She realised an implacability of hatred in their turning on her. But she did not lose her head. She quietly paid out money and turned away.

Those were dangerous moments, though, and she learned to be prepared for them. The Princess she was, and the fairy from the north, she could never understand the volcanic phallic rage with which coarse people could turn on her, in a paroxysm of hatred. They never turned on her father like that. And quite early, she decided it was the New England mother in her whom they hated. Never for one minute could she see with the old Roman eyes, see herself as sterility, the barren flower, taken on airs and an intolerable impertinence. This was what the Roman cabman saw in her. And he longed to crush the barren blossom. Its sexless beauty and its authority put him in a passion of brutal revolt.

When she was nineteen her grandfather died, leaving her a considerable fortune in the safe hands of responsible trustees. They would deliver her her income, but only on condition that she resided for six months in the year in the United States.

"Why should they make me conditions!" she said to her father. "I refuse to be imprisoned six months in the year in the United States. We will tell them to keep their money."

"Let us be wise, my little Princess, let us be wise. Now we are almost poor, and we are never safe from rudeness. I cannot allow anybody to be rude to me. I hate it, I hate it!" His eyes flamed as he said it. "I could kill any man or woman who is rude to me. But we are in exile in the world. We are powerless. If we were really poor, we should be quite powerless, and then I should die.—No, my Princess. Let us take their money, then they will not dare to be rude to us. Let us take it, as we put on clothes, to cover ourselves from their aggressions."

There began a new phase, when the father and daughter spent their summers on the Great Lakes, or in California, or in the South West. The father was something of a poet, the daughter something of a painter. He wrote poems about the Lakes or the redwood trees, and she made dainty drawings. He was physically a strong man, and he loved the out-of-doors. He would go off with her for days, paddling in a canoe and sleeping by a camp-fire. Frail little Princess, she was always undaunted: always undaunted. She would ride with him on horseback over the mountain trails till she was so tired, she was nothing but a bodiless consciousness sitting astride her pony. But she never gave in. And at night he folded her in her blankets on a bed of balsam-pine twigs, and she lay and looked at the stars unmurmuring. She was fulfilling her rôle.

People said to her, as the years passed, and she was a woman of twenty-five, then a woman of thirty, and always the same virgin dainty Princess, "knowing" in a dispassionate way, like an old woman, and utterly intact:

"Don't you ever think what you will do when your father is no longer with you?"

She looked at her interlocutor with that cold, elfin detachment of hers:

"No, I never think of it," she said.

She had a tiny, but exquisite little house in London, and another small, perfect house in Connecticut, each with a faithful housekeeper. Two homes, if she chose. And she knew many interesting literary and artistic people. What more!

So the years passed, imperceptibly. And she had that quality of the sexless fairies, she did not change. At thirty-three she looked twenty-three.

Her father, however, was ageing, and becoming more and more queer. It was now her task to be his guardian in his private madness. He spent the last three years of life in the house in Connecticut. He was very much estranged, sometimes had fits of violence which almost killed the little Princess. Physical violence was horrible to her, it seemed to shatter her heart. But she found a woman a few years younger than herself, well educated and sensitive, to be a sort of nurse-companion to the mad old man. So the fact of madness was never openly admitted. Miss Cummins, the companion, had a passionate loyalty to the Princess, and a curious affection, tinged with love, for the handsome, white-haired, courteous old man who was never at all aware of his fits of violence, once they had passed.

The Princess was thirty-eight years old when her father died: and quite unchanged. She was still tiny, and like a dignified, scentless flower. Her soft brownish hair, almost the colour of beaver fur, was bobbed, and fluffed softly round her apple-blossom face, that was modelled with an arched nose like a proud old Florentine portrait. In her voice, manner, and bearing, she was exceedingly still, like a flower that has blossomed in a shadowy place. And from her blue eyes looked out the Princess' eternal laconic challenge, that grew almost sardonic as the years passed. She was the Princess, and sardonically she looked out on a princeless world.

She was relieved when her father died, and at the same time, it was as if everything had evaporated around her. She had lived in a sort of hot-house, in the aura of her father's madness. Suddenly the hot-house had been removed from around her, and she was in the raw, vast, vulgar open air.

Quoi faire? What was she to do? She seemed faced with absolute nothingness. Only she had Miss Cummins, who shared with her the secret, and almost the passion for her father. In fact the Princess felt that her passion for her mad father had in some curious way transferred itself largely to Charlotte Cummins, during the last years. And now Miss Cummins was the vessel that held the passion for the dead man. She herself, the Princess, was an empty vessel.

An empty vessel, in the enormous warehouse of the world.

Quoi faire? What was she to do? She felt that, since she could not evaporate into nothingness like alcohol from an unstopped bottle, she must *do* something. Never before in her life had she felt the incumbency. Never, never had she felt she must *do* anything. That was left to the vulgar.

Now her father was dead, she found herself on the *fringe* of the vulgar crowd, sharing their necessity to *do* something. It was a little humiliating. She felt herself becoming vulgarised. At the same time, she found herself looking at men with a shrewder eye: an eye to marriage. Not that she felt any sudden interest in men, or attraction towards them. No! She was still neither interested nor attracted towards men vitally. But *marriage*, that peculiar abstraction, had imposed a sort of spell on her. She thought that *marriage*, in the blank abstract, was the thing she ought to *do*. That marriage implied a man, she also knew. She knew all the facts. But the man seemed a property of her own mind rather than a thing in himself, another being.

Her father died in the summer, the month after her thirty-eighth birthday. When all was over, the obvious thing to do, of course, was to travel. With Miss Cummins. The two women knew each other intimately, but they were always Miss Urquhart and Miss Cummins to one another, and a certain distance was instinctively maintained. Miss Cummins, from Philadelphia, of scholastic stock, and intelligent, but untravelled, four years younger than the Princess, felt herself immensely the junior of her "lady." She had a sort of passionate veneration for the Princess, who seemed to her ageless, timeless. She could not see the rows of tiny, dainty, exquisite shoes in the Princess' cupboard without feeling a stab at the heart, a stab of tenderness and reverence, almost of awe.

Miss Cummins also was virginal: but with a look of puzzled surprise in her brown eyes. Her skin was pale and clear, her features well modelled, but there was a certain blankness in her expression, where the Princess had an odd touch of Renaissance grandeur. Miss Cummins' voice was also hushed almost to a whisper: it was the inevitable effect of Colin Urquhart's room. But the hushedness had a hoarse quality.

The Princess did not want to go to Europe. Her face seemed turned west. Now her father was gone, she felt she would go west, westwards, as if for ever. Following, no doubt, the March of Empire, which is brought up rather short on the Pacific coast, among swarms of wallowing bathers.

No, not the Pacific coast. She would stop short of that. The South West was less vulgar. She would go to New Mexico.

She and Miss Cummins arrived at the Rancho del Cerro Gordo towards the end of August, when the crowd was beginning to drift back east. The ranch lay by a stream on the desert some four miles from the foot of the mountains, a mile away from the Indian pueblo of San Cristobal. It was a ranch for the rich: the Princess paid thirty dollars a day for herself and Miss Cummins. But then she had a little cottage to herself, among the apple-trees of the orchard, with an excellent cook. She and Miss Cummins, however, took dinner at evening in the large guest-house. For the Princess still entertained the idea of "marriage."

The guests at the Rancho del Cerro Gordo were of all sorts, except the poor sort. They were practically all rich, and many were romantic. Some were charming, others were vulgar, some were movie people, quite quaint and not unattractive in their vulgarity, and many were Jews. The Princess did not care for Jews, though they were usually the most interesting to *talk* to. So she talked a good deal with the Jews, and painted with the artists, and rode with the young men from College, and had altogether quite a good time. And yet she felt something of a fish out of water, or a bird in the wrong forest. And "marriage" remained still completely in the abstract. No connecting it with any of these young men, even the nice ones.

The Princess looked just twenty-five. The freshness of her mouth, the hushed, delicate-complexioned virginity of her face gave her not a day more. Only a certain laconic look in her eyes was disconcerting.— When she was *forced* to write her age, she put twenty-eight, making the figure *two* rather badly, so that it just avoided being a three.

Men hinted marriage at her. Especially boys from college suggested it from a distance. But they all failed before the look of sardonic ridicule in the Princess' eyes. It always seemed to her rather preposterous, quite ridiculous, and a tiny bit impertinent on their part.

The only man that intrigued her at all was one of the guides, a man called Romero: Domingo Romero. It was he who had sold the ranch itself to the Wilkiesons, ten years before, for two thousand dollars. He had gone away: then reappeared at the old place. For he was the son of the old Romeros, the last of the Spanish family that had owned miles of land around San Cristobal. But the coming of the white man and the failure of the vast flocks of sheep and the fatal inertia which overcomes all men, at last, on the desert near the mountains, had finished the Romero family. The last descendants were just Mexican peasants.

Domingo, the heir, had spent his two thousand dollars, and was working for white people. He was now about thirty years old, a tall, silent fellow with a heavy closed mouth and black eyes that looked across at one almost sullenly. From behind, he was handsome, with a strong, natural body and the back of his neck very dark and well-shapen, strong with life. But his dark face was long and heavy, almost sinister, with that peculiar heavy meaninglessness in it, characteristic of the Mexicans of his own locality. They are strong, they seem healthy. They laugh and joke with one another. But their physique and their natures seem static, as if there were nowhere, nowhere at all for their energies to go, and their faces, degenerating to misshapen heaviness, seem to have no *raison d'être*. As if, both as individual men and as a race, they had no *raison d'être*, no radical meaning. Waiting either to die, or to be aroused into passion and hope. In some of the black eyes, a queer, haunting mystic quality, sombre and a bit gruesome, the skull-and-crossbones look of the Penitentes. They had found their *raison d'être* in self-torture and death-worship. Unable to wrest a *positive* significance for themselves from the vast, beautiful, but vindictive landscape they were born into, they turned on their own selves, and worshipped death through self-torture. The mystic gloom of this showed in their eyes.

But as a rule the dark eyes of the Mexicans were heavy and half-alive, sometimes hostile, sometimes kindly, often with the fatal Indian glaze on them, or the fatal Indian glint.

Domingo Romero was *almost* a typical Mexican to look at, with the typical heavy, dark long face, clean-shaven, with an almost brutally heavy mouth. His eyes were black and Indian looking. Only, at the centre of their hopelessness was a spark of pride, of self-confidence, of dauntlessness. Just a spark in the midst of the blackness of static despair.

But this spark was the difference between him and the mass of men. It gave a certain alert sensitiveness to his bearing, and a certain beauty to his appearance. He wore a low-crowned black hat, instead of the ponderous head-gear of the usual Mexican, and his clothes were thinnish and graceful. Silent, aloof, almost imperceptible in the landscape, he was an admirable guide, with a startling quick intelligence that anticipated difficulties about to arise. He could cook too, crouching over the camp-fire and moving his lean, deft brown hands. The only fault he had was that he was not forthcoming: he wasn't chatty and cosy.

"Oh, don't send Romero with us," the Jews would say. "One can't get any response from him."

Tourists come and go, but they rarely *see* anything, inwardly. None of them ever saw the spark at the middle of Romero's eye: they were not alive enough to see it.

The Princess caught it one day, when she had him for a guide. She was fishing for trout in the canyon, Miss Cummins was reading a book, the horses were tied under the trees, Romero was fixing a proper fly on her line. He fixed the fly and handed her the line, looking up at her. And at that moment she caught the spark in his eye. And instantly she knew that he was a gentleman, that his "demon," as her father would have said, was a fine demon. And instantly her manner towards him changed.

He had perched her on a rock over a quiet pool, beyond the cottonwood trees. It was early September, and the canyon already cool, but the leaves of the cottonwoods were still green. The Princess stood on her rock, a small but perfectly-formed figure, wearing a soft close grey sweater and neatly cut grey riding-breeches, with tall black boots, her fluffy brown hair straggling from under a little grey felt hat. A woman? Not quite. A changeling of some sort, perched in outline there on the rock, in the bristling wild canyon. She knew perfectly well how to handle a line. Her father had made a fisherwoman of her.

Romero, in a black shirt and with loose black trousers pushed into wide black riding-boots, was fishing a little further down. He had put his hat on a rock behind him, his dark head was bent a little forward, watching the water. He had caught three trout. From time to time he glanced upstream at the Princess, perched there so daintily. He saw she had caught nothing.

Soon he quietly drew in his line and came up to her. His keen eye watched her line, watched her position. Then quietly, he suggested certain changes to her, putting his sensitive brown hand before her. And he withdrew a little, and stood in silence leaning against a tree, watching her. He was helping her across the distance. She knew it, and thrilled. And in a moment she had a bite. In two minutes she had landed a good trout. She looked round at him quickly, her eyes sparkling, the colour heightened in her cheeks. And as she met his eyes a smile of greeting went over his dark face, very sudden, with an odd sweetness.

She knew he was helping her. And she felt in his presence a subtle, insidious male *kindliness* she had never known before, waiting upon her. Her cheek flushed, and her blue eyes darkened.

After this, she always looked for him, and for that curious dark beam of a man's kindliness which he could give her, as it were, from his chest, from his heart. It was something she had never known before.

A vague, unspoken intimacy grew up between them. She liked his voice, his appearance, his presence. His natural language was Spanish, he spoke English like a foreign language, rather slow, with a slight hesitation, but with a sad, plangent sonority lingering over from his Spanish. There was a certain subtle correctness in his appearance, he was always perfectly shaved, his hair was thick and rather long on top, but always carefully groomed behind. And his fine black cashmere shirt, his wide leather belt, his well-cut, wide black trousers going into the embroidered cowboy boots had a certain inextinguishable elegance. He wore no silver rings or buckles. Only his boots were embroidered and decorated at the top with an inlay of white suède. He seemed elegant, slender, yet he was very strong.

And at the same time, curiously, he gave her the feeling that death was not far from him. Perhaps he too was half in love with death. However that may be, the sense she had that death was not far from him made him "possible" to her.

Small as she was, she was quite a good horsewoman. They gave her at the ranch a sorrel mare, very lovely in colour, and well-made, with a powerful broad neck and the hollow back that betokens a swift runner. Tansy, she was called. Her only fault was the usual mare's failing, she was inclined to be hysterical.

So that every day the Princess set off with Miss Cummins and Romero, on horseback, riding into the mountains. Once they went camping for several days, with two more friends in the party.

"I think I like it better," the Princess said to Romero, "when we three go alone."

And he gave her one of his quick, transfiguring smiles.

It was curious, no white man had ever showed her this capacity for subtle gentleness, this power to *help* her in silence across a distance, if she were fishing without success, or tired on her horse, or if Tansy suddenly got scared. It was as if Romero could send her *from his heart* a dark beam of succour and sustaining. She had never known this before, and it was very thrilling.

Then the smile that suddenly creased his dark face, showing the strong white teeth. It creased his face almost into a savage grotesque. And at the same time there was in it something so warm, such a dark flame of kindliness for her, she was elated into her true Princess self.

Then that vivid, latent spark in his eye, which she had seen, and which she knew he was aware she had seen. It made an inter-recognition between them, silent and delicate. Here he was delicate as a woman, in this subtle inter-recognition.

And yet his presence only put to flight in her the *idée fixe* of "marriage." For some reason, in her strange little brain, the idea of *marrying* him could not enter. Not for any definite reason. He was in himself a gentleman, and she had plenty of money for two. There was no actual obstacle. Nor was she conventional.

No, now she came down to it, it was as if their two "dæmons" could marry, were perhaps married. Only their two *selves*, Miss Urquhart and Señor Domingo Romero, were for some reason incompatible. There was a peculiar subtle intimacy of inter-recognition between them. But she did not see in the least how it could lead to marriage. Almost she could more easily marry one of the nice boys from Harvard or Yale.

The time passed, and she let it pass. The end of September came, with aspens going yellow on the mountain heights, and oak-scrub going red. But as yet, the cottonwoods in the valleys and canyons had not changed.

"When will you go away?" Romero asked her, looking at her fixedly, with a blank black eye.

"By the end of October," she said. "I have promised to be in Santa Barbara at the beginning of November."

He was hiding the spark in his eye from her. But she saw the peculiar sullen thickening of his heavy mouth.

She had complained to him many times that one never saw any wild animals, except chipmunks and squirrels and perhaps a skunk and a porcupine. Never a deer, or a bear, or a mountain lion.

"Are there no bigger animals in these mountains?" she asked, dissatisfied.

"Yes!" he said. "There are deer—I see their tracks. And I saw the tracks of a bear."

"But why can one never see the animals themselves?"—She looked dissatisfied and wistful like a child.

"Why it's pretty hard for you to see them. They won't let you come close. You have to keep still, in a place where they come. Or else you have to follow their tracks, a long way."

"I can't bear to go away till I've seen them: a bear, or a deer—"
The smile came suddenly on his face, indulgent.

"Well what do you want? Do you want to go up into the mountains to some place, to wait till they come?"

"Yes," she said, looking up at him with a sudden naïve impulse of recklessness.

And immediately his face became sombre again, responsible.

"Well," he said, with slight irony, a touch of mockery of her. "You

would have to find a house. It's very cold at night now. You would
have to stay all night in a house."

"And there are no houses up there?" she said.

"Yes," he replied. "There is a little shack that belong to me, what
a miner built a long time ago, looking for gold. You can go there and
stay one night, and maybe you see something. Maybe! I don't know.
Maybe nothing come."

"How much chance is there?"

"Well I don't know. Last time when I was there I see three deer
come down to drink at the water, and I shot two raccoons. But maybe
this time we don't see anything."

"Is there water there?" she asked.

"Yes, there is a little round pond, you know, below the spruce trees.
And the water from the snow run into it."

"Is it far away?" she asked.

"Yes, pretty far. You see that ridge there—" and turning to the
mountains he lifted his arm in the gesture which is somehow so moving,
out in the West, pointing to the distance—"that ridge where there
are no trees, only rock—"—his black eyes were focussed on the
distance, his face impassive, but as if in pain—"you go round that
ridge, and along, then you come down through the spruce trees to
where the cabin is. My father, he bought that placer claim from a
miner who was broke, but nobody ever found any gold or anything,
and nobody ever goes there. Too lonesome!"

The Princess watched the massive, heavy-sitting, beautiful bulk of
the Rocky Mountains. It was early in October, and the aspens were
already losing their gold leaves; high up, the spruce and pine seemed
to be growing darker; the great flat patches of oak-scrub on the heights
were red like gore.

"Can I go over there?" she asked, turning to him and meeting the
spark in his eye.

His face was heavy with responsibility.

"Yes," he said, "you can go. But there'll be snow over the ridge,
and it's awful cold, and awful lonesome."

"I should like to go," she said, persistent.

"All right," he said. "You can go if you want to."

She doubted, though, if the Wilkiesons would let her go: at least,
alone with Romero and Miss Cummins.

Yet an obstinacy characteristic of her nature, an obstinacy tinged
perhaps with madness, had taken hold of her. She wanted to look over

the mountains into their secret heart. She wanted to descend to the cabin below the spruce trees, near the tarn of bright green water. She wanted to see the wild animals move about in their wild unconsciousness.

"Let us say to the Wilkiesons that we want to make the trip round the Frijoles canyon," she said.

The trip round the Frijoles canyon was a usual thing. It would not be strenuous nor cold nor lonely: they could sleep in the log house that was called an hotel.

Romero looked at her quickly.

"If you want to say that," he replied, "you can tell Mrs Wilkieson. Only I know she'll be mad with me, if I take you up in the mountains to that place.—And I've got to go there first with a pack-horse, to take lots of blankets and some bread. Maybe Miss Cummins can't stand it. Maybe not! It's a hard trip."

He was speaking, and thinking, in the heavy, disconnected Mexican fashion.

"Never mind!"—The Princess was suddenly very decisive and stiff with authority. "I want to do it. I will arrange with Mrs Wilkieson. And we'll go on Saturday."

He shook his head slowly.

"I've got to go up on Sunday with a pack-horse and blankets," he said. "Can't do it before."

"Very well!" she said, rather piqued. "Then we'll start on Monday."

She hated being thwarted even the tiniest bit.

He knew that if he started with the pack on Sunday at dawn he would not be back until late at night. But he consented that they should start on Monday morning at seven. The obedient Miss Cummins was told to prepare for the Frijoles trip. On Sunday Romero had his day off. He had not put in an appearance when the Princess retired on Sunday night, but on Monday morning, as she was dressing, she saw him bringing in the three horses from the corral. She was in high spirits.

The night had been cold. There was ice at the edges of the irrigation ditch, and the chipmunks crawled into the sun and lay with wide, dumb, anxious eyes, almost too numb to run.

"We may be away two or three days," said the Princess.

"Very well. We won't begin to be anxious about you before Thursday, then," said Mrs Wilkieson, who was young and capable:

from Chicago. "Anyway," she added, "Romero will see you through. He's so trustworthy."

The sun was already on the desert as they set off towards the mountains, making the greasewood and the sage pale as pale-grey sands, luminous the great level around them. To the right glinted the shadows of the adobe pueblo, flat and almost invisible on the plain, earth of its earth. Behind lay the ranch and the tufts of tall, plumy cottonwoods, whose summits were yellowing under the perfect blue sky.

Autumn breaking into colour, in the great spaces of the South West.

But the three trotted gently along the trail, towards the sun that sparkled yellow just above the dark bulk of the ponderous mountains. Side-slopes were already gleaming yellow, flaming with a second light, under the coldish blue of the pale sky. The front slopes were in shadow, with submerged lustre of red oak-scrub and dull-gold aspens, blue-black pines and grey-blue rock. While the canyon was full of a deep blueness.

They rode single file, Romero first, on a black horse. Himself in black, he made a flickering black spot in the delicate pallor of the great landscape, where even pine-trees at a distance take a film of blue paler than their green. Romero rode on in silence past the tufts of furry greasewood. The Princess came next, on her sorrel mare. And Miss Cummins, who was not quite happy on horseback, came last, in the pale dust that the others kicked up. Sometimes her horse sneezed, and she started.

But on they went, at a gentle trot. Romero never looked round. He could hear the sound of the hoofs following, and that was all he wanted. For the rest, he held ahead. And the Princess, with that black, unheeding figure always travelling away from her, felt strangely helpless, withal elated.

They neared the pale, round foot-hills, dotted with the round dark piñón and cedar shrubs. The horses clinked and clattered among stones. Occasionally a big round greasewood held out fleecy tufts of flowers, pure gold. They wound into blue shadow, then up a steep stony slope, with the world lying pallid away behind and below. Then they dropped into the shadow of the San Cristobal canyon.

The stream was running full and swift. Occasionally the horses snatched at a tuft of grass. The trail narrowed and became rocky, the rocks closed in, it was dark and cool as the horses climbed and climbed upwards, and the tree-trunks crowded in, in the shadowy, silent tightness of the canyon. They were among cottonwood trees that ran up straight and smooth and round to an extraordinary height. Above, the tips were gold and it was sun. But away below, where the horses struggled up the rocks and wound among the trunks, there was chill blue shadow by the sound of waters, and an occasional grey festoon of old-man's-beard, and here and there a pale, dipping cranesbill flower among the tangle and the débris of the virgin place. And again the chill entered the Princess' heart, as she realised what a tangle of decay and despair lay in the virgin forests.

They scrambled downwards, splashed across-stream, up rocks and along the trail of the other side. Romero's black horse stopped, looked down quizzically at the fallen trees, then stepped over lightly. The Princess' sorrel followed, carefully. But Miss Cummins' buckskin made a fuss, and had to be got round.

In the same silence, save for the clinking of the horses and the splashing as the trail crossed stream, they worked their way upwards in the tight, tangled shadow of the canyon. Sometimes, crossing stream, the Princess would glance upwards, and then always her heart caught in her breast. For high up, away in heaven, the mountain heights shone yellow dappled with dark spruce firs, clear almost as speckled daffodils against the pale turquoise blue lying high and serene above the dark-blue shadow where the Princess was. And she would snatch at the blood-red leaves of the oak as her horse crossed a more open slope, not knowing what she felt.

They were getting fairly high, occasionally lifted above the canyon itself, in the low groove below the speckled, gold-sparkling heights which towered beyond. Then again they dipped and crossed stream, the horses stepping gingerly across a tangle of fallen, frail aspen stems, then suddenly floundering in a mass of rocks. The black emerged ahead, his black tail waving. The Princess let her mare find her own footing: then she too emerged from the clatter. She rode on after the black. Then came a great, frantic rattle of the buckskin behind. The Princess was aware of Romero's dark face looking round with a strange, demon-like watchfulness, before she herself looked round, to see the buckskin scrambling rather lamely beyond the rocks, with one of his pale buff knees already red with blood.

"He *almost* went down!" called Miss Cummins.

But Romero was already out of the saddle and hastening down the path. He made quiet little noises to the buckskin, and began examining the cut knee.

"Is he hurt?" cried Miss Cummins anxiously, and she climbed hastily down.

"Oh my Goodness!" she cried, as she saw the blood running down the slender buff leg of the horse, in a thin trickle. "Isn't that *awful*!" She spoke in a stricken voice, and her face was white.

Romero was still carefully feeling the knee of the buckskin. Then he made him walk a few paces. And at last he stood up straight and shook his head.

"Not very bad!" he said. "Nothing broken."

Again he bent and worked at the knee. Then he looked up at the Princess.

"He can go on," he said. "It's not bad."

The Princess looked down at the dark face in silence.

"What, go on right up here?" cried Miss Cummins. "How many hours?"

"About five," said Romero simply.

"Five hours!" cried Miss Cummins. "A horse with a lame knee! And a steep mountain!—Why-y!—"

"Yes, it's pretty steep up there," said Romero, pushing back his hat and staring fixedly at the bleeding knee. The buckskin stood in a stricken sort of dejection. "But I think he'll make it all right," the man added.

"Oh!" cried Miss Cummins, her eyes bright with sudden passion of unshed tears. "I wouldn't think of it. I wouldn't ride him up there, not for any money."

"Why wouldn't you?" asked Romero.

"It *hurts* him."

Romero bent down again to the horse's knee.

"Maybe it hurts him a little." he said. "But he can make it all right, and his leg won't get stiff—"

"What! Ride him five hours up the steep mountains!" cried Miss Cummins. "I couldn't. I just couldn't do it. I'll lead him a little way and see if he can go. But I *couldn't* ride him again. I couldn't. Let me walk."

"But Miss Cummins dear, if Romero says he'll be all right—?" said the Princess.

"I know it hurts him. Oh, I just couldn't bear it."

There was no doing anything with Miss Cummins. The thought of a hurt animal always put her into a sort of hysterics.

They walked forward a little, leading the buckskin. He limped rather badly. Miss Cummins sat on a rock.

"Why it's agony to see him!" she cried. "It's *cruel*!"

"He won't limp after a bit, if you don't take no notice of him," said Romero. "Now he plays up, and limps very much, because he wants to make you see."

"I don't think there can be much playing up," said Miss Cummins bitterly. "We can *see* how it must hurt him."

"It don't hurt much," said Romero.

But now Miss Cummins was silent with antipathy.

It was a deadlock. The party remained motionless on the trail, the Princess in the saddle, Miss Cummins seated on a rock, Romero standing black and remote near the drooping buckskin.

"Well!" said the man suddenly at last. "I guess we go back, then."

And he looked up swiftly at his horse, which was cropping at the mountain herbage and treading on the trailing reins.

"No!" cried the Princess. "Oh no!"—Her voice rang with a great wail of disappointment and anger. Then she checked herself.

Miss Cummins rose with energy.

"Let me lead the buckskin home," she said, with cold dignity, "and you two go on."

This was received in silence. The Princess was looking down at her with a sardonic, almost cruel gaze.

"We've only come about two hours," said Miss Cummins. "I don't mind a bit leading him home. But I *couldn't* ride him. I *couldn't* have him ridden, with that knee."

This again was received in dead silence. Romero remained impassive, almost inert.

"Very well then," said the Princess. "You lead him home. You'll be quite all right. Nothing can happen to you, possibly. And say to them that we have gone on and shall be home tomorrow—or the day after—"

She spoke coldly and distinctly. For she could not bear to be thwarted.

"Better all go back, and come again another day," said Romero, non-committal.

"There will never *be* another day," cried the Princess. "I *want* to go on."

She looked him square in the eyes, and met the spark in his eye.

He raised his shoulders slightly.

"If you want it," he said. "I'll go on with you. But Miss Cummins can ride my horse to the end of the canyon, and I lead the buckskin. Then I come back to you."

It was arranged so. Miss Cummins had her saddle put on Romero's black horse, Romero took the buckskin's bridle, and they started back. The Princess rode very slowly on, upwards, alone. She was at first so angry with Miss Cummins, that she was blind to everything else. She just let her mare follow her own inclinations.

The peculiar spell of anger carried the Princess on, almost unconscious, for an hour or so. And by this time she was beginning to climb pretty high. Her horse walked steadily all the time. They emerged on a bare slope, and the trail wound through frail aspen-stems. Here a wind swept, and some of the aspens were already bare. Others were fluttering their discs of pure solid yellow, leaves so *nearly* like petals, while the slope ahead was one soft, glowing fleece of daffodil yellow; fleecy like a golden fox-skin, and yellow as daffodils alive in the wind and the high mountain sun.

She paused and looked back. The near great slopes were mottled with gold and the dark hue of spruce, like some unsinged eagle, and the light lay gleaming upon them. Away through the gap of the canyon she could see the pale blue of the egg-like desert, with the crumpled dark crack of the Rio Grande canyon. And far, far off, the blue mountains like a fence of angels on the horizon.

And she thought of her adventure. She was going on alone with Romero. But then she was very sure of herself, and Romero was not the kind of man to do anything to her, against her will. This was her first thought. And she just had a fixed desire to go over the brim of the mountains, to look into the inner chaos of the Rockies. And she wanted to go with Romero, because he had some peculiar kinship with her, there was some peculiar link between the two of them. Miss Cummins anyhow would have been only a discordant note.

She rode on, and emerged at length in the lap of the summit. Beyond her was a great concave of stone and stark dead-grey trees, where the mountain ended against the sky. But nearer was the dense black, bristling spruce, and at her feet was the lap of the summit, a flat little valley of sere grass and quiet-standing yellow aspens, the stream trickling like a thread across.

It was a little valley or shell from which the stream was gently poured into the lower rocks and trees of the canyon. Around her was a fairy-like gentleness, the delicate sere grass, the groves of delicate-stemmed aspens dropping their flakes like petals. Almost like flowers the aspen trees stood in thickets, shedding their petals of bright yellow. And the delicate, quick little stream threading through the wild, sere grass.

Here one might expect deer and fawns and wild things, as in a little paradise. Here she was to wait for Romero, and they were to have lunch.

She unfastened her saddle and pulled it to the ground with a crash, letting her horse wander with a long rope. How beautiful Tansy looked, sorrel among the yellow leaves that lay like a patina on the sere ground. The Princess herself wore a fleecy sweater of a pale, sere buff, like the grass, and riding breeches of a pure orange-tawny colour. She felt quite in the picture.

From her saddle-pouches she took the packages of lunch, spread a little cloth, and sat to wait for Romero. Then she made a little fire. Then she ate a devilled egg. Then she ran after Tansy, who was straying across-stream. Then she sat in the sun, in the stillness near the aspens, and waited.

The sky was blue. Her little alp was soft and delicate as fairyland. But beyond and up jutted the great slopes, dark with the pointed feathers of spruce, bristling with grey dead trees among grey rock, or dappled with dark and gold. The beautiful, but fierce, heavy, cruel mountains, with their moments of tenderness.

She saw Tansy start, and begin to run. Two ghostlike figures on horseback emerged from the black of the spruce across the stream. It was two Indians on horseback, swathed like seated mummies in their pale-grey cotton blankets. Their guns jutted beyond the saddles. They rode straight towards her, to her thread of smoke.

As they came near, they unswathed themselves and greeted her, looking at her curiously from their dark eyes. Their black hair was somewhat untidy, the long rolled plaits on their shoulders were soiled. They looked tired.

They got down from their horses near her little fire—a camp was a camp—swathed their blankets round their hips, pulled the saddles from their ponies and turned them loose, then sat down. One was a young Indian whom she had met before, the other was an older man.

"You all alone?" said the younger man.

"Romero will be here in a minute," she said, glancing back along the trail.

"Ah Romero! You with him? Where you going?"

"Round the ridge," she said. "Where are you going?"

"We going down to Pueblo."

"Been out hunting? How long have you been out?"

"Yes. Been out five days." The young Indian gave a little, meaningless laugh.

"Got anything?"

"No, we see tracks of two deer—but not got nothing."

The Princess noticed a suspicious-looking bulk under one of the saddles: surely a folded-up deer. But she said nothing.

"You must have been cold," she said.

"Yes, very cold in the night. And hungry. Got nothing to eat since yesterday. Eat it all up."—And again he laughed his little meaningless laugh.

Under their dark skins, the two men looked peaked and hungry. The Princess rummaged for food among the saddle-bags. There was a lump of bacon—the regular stand-back—and some bread. She gave them this, and they began toasting slices of it on long sticks at the fire. Such was the little camp Romero saw as he rode down the slope: the Princess in her orange breeches, her head tied in a blue and brown silk kerchief, sitting opposite the two dark-headed Indians across the camp-fire, while one of the Indians was leaning forward toasting bacon, his two plaits of braid-swathed hair dangling as if wearily.

Romero rode up, his face expressionless. The Indians greeted him in Spanish. He unsaddled his horse, took food from the bags, and sat down at the camp to eat. The Princess went to the stream for water, and to wash her hands.

"Got coffee?" asked the Indians.

"No coffee this outfit," said Romero.

They lingered an hour or more in the warm midday sun. Then Romero saddled the horses. The Indians still squatted by the fire. Romero and the Princess rode away, calling *Adios!* to the Indians, over the stream and into the dense spruce whence the two strange figures had emerged.

When they were alone, Romero turned and looked at her curiously, in a way she could not understand, with such a hard glint in his eyes. And for the first time, she wondered if she was rash.

"I hope you don't mind going alone with me," she said.

"If you want it," he replied.

They emerged at the foot of the great bare slope of rocky summit, where dead spruce trees stood sparse and bristling like bristles on a grey, dead hog. Romero said the Mexicans, twenty years back, had fired the mountains, to drive out the whites. This grey concave slope of summit was corpse-like.

The trail was almost invisible. Romero watched for the trees which the Forest Service had blazed. And they climbed the stark corpse slope, among dead spruce fallen and ash-grey, into the wind. The wind came rushing from the west, up the funnel of the canyon, from the desert. And there was the desert, like a vast mirage tilting slowly upwards towards the west, immense and pallid, away beyond the funnel of the canyon. The Princess could hardly look.

For an hour their horses rushed the slope, hastening with a great working of the haunches upwards, and halting to breathe, scrambling again, and rowing their way up length by length, on the livid, slanting wall. While the wind blew like some vast machine.

After an hour they were working their way on the incline, no longer forcing straight up. All was grey and dead around them, the horses picked their way over the silver-grey corpses of the spruce. But they were near the top, near the ridge.

Even the horses made a rush for the last bit. They had worked round to a scrap of spruce forest, near the very top. They hurried in, out of the huge, monstrous, mechanical wind, that whistled inhumanly and was palely cold. So, stepping through the dark screen of trees, they emerged over the crest.

In front now was nothing but mountains, ponderous, massive, down-sitting mountains, in a huge and intricate knot, empty of life or soul. Under the bristling black feathers of spruce near by lay patches of white snow. The lifeless valleys were concaves of rock and spruce, the rounded summits and the hog-backed summits of grey rock crowded one behind the other, like some monstrous herd in arrest.

It frightened the Princess, it was *so* inhuman. She had not thought it could be so inhuman, so, as it were, anti-life. And yet now one of her desires was fulfilled. She had seen it, the massive, gruesome, repellent core of the Rockies. She saw it there beneath her eyes, in its gigantic heavy gruesomeness.

And she wanted to go back. At this moment she wanted to turn back. She had looked down into the intestinal knot of these mountains. She was frightened. She wanted to go back.

But Romero was riding on, on the lee side of the spruce forest, above the concaves of the inner mountains. He turned round to her, and pointed at the slope with a dark hand:

"Here a miner has been trying for gold," he said.

It was a grey, scratched out heap near a hole—like a great badger hole. And it looked quite fresh.

"Quite lately?" said the Princess.

"No, long ago—twenty, thirty years." He had reined in his horse and was looking at the mountains. "Look!" he said. "There goes the Forest Service trail—along those ridges, on the top, way over there till it come to Lucytown, where is the government road. We go down there—no trail—see, behind that mountain—you see the top, no trees, and some grass?"

His arm was lifted, his brown hand pointing, his dark eyes piercing into the distance, as he sat on his black horse twisting round to her. Strange and ominous, only the demon of himself, he seemed to her. She was dazed and a little sick, at that height, and she could not *see* any more. Only she saw an eagle turning in the air beyond, and the light from the west showed the pattern on him underneath.

"Shall I ever be able to go so far?" asked the Princess faintly, petulantly.

"Oh yes! All easy now. No more hard places."

They worked along the ridge, up and down, keeping on the lee side, the inner side, in the dark shadow. It was cold. Then the trail laddered up again, and they emerged on a narrow ridge-track, with the mountain slipping away enormously on either side. The Princess was afraid. For one moment she looked out, and saw the desert, the desert ridges, more desert, more blue ridges, shining pale and very vast, far below, vastly, palely tilting to the western horizon. It was ethereal and terrifying in its gleaming, pale, half-burnished immensity, tilted at the west. She could not bear it. To the left was the ponderous, involved mass of mountains all kneeling heavily.

She closed her eyes and let her consciousness evaporate away. The mare followed the trail. So on and on, in the wind again.

They turned their backs to the wind, facing inwards to the mountains. She thought they had left the trail: it was quite invisible.

"No," he said, lifting his hand and pointing. "Don't you see the blazed trees?"

And making an effort of consciousness, she was able to perceive on a pale-grey dead spruce stem the old marks where an axe had chipped a piece away. But with the height, the cold, the wind, her brain was numb.

They turned again and began to descend: he told her they had left the trail. The horses slithered in the loose stones, picking their way downward. It was afternoon, the sun stood obtrusive and gleaming in the lower heavens: about four o'clock. The horses went steadily, slowly, but obstinately onwards. The air was getting colder. They were in among the lumpish peaks and steep concave valleys. She was barely conscious at all of Romero.

He dismounted and came to help her from her saddle. She tottered, but would not betray her feebleness.

"We must slide down here," he said. "I can lead the horses."

They were on a ridge, and facing a steep bare slope of pallid, tawny mountain grass on which the western sun shone full. It was steep and concave. The Princess felt she might start slipping, and go down like a toboggan, into the great hollow.

But she pulled herself together. Her eye blazed up again with excitement and determination. A wind rushed past her: she could hear the shriek of spruce trees far below. Bright spots came on her cheeks, as her hair blew across. She looked a wild, fairy-like little thing.

"No," she said. "I will take my horse."

"Then mind she doesn't slip down on top of you," said Romero. And away he went, nimbly dropping down the pale, steep incline, making from rock to rock, down the grass, and following any little slanting groove. His horse hopped and slithered after him, and sometimes stopped dead, with forefeet pressed back, refusing to go further. He, below his horse, looked up and pulled the reins gently, and encouraged the creature. Then the horse once more dropped his forefeet, with a jerk, and the descent continued.

The Princess set off in blind, reckless pursuit, tottering and yet nimble. And Romero, looking constantly back to see how she was faring, saw her fluttering down like some queer little bird, her orange breeches twinkling like the legs of some duck, and her head, tied in the blue and buff kerchief, bound round and round like the head of some blue-topped bird. The sorrel mare rocked and slipped behind her. But down came the Princess, in a reckless intensity, a tiny, vivid spot on the great hollow flank of the tawny mountain. So tiny! Tiny as a frail bird's egg. It made Romero's mind go blank with wonder.

But they had to get down, out of that cold and drugging wind. The spruce trees stood below, where a tiny stream emerged in stones. Away plunged Romero, zigzagging down. And away behind, up the slope, fluttered the tiny, bright coloured Princess, holding the end of the long reins, and leading the lumbering, four-foot-sliding mare.

At last they were down. Romero sat in the sun, below the wind, beside some squaw-berry bushes. The Princess came near, the colour flaming in her cheeks, her eyes dark blue, much darker than the kerchief on her head, and glowing unnaturally.

"We make it," said Romero.

"Yes," said the Princess, dropping the reins and subsiding on to the grass, unable to speak, unable to think.

But thank heaven, they were out of the wind and in the sun.

In a few minutes her consciousness and her control began to come back. She drank a little water. Romero was attending to the saddles. Then they set off again, leading the horses still a little further down the tiny stream-bed. Then they could mount.

They rode down a bank and into a valley grove dense with aspens. Winding through the thin, crowding, pale-smooth stems, the sun shone flickering beyond them, and the disc-like aspen leaves, waving queer mechanical signals, seemed to be splashing the gold light before her eyes. She rode on in a splashing dazzle of gold.

Then they entered shadow and the dark, resinous spruce trees. The fierce boughs always wanted to sweep her off her horse. She had to twist and squirm past.

But there was a semblance of an old trail. And all at once they emerged in the sun on the edge of the spruce-grove, and there was a little cabin, and the bottom of a small, naked valley with grey rock and heaps of stones, and a round pool of intense green water, dark green. The sun was just about to leave it.

Indeed, as she stood, the shadow came over the cabin and over herself; they were in the lower gloom, a twilight. Above, the heights still blazed.

It was a little hole of a cabin, near the spruce trees, with an earthen floor and an unhinged door. There was a wooden bed-bunk, three old sawn-off log-lengths, to sit on, as stools, and a sort of fire-place, no room for anything else. The little hole would hardly contain two people. The roof had gone—but Romero had laid on thick spruce-boughs.

The strange squalor of the primitive forest pervaded the place, the squalor of animals and their droppings, the squalor of the wild. The Princess knew the peculiar repulsiveness of it. She was tired and faint.

Romero hastily got a handful of twigs, set a little fire going in the stone grate, and went out to attend to the horses. The Princess vaguely, mechanically put sticks on the fire, in a sort of stupor, watching the blaze stupefied and fascinated. She could not make much fire—it would set the whole cabin alight. And smoke oozed out of the delapidated mud-and-stone chimney.

When Romero came in with the saddle-pouches and saddles, hanging the saddles on the wall, there sat the little Princess on her stump of wood in front of the delapidated fire-grate, warming her tiny hands at the blaze, while her orange breeches glowed almost like another fire. She was in a sort of stupor.

"You have some whiskey now, or some tea? Or wait for some soup?" he asked.

She rose and looked at him with bright, dazed eyes, half comprehending, the colour glowing hectic in her cheeks.

"Some tea," she said, "with a little whiskey in it. Where's the kettle?"

"Wait," he said. "I'll bring the things."

She took her cloak from the back of her saddle, and followed him into the open. It was a deep cup of shadow. But above, the sky was still shining, and the heights of the mountains were blazing with aspens like fire blazing.

Their horses were cropping the grass among the stones. Romero clambered up a heap of grey stones and began lifting away logs and rocks, till he had opened the mouth of one of the miner's little old workings. This was his cache. He brought out bundles of blankets, pans for cooking, a little petrol camp-stove, an axe: the regular camp outfit. He seemed so quick and energetic and full of force. This quick force dismayed the Princess a little.

She took a saucepan and went down the stones to the water. It was very still and mysterious, and of a deep green colour, yet pure, transparent as glass. How cold the place was! How mysterious and fearful.

She crouched in her dark cloak by the water, rinsing the saucepan, feeling the cold heavy above her, the shadow like a vast weight upon her, bowing her down. The sun was leaving the mountain tops, departing, leaving her under profound shadow. Soon it would crush her down completely.

Sparks?—or eyes looking at her across the water? She gazed hypnotised. And with her sharp eyes she made out in the dusk the pale form of a bob-cat crouching by the water's edge, pale as the stones among which it crouched, opposite. And it was watching her with cold, electric eyes of strange intentness, a sort of cold, icy wonder and fearlessness. She saw its *museau* pushed forward, its tufted ears pricking intensely up. It was watching her with cold, animal curiosity, something demonish and conscienceless.

She made a swift movement, spilling her water. And in a flash the creature was gone, leaping like a cat that is escaping: but strange and soft in its motion, with its little bob tail. Rather fascinating. Yet that cold, intent, demonish watching! She shivered with cold and fear. She knew well enough the dread and repulsiveness of the wild.

Romero carried in the bundles of bedding and the camp outfit. The windowless cabin was already dark inside. He lit a lantern, and then went out again with the axe. She heard him chopping wood as she fed sticks to the fire under her water. When he came in with an armful of oak-scrub faggots, she had just thrown the tea into the water.

"Sit down," she said, "and drink tea."

He poured a little bootleg whiskey into the enamel cups, and in the silence the two sat on the log-ends, sipping the hot liquid and coughing occasionally from the smoke.

"We burn these oak sticks," he said. "They don't make hardly any smoke."

Curious and remote he was, saying nothing except what had to be said. And she, for her part, was as remote from him. They seemed far, far apart, worlds apart, now they were so near.

He unwrapped one bundle of bedding, and spread the blankets and the sheepskin in the wooden bunk.

"You lie down and rest," he said, "and I make the supper."

She decided to do so. Wrapping her cloak round her, she lay down in the bunk, turning her face to the wall. She could hear him preparing supper over the little petrol stove. Soon she could smell the soup he was heating: and soon she heard the hissing of fried chicken in a pan.

"You eat your supper now?" he said.

With a jerky, despairing movement she sat up in the bunk, tossing back her hair. She felt cornered.

"Give it me here," she said.

He handed her first the cupful of soup. She sat among the blankets, eating it slowly. She was hungry. Then he gave her an enamel plate with pieces of fried chicken, and currant jelly, butter, and bread. It was very good. As they ate the chicken he made the coffee. She said never a word. A certain resentment filled her. She was cornered.

When supper was over he washed the dishes, dried them, and put everything away carefully, else there would have been no room to move, in the hole of a cabin. The oak-wood gave out a good bright heat.

He stood for a few moments at a loss. Then he asked her:

"You want to go to bed soon?"

"Soon," she said. "Where are you going to sleep?"

"I make my bed here——" he pointed to the floor along the wall. "Too cold out of doors."

"Yes," she said. "I suppose it is."

She sat immobile, her cheeks hot, full of conflicting thoughts. And she watched him while he folded the blankets on the floor, a sheepskin underneath. Then she went out into the night.

The stars were big. Mars sat on the edge of a mountain, for all the world like the blazing eye of a crouching mountain lion. But she herself was deep, deep below, in a pit of shadow. In the intense silence she seemed to hear the spruce forest crackling with electricity and cold. Strange, foreign stars floated on that unmoving water. The night was going to freeze. Over the hills came the far sobbing-singing howling of the coyotes. She wondered how the horses would be.

Shuddering a little, she turned to the cabin. Warm light showed through its chinks. She pushed at the ricketty, half opened door.

"What about the horses?" she said.

"My black, he won't go away. And your mare will stay with him.—You want to go to bed now?"

"I think I do."

"All right. I feed the horses some oats."

And he went out into the night.

He did not come back for some time. She was lying wrapped up tight in the bunk.

He blew out the lantern, and sat down on his bedding to take off his clothes. She lay with her back turned. And soon, in the silence, she was asleep.

She dreamed it was snowing, and the snow was falling on her through the roof, softly, softly, helplessly, and she was going to be buried alive. She was growing colder and colder, the snow was weighing down on her. The snow was going to absorb her.

She awoke with a sudden convulsion, like pain. She was really very cold. Perhaps the heavy blankets had numbed her. Her heart seemed unable to beat, she felt she could not move.

With another convulsion she sat up. It was intensely dark. There was not even a spark of fire: the light wood had burned right away.

She sat in thick, oblivious darkness. Only through a chink she could see a star.

"What did she want? Oh, what did she want?"—She sat in bed and rocked herself wofully. She could hear the steady breathing of the sleeping man. She was shivering with cold, her heart seemed as if it could not beat. She wanted warmth, protection, she wanted to be taken away from herself. And at the same time, perhaps more deeply than anything she wanted to keep herself intact, intact, untouched, that no-one should have any power over her, or rights to her. It was a wild necessity in her: that no-one, particularly no man, should have any rights or power over her, that no-one and nothing should possess her.

Yet that other thing! And she was so cold, so shivering, and her heart could not beat. Oh, would not someone help her heart to beat.

She tried to speak, and could not. Then she cleared her throat.

"Romero," she said strangely. "It is so cold!"

Where did her voice come from, and whose voice was it, in the dark?

She heard him at once sit up, and his voice, startled, with a resonance that seemed to vibrate against her, saying:

"What? What is it? Eh?"

"I am so cold."

He had risen from his blankets, and stood by the bunk.

"You want me to make you warm."

"Yes."

As soon as he had lifted her in his arms, she wanted to scream to him not to touch her. She stiffened herself. Yet she was dumb.

And he was warm, but with a terrible animal warmth that seemed to annihilate her. He panted like an animal with desire. And she was given over to this thing.

She had never, never wanted to be given over to this. But she had *willed* that it should happen to her. And according to her will, she lay and let it happen. But she never wanted it. She never wanted to be thus assailed and handled, mauled. She wanted to keep herself to herself.

However, she had willed it to happen, and it had happened. She panted with relief when it was over.

Yet even now she had to lie within the hard, powerful clasp of this other creature, this man. She dreaded to struggle to go away. She dreaded almost too much the icy cold of that other bunk.

"Do you want to go away from me?" asked his strange voice. Oh, if it could only have been a thousand miles away from her! Yet she had willed to have it thus close.

"No," she said.

And she could feel a curious joy and pride surging up again in him: at her expense. Because he had got her. She felt like a victim there. And he was exulting in his power over her, his possession, his pleasure.

When dawn came, he was fast asleep. She sat up suddenly.

"I want a fire," she said.

He opened his brown eyes wide, and smiled with a curious tender luxuriousness.

"I want you to make a fire," she said.

He glanced at the chinks of light. His brown face hardened to the day.

"All right," he said. "I'll make it."

She hid her face while he dressed. She could not bear to look at him. He was so suffused with pride and luxury. She hid her face almost in despair. But feeling the cold blast of air as he opened the door, she wriggled down into the warm place where he had been. How soon the warmth ebbed, when he had gone.

He made a fire and went out, returning after a while with water.

"You stay in bed till the sun comes," he said. "It's very cold."

"Hand me my cloak."

She wrapped the cloak fast round her, and sat up among the blankets. The warmth was already spreading from the fire.

"I suppose we will start back as soon as we've had breakfast?"

He was crouching at his camp-stove making scrambled eggs. He looked up suddenly transfixed, and his brown eyes, so soft and luxuriously widened, looked straight at her.

"You want to?" he said.

"We'd better get back as soon as possible," she said, turning aside from his eyes.

"You want to get away from me?" he asked, repeating the question of the night in a sort of dread.

"I want to get away from here," she said decisively. And it was true. She wanted supremely to get away, back to the world of people.

He rose slowly to his feet, holding the aluminium frying-pan.

"Don't you like last night?" he asked.

"Not really," she said. "Why? Do you?"

He put down the frying-pan and stood staring at the wall. She could see she had given him a cruel blow. But she did not relent. She was getting her own back. She wanted to regain possession of all herself, and in some mysterious way, she felt that he possessed some part of her still.

He looked round at her slowly, his face greyish and heavy.

"You Americans," he said; "you always want to do a man down."

"I am not American," she said, "I am British. And I don't want to do any man down. I only want to go back, now."

"And what will you say about me, down there?"

"That you were very kind to me, and very good."

He crouched down again, and went on turning the eggs. He gave her her plate, and her coffee, and sat down to his own food.

But again he seemed not to be able to swallow. He looked up at her.

"You don't like last night?" he asked.

"Not really," she said, though with some difficulty. "I don't care for that kind of thing."

A blank sort of wonder spread over his face, at these words: followed immediately by a black look of anger, and then a stony, sinister despair.

"You don't?" he said, looking her in the eyes.

"Not really," she replied, looking back with steady hostility, into his eyes.

Then a dark flame seemed to come from his face.

"I make you," he said, as if to himself.

He rose and reached her clothes, that hung on a peg: the fine linen underwear, the orange breeches, the fleecy jumper, the blue and buff kerchief: then he took up her riding boots and her bead moccasins. Crushing everything in his arms, he opened the door. Sitting up, she saw him stride down to the dark-green pool, in the frozen shadow of that deep cup of a valley. He tossed the clothing and the boots out on the pool. Ice had formed. And on the pure, dark green mirror, in the slaty shadow, the Princess saw her things lying, the white linen, the orange breeches, the black boots, the blue moccasins, a tangled heap of colour. Romero picked up rocks and heaved them out at the ice, till the surface broke and the fluttering clothing disappeared in the rattling water, while the valley echoed and shouted again with the sound.

She sat in despair among the blankets, hugging tight her pale-blue cloak. Romero strode straight back to the cabin.

"Now you stay here with me," he said.

She was furious. Her blue eyes met his. They were like two demons watching one another. In his face, beyond a sort of unrelieved gloom, was a demonish desire for death.

He saw her looking round the cabin, scheming. He saw her eyes on his rifle. He took the gun and went out with it. Returning, he pulled out her saddle, carried it to the tarn, and threw it in. Then he fetched his own saddle and did the same.

"Now will you go away?" he said, looking at her with a smile.

She debated within herself whether to coax him and wheedle him. But she knew he was already beyond it. She sat among her blankets in a frozen sort of despair, hard as hard ice with anger.

He did the chores, and disappeared with the gun. She got up in her blue pyjamas, huddled in her cloak, and stood in the doorway. The dark-green pool was motionless again, the stony slopes were pallid and frozen. Shadow still lay like an after-death, deep in this valley. Away in the distance she saw the horses feeding. If she could catch one!—The brilliant yellow sun was half way down the mountains. It was nine o'clock.

All day she was alone: and she was frightened. What she was frightened of, she didn't know. Perhaps the crackling in the dark spruce wood. Perhaps just the savage, heartless wildness of the mountains. But all day she sat in the sun in the doorway of the cabin, watching, watching for hope. And all the time, her bowels were cramped with fear.

She saw a dark spot that probably was a bear roving across the pale grassy slope in the far distance, in the sun.

When, in the afternoon, she saw Romero approaching, with silent suddenness, carrying his gun and a dead deer, the cramp in her bowels relaxed, then become colder. She dreaded him with a cold dread.

"There is deer-meat," he said, throwing the dead doe at her feet.

"You don't want to go away from here," he said. "This is a nice place."

She shrank into the cabin.

"Come into the sun," he said, following her. She looked up at him with hostile, frightened eyes.

"Come into the sun," he repeated, taking her gently by the arm, in a powerful grasp.

She knew it was useless to rebel. Quietly he led her out, and seated himself in the doorway, holding her still by the arm.

"In the sun it is warm," he said. "Look, this is a nice place. You are such a pretty white woman, why do you want to act mean to me? Isn't this a nice place! Come! Come here! It sure is warm here."

He drew her to him, and in spite of her stony resistance, he took her cloak from her, holding her in her thin blue pyjamas.

"You sure are a pretty little white woman, small and pretty," he said. "You sure won't act mean to me—you don' want to, I know you don't."

She, stony and powerless, had to submit to him. The sun shone on her white, delicate skin.

"I sure don't mind hell fire," he said, "after this."

A queer, luxurious good-humour seemed to possess him again. But though outwardly she was powerless, inwardly she resisted him, absolutely and stonily.

When later he was leaving her again, she said to him suddenly:

"You think you can conquer me this way. But you can't. You can never conquer me."

He stood arrested, looking back at her, with many emotions conflicting in his face: wonder, surprise, a touch of horror, and an unconscious pain that crumpled his face till it was like a mask. Then he went out without saying a word, hung the dead deer on a bough, and started to flay it. While he was at this butcher's work, the sun sank and cold night came on again.

"You see," he said to her as he crouched cooking the supper, "I ain't goin' to let you go. I reckon you called to me in the night, and I've some right. If you want to fix it up right now with me, and say you want to be with me, we'll fix it up now and go down to the ranch tomorrow and get married or whatever you want. But you've got to say you want to be with me. Else I shall stay right here, till something happens."

She waited a while before she answered:

"I don't want to be with anybody against my will. I don't dislike you: at least, I didn't, till you tried to put your will over mine. I won't have anybody's will put over me. You can't succeed. Nobody could. You can never get me under your will.—And you won't have long to try, because soon they will send someone to look for me."

He pondered this last, and she regretted having said it. Then, sombre, he bent to the cooking again.

He could not conquer her, however much he violated her. Because her spirit was hard and flawless as a diamond. But he could shatter her. This she knew. Much more, and she would be shattered.

In a sombre, violent excess he tried to expend his desire for her. And she was racked with agony, and felt each time she would die. Because, in some peculiar way, he had got hold of her, some un-realised part of her which she never wished to realise. Racked with a burning, tearing anguish, she felt that the thread of her being would break, and she would die. The burning heat that racked her inwardly.

If only, only she could be alone again, cool and intact. If only she could recover herself again, cool and intact! Would she ever, ever, ever be able to bear herself again.

Even now she did not hate him. It was beyond that. Like some racking, hot doom. Personally he hardly existed.

The next day he would not let her have any fire, because of attracting attention with the smoke. It was a grey day, and she was cold. He stayed around, and heated soup on the petrol stove. She lay motionless in the blankets.

And in the afternoon she pulled the clothes over her head and broke into tears. She had never really cried in her life. He dragged the blankets away and looked to see what was shaking her. She sobbed in helpless hysterics. He covered her over again and went outside, looking at the mountains where clouds were dragging and leaving a little snow. It was a violent, windy, horrible day, the evil of winter rushing down.

She cried for hours. And after this a great silence came between them. They were two people who had died. He did not touch her any more. In the night she lay and shivered like a dying dog. She felt that her very shivering would rupture something in her body, and she would die.

At last she had to speak.

"Could you make a fire? I am so cold," she said, with chattering teeth.

"Want to come over here?" came his voice.

"I would rather you made me a fire," she said, her teeth knocking together and chopping the words in two.

He got up and kindled a fire. At last the warmth spread, and she could sleep.

The next day was still chilly, with some wind. But the sun shone. He went about in silence, with a dead-looking face. It was now so dreary, and so like death, she wished he would do anything rather than continue in this negation. If now he asked her to go down with

him to the world and marry him, she would do it. What did it matter!
Nothing mattered any more.

But he would not ask her. His desire was dead and heavy like ice
within him. He kept watch around the house.

On the fourth day as she sat huddled in the doorway in the sun,
hugged in a blanket, she saw two horsemen come over the crest of the
grassy slope, small figures. She gave a cry. He looked up quickly and
saw the figures. The men had dismounted. They were looking for the
trail.

"They are looking for me," she said.

"Muy bien!" he answered in Spanish.

He went and fetched his gun, and sat with it across his knees.

"Oh!" she said. "Don't shoot!"

He looked across at her.

"Why?" he said. "You like staying with me?"

"No," she said. "But don't shoot."

"I ain't going to Pen.," he said.

"You won't have to go to Pen.," she said. "Don't shoot."

"I'm going to shoot," he muttered.

And straight away he kneeled and took very careful aim. The
Princess sat on in an agony of helplessness and hopelessness.

The shot rang out. In an instant she saw one of the horses on the
pale grassy slope rear and go rolling down. The man had dropped in
the grass, and was invisible. The second man clambered on his horse,
and on that precipitous place went at a gallop in a long swerve towards
the nearest spruce tree cover. Bang! Bang! went Romero's shots. But
each time he missed, and the running horse leaped like a kangaroo
towards cover.

It was hidden. Romero now got behind a rock, watching for the
man to show some sign of himself. All was tense silence, in the brilliant
sunshine. The Princess sat on the bunk inside the cabin, crouching
paralysed. For hours, it seemed, Romero knelt behind his rock, in
his black shirt, bare-headed, watching. He had a beautiful alert figure.
The Princess wondered why she did not feel sorry for him. But her
spirit was hard and cold, her heart could not melt, though now she
would have given anything if it could have melted. If she could have
called him to her, with love.

But no, she did not love him. She would never love any man. Never.
It was fixed and sealed in her, almost vindictively.

Suddenly she was so startled she almost fell from the bunk. A shot rang out quite close, from behind the cabin. Romero leaped straight into the air, his arms fell outstretched, turning as he leaped. And even while he was in the air, a second shot rang out, and he fell with a crash, squirming, his hands clutching the earth towards the cabin door.

The Princess sat absolutely motionless, transfixed, staring at the prostrate figure. In a few moments the figure of a man in the Forest Service appeared close to the house: a young man in a broad-brimmed Stetson hat, dark flannel shirt, and riding-boots, carrying a gun. He strode over to the prostrate figure.

"Got you, Romero!" he said aloud. And he turned the dead man over. There was already a little pool of blood where Romero's breast had been.

"Hm!" said the Forest Service man. "Guess I got you nearer than I thought."

And he squatted there staring at the dead man.

The distant calling of his comrade aroused him. He stood up.

"Hallo Bill!" he shouted. "Yep! Got him!—Yep! Done him in, apparently."

The second man rode out of the forest, on a grey horse. He had a ruddy, kind face and round brown eyes dilated with dismay.

"He's not passed out?" he asked anxiously.

"Looks like it," said the first young man coolly.

The second dismounted and bent over the body. Then he stood up again and nodded.

"Yea-a!" he said. "He's done in all right. It's him all right, boy! It's Domingo Romero."

"Yep! I know it!" replied the other.

Then in perplexity he turned and looked into the cabin where the Princess squatted staring with big owl eyes from her red blanket.

"Hello!" he said, coming towards the hut. And he took his hat off. Oh, the sense of ridicule she felt! Though he did not mean any.

But she could not speak, no matter what she felt.

"What'd this man start firing for?" he asked.

She fumbled for words, with numb lips.

"He had gone out of his mind!" she said, with solemn, stammering conviction.

"Good Lord! You mean to say he'd gone out of his mind.—Whew! That's pretty awful. That explains it then. Hm!"

He accepted the explanation without more ado.

With some difficulty they succeeded in getting the Princess down to the ranch. But she too was now a little mad.

"I'm not quite sure where I am," she said to Mrs Wilkieson, as she lay in bed. "Do you mind explaining."

Mrs Wilkieson explained, tactfully.

"Oh yes!" said the Princess. "I remember. And I had an accident in the mountains, didn't I? Didn't we meet a man who'd gone mad, and who shot my horse from under me?"

"Yes, you met a man who had gone out of his mind."

The real affair was hushed up. The Princess departed east in a fortnight's time, in Miss Cummins' care. Apparently she had recovered herself entirely. She was the Princess, and a virgin intact.

But her bobbed hair was grey at the temples, and her eyes were a little mad. She was slightly crazy.

"Since my accident in the mountains, when a man went mad and shot my horse from under me, and my guide had to shoot him dead, I have never felt quite myself."

So she put it.

Later, she married an elderly man, and seemed pleased.

Explanatory Notes

The Woman Who Rode Away

5:8 **Sierra Madre**   A mountain range in western Mexico, rich in silver and copper. Lawrence travelled in this area in October 1923 and, from Navojoa, Sonora, visited a silver mine in the mountains at Minas Nuevas near Alamos close to the state border between Sonora and Chihuahua. The setting for the main part of the story is based on this region, and other elements draw on the various Native American peoples of the area. However, Lawrence also drew significantly on the topography and native cultures of New Mexico (see notes 35:14–15 and 186:34).

5:29–31 **portales ... dead dog**   Covered wooden walkways ... Lawrence describes a similar scene on his visit to the mountain village of Alamos; see *Letters* iv. 506.

5:35 **The great war**   First World War, 1914–18.

6:16 **Like any Sheik**   *The Sheik* (1921) was a film starring Rudolph Valentino (see note on 75:36–7). The association is sustained with the reference to 'invincible slavery' (6:24).

6:34 **El Paso**   City in Texas on the border with Mexico.

8:21 **Torreón**   City in central Mexico.

8:23 **Navajo ... Aztec or Totonac [8:28]**   The Navajo are the largest Native American group of the Southwest; the Yaquis are a smaller group in north-west Mexico. The Chilchuis are, apparently, invented, but their description draws on Lawrence's knowledge of Mexican and Southwest American peoples. Montezuma II (d. 1521) was the emperor of the Aztecs, who ruled Mexico at the time of the Spanish conquest (1519–21). The Totonacs were another ancient Mexican people.

8:38 **Cuchitee**   Probably a fictitious place.

9:26 **roan**   Horse whose main colour is thickly interspersed with hairs of another colour.

11:31, 34 **Adios! ... serapes**   An all-purpose greeting, also used for goodbye (Spanish) ... brightly decorated woollen wraps or shawls.

14:28 **tortillas**   Soft flat-bread made from cornflour.

15:13 **Her horse was hobbled**   It had had two of its legs tied together to prevent it straying.

16:34 **barranca**   Canyon or gorge (Spanish).

23:32 **caciques**   Native American chiefs (Spanish).

25:16 **dance**   Lawrence also describes ceremonial dancing in, for example,

The Plumed Serpent (1926; ed. L. D. Clark, Penguin, 1995) and in three essays ('Indians and Entertainment', 'Dance of the Sprouting Corn' and 'The Hopi Snake Dance') in *Mornings in Mexico* (1927).

26:18 *Mene . . . Upharsin* Cf. Daniel v. 5–28. Daniel interpreted the words that appeared on the wall at King Belshazzar's feast as God's judgement on the king, foretelling his downfall. Thus, a proverbial reference to signs of impending trouble or disaster.

29:30 **like a basilisk's** The basilisk is a Central American lizard, but it is also the name of a mythical creature (also known as a cockatrice) whose glance was said to be fatal to any living thing.

30:18–19 **like a scorched eagle** See Lawrence's poem 'Eagle in New Mexico' (*Birds, Beasts and Flowers*, 1923).

32:24 **descended by a ladder** The description of this chamber is suggestive of a ceremonial 'kiva' of the Hopi of Arizona, which is often partly subterranean and entered from above. Lawrence visited Hopi country in August 1924.

32:38 **amole** The Mexican name for various plants used for making soap (Spanish).

34:3 **obsidian** A black, glassy, volcanic rock that the Aztecs used to make sacrificial knives.

35:14–15 **a strange amphitheatre** The setting is based on an actual place above the village of Arroyo Seco near Taos, New Mexico, where there is an ancient ceremonial cave that Lawrence visited on horseback in May 1924.

St. Mawr

41:15 *museau* Literally, the muzzle or snout of an animal, but often used figuratively for the human face (French). Cf. 'muzzles' (55:20).

41:18–19 **an outsider . . . like a sort of gipsy** The theme of 'the outsider' is a central one for Lawrence and he developed it specifically through the figure of a gipsy in another novella written not long after *St. Mawr*, *The Virgin and the Gipsy* (December 1925–January 1926; published posthumously in 1930; collected in *The Virgin and the Gipsy and Other Stories*, ed. Michael Herbert, Bethan Jones and Lindeth Vasey, Cambridge University Press, 2006). See also the biography by John Worthen, *D. H. Lawrence: The Life of an Outsider* (Allen Lane/Penguin, 2005).

41:25 **Palermo, Biarritz** The capital of Sicily and a fashionable sea resort in south-west France respectively.

41:31–3 **Rico . . . Sir Henry** Rico's name would appear to derive from Enrico, the Italian form of Henry, his actual name, and is possibly Lou's pet name for him from their early days together in Italy – or part of his pose of 'being an artist' (41:35). A baronet is an hereditary title in Britain, ranking below the peerage and nobility. Australia was a British colony until 1901 (see 54:9).

41:37 **Capri** Famous island in the Bay of Naples and something of an expatriate artists' colony during the 1920s. Lawrence visited it for two months in 1919–20 and, more briefly, in 1921 and 1926.

42:12 *gamine*   Worldly or 'street-wise'; the feminine form of *gamin*, meaning 'street urchin' (French).

42:24 **Umbria**   Region of central Italy.

42:36–7 **Cézanne ... Renoir ... the Rotonde**   The acute accent in Cézanne's name was omitted in Brett's typescript and in the English and American first editions, and uncorrected in the Cambridge edition of 1983 even though, in other similar instances, the Cambridge editor did correct missing accents (as at 137:34 and 158:19); it has been added here (see A Note on the Texts). Paul Cézanne (1839–1906) and Pierre-Auguste Renoir (1841–1919) were leading French Impressionist (and, in the case of Cézanne, Post-Impressionist) painters. The Rotonde was a café-brasserie in Montparnasse, on the Left Bank in Paris, associated with the bohemian café-culture of the period, though retaining a certain bourgeois character of its own.

43:6 **grape-shot**   Originally, a type of ammunition made up of small iron balls that scatter when fired from a cannon.

43:21 **Les Halles**   Paris's old central food market.

43:22 **the old Adam**   A proverbial reference (in allusion to original sin) to man's worldly or sensual nature. A favourite image for Lawrence, often used with sexual connotations. See, for example, his early short stories 'The Old Adam' and 'New Eve and Old Adam' (written in the early 1910s and published posthumously in 1934; collected in *Love Among the Haystacks and Other Stories*, ed. John Worthen, Penguin, 1996).

44:11 **Platonic**   Non-sexual, spiritual (by reference to Plato's idealist philosophy).

44:20 **ménage**   Literally, 'household' or 'married couple' but here also with the sense of an 'arrangement' (French).

44:35 **the war**   First World War, 1914–18.

44:39 **Geronimo**   This may be an allusion, possibly ironic, to the famous Apache warrior Geronimo (1829–1909) – though a man called Geronimo did some casual work on the Lawrences' ranch in the summer of 1924 (see note on 160: 18).

45:8 **shell-shocked**   The term first emerged during the First World War to describe psychological and psychosomatic symptoms resulting from war trauma.

45:14 *Apache*   A gangster or street thug (colloquial French, also used in English).

45:17 **Phoenix**   On the surface, the name derives from the character's original home in Phoenix, Arizona, but it also refers to one of Lawrence's favourite images, the mythical phoenix bird that consumes itself in flames every 500 years and is then reborn from its own ashes – and is thus a symbol of resurrection and of uniqueness.

45:24 **the Park ... the Row** [45:30]   London's Hyde Park ... Rotten Row (see also 45:40), a bridle path where, traditionally, the fashionable and well-to-do paraded on horseback, especially during the 'season' (see note on 62:15).

45:34–6 *beau monde . . . grand monde . . .* Pincio   Fashionable world . . . world of high society (French). The Bois de Boulogne and the Pincio were famous parks in Paris and Rome where it was fashionable for the upper classes to be seen.

46:7 **argus-eyes**   In Greek mythology, the watchman Argus had a hundred eyes.

46:20–21 **Abraham Lincoln . . . Arthur Balfour**   Lincoln (1809–65), 16th President of the USA (1861–5) who led the Union states in the American Civil War, was regarded as a staunch advocate of democracy. Arthur James Balfour (1848–1930), a prominent British politician and prime minister (1902–5), had a reputation for aristocratic aloofness; he was also a distinguished philosopher, with several books to his name. It seems Lawrence had read at least one of his essays, 'Creative Evolution and Philosophic Doubt' (1911) (see Lawrence's *Letters* i. 359). He is mentioned again at 80:22.

47:10 **form, marvellous form . . .** *tableau vivant*   A barbed reference to formalist theories of art current at the time and particularly to the theory of 'significant form' put forward by one of Lawrence's Bloomsbury acquaintances, art critic Clive Bell (1881–1964) in *Art* (1914). See also Lawrence's essay, 'Introduction to These Paintings' (1929; *Late Essays and Articles*, ed. James T. Boulton, Cambridge University Press, 2004), in which he presents a more developed critique of such theories. *Tableau vivant*, literally 'living picture' (French), has the sense of a set-piece scene or situation.

47:19 **sorrel . . . mews**   Reddish-brown colour . . . urban stables, usually set round an open yard.

47:34 **think"**   In the Cambridge edition of the text, the closing quotation marks were accidentally printed as two single inverted commas (''): this has been corrected here. (See A Note on the Texts.)

48:4 **bay**   Chestnut-coloured or, as on 48:16, 'red-gold'. The related archaic word, 'bayard', may give some insight into Lawrence's choice of colour here. It can mean simply 'a bay horse', but also 'a spirited horse' or 'a knight of good fame' (*Collins English Dicitionay*); in another sense, to do with excessive self-confidence, it 'alludes to the name of the magic steed given (in medieval romance) by Charlemagne to Renaud de Montauban, which was celebrated as a type of blind recklessness' (*New Shorter Oxford English Dictionary*).

48:11 *St. Mawr . . .* **The man repeated it with a slight Welsh twist** [48:20]   The precise derivation and significance of the horse's name is open to speculation. Lawrence is reported to have pronounced the name as 'Seymour' (an old English name apparently derived from St. Mawr), so there may be a play on the sense of 'see more', given the depiction of the horse as a vision-inspiring creature with 'questioning eyes' (see, for example, 50:35–51:25). 'Mawr' is 'big' or 'great' in Welsh, which makes the name mean something like 'Great Saint'; there is a well-known Welsh hymn called 'Jesu Mawr' ('Jesu' pronounced 'Yessi'), 'Great Jesus' – and the same Welsh phrase is used colloquially as a blasphemous oath. St. Maurus, one of two principal followers of St. Benedict, is credited with introducing the Benedictine rule into France at St. Maur-sur-Loire in 543. Lawrence, who spent two years in Cornwall (1915–17), would also have been familiar with the name of the Cornish town, St. Mawes; for two months he lived near to St. Merryn, Padstow.

48:18 **Isn't that the ticket** Colloquial expression meaning 'Isn't that right?'

49:22 **hackney** A riding horse.

49:31 **the forest of Dean** In Gloucestershire in the west of England. Lawrence had visited friends at Upper Lydbrook, in the forest, at the end of August 1918.

51:1–2 **his great body glowed red with power** See Revelation vi. 4: 'And there went out another horse that was red: and power was given to him that sat thereon . . .'. Part of the inspiration for *St. Mawr* came from Lawrence's visit to the writer Frederick Carter in Shropshire in January 1924 (see note 62:18–29). Lawrence had read Carter's manuscript on the symbolism of Revelation in the summer of 1923, and later wrote his own book on Revelation, *Apocalypse* (1929–30; published posthumously 1931; ed. Mara Kalnins, Penguin, 1995), in which he argues that the horse is one of our most powerful symbols, a 'link with the ruddy-glowing Almighty of potency' (101:28–29).

51:18 **ban** From Old English *bannan*, 'to curse': an edict, command or sentence. See also previous paragraph: 'it forbade her'.

52:7 **black fiery flow in the eyes** The recurrent imagery of darkness and fire associated with St. Mawr's eyes echoes Lawrence's discussion of the 'sensual root' of vision in 'The Five Senses', chap. 5 of *Fantasia of the Unconscious* (written 1921; published 1922); see especially pp. 101–2, where he discusses horse vision and refers to 'the dark eye which glances with a certain fire' (*Psychoanalysis and the Unconscious and Fantasia of the Unconscious*, ed. Bruce Steele, Cambridge University Press, 2004).

52:15 **May we offer the penny?** A variation on the common saying, 'A penny for your thoughts?' (i.e. 'What are you thinking about?').

54:1 **like John the Baptist's** See Matthew xiv. 6–11 and Mark vi. 22–28 for the Biblical account of Herod delivering up the severed head of John the Baptist to Salome.

54:4–5 **the famous "talking heads" of modern youth ... Mephistophelian** The description of Rico throughout this paragraph seems to owe something to the artfully made-up 'talking heads' of the silent movies of the period, and may be intended to suggest what Lawrence later referred to as the 'ready-made notion of handsomeness' associated with film stars such as Rudolph Valentino (1895–1926) in his essay 'Sex Appeal'

Explanatory Notes

(1928; *Late Essays and Articles*, ed. James T. Boulton, Cambridge University Press, 2004, p. 146). Rico's 'curved mouth thrilling to death to kiss' anticipates a similar image in Lawrence's poem 'When I Went to the Film' (*Pansies*, 1929) and in his painting 'Close-Up (Kiss)' (1928). See also the earlier suggestion that Lou 'might be on the movies' (46:30). Mephistophelian, fiendishly or fatally attractive, from Mephistopheles, the evil spirit who persuades Dr Faust to sell his soul to the devil in the German legend that inspired the dramas *Doctor Faustus* by Christopher Marlowe (1564–93) and *Faust* by Goethe (1749–1832). See also 99:31–2.

54:18 *suffisance* Self-sufficiency, self-conceit (French). Later used to describe Lewis (126:24).

54:31–2 Mahomet ... mountain From the proverbial saying, 'If the mountain will not go to Mahomet (Muhammad), Mahomet will go to the mountain.'

55:17 Hippolytus Virgin-prince and huntsman of Greek legend who was killed by his own chariot horses when they bolted and dragged him along the ground after being attacked by a sea monster. Hippolytus had been falsely accused of rape by his stepmother, Phaedra, and his father, King Theseus, had then called upon the sea-god Poseidon to destroy him.

55:29 to get him going Lawrence revised this in the Eton proofs (see A Note on the Texts) to 'to get the horse going' but, evidently, he did not make the same change in the other sets of proofs as the English and American first editions do not have this reading.

56:4 without posting Without rising and falling in the saddle. See also 57:10 where, by contrast, 'Lou posted'.

57:8 Medusa The most famous (and only mortal) of the three monstrous Gorgons of Greek mythology: anyone who looked at her serpent-covered head would be turned to stone.

58:18 Queen Victoria ... Queen Alexandra [58:30] (1819–1901) British monarch, reigned 1837–1901 ... (1844–1925) widow of King Edward VII (1841–1910, reigned 1901–10) and mother of King George V (1865–1963, reigned 1910–36).

58:35 Mayfair Expensive, upper-class quarter of London.

59:6 Pullman-boy Railway-carriage attendant.

60:40 Sèvres paintings or Dresden figures The grave accent in 'Sèvres' was omitted in the typescript and in the first English edition, and this reading was accepted in the Cambridge edition. However, it was corrected for the first American edition, for which Lawrence saw the proofs, and has therefore been accepted here. (See A Note on the Texts.) Sèvres, just outside Paris, was famous since the 18th century for its finely painted porcelain; the porcelain factory at Dresden in Saxony (now Germany) was renowned for its highly decorative figures.

61:7, 9 *élan* Energy, spirit or uplift (French). The word 'vitality' is used a few lines below (61:18), suggesting a possible allusion to the theory of an *élan vital* ('life force' or 'vital impulse') first put forward in 1907 by the French philosopher, Henri Bergson (1859–1941).

61:33 **let's-be-happy** The apostrophe was omitted in the typescript and the first English edition, and this reading was accepted in the Cambridge edition. However, it was corrected in the first American edition, for which Lawrence saw the proofs, and has therefore been accepted here. Two other occurrences of 'lets' in the typescript at 65:2–3 were corrected for both first editions and then emended silently in the Cambridge edition. (See A Note on the Texts.)

61:36 **fiery and terrible** Lawrence revised this phrase in the Eton proofs (see A Note on the Texts) to 'fiery and different' but this change was not made in the other sets of proofs for the English and American first editions. Lawrence was perhaps thinking of reinforcing the motif of difference and otherness with which St. Mawr is associated.

61:39 **Claridge's ... the Carlton** Fashionable and expensive hotels in central London.

62:4 **Barmecide food** A 'Barmecide Feast' is an illusory feast, after the story in the *Arabian Nights* where a rich Barmecide prince offers an illusory feast to a beggar, who makes such a good show of enjoying it that he is then given a real one.

62:15 **the season** London's annual social round for the upper-class and well-to-do, taking place mainly from May to July.

62:18 **Shropshire ... big Church [62:29]** A county in the mid-west of England, bordering on Wales of which Shrewsbury (62:27) is the county town. Mrs Witt's Georgian house is based on an old rectory once rented by Frederick Carter (1883–1967), a writer and artist with interests in astrology and the occult. Lawrence, who had corresponded with him since December 1922, visited him in Shropshire in early January 1924. Many other aspects of the story's locale are drawn from this visit, described by Carter in *D. H. Lawrence and the Body Mystical* (London, 1932, pp. 33–42). The village here called Chomesbury (70:22) is modelled on the actual village of Pontesbury, ten miles or so south-west of Shrewsbury. The name of Corrabach Hall (62:22) may have been suggested by Pulverbatch Hall in this vicinity. See also 84:16 and the note on 87:19–20.

62:31–4 **grave-stones ... grey** Mrs Witt's elegiac mood here may be a deliberate allusion to the famous poem by Thomas Gray (1716–71), 'Elegy in a Country Churchyard' (1742–50). The poem is alluded to more directly later in the story (113:7).

62:34 **the Dean ... curates** Dean Vyner would seem to be modelled on the High Church vicar of Pontesbury whom Lawrence encountered in 1924 (see note on 62:18). It is not clear why Lawrence made him a Dean (unless to disguise the origin of the character while retaining an emphasis on his High Church allegiance); but if, as seems to be the case, he is intended to be a rural dean (a senior clergyman appointed by the bishop to oversee a group of parishes in the diocese), then his title is incorrect, as a rural dean would not be addressed as 'Dean'. Curates are non-beneficed clergy who assist a vicar or rector.

62:39–40 **passing-bell** A bell tolled at someone's passing-away.

63:5 **parvenu** Social upstart (from French).

63:6 **Yankee ... Yankee** In Europe, used of all Americans, but in the USA referring only to those from New England and other northern states – Mrs Witt is from the south.

63:16 **her own pew ... old house** It was traditional for the gentry to have a private pew in the parish church.

63:20 **Mile End** Lawrence may have been remembering the village of Mile End in the Forest of Dean from his visit nearby in August 1918 (see note on 49:31).

64:12 **gone dry** A reference to Prohibition (1919–33) when the manufacture and sale of alcohol was banned in the USA.

64:17–19 **one mothers' meeting, one sewing-bee ... Band of Hope** The typescript, English and American first editions and the Cambridge edition (see A Note on the Texts) have 'one mother's meeting'; the placing of the apostrophe (presumably a mistake) has been corrected here. Mothers' meetings were parish gatherings for women and often involved some religious instruction along with more general discussion. A 'bee' was a social gathering at which some form of communal activity – in this case, sewing – took place. The Band of Hope was a Christian temperance association for the young, founded in the mid-19th century.

64:20–21 **Wesleyan and Baptist chapels ... true-blue episcopalian** The opposition here is between the nonconformist churches and the mainstream Church of England. True-blue signifies constancy or steadfastness (originally by reference to a lasting blue dye).

65:32 **Chester** County town of Cheshire, 30 miles north of Shrewsbury.

67:33–4 **in the picture** Looking modish, just the part. See also *The Princess* 199:11.

68:25 **currants** The word is used in the general sense of 'berry fruits' (cf. also 70:37) and probably refers to the bilberries that are common in this area (see 62:20).

68:32–3 **Belle-Mère** Mother-in-law (French). See 109:39–110:4 for Mrs Witt's further word-play on 'bell-mare'.

68:39 **it's my duty** The apostrophe was omitted (presumably inadvertently) in the typescript, the first English edition and, subsequently, the Cambridge edition; however, it was corrected for the first American edition (for which Lawrence saw proofs) and that reading has been adopted here. (See A Note on the Texts.)

69:31 **martingale** A strap running from the bridle to the girth to stop a horse from throwing its head back.

71:26 **gaiters** Covering for the lower leg as protection against mud.

73:33–4 *la patrona* The boss (Spanish).

75:9 **bobbed hair** Wearing the hair short in a 'bob' became fashionable for young women in the 1920s. For many, it was a statement of modernity and a challenge to traditional gender stereotypes.

75:32 **I had so much** *go* The word is used in a similar way by Lawrence in *Women in Love* (1920), where Gudrun and Ursula discuss the '*go*' of Gerald Crich (Penguin, 2006, 48:33–6).

75:33–5 **'Those maids ... generation.'** A line from the first section of 'June in Town', a poem by Ford Madox Ford (1873–1939), first published in *Country Life* in 1907 and collected in *Songs from London* (1910). Perhaps because of the ballad rhythm, Lawrence seems to have misremembered the line as three separate ones, and the punctuation also therefore differs from the original (Ford, *Selected Poems*, ed. Max Saunders, Carcanet, 1997). An influential critic and editor of the period, Ford founded the *English Review* in 1908 and played an important part in establishing Lawrence's early career as a writer.

75:36–7 **the harem type ... the lattice** A common saying suggesting a type of woman happy to be subordinate and passive in marriage; a related use of 'harem type' appears at the end of Lawrence's short story 'Mother and Daughter' (written 1928, published 1929; collected in *The Virgin and the Gipsy and Other Stories*, ed. Michael Herbert, Bethan Jones and Lindeth Vasey, Cambridge University Press, 2006). A lattice screen typically partitioned off the harem from other quarters in an Arabian house. The 1920s saw a major fashion for all things Arabian, fuelled by popular films such as *The Sheik* (1921, starring Rudolph Valentino) and *The Thief of Baghdad* (1924, starring Douglas Fairbanks). Lawrence definitely saw (and enjoyed) the latter film, and he alludes to the former several times in his work of the 1920s.

77:7 **like one of the fates** In classical mythology, the three fates determine the life-cycle of each person: Clotho spins the original thread of life; Lachesis winds and measures it; and Atropos cuts it with her shears at the allotted time. Clearly, Mrs Witt is seen as Atropos here, and at 78:1 with the reference to her 'terrifying shears'.

77:20 **faun-like** In Roman mythology, fauns were minor rural deities represented as half-human, half-goat. The name comes from the Roman god of nature and fertility, Faunus, who is often identified with the Greek god Pan and, similarly, fauns are often identified with the Greek satyrs. See also the notes on 84:31 and 84:38.

77:38 **he knew which side his bread was buttered** Proverbial expression meaning 'he knew what was in his own best interests'.

78:6 **aureole** Halo.

81:3–5 **quick ... quick** The context makes clear that the word is used here to mean both the opposite of slow and 'alive' or 'living', as in 'the quick and the dead' (from the Apostles' Creed in the Book of Common Prayer). The latter usage is common throughout Lawrence's works.

82:4–7 **wonder ... wonder** Another key word for Lawrence, especially in this period of his career. In his essay 'Hymns in a Man's Life' (1928), for example, he writes: 'And when the wonder has gone out of a man, he is dead. ... the most precious element in life is wonder' (*Late Essays and Articles*, ed. James T. Boulton, Cambridge University Press, 2004, p. 131).

82:34 *empressé* Over-eager, exaggerated (French).

83:1–2 **the Devil's Chair** See note on 87:20.

83:18 **Women's clothing takes up so little space** This is a correction of the typographical error in the Cambridge edition that reads 'Women's clothing take up so little space'. (See A Note on the Texts.)

83:30 *L'uomo è cacciatore* In the typescript, all uncorrected accents appear as vertical marks and in both first editions and in the Cambridge edition the accent in this Italian phrase (meaning 'Man is a hunter') was printed incorrectly as an acute instead of a grave; it has been corrected here. (See A Note on the Texts.)

83:38 *game*! A pun (entirely lost on Fred) on game's two meanings of 'willing' and 'a creature hunted for sport'. Cf. Tennyson's *The Princess* (1847), section 5: 'Man is the hunter; woman is his game'. See also Lawrence's essay, 'Man is a Hunter' (1926), where he says that the phrase '*L'uomo è cacciatore*' is popular among Italians (*Sketches of Etruscan Places*, ed. Simonetta de Filippis, Penguin, 1999, p.219).

84:2 **the bottomless pit** Hell; see Revelation xx. 1–3.

84:4–5 **as if virtue had gone out of him** Cf. Mark v. 30.

84:31 **like Pan's ... the Great God Pan [84:35]** The Greek god of wild nature, of fertility, and of shepherds and their flocks. Pan is usually represented as half-man and half-goat and associated, amongst other things, with sexuality. Lawrence makes extensive reference to the myth of Pan throughout his writings of the 1920s. See, for example, his essay 'Pan in America', which he wrote at the same time as *St. Mawr*, in May–June 1924 (first published 1926; collected in *Phoenix: The Posthumous Papers of D. H. Lawrence*, ed. Edward D. McDonald, Viking Press, 1936). See also notes on 85:19–20 and 96:30–31.

84:38 **satyrs ... nymphs [85:4]** Minor woodland deities, half-man, half-goat, associated with Pan and the vital forces of nature, especially sexuality; the word is now synonymous with 'a lecherous person'. Nymphs, youthful and beautiful minor female deities, were associated with rivers, grottoes, trees and mountains.

84:40 **Even our late King Edward** The allusion is to Edward VII's (see note on 58:18) reputation as a womanizer, especially before his accession (when, for example, he was cited in two divorce cases). The line (inserted by hand in the typescript by Lawrence) was cut from some copies of the original English edition of *St. Mawr* at the request of one large bookseller, W. H. Smith and Son.

85:12 **Mr Wells' Outline** A very popular text of the 1920s, *The Outline of History, Being a Plain History of Life and Mankind* (1920) by H. G. Wells (1866–1946); also mentioned at 94:29.

Explanatory Notes

85:19–20 **If you ever saw ... you died** A contemporary myth of Pan, popularized by the writer Arthur Machen (1863–1947) in his novella *The Great God Pan* (1894), suggested that a direct encounter with Pan would lead to madness or death. Lawrence draws further on this myth in his comic short story, 'The Last Laugh' (1925; collected in *The Woman Who Rode Away and Other Stories*, ed. Dieter Mehl and Christa Jansohn, Cambridge University Press, 1995).

85:31 **your third eye** A reference to the occult belief that we possess a third eye of spiritual consciousness and perception at the centre of the forehead. Lawrence refers again to 'the mystic eye or "third eye" ' in *Apocalypse* (ed. Mara Kalnins, Cambridge University Press, 1980, 107:16).

87:19–20 **An excursion ... to ... the Angel's Chair and the Devil's Chair** This excursion is based on a walk Lawrence took with Frederick Carter in January 1924 (see note on 62:18–29). The two men walked about six miles south-west of Pontesbury to the Stiperstones, a ridge of craggy rocks that provides a high viewpoint into Wales from around 1,760 feet above sea level. In the account he later wrote of the walk, Frederick Carter says that lead had been mined in the area since Roman times (see 90:7–8).

87:25 **monkshood flowers** Purple, hooded flowers of the aconite family, and extremely poisonous.

90:20 **ling** A type of heather.

91:4 **Montgomery ... Merioneth [91:9]** Montgomery or Montgomeryshire was formerly a county of Wales, its name taken from the town of Montgomery, which is about ten miles west of the Stiperstones, just over the border in Wales ... Merioneth, a former county and now part of Gwynedd, is further to the north-west of Wales.

93:24 **prussic acid** Poison derived from Prussian blue pigment.

94:24, 26 *joie de vivre* **... a brick** Joy of living, joyousness (French) ... upper-class idiom for a good fellow or staunch friend.

94:34 **the famous Needle's Eye** Described further on 95:7–8. Lawrence may have been thinking here of a more widely-known Needle's Eye at another regional landmark, The Wrekin, some ten miles east of Shrewsbury.

96:30–31 **panic ... panic** The repetition here suggests an intentional consolidation of the Pan motif in the story: the word 'panic' comes from the Greek for 'fear excited by Pan', as the goat-god was said to startle travellers and inspire uncontrollable fear and dread.

97:38 **a dead adder ... its head crushed [97:40]** Cf. Genesis xlix. 17: 'an adder in the path, that biteth the horse heels, so that his rider shall fall backward' ... and Genesis iii. 15: 'it shall bruise thy head, and thou shalt bruise his heel'.

99:23 **bolshevism** Revolutionary socialism or communism, from the Bolshevik Party who led the Russian revolution in 1917.

100:18–19 **The accumulation of life and things** Cf. Lawrence's satirical story, 'Things' (1928; collected in *The Virgin and the Gipsy and Other*

Stories, ed. Michael Herbert, Bethan Jones and Lindeth Vasey, Cambridge University Press, 2006).

100:23 –4 **The dead ... their dead** Cf. Matthew viii. 22. Lawrence also uses the phrase in *Women in Love* (Penguin, 2006, 327:29).

100:38 **young Edwards'** The phrase has been emended from 'young Edward's' as Lawrence is presumably referring to the character of Frederick Edwards (82:37), who is called Young Edwards (96:19) but more usually Fred (83:19, 26, 39; 95:39). It is possible that he may be the same character as Sir Edward Edwards (65:33), and Mrs Vyner does refer to Fred Edwards as Eddy Edwards at 107:27 –8, so it could be correct to say 'young Edward's' if we took that to be his first name; but it does not seem likely that Lou or the narrator would be thinking of him here in first-name terms. (See A Note on the Texts.)

101:31 **slavish malevolence ... real freedom [102:2]** This discourse has roots in the ideas of Friedrich Nietzsche (1844–1900), and especially his concept of 'slave-morality', which he develops in chap. 9 of *Beyond Good and Evil* (translated into English in 1909); it appears again in very similar terms in section eight of Lawrence's novella, *The Virgin and the Gipsy*.

104:3 *laisser-faire* Non-intervention, letting things take their course (French).

106:7–8 *Pino-real ... pinavete ... piñón* Royal pine ... fir ... pinyon or 'nut' pine (Spanish).

107:16 **a bad egg** A good-for-nothing (colloquial).

107:31 **It's a bit thick** Rather excessive or unreasonable.

108:13 **an order** A court order.

108:40 **worked the bell-handle** Rang for the maid.

109:15 *My head ... runneth over* Comic play on Psalm xxiii. 5, 'my cup runneth over'.

110:22 **a seated pillar of salt** This reference to the story of Lot's wife who was turned into a pillar of salt for looking back at the destruction of Sodom and Gomorrah (Genesis xix. 26) playfully suggests Mrs Witt's power as a Medusa figure (57:8), and even Lou is 'petrified' here (110:35). However, the pillar of salt image is also used of Mrs Witt herself near the end of the story (171:40).

111:36 **dryad** In Greek mythology, a tree nymph (see note on 85:4).

112:24–5 *Oh Death where is thy sting-a-ling-a-ling?* From a song popular in the British Army during the First World War, playing on 1 Corinthians xv. 55.

112:28 *slicker* Mackintosh, waterproof coat (USA).

113:13–14 **Kind Words Can Never Die** The title of an evangelistic hymn from the American Civil War, 1861–5.

113:21 **Amazon** The Amazons were a mythical race of fierce female warriors.

114:35 **made a little *moue*** From the French, *faire la moue*, to pout or pull a face.

115:14 **geld** Of horses, to castrate.

117:4–5 **apples ... of "Knowledge"** A reference to Eve's forbidden fruit from the tree of knowledge in the Garden of Eden (Genesis ii. 9). See also a similar statement in chap. 4 of *Lady Chatterley's Lover* (1928; Penguin, 2006, p. 37). See also 134:34–6.

117:23–4 **little quotation-mark's moustaches** This appears in the typescript, the first English edition and the Cambridge edition, but the first American edition has 'little quotation-marks moustaches'. This reading could be seen to be technically correct, as the intention seems to be to describe the moustaches as looking like *pairs* of quotation marks (the singular form would seem to mean 'the moustaches of the quotation mark'). However, this is open to interpretation and we cannot be sure that Lawrence himself made the change to the proofs for the American edition. (See A Note on the Texts.)

117:35 *Ay, qué gozo!* 'Oh, what joy!' (Spanish).

119:29 *A rivederci* Goodbye; until we see each other again (Italian).

121:36 **Prince of Wales** Edward (1894–1972), eldest son of King George V, was Prince of Wales from 1911–36, when he became King Edward VIII (abdicating in the same year). Fashionable, sporty and good-looking, with a fast and glamorous lifestyle that was widely reported in the press, his is an appropriate image to capture those aspects of the 'roaring twenties' that Mrs Witt is reacting against here.

121:39 *Dio benedetto!* 'Blessed God!' (Italian).

122:4 **Cleopatra ... asp, as she tried her pearls in wine [122:26]** Cleopatra (68–30 BC), the last queen of Egypt, was the lover, first, of the Roman general Julius Caesar and then of Mark Antony. She is said to have dissolved a pearl in her wine in order to impress Antony with her wealth, and – after she and Antony were defeated by Octavian at the battle of Actium – to have committed suicide by the self-inflicted bite of a poisonous snake or asp.

123:40 *Little Jack Horner ... corner* Line from the well-known children's nursery rhyme.

124:7 **chétif** Undeveloped, stunted, or puny (French).

126:39 **puther** Variant of 'pother', a disturbance, commotion or confusion.

128:15 **pig-nuts** Edible woodland tubers, also known as earth-nuts (or, in the past, the more descriptive earth chestnuts), particularly enjoyed by pigs. Cf. Caliban in Shakespeare, *The Tempest* (1611), II. ii: 'And I with my long nails will dig thee pig nuts.'

133:16–17 **Flora ... in the bud ... in full blow** A play on Flora's association with flowers: as we are told on 134:19, Flora was the Roman goddess of flowers and spring. Fiorita and Florecita (133:29) are the Italian and Spanish diminutives of Flora, and the *Collyposy* (133:31) is a cauliflower, a posy being a small bunch of flowers.

133:18–19 **Shylock ... shekels** Allusion to Shakespeare, *The Merchant of Venice* (1596–8), IV. i, where the moneylender, Shylock, comes to demand a forfeit of a pound of flesh from his rival, Antonio. Hebrew coins were called shekels.

133:35 à la *Mademoiselle de Maupin* 'Like' or 'in the style of' (French) the heroine named in the title of the novel (1835) by Théophile Gautier (1811–72), who travels on horseback disguised as a man.

134:26–7 Aspasia . . . intaglio of Priapus   Greek courtesan and mistress of Pericles . . . an intaglio is a design cut into a semi-precious stone; Priapus is the god of the phallus and fertility.

134:40–135:1 the Yankee . . . Arthur   Reference to *A Connecticut Yankee in King Arthur's Court* (1889) by Mark Twain (1835–1910).

135:24 Father Abraham   Abraham was the founding father of the Hebrew nations according to Genesis xvii. 1–8.

136:7–9 Cassandra . . . dying   Cassandra was seized at the fall of Troy and, in some accounts, raped by Ajax. Iphigenia, the priestess of Artemis (virgin huntress and moon-goddess), was on the point of sacrificing Orestes to the goddess when she recognized him as her brother and helped him to escape. Adonis was a surpassingly beautiful youth fatally wounded by a boar and grievously mourned by his lover, Aphrodite (goddess of love). King Charles II (reigned 1660–85) was said to have apologized on his deathbed for taking 'an unconscionable time dying'.

136:15 gaillardias   Showy flowers of the daisy family.

136:20 *Oh my love . . . rrose*!   The first line of the famous lyric by Robert Burns (1759–96), 'A red red Rose' (1794), which is often set to music.

137:3 libido   From the Latin for 'desire' or 'lust', and used in Freudian psychology to refer to the fundamental psychic drive behind life, especially associated with sexual desire – though Lou is clearing using the term ironically here.

137:33–5 the Royal Academy . . . László . . . Orpen   Institution founded in 1768 for the advancement of the arts. Philip Alexius László (1869–1937) and Sir William Orpen (1878–1931) were fashionable portrait painters of the period.

138:5 a . . . pig in clover   Proverbial phrase for wallowing in comfort and luxury.

138:23 *the Tyrol*   Alpine region of Austria.

140:9 the scribe and the Pharisee   See Matthew xv. 1–20 and xxiii where Christ condemns the scribes and Pharisees for their hypocrisy in promoting the letter rather than the spirit of the law. The playful allusion perhaps suggests that Lou is the Pharisee who writes long and involved letters of self-justification, while Mrs Witt simply writes down what she must in perfunctory fashion; or it might be that Lou is the scribe who dutifully writes everything down, while Mrs Witt is the Pharisee who speaks but does not act.

140:15–16 *Noli me tangere*. Touch me not . . . Father   See John xx. 17; Christ's words to Mary Magdalene after the resurrection. *Noli me tangere* (Latin: touch me not) is from the Vulgate translation. Lou repeats the phrase at 120:20, adding *homine* (O man). Lawrence uses the phrase frequently in his works, especially in the 1920s.

140:33 *the Corpus delicti*   The substance or evidence of the crime; literally, 'the body of the crime' (Latin).

141:8 **agate**   A precious stone composed of layers of coloured quartz.

143:3–4 **the Honorable Laura Ridley**   Possibly based loosely on Lawrence's friend, Dorothy Brett (see note on 179:2).

144:37 **gimlets**   Boring tools.

147:5–6 **the dim, dissolving edges of a dream**   The description of a disappearing England may owe something to a passage in H. G. Wells' novel, *Tono-Bungay* (1909), where a new social order is felt to be coming into being, but 'just as in that sort of lantern show that used to be known in the village as the "Dissolving Views", the scene that is going remains upon the mind . . . and the newer picture is yet enigmatical' (ed. Patrick Parrinder, Penguin, 2005, pp. 14–15). Lawrence had praised *Tono-Bungay* as 'a great book' on its publication (*Letters* i. 127).

149:1 **hock**   German white wine from the Rhine region.

149:15, 16 **Plus ça change, plus c'est la même chose . . . On n'est pas mieux ici**   'The more things change, the more they remain the same' (French), proverbial for 'nothing really changes' . . . 'It's no better here' or 'We're no better off here' (French).

150:30–31 **a pearl before swine**   Cf. Matthew vii. 6.

151:10–11 **cinematograph**   An early apparatus for showing motion-picture films.

151:29 **Zane Grey**   (1872–1939), best-selling author of novels of the Wild West, many of which were adapted for the cinema.

152:25 **Coué**   Emile Coué (1857–1926) was a French pharmacist who popularized a system of self-cure or self-help in his book, *Self-Mastery Through Conscious Auto-Suggestion*. Couéism was all the rage in the early 1920s and he became, briefly, an international celebrity. Extravagant successes were claimed for the technique, which included daily repetition of the phrase 'Day by day, in every way, I am getting better and better'.

152:39 **Ça ne change jamais**   Things never change (French).

153:12 **the mayonnaise intimacy**   In the first American edition (see A Note on the Texts), this phrase was altered to 'the salad-bowl intimacy'. If this reading derived from an authorial change made in the proofs, it would constitute a considered change to the latest state of the text over which Lawrence had any direct influence – but we cannot be sure it was Lawrence who made the change.

156:8 **cocotte**   Loose woman or prostitute (French).

157:12 *Merci, mon cher!*   'No thank you, my dear!' (French).

158:19 *Quién sabe!*   'Who knows!' (Spanish).

158:37–8 **Vestal Virgins . . . holy fire in the old temples**   Virgin priestesses who tended the sacred fire and shrine of Vesta, the goddess of the hearth, in Rome.

159:6 **mesa** A high plateau or tableland in the American Southwest (from Spanish).

159:31 **Apollo** Identified with sun and light, Apollo was one of the major Greek deities, the god of oracles, prophecy and healing, and also of poetry and music.

160:18 **the ranch itself** This ranch, and the detailed description of it, is based on the Lobo (later Kiowa) Ranch in the foothills of the Rocky Mountains north of Taos, where Lawrence and his wife lived from May to October 1924 during the writing of *St. Mawr*. For parallel, non-fictional descriptions, see Lawrence's essay 'New Mexico' (written 1928 and first published 1931; collected in *Phoenix: The Posthumous Papers of D. H. Lawrence*, ed. Edward D. McDonald, Viking Press, 1936) and a letter to his niece of 31 August 1924 (*Letters* v. 110–12).

161:6 **mariposa lilies** See the description at 169:1–6.

163:8 **padres** Spanish for 'fathers': the male goats of the herd.

163:31 **pithed, to use one of Kipling's words** A word coined by Rudyard Kipling (1865–1936) in his story 'With the Night Mail' (1905), collected in *Actions and Reactions* (1909).

164:27 **ithyphallic** Phallic; 'ithyphallic' normally refers to phallic rites at festivals celebrating Dionysus (or Bacchus), the god of wine.

165:22 *ne plus ultra* Not to be surpassed (French).

165:32, 34 **adobe ... cotton-wood tree** Type of reddish clay used for building, typical of the Southwest region ... tree of the poplar family with fluffy white seeds.

166:15 **like pillars of cloud by day** Cf. Exodus xiii. 21–2; also *The Rainbow* (1915; Penguin, 2006, 91:35).

167:19 **Mother Hubbard** From the nursery rhyme, 'Old Mother Hubbard' (1805).

168:17–18 **dead-nettle ... columbines** A non-stinging plant resembling a nettle ... columbines (*Aquilegia vulgaris*) are so-called because their small bell-shaped flowers with five petals are said to resemble a cluster of doves; *columba* is Latin for 'dove' (168:20).

169:24 **cornelian** Reddish-white or flesh coloured, from the precious stone of this name.

171:6 **the "dragon," ... Augean stables [171:14]** The dragon Lagon guarded the golden apples in the garden of the Hesperides; according to Greek myth, the hero Heracles (Hercules) was set the task of stealing them as the eleventh of his twelve labours. Heracles also took part in the epic quest of Jason and the Argonauts to obtain the Golden Fleece, likewise guarded by a dragon. The fifth of his labours was to clean, in a single day, the stables of Augeas, king of Elis, which had not been touched for thirty years.

171:40 **Las Chivas** The goats or she-goats (Spanish). The name may also echo the word 'kiva', a ceremonial chamber of the Native Americans of the Southwest (see Keith Brown, 'Welsh Red Indians: D. H. Lawrence and

St. Mawr,' in *Rethinking Lawrence*, ed. Keith Brown, Open University Press, 1990, pp. 25–6). See also note on 32:24.

172:5 **arroyo**   Gully or ravine cut by a watercourse (Spanish for 'stream').

172:34 **a cold egg**   An abandoned egg, incapable of hatching; sterile, dead.

173:27 **to pay . . . out**   To take revenge on, to punish.

174:20 **"What is the something bigger? And *pray*, what is it bigger than?"**   This is a puzzling response from Mrs Witt to what Lou has just said, as Lou has not used the word 'bigger' in this part of the dialogue, and does not utter the words to which these words might be an appropriate reply until 175:21–2. It is possible that, at some point during the writing or revising of the story, Lawrence rearranged the sequence of the dialogue in these final pages but then failed to correct this apparent discontinuity; however, there is no evidence of such a rearrangement in the surviving typescript, so, if it occurred, it must have been at the manuscript stage. (See A Note on the Texts.)

The Princess

179:2 **The Princess**   One possible source for the title and (indirectly) some aspects of the story, may be Tennyson's poetic medley, *The Princess* (1847). It has also been suggested that the story draws ironically on elements of the fairy-tale of 'The Sleeping Beauty', with Dollie representing a version of the sleeping princess. The character of Dollie seems to have been modelled loosely on Lawrence's painter friend, the Hon. Dorothy Eugenie Brett (1883–1977), whose father, Viscount Esher, owned an ancestral castle in Scotland.

179:8–9 **blued . . . Stuart**   Members of the royalty (and aristocracy) were said to have blue blood. The Stuarts were kings of Scotland from 1371 and of England from the accession of King James VI of Scotland as James I of England in 1603 (to the death of Queen Anne in 1714).

179:16, 17 **sporran . . . Ossianic past**   A pouch or purse worn on the front of a kilt . . . the legend of Ossian or Oisin, son of Fingal, a Gaelic bard and warrior of the 3rd century, was popularized in the 18th century by the poems of James Macpherson (1736–96), which he claimed, falsely, to have translated from original manuscripts.

179:34 **Not all there**   Lacking in some mental faculties.

180:31 **contadina . . . ayah**   Peasant woman (Italian) . . . an Indian nurse-maid or governess, especially in European households (from Portuguese).

181:21 **the last of the royal race of the old people**   Lawrence draws on the mythology of the Tuatha De Dannan (or Danaan), a legendary race of heroes worshipped as gods by the ancient Irish and thereafter part of Irish fairy folklore.

181:31 ***noblesse oblige***   Old French, meaning that nobility brings with it certain duties and obligations (literally, nobility obliges).

182:6 **changeling**   A sickly or otherwise abnormal child that was said to have been secretly left by fairies in exchange for a healthy child.

182:8, 10 **Milan point ... spinet** Fine needle-worked lace from Milan ... small keyboard instrument similar to a harpsichord, with plucked strings.

182:31 **Zola and Maupassant ... Nibelung poems [182:36]** Emile Zola (1840–1902) and Guy de Maupassant (1850–93), leading writers of the French naturalist school; Leo Tolstoy (1828–1910) and Fyodor Dostoevsky (1821–81), well-known Russian novelists; *The Decameron*, a collection of stories by Giovanni Boccaccio (1313–75); *Das Nibelungenlied*, a medieval German epic poem based on old Scandinavian legends. The contrast between the Princess's responses to the French and Russian writers is perhaps explained by the coolly detached and unemotional style of the former and the more passionately engaged art of the latter: she is evidently 'confused' by passion and emotion, but able 'to understand things in a cold light perfectly, with all the flush of fire absent' (182:37–8).

183:5 **Roman cabman** This character anticipates the guide Romero later in the story (187:25ff), as this section (182:39–183:31) sketches in the terms of the opposition to be developed between the Princess and Romero.

183:9–10 **Caliban ... the perfect lotus** The brutish slave of Prospero in Shakespeare's *The Tempest* ... the Buddhist symbol of Nirvana, the highest state of refinement and peace for the soul.

183:11 *beauté mâle* Male beauty (French).

186:28–9 **westwards ... the March of Empire** Allusion to *On the Prospect of Planting Arts and Learning in America* (1752) by Bishop Berkeley (1685–1753): 'Westward the course of empire takes its way.'

186:34 **Rancho del Cerro Gordo** Ranch of the Big Hill (Spanish). From here, the setting is based on the foothills of the Rocky Mountains, north of Taos, New Mexico. From December 1922 to March 1923 Lawrence lived at the Del Monte Ranch, Questa (17 miles from Taos) and from May to October 1924 and April to September 1925 at Lobo (later Kiowa) Ranch, two miles further on. The Rancho del Cerro Gordo is based on the Del Monte Ranch, which was run partly as a farm and partly as a dude ranch by the Hawk family, who are probably the models for the Wilkiesons (187:26). The ride taken by Dollie and Romero (194 ff.) draws on an excursion to Lake Columbine, in the Rocky Mountains, made by Lawrence with Brett and others in late August 1924.

186:37–8 **pueblo of San Cristobal** A village north-west of Taos; pueblo (the Spanish word for 'village') has come to refer to both the settlements and the people of a major group of Native Americans in the Southwest known as the Pueblo peoples.

188:5 *raison d'être* Reason for existence; justification, purpose (French).

188:9 **the Penitentes** An ascetic Hispanic Christian sect in New Mexico which, as the name suggests, devotes itself to a penitential form of worship. Cf. Lawrence's poem, 'Men in New Mexico' (*Birds, Beasts and Flowers*, 1923) where he talks of the Penitentes lashing themselves 'till they run with blood'.

190:11 **half in love with death** Allusion to Keats' poem, 'Ode to a Nightingale' (1819), stanza 6, l. 2.

190:39 *idée fixe* A fixed idea; an obsession or artificial notion (French).

192:22 **placer** A mining term for a place where loose surface soil is sifted for gold (from Spanish).

194:6 **adobe** See note on 165:32.

194:30, 32 **withal . . . piñón** At the same time . . . pinyon or 'nut' pine.

195:6 **old-man's-beard . . . cranesbill** Clematis . . . geranium.

195:13 **buckskin** Horse of light buff colour, common to the Southwest.

199:11 **in the picture** See note on 67:33–4.

199:14 **devilled egg** A mustard-seasoned egg, roasted or grilled. The introduction of the word 'devil' here is perhaps not entirely circumstantial; it links with the earlier motif of fairy demons and strikes an ironically darker note against the Princess's innocent sense of a fairyland 'paradise' (199:4).

200:14 **stand-back** Stand-by, reserve.

204:1 **squaw-berry** A shrub of the dogwood family *(Cornaceae)* with edible berries.

205:37 **bob-cat** American lynx, with a 'bobbed' tail.

205:40 *museau* See note on 41:15.

206:14 **bootleg whiskey** Illicitly traded whiskey during Prohibition (see note on 64:12).

207:17 **coyotes** Members of the dog family native to North America, also known as prairie wolves.

214:11 **Muy bien!** Very well! (Spanish).

214:17 **Pen.** Penitentiary.

PENGUIN CLASSICS

SONS AND LOVERS D. H. LAWRENCE

The marriage of Gertrude and Walter Morel has become a battleground. Repelled by her uneducated and sometimes violent husband, fastidious Gertrude devotes her life to her children, especially to her sons, William and Paul – determined they will not follow their father into working down the coal mines. But conflict is inevitable when Paul seeks to escape his mother's suffocating grasp by entering into relationships with other women. Set in Lawrence's native Nottinghamshire, *Sons and Lovers* (1913) is a highly autobiographical and compelling portrayal of childhood, adolescence and the clash of generations.

In his introduction, Blake Morrison discusses the novel's place in Lawrence's life and his depiction of the mother-son relationship, sex and politics. Using the complete and restored text of the Cambridge edition, this volume includes a new chronology and further reading by Paul Poplawski.

'Lawrence's masterpiece ... a revelation' Anthony Burgess

'Momentous – a great book' Blake Morrison

Edited by Helen Baron and Carl Baron
With an introduction by Blake Morrison

www.penguin.com

PENGUIN CLASSICS

LADY CHATTERLEY'S LOVER D. H. LAWRENCE

Constance Chatterley feels trapped in her sexless marriage to the invalid Sir Clifford. Unable to fulfil his wife emotionally or physically, Clifford encourages her to have a liaison with a man of their own class. But Connie is attracted instead to Mellors, her husband's gamekeeper, with whom she embarks on a passionate affair that brings new life to her stifled existence. Can she find true equality with Mellors, despite the vast gulf between their positions in society? One of the most controversial novels in English literature, *Lady Chatterley's Lover* is an erotically charged and psychologically powerful depiction of adult relationships.

In her introduction, Doris Lessing discusses the influence of Lawrence's sexual politics, his relationship with his wife Frieda and his attitude towards the First World War. Using the complete and restored text of the Cambridge edition, this volume includes a new chronology and further reading by Paul Poplawski.

'No one ever wrote better about the power struggles of sex and love'
Doris Lessing

'A masterpiece' *Guardian*

Edited by Michael Squires
With an introduction by Doris Lessing

PENGUIN CLASSICS

THE FOX/THE CAPTAIN'S DOLL/THE LADYBIRD
D. H. LAWRENCE

These three novellas show D. H. Lawrence's brilliant and insightful evocation of human relationships – both tender and cruel – and the devastating results of war. In 'The Fox', two young women living on a small farm during the First World War find their solitary life interrupted. As a fox preys on their poultry, a human predator has the women in his sights. 'The Captain's Doll' explores the complex relationship between a German countess and a married Scottish soldier in occupied Germany, while in 'The Ladybird', a wounded prisoner of war has a disturbing influence on the Englishwoman who visits him in hospital.

In her introduction, Helen Dunmore discusses the profound effect the First World War had on Lawrence's writing. Using the restored texts of the Cambridge edition, this volume includes a new chronology and further reading by Paul Poplawski.

'As wonderful to read as they are disturbing … Lawrence's prose is breath-taking' Helen Dunmore

'A marvellous writer … bold and witty' Claire Tomalin

Edited by Dieter Mehl
With an introduction by Helen Dunmore

PENGUIN CLASSICS

ASPECTS OF THE NOVEL
E. M. FORSTER

'The final test of a novel will be our affection for it, as it is the test of our friends'

First given as a series of lectures at Cambridge University, *Aspects of the Novel* is Forster's analysis of this great literary form. Here he rejects the 'historical' view of criticism – 'that demon of chronology' – that considers writers in terms of the period in which they wrote and instead asks us to imagine the great novelists at work together in a circular room. He discusses aspects of people, plot, fantasy and rhythm, making illuminating comparisons between such novelists as Proust and James, Dickens and Thackeray, Eliot and Dostoyevsky – the features shared by their books and the ways in which they differ. Written in a wonderfully engaging and conversational manner, this penetrating work of criticism is full of Forster's habitual irreverence, wit and wisdom.

In his new preface, Frank Kermode discusses the ways in which Forster's perspective as a novelist inspired his lectures. This edition also includes the original introduction by Oliver Stallybrass, a chronology, further reading, appendices and an index.

Edited by Oliver Stallybrass

With an introduction by Frank Kermode

PENGUIN CLASSICS

MOLL FLANDERS   DANIEL DEFOE

'I grew as impudent a Thief, and as dexterous as ever *Moll Cut-Purse* was'

Born and abandoned in Newgate Prison, Moll Flanders is forced to make her own way in life. She duly embarks on a career that includes husband-hunting, incest, bigamy, prostitution and pick-pocketing, until her crimes eventually catch up with her. One of the earliest and most vivid female narrators in the history of the English novel, Moll recounts her adventures with irresistible wit and candour – and enough guile that the reader is left uncertain whether she is ultimately a redeemed sinner or a successful opportunist.

Based on the first edition of 1722, this volume includes a chronology, notes on currency, and maps of London and Virginia in the late seventeenth century.

Edited with an introduction and notes by David Blewett

PENGUIN CLASSICS

JANE EYRE   CHARLOTTE BRONTË

'I am no bird and no net ensnares me. I am a free human being with an independent will'

Having endured humiliation and loneliness in the home of her heartless Aunt Reed, and the harsh regime of Lowood, a charity boarding school, the orphaned Jane Eyre survives her childhood unbroken in spirit and integrity. When she takes up a post as a governess at Thornfield Hall, she also finds love with her employer, the dark and sardonic Mr Rochester. But her discovery of Rochester's terrible secret forces Jane to follow her own moral convictions, even if it means giving up her chance of happiness. Although many were shocked by its depiction of a woman's bold and passionate search for independence and love on her own terms, *Jane Eyre* was an immediate success when it appeared in 1847 and remains one of the most popular of all English novels.

In his introduction, Michael Mason discusses the literary critical history of *Jane Eyre*. This edition includes suggestions for further reading, notes and a new chronology.

'The masterwork of a great genius' William Makepeace Thackeray

Edited with an introduction and notes by Michael Mason

PENGUIN CLASSICS

PAMELA   SAMUEL RICHARDSON

'I cannot be patient, I cannot be passive, when my virtue is in danger'

Fifteen-year-old Pamela Andrews, alone and unprotected, is relentlessly pursued by her dead mistress's son. Although she is attracted to young Mr B., she holds out against his demands and threats of abduction and rape, determined to defend her virginity and abide by her own moral standards. Psychologically acute in its investigations of sex, freedom and power, Richardson's first novel caused a sensation when it was first published, with its depiction of a servant heroine who dares to assert herself. Richly comic and full of lively scenes and descriptions, *Pamela* contains a diverse cast of characters, ranging from the vulgar and malevolent Mrs Jewkes to the aggressive but awkward country squire who serves this unusual love story as both its villain and its hero.

This edition incorporates all the revisions made by Richardson in his lifetime. Margaret A. Doody's introduction discusses the genre of epistolary novels, and examines characterization, the role of women and class differences in *Pamela*.

Edited by Peter Sabor with an introduction by Margaret A. Doody

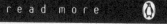
PENGUIN CLASSICS

FRANKENSTEIN MARY SHELLEY

'Now that I had finished, the beauty of my dream vanished, and breathless horror and disgust filled my heart . . .'

Obsessed by creating life itself, Victor Frankenstein plunders graveyards for the material to fashion a new being, which he shocks into life by electricity. But his botched creature, rejected by Frankenstein and denied human companionship, sets out to destroy his maker and all that he holds dear. Mary Shelley's chilling gothic tale was conceived when she was only eighteen, living with her lover Percy Shelley near Byron's villa on Lake Geneva. It would become the world's most famous work of horror fiction, and remains a devastating exploration of the limits of human creativity.

Based on the third edition of 1831, this contains all the revisions Mary Shelley made to her story, as well as her 1831 introduction and Percy Bysshe Shelley's preface to the first edition. It also includes as appendices a select collation of the texts of 1818 and 1831 together with 'A Fragment' by Lord Byron and Dr John Polidori's 'The Vampyre: A Tale'.

Edited with an introduction by Maurice Hindle

THE STORY OF PENGUIN CLASSICS

Before 1946 …'Classics' are mainly the domain of academics and students, without readable editions for everyone else. This all changes when a little-known classicist, E. V. Rieu, presents Penguin founder Allen Lane with the translation of Homer's *Odyssey* that he has been working on and reading to his wife Nelly in his spare time.

1946 *The Odyssey* becomes the first Penguin Classic published, and promptly sells three million copies. Suddenly, classic books are no longer for the privileged few.

1950s Rieu, now series editor, turns to professional writers for the best modern, readable translations, including Dorothy L. Sayers's *Inferno* and Robert Graves's *The Twelve Caesars*, which revives the salacious original.

1960s The Classics are given the distinctive black jackets that have remained a constant throughout the series's various looks. Rieu retires in 1964, hailing the Penguin Classics list as 'the greatest educative force of the 20th century'.

1970s A new generation of translators arrives to swell the Penguin Classics ranks, and the list grows to encompass more philosophy, religion, science, history and politics.

1980s The Penguin American Library joins the Classics stable, with titles such as *The Last of the Mohicans* safeguarded. Penguin Classics now offers the most comprehensive library of world literature available.

1990s The launch of Penguin Audiobooks brings the classics to a listening audience for the first time, and in 1999 the launch of the Penguin Classics website takes them online to a larger global readership than ever before.

The 21st Century Penguin Classics are rejacketed for the first time in nearly twenty years. This world famous series now consists of more than 1300 titles, making the widest range of the best books ever written available to millions – and constantly redefining the meaning of what makes a 'classic'.

The Odyssey continues …

The best books ever written

PENGUIN 🐧 CLASSICS

SINCE 1946

Find out more at www.penguinclassics.com